LIBBY RICE

A SECOND CHANCES *Novel*

ART-CROSSED
Love

ISBN: 099035363X
ISBN-13: 978-0-9903536-3-8

This is a work of fiction. Names, characters, places, and incidents are the product of the author's imagination or are used fictitiously. Any resemblance to actual events, locales, or persons, living or dead, is coincidental.

Gateway Publishing Ltd.
P.O. Box 1414
Golden, Colorado 80402

Cover design by Viola Estrella
Edited by Kathie Middlemiss

DEDICATION

For Tom, who proves all the good ones aren't gone.

ACKNOWLEDGMENTS

One would think an author's second book might be easier than the first. Not so in this case. Art-Crossed Love is near and dear to me because of the way I struggled to get the story out as I'd envisioned, and because of the people who helped me along the way.

My beta readers were invaluable: Jennifer Maitlen, Larie Brannick, Lorna Bryan, Viola Estrella, Lindsey Donakowski, Kimberley Anderson, Julie Sheridan, Krista Hwang, Spice Jones, and Judy Adams. You helped in every way imaginable, from reading the book to great conversation about books to good wine. Every moment was precious!

Thea Harrison was a heavy in my corner when I needed advice about this business from a tried-and-true professional. She shared her experience and valuable insight, often at the drop of a hat, and for that I'm eternally grateful, for both her genuine friendship and her impressive mind. Courtney Milan offered endless practical advice from the standpoint of a woman who knows more about how to succeed in publishing than almost anyone I know. She answers little-guy questions with patience and heart. To her, everyone has a place at the table, and she wants nothing more than to see each new author take a seat.

To my closest non-writer friends, thank you! To Pam for your calls and notes and flowers, to Kim and Keri for having wine made with my covers as labels (!), to Dave for letting me drive your new BMW, to Spez for buying whole boxes of books and then giving them to me along with a nice filet mignon, to Lisa for your wise encouragement, to Eleanor for all the homemade meals, to Anya for poking at me to go faster and harder and better. Books, it seems, are a team effort.

Finally (and always), thank you, Tom. I can't imagine doing this, or anything, frankly, without you there to tell jokes, write songs about breakfast burritos, and generally make this whole writing thing seem like a wise decision, even on the days it (quite objectively) is not.

Kintsukuroi

"To repair with gold." The art of repairing pottery with gold or silver lacquer and understanding that the piece is more beautiful for having been broken.

CHAPTER 1

February—Boulder, Colorado

Cole set the prostitute's money on the nightstand, wondering if his wife's angel was laughing as hard as the living woman would have. Low light from an overhanging lamp highlighted Ben Franklin's sagging jowls, and Cole flicked his gaze toward the cash. "We agreed on four hundred?"

"Yes," she said. "Thanks." Her voice held the cultured tones of the upper class. This wasn't your average streetwalking hustler, but an expensive call girl living the good life. Boulder, Cole was learning, didn't offer much variety in the way of hired sex. For cheap love, a guy drove to Denver.

Ms. Jewel, or at least the woman who called herself that, reached across a foot of empty space separating their respective queen beds. The hotel might be respectable, but he hadn't splashed out for a suite. Most of her customers didn't, she'd told him, and he wanted the pictures to be representative of a normal gig.

Long, tapered nails scratched lightly over his thigh in a less-than-subtle suggestion. In her mid-thirties, Ms. Jewel looked to be a willing—more like eager—twenty-five, but her caress didn't stir anything but mild curiosity. No surprise there.

Cole hadn't come to fuck.

He halted her progress with a gentle hold on her slim wrist. "Beautiful, definitely, but you know why we're here."

"Close-ups and conversation," she acknowledged with a sly smile, "but a girl can hope." Drawing back with a languorous pull, Ms. Jewel stretched along the edge of the bed before propping her head up with one hand. With the other, she stroked along the curvaceous silhouette her pose presented to great advantage.

1

Facing off against a preening whore, who looked ready to pounce, only added weight to the digital camera in Cole's lap. *God*, the fall from regular contributions at *Time* to freelancing for Boulder's local daily had been far. In slow increments, he raised his bulky equipment and snapped a candid shot of this evening's companion, from the neck down, as agreed.

The woman's presence in his frame proved that pimping wasn't nearly as rare in Mayberry-esqe Boulder as one might think. Five minutes on Craigslist could get a man—or a woman, for that matter—a wealth of by-the-hour entertainment. Yet paid or not, the camera couldn't help but love Ms. Jewel's creamy cleavage and healthy, smooth skin. While hookers might abound in this hotbed of high-tech employment, they were the consensual kind, not drug-addicted runaways or kidnap victims without other options. No, Boulder hookers drove fast cars and lived in sleek apartments, pandering to white, well-salaried, workaholic techies who paid the bill before the sex, cringed at physical force, and felt a desperate need for affection.

All in all, Boulder made hooking look pretty good.

Cole stood and began a series of photographs in rapid succession, almost like he was shooting the cover of Vogue, only he wouldn't Photoshop or airbrush or taint the photos in any way. What he saw, readers would get. "Tell me how you started."

He didn't have to ask the question. Cole was just the photographer. A journalist would write the words, while Cole would provide the pictures. But a talking subject relaxed, and a relaxed subject made for better shots.

So talk he would.

His model didn't hesitate. "I enjoy sex." There was that smile again. This time she rolled onto her back and cupped her breasts. They were covered—he'd managed to axe every one of her efforts to strip—but barely. A skimpy sundress skimmed the top of her areolas, and without a bra, her nipples might as well have been giving a dance recital on her chest.

"I suppose that's a good trait in your profession." Probably too glib, but she didn't notice.

"Yes. I'm also attractive." *And humble.* "School was never my thing, and after the fifth offer, I finally took the money and rode, so to speak."

Damn if she didn't get a smile out of *him* with that one. "And?"

Ms. Jewel didn't spread her legs. She also didn't clamp them together. The thin material of her dress made her lack of undergarments all the more obvious when she went limp and relaxed against the bed. "Since I liked the... physical aspects of the work, I let them make me rich. Lines of good-looking nerds at the door have secured my future." Her teasing look said, *want to be next?*

Cole took a picture of her long fingers. They thrummed her hardened nipples with no sign of fatigue. He really ought to put a stop to her little show, which hadn't been on the agenda, but he couldn't quell the curiosity she'd sparked with that touch to his thigh. How far would this sexpot have to go to turn him on? If she slid that hand down into her heat, would he finally get hard? If she moaned? What if she lifted the dress to her waist and went ahead with the spread she'd been threatening?

"Enough," he clipped. "Gorgeous as you are, this isn't *Playboy*, and I'm not interested." Because every last one of his wonderings had the same answer: *nothing*. She could play and pant, even moan and masturbate for his eyes only, and he wouldn't respond. Pleasure had died along with Kate. In its place, he felt nothing good, only a burning desire to be close to the woman he'd loved, only a visceral need to visit her grave, only an unswerving willingness to sacrifice a rising career to accomplish those goals.

No matter how succulent the woman, a whore in a hotel room could never thaw the ice. Cole stuffed his camera and a few scribbled notes in his duffle. The evening couldn't be called photojournalism at its finest, but he had several decent pictures and enough information to cobble together semi-informative captions. Ms. Jewel had her cash. The local paper would buy this shit and assemble a story that wouldn't surprise anyone. Yes, the world's oldest profession made its home on street corners and casinos and the Mustang Ranch. But prostitution had also infiltrated lily-white bastions of education and accumulated wealth, granola moms with thousand-dollar strollers be damned.

When he touched the door handle, tasting escape, she posed a question with the barest hint of contempt in her voice. "And you, Mr. Rathlen? What are you doing here? You were one of Boulder's best-loved sons, traveling the world, having your photos featured in all sorts of fancy publications. I swear I saw your Tsunami shots in *National Geographic*."

"I was," he admitted. "You did." But they both knew what she meant. *Now you're photographing a hometown hooker for the local daily.*

No longer. Thirteen months and seventeen days had passed without a care for the fact that Kate wouldn't have chosen mediocre. Ms. Jewel, who sold her body for money, at least had the decency to excel at it. Perhaps she hadn't been forced into this line of work, but few made her kind of choices without glimpses of pain.

The woman mocking him from the bed hadn't jumpstarted his cock, but she'd done a number on his head. Cole would be making some calls come morning.

******

June—New York City

"You don't look like your headshots."

Cole paused his perusal of a painting that monopolized an entire wall of one of the Meatpacking District's chicest galleries. Though the disembodied voice came from behind him, he knew the smooth tones interrupting his study belonged to Lissa Blanc. He drew out his response, glancing between the canvas and the nearby placard that described it. "And this painting doesn't look like a park."

"Your pictures make you look friendlier. Smaller. *Happier.*"

She didn't wait for his rebuttal before circling around to tap the crimson drywall next to her work with a matching fingertip. "What do you feel when you look at it? Not like you're in a park, but maybe you think of being young and carefree?" Her lips curled into a parody of a smile, like she was being forced into used-car sales at gunpoint. "Maybe you see something you want to *purchase.*"

"You're kidding." *Morning Park* was more interesting for what it lacked. Chunks of the car-sized canvas had been left bare. Where she'd seen fit to add paint, serrated jags of black and green crawled out from the edges toward a thin seam of yellow that unevenly bisected the disarray. The mess had all the qualities—if you could call them that—of the prints his wife had framed.

Kate had loved her "Blancs"—not that Lissa had reached that lofty, last-name-only level of acclaim—while Cole had wanted to use them as bonfire kindling. Where his wife had touted Lissa as an up-and-coming genius, *mark her words*, Cole had questioned the mental faculties, let alone the artistic integrity, behind paintings that could potentially be copied by a posse of well-trained five-year-olds.

Lissa stiffened, all the welcome-to-the-big-tent theatrics draining away in an instant. "Unlike you, Mr. Rathlen, I don't consider my work a joke."

He bit his tongue. She flushed when she got mad. The pinkening of the smooth skin rising above her black corset held his interest more than the paint she'd thrown at the canvas. "I'm critical, Ms. Blanc. I have *not* called you a joke."

Mostly because circumstances hadn't thrown him the chance. He was a photographer, not an art critic, so other than becoming a bona fide Internet troll, he lacked a platform to rant about the "talent" his wife had so admired.

"Sorry," Lissa sneered, examining her nails. "I was having a gin and tonic in my mind just now and missed your point." Slender arms wound across her chest. "What gives *you* the right to criticize work you can't possibly understand?"

"A mouth," he said dryly, "and a rampant superiority complex." Might as well be honest. Certainly less had allowed fools to masquerade as fine minds.

Turning to the painting once again, he marveled at the blobs Kate would have called brilliant. *"There,"* she'd have informed him, *"where the green prowls toward the black but can't reach it for the yellow. That's the essence of disrupted nature—a park."*

"What's interesting about you," Cole told Lissa casually, "is what you *don't* understand. Art is more than critical acclaim. If great, ordinary people connect with the work."

And pay for it. He let the undeniable thrust of his words hang between them. Lissa had wormed her way into a few of New York City's most hallowed show spaces, but a big seller she was not.

Her do-or-die smile receded. Inexplicably, Cole wanted that particular danger to return. But professional relationships, like all others, began best in honesty.

"I hear the highway business is booming these days." He paused, eyeing her famously philanthropic parents in the crowd. Together they ran one of the country's largest construction companies. "Rumor has it these swank gallery showings have more to do with your family's heavy machinery than your hand with a brush."

The red blooming on her chest darkened to an angry purple. He got his smile back, but only in the form of a tight stretch of lip set against clenched teeth. A shame, because apparently unlike him, Lissa Blanc was photogenic as hell. The pictures he'd seen had portrayed her looks with staggering accuracy. They'd highlighted the thick chestnut hair that now gleamed auburn in the light and revealed the dark eyes that assessed him with cool intensity, at odds with the delicacy of the surrounding bone structure. They'd even done justice to her skin, showcasing the exact shade of white tulips, at least when she wasn't flushed with anger or frustration.

Most of all, her pictures had hinted that Lissa Blanc would be magnificent were she to stretch those generous lips wide with the proper smile she withheld.

"So that's it. *You don't like it.*" Lissa stated the obvious, probably still mentally sucking gin and tonics. "You sought me out for an appointment, then traveled to Manhattan, all to share your—with all due respect—less-than-worthy disdain."

"No." Taking her in, he drifted closer and breathed deep. Notes of fruit and an unrecognizable spice hit like an apple orchard in August, one he badly wanted to explore. Kate had smelled like Chanel No 5.

He froze, rejecting the thrall of long-denied senses rushing to life. Betrayal started small. First an innocuous observation, then… a crisis. Had Cole not believed in the power of temptation so ardently, he'd still have a wife.

Shame lashed at the part of him he kept on lockdown, not for insulting Lissa's painting or for tearing a chink in her armor, but for enjoying the tease and wondering what color she'd turn next.

He cleared his throat. *Yet Lissa's the one I need, the one Kate would have chosen.* Choosing Lissa himself—no matter how distracting the woman *or* how virulently he disagreed with his wife's prematurely-silenced admiration—would pave a path to absolution.

Without uttering a single superfluous syllable, he made his point. "I want you to paint for me."

******

Finally. Lissa couldn't block the triumph she knew chased across her face. "So the insults have been code for 'Love what you've done here'?"

He made a show of visually inspecting the room. "We'd study the most intriguing places in the world, contrasted in ink—that would be me—and oil, which would be you. Not this drivel."

She could only stare. This was a helluva reach across the aisle—first the judgment and then an insult on the heels of an offer—all from the mouth of an apparent Gold Coast surfer turned beloved travel and journalistic photographer. Disheveled dark blond threaded through platinum strands that needed a healthy trim. He flaunted his irreverence in a pair of too-casual, but delectably low-slung jeans that magnified the leanness of his hips in contrast to breadth of his shoulders. The fine lines fanning from his blue eyes spoke of long outdoor photo shoots and a careless take on sunscreen. They made him look capable, experienced, disenchanted. Anything but old.

Rolling stiff lips inward, Lissa released with a pop. Obviously he hated her work, and worse, she feared he might be right. Plus, someone else had heard his verbal slap. Her closest friend had been hovering nearby for long, embarrassing minutes. The soft gasp that sounded at Cole's slight had labeled Scarlet for the eavesdropper she was, a taken-aback one at that.

"You called my work drivel," Lissa growled. *Yet you own some of it.* After Cole had requested this meeting with all the enthusiasm of a fashion designer locked in a Wal-Mart, she'd done her homework. He'd mostly worked freelance, selling to the likes of *National Geographic* and *Time* and *Lonely Planet.* Somewhere along the line, this producer of safe, aesthetically faithful images—whether of mountains or cathedrals or indigenous tribes—had purchased two of her most free-thinking examples of abstract expressionism. She had the sales receipts to prove it.

"D-r-i-v-e-l," she snarled over her shoulder. "Scarlet, tell me why I should hear this guy out."

Cole peered around her, looking unconcerned. Then, without warning, he jerked the conversation from Lissa and handed it to their unrepentant spy. "Yeah... Scarlet, is it? Let's hear why your friend ought to listen."

Scarlet's guileless answer came fast and *way* too sure. "He wants you from the Louboutins up, Liss. And every woman deserves that..."

Lissa didn't hear the rest. Her evening shattered. Through a haze of mortification, she watched Cole's eyes shutter, then light with slow, cold fire. Apparently Scarlet hadn't said something merely revealing or embarrassing, but very, very wrong.

Mentally tunneling inward, Lissa felt her body turn. The movement imparted a strange sensation, the feeling of taking action without giving her limbs instruction. Then Cole was talking, but she was louder, rambling about Scarlet getting out more, anything to mask embarrassment with noise.

Finally, the all-business in Cole's tone permeated the fog. He spoke of a grant from the National Endowment for the Arts to his small company, of wanting her to hire on for a project. At the same time, his voice, his words, his posture, even the look on his face screamed that getting into business with Lissa might constitute his worst nightmare. Still, he went on. "That means funding, promotion, name recognition, and an end to all… this."

With that last insult, the night officially went from bad to worse. "Funding for your company, you mean. How do *I* get paid?" Since he'd so eloquently pointed out that, currently, she did not.

"You'd have a contract with Rathlen Images, including a monthly salary deducted from the grant for the duration of the project." When she stepped forward, mildly intrigued, he clarified, "The money's not much—barely enough to cover basic expenses for someone like you. But then you don't need *me* to get rich."

Mouth gaping, Lissa pictured a wildly colorful farewell. "I don't need *you* to—"

"It's the *opportunity* you need, a chance that just so happens to take the form of a grant awarded to *me* to be completed at *my* discretion. I think we can both estimate the reputational benefits of a successful collaboration, dollar signs aside."

A new and patient presence prickled along Lissa's side. Soon a gentle tap on her shoulder shredded her fantasy sendoff before it could truly begin. When she turned, her father did the worst thing he could do in front of their particular audience. A check landed in Lissa's palm, its weight at once negligible and the heaviest thing she'd ever held. Fatigue shadowed her father's eyes, and she reminded herself the Blanc fortune hadn't sprung from a silver tongue or a big inheritance. Robert Blanc had earned every penny. Decades of early mornings and late nights had begun to fray his urbane edges.

Humiliation scorched her insides at the thought of what Cole was witnessing—first Scarlet, and now this. The intelligence shining in Cole's blue, blue gaze promised to put two and two together. Slowly, she closed her mouth and collected her thoughts, vying to reach a place of gratitude rather than resentment.

Memories threatened from her mind's periphery, lashing her with the reasons she wouldn't tell her father no. The scenes in her head conjured a time when the gilded name *Blanc* had tended toward tarnish.

Money had waned. Changes had followed.

In her case, the setback had invited sticks and stones rather than words that could never hurt her. Refusing to wince, Lissa reminded herself that those days of fearful pandering for acceptance were long over. Waves of gratitude for her parents' enduring support pushed her aging unease back into the well where it usually resided. Now her worst fate involved scathing reviews that implied if never a Blanc, then always a joke.

Asphalt heiress, they'd whisper. But the slight was nothing new.

Let them come. Because she *was* a Blanc, with the might of her family's recovered industrial empire at her back. Her parents didn't know the toll on their temporary fall from grace—she'd made damn sure of that—but they *suspected.* Now checks were written and strings were pulled in the name of atonement.

And goddamn her for needing the handout.

Lissa began in a tone that was infinitely milder than the one she'd blasted at Cole. "*Dad.*"

"Sweetheart," he said, not realizing his ill-fated timing, "you have to sell at least twenty-five percent tonight for the show to carry. Otherwise the gallery will balk at keeping you on display for the full two weeks. You know how your mother and I love your paintings."

With that, he closed her limp fingers around the paper and left her standing there, shaking, check in hand. Glancing down, Lissa confirmed the amount—*blank*—carte blanch to do what was needed to sustain the dream of her art for another day.

Epic. Fail.

When she looked up, she saw judgment staring back at her, not curiosity. Cole had reached the right conclusion.

"Don't say anything you'll regret." She choked on the warning, not managing the heat needed to fire the threat.

Cole responded with a flat stare, as though nothing Lissa could say or do could possibly cause him an ounce of remorse. "You'll paint the realities I photograph. Abstract is in your past." No longer did Cole concede to the language of possibility. Her dad's check had turned "*if*" into "*when.*"

Looking around, Cole added a droll, "Perhaps it's time. Hmm?"

The offer remained on the table despite his seeing the damning truth of her illustrious career. That alone told Lissa he had a mighty strong motive for seeking her out. Perhaps Scarlet was right. Cole *did* want her, but not for sex and not for talent.

For what, then?

If Cole was a question with no answer, Lissa was a woman fresh out of the luxury to refuse. He'd distilled her choices so succinctly—keep selling pictures to Daddy, or take a chance on a man and an opportunity that actually derived from her art.

No matter how tenuously.

Cole came with *earnable* pay. Perhaps failure with him would beat the undeserved "success" crumpled in her fist.

Darting a quick glance at Scarlet, whose eyes bugged in blatant do-this-or-I'll-kill-you command, Lissa asked Cole one final question. "Where're we going?"

Her surrender brought a biting smile. "To my estate in Colorado for training. Then to the wilds of India, city girl."

Satiny paper slid between her fingers. She looked down to see a glossy card he'd placed in her hand. The front depicted a socked-in picture of Mt. Everest. Cole's, naturally. The black back listed his name, e-mail, and a cell number in white letters.

Looking up, she realized his index finger still rested on the back of her hand. He tapped once. Twice. Then she felt the lightest pinch.

"Don't forget your shots."

CHAPTER 2

October—Outside Nederland, Colorado

"*Near Boulder,*" Cole had promised.

Lissa guessed that little lie would be the first of many. She'd trundled her rented SUV past Pearl Street fifty minutes ago. The GPS had directed her into an upwardly winding canyon and through a small mountain town. The welcome sign had read, "Nederland." Fifty feet beyond, a billboard enthusiastically invited her to attend "Frozen Dead Guy Days—March 2nd-4th!"

Uh, yeah.

Past Nederland—*and over the hill and through the woods*—she continued along a two-lane highway until finally turning off onto a not-so-graveled road. Uneven ruts jolted Lissa over what she hoped would be the last leg of her journey to Cole's so-called "estate."

When the ruts morphed into a tree-lined driveway, she slowed the car, stunned at the sight that rose in the distance. At least he hadn't lied about *this.*

A half-mile later, the drive ended with a two-story plantation house. More a nod to authenticity than size, the aberration boasted black iron verandas and an arched doorway. Six white columns guarded the front façade. Lissa looked around for the sugarcane and cotton fields that surely interspersed the miles of unmolested pines sprouting between rock outcroppings. Stepping out onto a graveled parking circle, she swore the wind whispered, "Frankly, my dear, I don't give a damn."

Leaving her bags, she wandered up the front steps. Curling letters across a brass knocker read, "Melina." Before she could lift the handle, the door flung wide. A tall man with a shock of disobedient white hair motioned her inside with a lopsided grin.

10

Cole's house offered a cool foyer and an immediate welcome. The entry led to a central staircase that widened into a balconied landing above. A chandelier sparkled in her right peripheral vision. Flecks of light from the front windows reflected through its crystals, swirling over a dining room containing a long table of natural oak planks. Eight high-backed chairs flanked the table's edges, giving an impression of sturdy function over form.

On her left, a leather couch and matching lounger beckoned from a den. Situated in front of a neat stone fireplace, the setting abandoned the pomp and circumstance of the massive white pillars outside in favor of a blended approach to southern grandiosity and mountain practicality.

A comforting tingle shimmied down Lissa's spine. *Home.* As unexpected as it was inappropriate, the feeling persisted.

Her beaming welcome wagon didn't seem to notice her surprise. "I've been waiting all morning on baited breath."

She held a hand out in greeting, but instead of a handshake, she got a plastic freezer container.

"Hold on," he said. "I'll see to your bags."

The man brushed past, descending on her open trunk while she babysat what appeared to be a dish of lasagna, gawking at the surroundings.

Outside, the man hoisted a round of luggage without a single flustered look at her failure to pack light. Two trips had him dropping the last of her bags to the gleaming parquet floor. He retrieved the lasagna and began to vigorously pump her now-free hand. "I'm Kent Rathlen, Cole's uncle."

"I'm—"

"I *know* who you are, Ms. Big Artiste." He said art-eest with the flair of a true Francophile. Still grinning, he lifted her hand and gave her knuckles a loud smack of a kiss. "Too bad you're here for Cole."

"I wouldn't say here *for* Cole. I'd characterize it as—"

"I know, I know. You're here to change the world with your knowledge. But, my dear, you'll do that *with* Cole."

Then he *bowed*, like she was a princess and he her loyal servant.

As though their intro was totally normal, Kent held up the Tupperware. "Hungry? I've been loading Cole's freezer with these dinners I make at Supper Solutions down in Broomfield. That man can't feed himself, let alone a pretty girl."

Cole's uncle had driven an hour to fill the freezer? "You do this often?" She followed him through the dining room and into a bright, open kitchen that ran the rear length of the house. Her arrival had obviously interrupted the unloading of bags full of chicken picante and flank steak with lemon marinade. A cherry cobbler peeked from the bottom of a stack.

Kent looked away a bit sheepishly. "Like I said, he's not good about food, and we Rathlens have to be." He beat his chest with an open palm.

"Salads with olive oil and vinegar for me." He picked up the flank steak and examined it wistfully. "*Mostly*," he added with a sigh. "My heart doctor put the brakes on the good stuff. Cole's the opposite. Months of Skittles and sandwiches have left him lean, but he's getting back to his fighting weight."

Brushing his hands together, Kent shut the freezer door and toggled his head back and forth between her and the handle. "Take out what you want the night before. The supper lady taped cooking instructions to each container. Follow the steps, and you two won't starve."

Where the hell was Cole? And why had he existed for months on Skittles and sandwiches? Even she could do better than that.

"Thanks," she offered. "I'm sure we'll get along just fine."

Kent nodded, and even though they'd been acquainted for all of ten minutes, she'd swear to a speculative twinkle in his eye. "Food-wise," he said, "you certainly will."

A beat of silence passed. Lissa thrust her hands into her pockets and opened her mouth to ask whether Cole had a latent Civil-War fixation when slow, heavy footsteps sounded behind her. She spun around, expecting to see a tardy Cole slink into the kitchen. Instead, she found the largest, furriest dog in the history of the universe. He kept coming, breathing so hard he could double for a phone stalker in a horror flick.

"Sasha gets hot," Kent provided helpfully.

She would too, with a hundred pounds of hair. "He's a she?" A girl-dog couldn't possibly get so big.

"Sasha's all—"

"Man."

The muffled voice carried sarcasm, not apology. Momentarily flicking her attention upward, Lissa saw Cole enter on the heels of his beast. She ignored him for the time being, content to watch Sasha turn in a circle, plant his rump on her foot, and arc his nose backward toward hers. Brown eyes the size of silver dollars said, *We're going to be very, very good friends.*

Cole loomed in the kitchen entrance, arms folded over an impressive chest.

Must be all the flank steak.

"Sasha's a Russian male's name," he explained evenly. "Remember Peter and the Wolf? Sasha's a man-bird."

Before she could help it, Bruce Springsteen's Born in the USA phantomed between her ears. "I have two friends who've named their girls Sasha. This is *America*—where you live, by the way—and where Sasha's a *girl's* name."

The St. Bernard obviously didn't care about his nationality. He wanted to make out, and he proved it by nuzzling into her chest, leaving a smear of spit across the cream silk of her shirt. She gave in and stroked his head and ears, earning another slobber stripe.

Close friends already.

Stillness stretched across the kitchen until Kent clasped his hands with a booming clap. "Until next week, then." Out of nowhere, he produced a jumbo bag of Skittles, slapped the candy on the granite island, and shuffled out, leaving her with a brooding Cole and a slobbering dog.

She'd never been good with silence. "Family-delivered meals?"

Cole blinked. "Family-delivered life?"

If only you knew. "Not necessarily," she replied, keeping her tone smooth and light like he hadn't hit a nerve. "And not this time."

He ripped the Skittles open with a practiced tear. Eating one candy at a time, he nodded, more than a little circumspect. "We'll see."

At her feet, Sasha let out an extended groan. He collapsed his limbs away from his body, sending him crashing into the kitchen tile with a force that would shatter a lesser dog's elbows. Unfazed, he yawned and began to lick at his outstretched legs.

Shaking her head, Lissa soldiered on. "I hadn't planned on staying *here*."

"That explains why four of your suitcases are stacked inside my front door."

She shrugged. "Your uncle works fast."

Cole ambled out to her luggage with her and Sasha trailing behind. "He knows my place will have to do. You won't find a Four Seasons in Nederland."

"Which, if I recall correctly, was supposed to be Boulder."

He slung the strap of her duffle over his shoulder and picked up the three remaining cases. "We're headed to *India*, dollface"—he delivered the endearment with a healthy sneer—"where half the population lacks a functioning toilet. Consider Ned part of your training." He started up the wide stairs, talking over his shoulder. "Harry Winston isn't down the street—"

"Because there isn't a street."

"—but I'm sure you'll make due, determined professional that you are."

"I've spent time in the country, you know. My family has a property in upstate New York. Summers? Holidays? All there."

"And what was that like?"

Manicured lawns and fountains. A chef and a gardener. Poodles and ponies lining the ice rink down the lane. "Rugged." She cupped one of Sasha's drooping jowls, then dropped it and followed her grudging bellhop. "Overrun with mutts."

Cole veered left at the top of the stairs and headed for the first door. "You lie about as well as you paint."

Ouch. "And your condescension far outshines your photographs." What was a little fib among non-friends?

Inside her room, buttercup walls reflected the midday sun against a lavender duvet and a vaulted wooden ceiling. A rocking chair fluttered in the chilled breeze pushing its way through a bay window. She even spied a canopy bed and, at its foot, a wood-burning fireplace with an attendant stack of logs.

The air wrapped its arms around her with a gentle squeeze. Surely she was falling too hard for a foreign bedroom, one that could never truly be hers. Yet an undeniable recognition pulsed in her chest. "Magnificent," she breathed. "Who did this?"

"This?"

"The house. All of it."

The last suitcase plunked to the floor, and Cole's fingers crept into a tight clench above the handle.

An eerie stillness descended on their already strained conversation. Silly, really. It wasn't as if she planned to steal his decorator.

"My wife."

Lissa might be slow, but after checking his credentials and tolerating *weeks* of phone prep, she knew the man didn't have a damn wife, which, given his sudden tension, probably meant an ugly divorce. And people never fully appreciated her compliments on their exes' exquisite tastes.

"Never mind. *Gawd*, this place is awful. Good thing you got rid of her. She had to have been—"

"An architect." Cole straightened, totally missing the joke and revealing nothing beyond a stark refusal to share himself. "Kate designed multi-million-dollar homes for Boulder 'hippies.' I took advantage of the outdoor photo ops and a suitable jumping-off point for international work."

Lissa studied Cole intently. Belligerence didn't bruise the edges of his speech like it had before. Instead, the words—notably *past-tense*—floated through the air like a prayer, each one seeming to drag him further into another, happier time.

"Melina grew from there," he explained, "from a displaced southerner who brought a piece of Savanna with her."

When Cole's big hands slid along the edge of the doorframe, petting the wood like a lover, Lissa knew she'd guessed wrong. This wasn't a man who'd said good riddance to a woman he felt better off without.

She began a slow spin but didn't make it far. A massive print took up most of the opposite wall. *Her* print. *Redemption* presided over the room, a fusion of color, line, and form that had never failed to infuse her with a sense of warmth, of being cherished.

She'd known he owned it, but seeing her favorite work hung with care in the house his wife built... "You still love her."

A careful answer bounced off her back. "Always."

Glimmerings of disappointment balled in Lissa's stomach, and she refused to turn and acknowledge the defiance she knew she'd find etched in his features. The writing—or the painting, she should say—was on the wall. "She's why I'm here, isn't she? You love her, and she loves my work. You're using me to prove yourself to a woman."

Damn, damn, damn.

Blinding drive had rendered Lissa purposely obtuse, so much so she'd rationalized *why* Cole might choose a partner he didn't particularly care to work with, one he didn't respect. Instead of addressing the obvious, she'd allowed herself to be persuaded by Cole's persistence and her desperation.

Liar, you turned a blind eye because he looks hot and acts cold, and you wanted the pleasure of thawing him out.

Stunned by her own naiveté, she sputtered, "Is this some kind of game? Desperate husband proves his willingness to sacrifice by working with the lowly, struggling abstract expressionist who happens to appeal to his estranged wife?" Sure, Lissa faced challenges. Many viewed her marginal success as a nepotistic boon, but to be a pawn in a man's marital discord?

"I wish," he said quietly.

She could do nothing but laugh. "Where is she?"

"Here." The answer catapulted her way, quick and low, like a well-placed dart. *Surprise!*

Her head snapped around before the blow could land.

But Cole didn't look defiant, not like she'd suspected. His gaze rested on the painting hanging across the room, eyes soft and head cocked, a stolen moment that ended the second he noticed Lissa's attention. A subtle tremor rippled through his body, and he began to slowly inch from the room, that familiar veneer of indifference falling into place.

"She's buried outside, beneath the rock garden she always wanted."

CHAPTER 3

An enduring silence followed Cole's announcement. Lissa drew a breath, but the air didn't do any good. Pithy responses had always come easy. Yet Cole's news left her opening and closing her pout like Clara's nutcracker. When she didn't snap into action, he turned and walked away.

After a few warbles, Lissa started down the hall in slow, quiet pursuit, each hesitant step calling forth the realization that she'd have to let him go. *This time.* The unyielding lines of his retreating back and his silently swinging arms told her to leave well enough alone for at least a little while.

A day? Two?

In the end, she returned to her room without uttering a single word. *Let him play mysterious lord of the manor.* Her bedroom didn't harbor any such demons and welcomed her with open arms. In fact, all of Melina held a warm charm her uptown brownstone in Manhattan couldn't duplicate. Now she knew why—Kate Rathlen, the architect who'd obviously stolen Cole's heart, had built him a love nest and then been torn away, leaving her husband to feather that nest alone.

Lissa instinctively tore through the suitcase that held her painting supplies. A working studio could soothe almost anything. In minutes, a familiar setup—an adjustable easel, jars of brushes, a palette, scrapers, water-soluble oil paints, rags, acrylic gesso, and finally a bare canvas—began to ease the frayed nerves pitching to and fro inside her chest.

Aligning her easel with the window, she surveyed a vista that stretched away from the house. Miles separated her from a group of peaks jutting into a cloudless afternoon sky. She couldn't remember the last time she'd seen that kind of uninterrupted blue. Between her and those mountains lay a world of possibility.

Before she could overthink the kinks of her arrival or what Cole had revealed, she gathered dollops of color on her palette and dove in, instinctively checking and dabbing and then looking again. Paint flayed the canvas in short, whipping strokes until an image began to take shape, but not one of rocks or trees or wild azure skies. The painting radiated life of the angry variety. Not a man, but the essence of one.

From the intermingling streaks of red and blue and black, a clear color break evoked a strong jaw. Above, three dark slits suggested a pair of hopeless eyes and a mouth held slightly ajar. Only these basic nods to the human face interrupted the pandemonium of furious color that cried *unfair.*

No forehead, no neck, no hair—nothing to indicate the owner of such torment. But when Lissa brushed two menacing yellow slashes over the fathomless eyes, she jerked in shock. She'd painted with a sense of floating detachment, but suddenly recognition streaked from her shaking fingers to her incredulous mind. This wasn't a general sense of anger and pain. She'd painted Cole wrapped in a furious grief he could neither release nor share.

Her peaceful landscape had morphed into the coming of Cole's personal apocalypse. This wasn't supposed to be about him. Sure, life had dumped her in Colorado to paint what he demanded, but this particular effort had been about *her*, about the release painting always brought.

Now he'd polluted her art with his secrets. A painful past hadn't shown up in her research. In an age of oversharing, she tended to forget that unless a person became extremely famous, he controlled his own flow of personal information. Cole maintained a flashy, picture-rich website and was on the usual suspects in terms of social media, but only in a professional capacity. No talk of lost loves and lingering sorrow.

Needing to escape the evidence of her subconscious fascination with Melina's owner, Lissa slammed her brushes into a glass of water and left the painting to brood. On the front steps, she barreled into a super-sized Cole. The man had light hair like Cole's, but instead of a tangled free-for-all, his had been trimmed close to the scalp. His face was set in familiar sharp angles, but where Cole was tall and lean with a seductive, almost feline quality to his striated lines, this guy was built like a citadel. A predatory one she could envision eating babies for breakfast.

Before she could tumble down the stairs, he steadied her with an arm that looked capable of lifting a subway car. "You must be the painter."

The deep voice held a note of curiosity, not the threat his looks telegraphed. Maybe he *hadn't* come to rape and pillage. "You *have* to be a brother."

He nodded, then held up a grocery bag. "I brought food."

"You people come twice a day?"

He didn't budge. "Uh, *no.*"

She retreated into the house, letting him fall in step behind her. "Kent was already here."

"Shit," he said without much rancor. "This was my week. *I think.* I'm

Trevor, by the way."

"Lissa," she provided over her shoulder, automatically heading for the kitchen. "What does Cole think of the coddling?" At least she'd learned *why* the family insisted on stopping in. If one of her brothers ever lost a spouse, she, too, would pull some serious, *Oh, just passing through.*

Trevor set the bag on the counter and began extracting more freezer containers full of pre-made meals. What did the Rathlens have against TV dinners? "Mostly"—he held up another bag of Skittles—"Cole stays quiet. But the food seems to disappear."

Lissa eyed Trevor with open speculation, wondering how much info she could pry out of this maybe not older, but definitely *bigger*, brother. "Any other family members I should expect? Maybe there's a random food-truck owner in the mix? I'm a sucker for a cupcake from a truck."

Kent pulled out box of brownie mix. "Afraid these will have to do. Once I make them, that is."

The giant *baked*. Too bad a burnished wedding ring hugged his finger. "Cole told me about Kate."

The unloading came to a sharp stop. "Did he now?"

Lissa nodded. "He mentioned that his wife is buried here at Melina and then disappeared." Calling it "mentioned" might be too casual. "Can I ask what happened?"

Trevor folded his reusable bag with a resigned smile, flashing a pair of dimples set low on his cheeks. "You can ask," he conceded. "You already know her name and that she's gone, so I think you're doing all right for a couple of hours. Keep at it. Cole takes a bit of tenacity."

The dregs of the caution Lissa had felt on the front steps drained away. Dimpled goliaths who delivered food to grieving brothers using reusable totes didn't eat babies.

"Why?" she asked.

"Mostly because he's a stubborn sonofa—"

"No, why won't you tell me the story?"

His eyes turned thoughtful. "Kate is Cole's story to tell." Then he paused, musing on the statement for a moment before his lips parted as if to go on. Slowly, he closed his mouth and shook his head with a shrug, as if to say, *Sorry, can't help.*

She sighed. Wouldn't Trevor explain if Kate's death had been run of the mill? Of course, few deaths were when they occurred in a person's late twenties or early thirties. "At least tell me what's up with the food."

This time Trevor capitulated, barely. "We want Cole to eat." He opened the new bag of Skittles and helped himself, not noticing that Kent's duplicate beckoned from next to the fridge. "Cole wasn't doing enough of that for a while. Now he is."

"When did she die?"

Trevor cast Lissa an indulgent look, but one that said she was pushing her luck. "Two years come January."

A hazy picture began to form in Lissa's mind. Cole had lost his wife to... *fill in the blank*... more than a year before. In the aftermath, he'd holed up in Timbuktu, letting basic necessities, like eating, slide. The family had rushed in to remedy that most pressing problem, but feeding a man only went so far. Now Cole kept his body in fighting form but had become reclusive and antisocial. At least that was her guess given her strained interactions with him in New York, on the phone, and now at Melina.

Time had obviously come for Cole to get back in the saddle, which is where Lissa came in. He'd received a prestigious grant, probably resting on past laurels, and while Cole didn't *want* to work with the likes of her, he felt obligated by the loss of a woman who'd been Lissa's Number One Fan.

Lissa had to chuckle. Leave it to her to channel her big break through post-mortem favoritism. At least her dad believed *living* people might appreciate her work.

Knowing what she did, she wondered whether Cole had owned up to scraping Lissa off the bottom of the barrel. "What has Cole said about *me* being here?"

"Very little," Trevor said, "but he rarely explains. Don't mistake tight-lipped for insult."

"You know nothing?"

"Not 'nothing.'" Without a hitch, Trevor repeated the bones of the project—Cole would take photographs, and Lissa would paint the same scenes, first here and then in northern India.

On the phone before her arrival, Cole had been adamant about strict adherence to representationalist ideals. Lissa was to keep it real, so to speak. Her paintings were to depict his chosen sights *exactly* as seen in real life. "Do you know what I paint?"

Trevor's tone edged toward flippant. "I'm hoping whatever's in front of you."

"No." Barely ever, in fact.

"So enlighten me."

Might as well lay it out. "I'm an abstract expressionist. That's emotional, subconscious creation. Think highly idiosyncratic and often seen as anarchic, even radical."

Instead of showing surprise or worry over the success of his brother's project or the unique choice in partners, Trevor burst out laughing in hard belly-clenching hilarity that doubled him over his handful of candy. "This," he wheezed, "is going to get good." A few chuckles later, he managed, "You... are... perfect."

What the hell? "How so?"

Trevor unfurled from his slouch, and she could tell he fought for a straight face. "Hit him over the head with this, Lissa. Go for shock and awe." When she didn't jump in, he grew serious. "Cole's dug so deep into his rules, like he's afraid to believe in, or even imagine, anything that isn't staring him in the face. If you can change his ways, even a little, that's progress."

Healing Cole. The idea hadn't occurred to her, though changing him had. She and Cole were about to embark on an intensely creative process, one that would require them to rely on each other, believe in each other, respect each other. Together for all the wrong reasons, success would elude them until she shook her partner to his foundations.

Lissa returned Trevor's infectious grin, concealing the ball-busting plan forming behind her innocent façade.

She knew exactly what to do.

CHAPTER 4

The next morning Cole cranked a winch, hoisting steel high into the air. He intended to feed deer, not attract bears. Dry wind whistled through the dimness lingering between the trees clustered a quarter-mile from the house, swinging the heavy container to and fro on its chain and threatening to send feed flying. Each wind-and-weight-defying pull of the lever sparked against the flint of his memory.

Lissa thought him stoic. *Yank*. If only she knew what he wanted to do with her taunts. *Push*. With the mouth that delivered them. *Repeat*. Each time she'd spun one of her caustic remarks—the frozen food, the salivating dog, the delight at his stiff discomfort over her incessant questions—he'd wanted to toss her to the nearest surface, flat or otherwise, and show her a thing or two about stiff and the ways she could loosen him up.

After endless months without so much as a spark, he'd woken up in the pre-dawn darkness with the *wrong* name on his lips. Instead of blond hair and soft curves, he'd envisioned a sleek brunette with intense brown eyes and delicate hands that his dream-self had wasted little time placing on his body. He'd slid over her, skin to skin, until the wrongness of it had jerked him awake.

Sasha had no such qualms. The animal hadn't come to bed last night. When Cole had gone looking, he'd found his dog glued to Lissa, head to that tantalizing chest, while she'd stroked along his glossy coat and cooed in his ear.

Traitor.

Finished with his chore, Cole prowled out from the trees toward the house. He planned to start Lissa's training with something easy, say, a chair sitting empty on the veranda. Surely the woman could paint a recognizable replica of a piece of furniture, and simplicity in form and function would facilitate a direct comparison between his photograph and her painting.

21

From there, they'd work their way up to more complex objects, then landscapes, animals, people, and so on.

With the maze of trees receding behind him, Cole shifted his focus forward and stopped short. Barely past dawn and Lissa stood, easy as you please, in the driveway. Her easel faced the house, and she appeared to be mixing colors on a worn palette.

Fitted jeans tapered to where they slid into a pair of leather riding boots. On top, a thick sweater hung just below the waist. Its bulk merely highlighted the pert perfection below.

Nearly two years had passed. Intellectually, he knew he had every right to enjoy the view, though he had to remind himself again that Lissa's slender, almost fragile appearance masked the heart of a flame-spitting dragon.

He jerked his gaze to her work.

The canvas should have been blank, primed to be the recipient of the training *he* had in mind. Instead, swirls of anemic color united in indistinguishable shapes sure to have an unreasonable explanation.

After weeks of telecon prep over how the project would unfold, she still balked at painting a scene's likeness, insisting that true divergence in their respective art forms lie in how each interpreted what they saw, not simply in which tools they used to depict life on paper or canvas.

"*You demand regurgitation*," she'd spat at the end of their last call.

How wrong she was. Talent didn't lie in morphing a scene into whatever you wanted it to be; magic came with the discipline and restraint required to show life for what it truly was.

The mixing stopped, and she set the palette down on a nearby folding table. "I know you're there."

"Amazing, your powers of deduction."

He approached from behind. Her body partially shielded the developing work, but a man would have to be blind to miss the two arched shapes occupying opposite corners of the image. The silhouettes gave the impression of a wrenching tear—two halves of a whole that couldn't reunite for the road winding between them.

A road strangely reminiscent of the one he and Lissa presently occupied.

Each arching mass looked to have been flooded with rich color—red— before life had leached it away, leaving only a faded white stain and an occasional flash of former glory behind dilapidated windows.

Cole stepped forward to see the rest. Like a Taser gun, her meaning arced out of the canvas and zapped him in the chest. His lips mouthed a question, but no sound came out. An answer would be superfluous anyway.

He already knew.

"The house," Lissa explained without prompting. She sounded confident on the surface, but he heard the faintest tremor beneath her ease.

She knew she'd overstepped. Their first full day, and she'd done her best to blow them up.

He closed his eyes and let his head fall back against his shoulders. "Why?" he drawled. Her wayward brush had tracked him like prey, as though she'd looked through some forgotten, unshuttered window to his life and thrown the vision to the canvas.

"This is what I see." Her answer didn't hold sarcasm or spite, but something worse, the soberness of true belief.

A hand brushed against his arm. He opened his eyes and stepped away, forcing his retreat to be deliberate, controlled. "*Never* touch me." That kind of intimacy still felt reserved for another, not a witch who tried to manipulate him with visceral reminders of a past he already couldn't forget.

She drew back casually. "All right. But you have to communicate. What does the painting tell you?"

The same touchy-feely question had come up at the gallery, then too often on the phone. Next she would ask, *What do you feeeeeel?* He couldn't stop the growl that sounded from deep in his chest. "That you're a haughty, self-righteous bitch who's ignored everything I've said since I found you in that gallery in New York. You accepted the job with no intention of doing what's required."

To her credit, she barely bristled. "Job?" she asked. "I woke up in an empty house, walked out the front door, and painted something all by my lonesome while you roamed the countryside. That job? My work won't always be for you."

"You need to acclimate," he lied, knowing he avoided the house and their work, not because of Lissa's needs, but because her very presence cast a shadow in the shape of the accusations that had killed Kate. *His* accusations. "And this isn't for me? *A picture of my house, interpreting my life, thrown in my face?*" The washed-out image drew him back, and he recoiled at the truth swirling through wet paint.

He took one step, then stopped, bringing his body into alignment with the edge of her canvas. Without turning, he spoke, low and mean. "You think you have the answers, that you can waltz in here and change my philosophy by eliciting a trumped-up emotional response that I will *never* give you. You. Know. Nothing."

Fire crawled over his skin, painful and destructive and demanding. His mind offered up only a single option for putting it out. *Destroy.* Perfectly calm, Cole lifted Lissa's debacle high in the air, feeling his fingertips sink into viscous paint. Then he let go. Initially the canvas caught the wind and flew high, but suddenly a corner wrenched from the strong updraft, and the painting darted downward, landing face down on a pile of rocks about twenty feet out.

Lissa's pained gasp barely registered as he marched forward toward the front porch. "Never again."

"You're damn right it won't happen—"

A sudden gust hit the moment his foot fell on the first step. Behind him, her easel crashed, and he smiled. Even the wind had done its part, but he'd beat nature to the punch, toppling the lie and destroying the *house that wasn't*.

He spoke to the air in front of him. "Someone made a mistake in teaching you life is easy." Everything down to the exclusive brand of her fucking jeans spoke of an ease not earned. Lissa would soon discover life could get hard.

His queen of comebacks fell conspicuously silent, yet he didn't bother to look back. He couldn't.

Because instead of Kate's perfect creation, a house pulled from his wife's past but built for her future—her now nonexistent future—Lissa had cast Melina as a shelled-out mutation of a home.

Lissa had painted a shattered house, one physically morphed into the bloody, beating remnants of a broken heart.

******

A day later, Lissa tried not to resent Cole's silent treatment even though time had flown with all the unpacking and settling in. After trucking her easel upstairs—perhaps Cole would unwind if she hid the evidence—she'd stowed the disastrous painting of the house and set a blank canvas in its place. If he stopped by her room, she wanted the expanse of white to remind him she'd come to Colorado for a *reason*, one he seemed content to ignore. Jeans and paint-splattered shirts had been stowed in an antique dresser beneath the window. A sole New Yorkish dress looked lonely in the closet—black and mini and Escada Couture.

Won't be needing that.

Two photos graced her bedside table. Her parents waved from the foreground of the first painting she'd ever sold. Her big brothers brandished the second. Pictures invited curiosity, she knew, but she needed the constant reminder of the importance of this trip. Not *all* her work could grace the Blanc family halls.

She traced a finger over one scene and then the other, smiling slightly to herself, stuck in the void between apprehension and appreciation.

Someone made a mistake in teaching you life is easy. Cole's words had hit like well-aimed arrows, and not of the Cupid variety. At least she knew which camp he fell into. The naysayers tended toward one of two options—push Lissa away or pull Lissa close. The pushers openly mocked her "illegitimate" success. The pullers beguiled her in an effort to see how much of that "luck"—or connections or money or opportunity—could rub off on them.

Cole was a clear pusher, and frankly, she liked those better. At least they were honest.

A hank of hair chose that moment to abandon the clip that couldn't quite contain her pony tail. Ruler straight despite a healthy dedication to volumizing shampoo, her hair liked to slip from its confines and lay flat against her head in an antagonizing refusal to hold body. She imagined her looks mattered about as much to Cole as couponing did to Donald Trump, but hell, she had nothing to lose and everything to gain. After the disaster in the driveway, she could at least try to make herself presentable.

Her trek to the spare bathroom two rooms down took her past Cole's bedroom door across the hall. His rumpled bed sat in silence. Nothing personal hinted at the room's inhabitant. A dresser and two night stands held a clock and a box of tissues between them. No pictures or knickknacks, not even a stray piece of clothing or a random shoe littered Cole's studied order, dimmed by heavy shades that blocked the rising sun from cheering the space.

Earthy scents of pine and sandalwood filled her nostrils. Despite his obvious efforts to disappear within the emptiness, the room bore his mark. The hard edges and sanded planks had absorbed his essence without permission.

Even her limited view of the room told her much, and temptation threatened. If she saw a little more… *Not a chance.* Forcing herself to put one foot behind the other, she backed away from his open door as quietly as she'd arrived.

The copper tub in her bathroom resembled a huge gravy boat. The New Yorker in Lissa marveled at the concept. So often her life demanded three-minute showers, never a leisurely soak in a tub that might have been filled by Mammy herself.

A wicker basket held sumptuous washcloths and a bottle of gardenia bubble bath. She tended toward tasty scents—from oranges to candy canes. They spurred her appetite, a good thing for a skinny girl, and always seemed approachable. Today she availed herself of the luxuries on tap. She sank deep into the tub, telling herself one didn't indulge in low-grade anxiety in these circumstances. Old world tubs and Egyptian-cotton towels required a certain amount of stress amnesia.

She sighed heavily. She and Cole would adapt.

Heat leached into her muscles, and she slumbered against a neck pillow. Eventually the creeping chill of the water brought her around. Stretching languidly, she climbed from the tub, wet and glistening, her hair streaming rivulets of flower-scented water over her shoulders.

After toweling dry and tossing the cloth down a chute she assumed terminated in a basement laundry room, she rummaged through the basket in search of body lotion. Already, the dry Colorado air had her skin feeling like the surface of Mars. When the search came up empty, she looked under the sink and in the mirrored vanity.

Nothing, which was surprising given the well-stocked state of Cole's home.

He'd either gotten in touch with his feminine side after his wife's death or someone came by regularly to make sure the place stayed clean and comfortable. From what she'd seen, an aunt probably showed up the day after Uncle Kent delivered the meals to wash the linens and line the waste-paper baskets with scented trash bags.

Opening the laundry chute, she peered into blackness. The *last* towel was long gone. With a quiet twist, she opened the bathroom door and peered into the hallway. All was clear and quiet, so she snuck a toe out onto the carpeted runner, then another. When that proved successful, she flew out the door and lurched into her quietest ball-of-the-foot giraffe run toward the body creams she'd unpacked in her room.

"This can only be penance for your last painting or bribery for your next one."

Cole's rumbling voice took her so off guard she lurched to a stop. There he stood, behind a panting Sasha in his doorway. Heat flared in her cheeks. "What's that supposed to mean?"

He cleared his throat. "Nice ass?"

Her jaw dropped, arms flying to cover her breasts. She tried to speak, to yell at him for his open regard, but she only sputtered, watching his gaze wander over her body, lingering in all the places she tried ineffectually to hide. Sasha lumbered forward. His wobbly-gaited oblivion broke the spell, and she whirled toward her room.

Inside, she took her time. With any luck, Cole would disappear while she slathered herself in lotion and dressed in an alternate pair of jeans since the clothes she'd planned were stranded down the hall. After about five minutes, she opened her door and stepped out, prepared to act like the morning had been perfectly ordinary.

Cole stood with a shoulder propped against his doorjamb, arms folded across his chest in a way that drew her eyes to tanned, vascular forearms. His loose-hipped stance and ruffled blond hair still screamed laid-back. *Not a care in the world. Life's a prize for the plucking.* In sum, an easy-going illusion. Cole's serious eyes shared nothing but color with the ocean. His obvious erection was anything but a joke.

She swallowed loudly. "I didn't know you were"—*so incredible when aroused?*—"still up here." *We needed anything but this.*

He didn't budge, but the glimmerings of a grin played about his lips. "No need to apologize."

"I wasn't."

He let out a derisive snort.

"You called it penance or bribery," she said, recalling the revealing words he'd blurted out, "when yesterday you led me to believe you were immune to such things. What did you say?" She looked around as if an answer might slide of the walls. "Ah, yes, that you don't have 'emotional responses.'"

The smile he'd been building died a quick death. "I still have a dick."

Her body flinched in all the wrong places, pulsing involuntarily at what his statement laid bare. She ignored the insinuation. "Fair enough."

"Let's keep this battle above the belt." Then, *Jesus Christ*, he licked his lips.

At first she nodded. Then, realizing what the move admitted, she shook her head hard enough to rattle her shoulders. "I haven't considered your dick part of the war."

He pushed off the door frame and sauntered forward, past her frozen position outside her room and down the curving staircase. His hands didn't touch, but his eyes sure did. Once he'd disappeared from view, his voice trailed up from the landing below.

"See that you never do."

CHAPTER 5

"Forget it." Lissa stared Sasha down. The dog stood beyond the threshold of Cole's darkened room. She'd followed him upstairs when he'd seemed intent on luring her away from her post in the kitchen where she'd been lying in wait for Cole, keen on a redo after her cameo as a nudist.

She didn't plan to flaunt her bare assets again, but her mistake had sure pulled him from his shell, if only momentarily. The morning's embarrassing interlude had at least proven one thing—Cole Rathlen was as human as any other red-blooded male with, in his own words, a well-functioning dick.

Not that she cared. His ravenous look when she'd struggled to cover herself had been an annoyance. *Really*. The ache that had settled in her center signified mere appreciation for his spontaneous flare of feeling, a glimpse of life behind the forty-foot walls surrounding him. Because art needed fire, and from what she'd seen, Kate's death had left him spitting ice.

So, naturally, after choking down a dinner of reheated beef enchiladas, she'd collected all the half-eaten bags of Skittles from the kitchen and dining room and piled them in front of her like bait. After polishing off the first bag, Sasha's eyes had finally rolled skyward. With a jerk of his cinder-block head and an impatient huff, he'd pranced out of the room, tail in the air. Thirty seconds had ticked by before he'd returned for a repeat performance.

He might as well have held a sign. *Come with me, stupid human.*

She stared at the sparse furniture through Cole's open door. Rummaging around his room could only end *badly*. If she got caught, well, *entrapment-via-dog* probably wouldn't cut it.

"Are there more Skittles in there, beastie?" Maybe she could do a quick sweep.

Sasha bent low over his forelegs and "jumped." He totally cleared at least a half-an-inch beyond the tips of the Berber. Then he moseyed over and sat next to the unmade bed, leaning against an exposed sheet. When he straightened, she grinned at the hair imprint left in his wake.

After a few more halfhearted refusals the dog ignored, she decided to take a look. What could Cole do? Go missing and refuse to get their work started? Oh, wait...

As soon as she turned on the light, Sasha sank to his belly, shoving his massive head under the bed until his shoulders wedged between the frame and the floor. Then came a low whine, more like a dog yodel. Every few seconds, he gathered renewed strength and surged forward, only to be repelled with the realization that the space still couldn't accommodate a dog the size of an adolescent water buffalo.

Lissa peered over her shoulder toward the hall, then back at Sasha. A smart woman would abandon the dog and plead ignorance when asked why he'd been found shoved beneath the bed like a woman who'd poured herself into an ill-fitting dress.

She made it to the top stair before Sasha let out a subdued bark. That muffled *woof* sealed her fate. Rushing the bed, she lowered to her knees and stroked Sasha's wiggling rump. She ought to want a cigarette to calm her nerves. Or a drink. After all, she was about to crawl under the furniture of an absentee widower who'd made privacy his life's quest. But she didn't smoke. And she only drank this late if, rather than signifying the beginning of a new day, the toast closed an old one.

Chin down, she wiggled under the box springs to the tune of Sasha's heavy panting, reaching forward until she swiped what felt like a dusty picture frame. *Jackpot*. Perhaps she'd found the stash of personal loot Cole kept hidden from view. She wouldn't pull the picture out. Action that drastic would be too invasive, even for her. Up till now, she had a damn good reason to... what? Lie face down under Cole's bed, manhandling his private possessions on her third night as a guest in his home?

"*Shit*." She splayed her arms to scramble out.

"Find what you're looking for?"

The bland voice came from above and might as well have grabbed her by the ankle and dragged her back into the light. Disoriented and embarrassed, she surged upward. But she'd forgotten her cramped position. Pain bit into the back of her skull where a screw—or maybe a nail or a protruding edge of the bed frame?—gouged the tender flesh behind her ear.

Her teeth sank reflexively into her lower lip. She was forever throwing herself at sharp objects. This particular run-in with Cole had to center on her ability, on forming a plan, not on a haphazard scrape. Nor would she give the man the satisfaction of knowing his sudden presence had scared her. With extreme care, she braced her palms against the floor and pushed. Her sweaty hands slipped at first, but she regrouped, sliding her body along until her head cleared the bed above.

"No," she groaned, the answer muffling against a rug.

"What?"

She craned her neck to look at him. "I did *not* find what I was looking for." *Not a fucking Skittle in sight.* Though it appeared she'd caught his attention without the bite-size rainbows of fruit flavor.

With a casual movement, she shagged her dark hair, efficiently covering the throbbing cut in her scalp. Taut moments dragged by in silence. Finally, he held out a hand, even though the rigid angles of his jaw said help was the last thing he wanted to offer.

His fingers were warm and calloused against hers—another sign of life.

"First," he said, "you're naked in my hall. Now you're writhing beneath my bed. I thought we had an agreement."

"We did. You're supposed to think with the *other* head. The one *above* the waist."

"I would if—"

"*I'm* supposed to paint pictures. Remember that agreement? Besides, Sasha"—who'd fled at the first sign of trouble—"*really* wanted under the bed."

A smooth lift deposited her on her feet. She wasn't prepared for the sudden lightheadedness that sent her swaying. Clutching his wrist, she closed her eyes and took a deep breath—in through the nose, out through the mouth.

"Problem?"

"Got up too fast," she murmured, intent on handling the wound in private. A little hot water, a dash of Neosporin, and she'd be set. "That hereditary low blood pressure gets me every time."

Steady hands gripped her shoulders, pushing toward the mattress. When she opened her eyes, Cole was studying her with slit-eyed suspicion. Irritation blanketed his expression, but so did concern. "Sit."

Probably a fine idea. Blood trickled along the base of her neck, crawling in a way that provided a constant reminder that she was hurt and *leaking*. Nausea roiled low in her stomach, far outweighing any attendant pain. When she opened up to ask about her training, saliva seeped uninvited from the roof of her mouth. Instead of demanding a plan for their first test run, she whimpered and swallowed convulsively.

"Breathe." He pulled her hair behind her shoulders, gripping the mass at the base of her neck in a makeshift ponytail. She felt the moment he saw the blood in the tightening of his fist and the responsive sting in her scalp.

She waited for a caustic, cynical response, but his voice held only alarm when he asked, "What did you do?"

"Moi? It was your bed that attacked me."

He didn't smile. "You live a dangerous life, Lissa Blanc." Gentle now, he pulled her hair aside and examined the wound. His touch remained soft and calm, but his voice stretched tight over his next words. "You should have told me."

"You caught me with my head in the proverbial cookie jar." She panted. "I didn't figure much sympathy would flow my way." Her voice soared higher and faster with each syllable, and now her deep breathing had gone shallow. A mere scratch and she was falling to pieces.

"Tetanus current?"

"Yes," she lied. If she could handle needles, she'd have put her father's resources to better use and become a doctor. This artist crap was overrated.

Up close, she focused on the sea blue of Cole's irises. Her vision hitched, swimming with another man—a blue-eyed boy, actually—yelling in her face while blood slipped down her neck.

"Come on." He supported her slow progress to the bathroom with a gentle arm around the waist. When she finally sat on his toilet, he pressed a cold washcloth into her hands. "Lay this against your cheeks."

The disturbing memory disappeared with the plunk of first-aid supplies on the sink. Before she knew it, he was swabbing at the wound in soft but efficient swipes.

"Why are you being so nice?"

He tugged at the washcloth. When she released it, he traced the cool, wet material across her lips, then down and around to the back of her neck, stripping away the blood. "Why do you think I'm incapable of nice?"

"I don't—"

A light grip settled on her chin, tipping her head back for a look that told her not to bother with the placating bullshit. *Fine.* "You haven't seemed particularly taken with me." *Kind of like that blue-eyed boy.*

The cloth stilled against her skin. In her peripheral vision, she saw tension gather at his temples and in the set of his jaw. "You were hurt," he said simply, as though her minor injury explained his about-face.

He smoothed a breathable bandage over the cut and stepped back, staring down at her still-upturned face. "You're not anymore."

A smile tugged at her lips. "Thanks to you." Could this be the beginning of a truce?

The warmth rebounded off the harsh planes of his expression. "Now what the hell were you doing in my room?"

She closed her eyes to block him out. *Guess not.*

******

Four strides took Cole to the bed, where he crouched down and reached blindly beneath, exactly where he'd found her wedged tight. "Let's have a look. Maybe you found something good."

31

With a jerk, a painting slid free on a soft swish of frame against floor. He dusted his hands together. "Nope." The "p" reverberated through the increasingly airless space.

Not a print this time. An original—*another of Lissa's*—lay flat at his knees.

Two days ago, she'd seemed touched by the fact that her painting hung in the spare bedroom. Collecting dust under the bed didn't have the same affect. The ivory sweep along her cheeks drained to an ashen white. "Did you take it down when she died, or was the removal for my benefit?"

"Been under there for weeks." Originally, he'd stored the painting in the hall closet. Then he'd moved it to the pile of junk stacked in the basement before experimenting with several other failed storage attempts. He should have known hiding the thing under the bed would only cause trouble.

"I knew you owned two," she said, "but that's not supposed to be one of them."

Cole stroked his knuckles along the frame. "This one was a gift." He looked up. "Everyone knew she liked your stuff. Kate only had it a short while before she died, but every day she lined treats along the top of the frame." He glanced down the hall for the fur bandit that had roped Lissa into his game. "You can guess the rest."

She crouched next to him by the bed. "Sasha."

Nodding, he explained, "He'd sit underneath the frame until Kate found him and ran him through his repertoire of tricks. I guess the frame still smells like Beggin' Strips. That, or the dog's smarter than we think. Floor level obviously isn't working."

She reached for the painting—only about the size of a cake pan—and pulled it into her arms. She had the palest limbs, as though her translucent skin was made of rice paper. He got the feeling she considered herself something of a blunt instrument, but from his vantage point, she was pure grace, long and supple and fluid. That's why her mouth kept surprising him. Those delicate looks gave the impression of fragility, of being *kind*.

But nice girls didn't parade their goods in front of strangers or sneak through forbidden bedrooms.

Earlier that morning he'd come upstairs on a quick errand and heard the running bathwater. Frankly, he'd stuck around to catch her unawares, wanting to lay some ground rules after her stunt on the front drive.

The bathroom door had clicked open. Instead of a fight, he'd gotten a flash of snowy skin and dripping auburn locks. Panic had dragged a wild, shaky breath into his lungs before a blast of lust had nearly flattened him. Smooth skin. High breasts. The barest flare at slender hips.

His wife had been petite and curvaceous, a va-va-voom body paired with the sweet mannerisms of a true southern lady—soft-spoken and cautious, considerate and well-mannered. Sometimes so, so sad.

Pretty much Lissa's antithesis.

Yet one look at Lissa's lithe form glistening from her bath, and he'd gotten harder than he'd been in recent memory. Make that long-term memory. He wondered if she'd be as aggressive in bed as she was out of it.

For now, though, the hellion appeared stricken. Without a word, she stared at Kate and Sasha's favorite Blanc, jaw slack and eyes dull. Even though he hated to admit it, the small piece packed an emotional punch. A vortex of black and red gave the impression of lost control amid drops of ice blue that fell like rain, either to mourn or to end the chaos. He couldn't tell which.

"I'll take it," she said quietly, "and hang it in my room."

He grabbed the painting and slid it beneath the bed with a smart flick of the wrist. "No."

For a moment, she studied him, probably plotting how to get her way. Then she shrugged, rising from the floor. The supposedly casual movement left her stiff, a marked tension creeping between her shoulder blades. The glimmer of humor she'd shown at hearing Sasha's antics had drained away.

"Why not?" Her question flew in a pointed verbal thrust.

Don't know. "Of all your paintings, that one intrigues me the most. The rest are either nonsensical or nauseating. Parks and sunshine and fireflies. Until I saw that"—he pointed to the gap where the painting had disappeared beneath the bed—"I doubted you had anything in you but kitsch. Manufactured squares of fun for everyone."

She smiled, but the expression reflected challenge, not joy.

"That painting is all about pain. I see blood and tears, Lissa." He traced a fingertip down her check. "I wonder why?"

Her eyes flickered with an emotion he couldn't name. He'd guess sorrow, but her increasingly defiant stance belied melancholy.

She took a deep breath and eased her shoulders away from her ears. "I was young—"

"Yet you still sell the thing, ship it out to people like my wife."

"—and young people do *angst*. Not to worry. As you've said, what did I have to be upset about?"

"That's what I'm trying to figure—"

The cluck, cluck, cluck of her tongue paused the inquisition. Then, "Okay, and in the interest of full disclosure, we can discuss what exactly happened to your wife who's *buried in the backyard.*"

He flinched at the indelicate truth. The woman knows how to change the subject.

"Too much emotion for you?" she asked. "Looks like you're having another one of your elusive *responses.*"

Long months had passed with him trying to shut people out. He'd gotten used to evading probing questions, not asking them. Lissa baffled him with her defensive attack when he'd actually sought to engage.

So this is what it feels like.

She held herself too still, completely detached, so different from the mocking wit she generally kept at the ready. How alike they were. But then, for the briefest instant, that same emotion he'd noted moments before flashed in her eyes. Looking closely, he noted her shallow pants and the way her pulse fluttered wildly at her throat.

Not sadness, he mused. *Fear.*

Not fear of him or of coming to any harm—she stared him down with the regalness of a queen ready to do battle, physical or otherwise—but fear of what he might learn with his probing.

His little artist had a secret.

He grabbed her arm in a gentle hold. "First, tell me about the nicks under your chin."

She yanked away, gritting out, "Dog bite."

"Mmmhmm. And the serrated line at the top of your spine?"

A hand flew to the back of her neck. "What—"

"Next time you play damsel in distress and need a patch-up, wear a tighter shirt." At her shocked look, he went on. "You prod and dig and sneak around, but you expect privacy in return. Not gonna happen."

Her composure returned in a blink. Without so much as a shake of her head, she walked toward the door in a gliding stride that said his discovery didn't bother her a bit. Three times now, she'd gotten a rise out of him. Months and months of numbness, and each time she lobbed a grenade in his direction, he blew up. When he turned the tables, she rebuffed him with ease.

Cole might have resisted her sass, might never have given in to her brash demands for information about Kate, but knowing she used the questions as a shield to keep a painful past on lockdown? Maybe he'd have to give if he was going to get.

Chew on this, little snoop. Steeling himself, he said, "Kate wanted to die."

Lissa's retreating form jerked to a standstill. "Are you saying—?"

"*Yes.* My wife flung herself from a cliff not ten miles away. She's buried here because this house actually made her happy. You didn't know the half of it when you painted this place. *Everything* about Melina, including me, is broken."

CHAPTER 6

Shock thrummed along the insides of Lissa's veins from her heart to her head, finally pulsing at her temple in a steady, painful beat.

"*Goddamn you.*" Air eddied against the constricted walls of her throat, and she gasped, wanting to rail at him. Her instincts had warned that Cole wasn't whole, and yet she'd ignored the message. As angry as she was with him for involving her in a farce, she was more disappointed in herself for the willful blindness.

"When were you going to tell me?" *I'm a naïve, gullible,* desperate *fool.*

Still facing away, she practically heard his shrug. "I wasn't."

Groaning, she whispered, "Of course not. And still we're to rely on each other, form two parts of a functioning whole. You *lied* to me."

Talent, not connections, had finally earned her a part in something meaningful. But not for long.

Kate's unexplained death had been one thing—a heart-wrenching tragedy that had understandably left Cole wounded and angry because loss sucked. But suicide? He might *never* overcome the grief, let alone the guilt.

When he next spoke, he was standing right behind her. A finger found the mark at the base of her neck, a reminder, she supposed, that they both kept secrets. "How is my wife your business?"

Because her ghost is standing between us as surely as her body would have. She stared at the floor. "Why haven't we started work?"

Silent moments dragged by, each longer than the last. When he didn't answer, she spun to face him, chin to chest. "You said it yourself. Because she broke you, and Humpty Dumpty hasn't been put back together again. Kate's my business because *your* problem is now *my* problem."

"One amongst many, huh?" He stalked back to the bed and pulled the painting out, holding it in her direction. "Dark times you want to forget? Kind of like the marks under your chin and on your neck."

"Old," she ground out. "Faded and forgotten, unlike your wife."

"Divulge, then, if it's all so meaningless." His voice dipped. "Otherwise, you're hiding a past that has tainted your painting. And since you're here to paint, we can talk about two in the fucked-up pool. Two who have put the project at risk. *Two* liars."

Her mind registered the rigid set of his shoulders and the slight tremor in the picture frame suspended from his hand. Tension poured off the muscle definition that had gone taut beneath his T-shirt, telling her to tread lightly... "I didn't lie!" She'd *omitted.* "I was hurt." *Forever* ago. "And I painted it out."

"You practically admit to using art as nothing more than an emotional conduit. You paint *feelings*, Lissa. You're incapable of painting anything real."

Maybe. But the hang-ups were mutual. "I guess we're in trouble because you're incapable of seeing potential. Kate's death tapped every ounce of creativity you've ever possessed. Your photographs *only* show what's real, and they're staid. Boring. *Safe.*"

He moved fast. Before she could regret the indelicacy of her accusation, he'd crowded her into the doorframe with the length of his body. Then, softly, against the top of her head, he said, "Big words for a little girl."

The taunt was all wrong, but the tone was low, melodious. Cole's voice wound an intricate pattern through Lissa's insides, squeezing and loosening and preparing a clear path for entry.

"No," she whispered. "True ones." Lissa had long finished fearing those bigger than her. She couldn't back down now. Unsurprisingly, she didn't want to. *But for all the wrong reasons.* He was so close and so angry and so gorgeous. Warm air fanned across her cheek with each of his measured breaths, a mental count to ten. With every thudding heartbeat, a hardness grew against the more pliant flesh of her stomach.

"Hurt how?" he asked.

The question barely penetrated. If he lifted her a few inches, that steely length would fall right where it could do some good.

A light touch skated down one arm, and he actually clasped her fingers. Held. "You said you were hurt, Lissa. *How?*"

Chest heaving with emotion, she answered the only way she could. "You're not the only one who thinks I've had it easy."

Her painting sailed across the room, landing softly on his comforter and freeing his other hand. "That's cryptic bullshit. At least I talk straight. You know my wife's dead. She took her own life. I'm torn up about it."

"Pain is black-and-white for you." *Like art.* "For me, it's a table of colors. Every experience brings a new shade."

"Try me."

She struggled to haul oxygen into her lungs. Technically, years of yoga and beating the streets of New York City had left her physically capable of a little adrenaline-fueled sparring, but New York had something Colorado didn't—oxygen.

And forget the mile-and-a-half above sea level. She'd stopped breathing with Cole's cringer about Kate. Every word since had made matters worse.

Suddenly both of Cole's arms were around her. A strong hand worked in large circles over her back. "Inhale, Liss."

She gulped down a breath.

"Now push it out. Nice and slow."

Again, her body automatically responded to his smooth, velvety instructions.

A sweep of his pelvis rubbed their lower bodies together in a rough grind. *So fucking tantalizing.* But when she heard his low, tortured groan before a guttural, "Talk," she snatched herself away. All the "tell me" and "no, you tell me" was interfering with their bout of accidental foreplay.

Ignoring the way her nipples stabbed into the backside of her bra, Lissa decided on a consolation prize. Obviously, he wouldn't be forthcoming until she opened up. At least a little.

"My parents underwent a rough patch when I was in high school. Money-wise, that is. The construction business is volatile. My brothers had made it through school, but I hadn't, and private tuition was *insane*. I transferred to public school at sixteen, as a precaution mostly, but also because my parents had modest upbringings. They thought the experience would be good for my character, or at least a worthwhile experiment. Long story." She cleared her throat, now unable to breathe out of a swimming, lightheaded need instead of panic. "But the first time a Bentley dropped me off at the curb—they were cautious about new spending but not offloading valuables—I became an instant aberration. My neck eventually had a run-in with the eyelet of a faux combat boot. I *used* to be torn up about it."

His hand clenched on her lower back. "Boot to spine?"

So he believed her? Most didn't believe a privileged girl could be a target. "That's what I said."

The grind of his jaw rasped against her ear. "How long?"

"Cole"—she sighed into his shoulder—"it doesn't take much time to kick a girl." Or call her a rich cunt. Or cut off her ponytail with a pair of sewing scissors stolen from the home-ec room.

"No," he corrected, "how long did this go on?"

"The three years leading to graduation."

Till now, Cole had given every impression of agreeing with those kids, had made it clear he saw Lissa as barely decorative and otherwise useless. Now outrage seeped from his pores along with a low curse he pushed out beneath his breath. "Your parents left you to deal, totally unprepared."

"They didn't know. They'll *never* know." Kind of. Details remained unsaid, but after the company, and the checkbook, had undergone an *obscene* recovery, her parents had displayed a not-positive-but-pretty-sure kind of guilt. If they could, they'd bring her a charmed life on a flatbed truck, all because they *thought* their choices *might* have hurt their baby girl.

Yet helping her only served to convince people she couldn't help herself.

Letting Robert and Karen Blanc assuage their guilt meant she'd never turn them down, not overtly at least, no matter how many Coles called her a talentless hack out of jealousy over the heavies in her corner. The perks of being Daughter Blanc would stop when she attained a level of success that made them unnecessary. The end.

Enter Cole, who offered escape from her reputation but corrupted the plan with his unexpected drama.

The hands bracketing her dropped, but Cole didn't retreat, not an inch. "You were young and the bullying endless. That painting on the bed contemplates the injury."

"I'm not that nice." She shook her head against the doorframe. "More like the *Revenge*."

CHAPTER 7

Morning brought the dry, pungent scent of fall and a thread of gold through the aspens dotting the hills. Through bleary eyes, Cole watched Lissa tackle breakfast outside his bedroom window. She sat on a bench swinging from a tree behind the house, eating a bowl of Fruit Loops and looking like she'd lost the sleep lottery.

Bullied. The word didn't seem to fit Lissa's insouciant exterior, though Cole was beginning to realize her devil-may-care attitude had been carefully crafted. She hid a deep vulnerability with jokes and sarcasm.

All through the night, he'd thought of her curled on the floor of a dim high-school hallway, defending herself against blows from above. She'd hid her struggles from the people who cared about her and assured herself the punishment would stop if she were worthy.

The physical threat had ended. The theory that Lissa was nothing but a spoiled child playing at a career had not, and Lissa had come to equate "worthy" with artistic recognition and respect.

From what Cole could tell, Lissa allowed her parents to pamper her out of guilt for their tender sensibilities. True redemption would only come once she'd made a way for herself in the glittering—and competitive, cutthroat, small, incestuous, and judgmental—world of New York art. The more help she took from her family, especially in the way of strings-pulled gallery showings and special exhibitions, the more she was seen as a spoiled poser.

Worse, she saw Cole as the secret to her success, either that, or the last roadblock preventing it. Cole was definitely the latter, and despite his dawning understanding of her situation, he had zero inclination to budge.

Not until the little hellion learned to cooperate. And follow orders. And respect his space. And stopped making his brain instantaneously combust with images of her sucking his cock.

With an exhale that was more growl than sigh, Cole refocused on the woman below. Today she wore a familiar cable sweater. The chunky knit emphasized the sleek lines of the endless legs she'd encased in another pair of fitted jeans and again tucked into those tall, sexy boots.

And he'd thought himself a breast man. Apparently, he was *ass all the way*.

Appreciation for Lissa's physical treasures brought relief along with unease. Each time her body reminded him he was still alive, her mouth questioned why his wife wasn't. *What exactly happened to your wife? Why's she buried in the backyard?*

Tit-for-tat questions hadn't shut her up. *Nothing* seemed to shut the woman up.

At this rate, Lissa was going to get her answers. Then their situation would lurch from bad to worse.

Once she knew...

Below, Lissa shifted on the swing, leaning over a rickety side to set one of Kate's prized ceramic bowls in the dirt. She propped a foot on the tree's trunk and used the leverage to shove sideways, twisting the supporting ropes round and round. On each rotation, she kicked the trunk with the heel of her boot until the ropes coiled like a torsion spring on a tilt-a-whirl.

Letting go, she spun wildly, a woman who still found joy in turning her face to the sun. Right then, with her unwelcomed questions silenced by laughter, Lissa was magnificent.

Snap!

The first rope broke, its frayed end plummeting as the chair swung from beneath her. She hit the ground in a crunch of busted pottery.

He whirled on his heel. She'd probably broken her tailbone, not to mention Kate's bowl. But when he burst outside, she'd rolled off the dish in a huff, looking irritated but uninjured.

Fine by him. Not like he'd rushed to the rescue with the intention of coddling her.

Again.

Lissa dusted her knees and frowned upward. "Twice." Her peace fingers shot into the air. "That's how many times your house has tried to kill me."

"Because you're a menace."

Her eyes narrowed. "More like a delicate flower stuck confronting a series of booby traps I can only believe you've set. But don't worry. When I mentioned revenge last night, I meant the retaliation I'd wanted, not what I ever actually got. You needn't worry that I'll attack you in your sleep."

He looked skyward like her revelation was *such* a relief. "I liked that bowl." Why didn't he care that she'd broken it?

She rose to her feet on a slow push, rubbing at her backside. "*I* liked my ass."

His fingers twitched because, fuck, so did he. He stuck out his lower lip. "Poor baby, want me to make it better?"

A purr escaped her chest. "Only in your twisted fantasies, where you're the boss, and I'm a rare form of biddable." She bent to pick up the shattered dish, a movement that stretched her jeans tight over the twin globes that would fit perfectly in his hands. His skin heated before he could control the sensation, sending pulses of hundred-proof lust straight to his hardening cock. Those long legs left her rear at the perfect height for him to sink hilt-deep.

He killed the view with a swift shake of his head. Three days with Lissa felt like a month of shock therapy. Each of her "surprises"—streaking, snooping, whatever the hell this was—stole a little more control. But *she*, not he, was here to be trained. *She*, not he, would bend, maybe even break. He crammed the boredom of a three-hour infomercial into his voice when he said, "Charming."

She snapped up, juggling a stack of ceramic shards. "What?" she asked, sounding surprised, as if her little ass-sway hadn't been figured into her grand plan to wear him down.

"Grab your stuff." Approaching the bench that now hung drunkenly from one rope, he pulled a pocket knife from his cargo pants and sawed through the remaining support.

"As in?"

He dragged the fractured bench behind him, not taking care to prevent further damage. The damn thing had dumped Lissa. Could've hurt her. The swing's lifecycle had officially met an end. "Your paints, brushes. *Brain*."

She followed. "Finally, the prodigy remembers our goal."

"If only I could forget." He threw the seat onto a pile of logs. More bonfire fodder. "Meet me here in ten."

She met him in twenty-five.

"I had to fix the easel," she explained with a smirk that undercut her excuse.

He grabbed the tripod and slid it into the truck. Sure enough, she'd duct-taped a leg—probably a mishap from the unexpected wind gust on that first morning. Yet he had a feeling her delay said more about their power struggle than broken equipment. Lissa obviously nursed a belief that she was in charge, that if she proved sufficiently difficult or contrary or even provocative, he'd give in, tell her everything, and be cured of whatever affliction caused him to cling to the dowdy notion of art reflecting reality. Too bad his quest wasn't about art, but life.

Today would be a lesson, just not the kind she'd been gunning for.

******

Switchbacks of dirt trail separated Lissa from Cole, and each hard-won step left her farther and farther behind. To Lissa, the distance felt not only physical, but metaphorical. Cole marched ahead with a few too many worried backward glances. He bore a hefty backpack like a second skin, and every step communicated a stamina she had to grudgingly respect. Her smaller tools were secure in a nap sack, but the easel proved unwieldy as she shifted it from one shoulder to the other. As Cole knew, most of her paintings had been completed in the studio. With each step, he proved she was unprepared for what he had in store—art on the road.

All her, "How hard can it be?" died over the first mile of path that was closely hemmed with color. Brackish moss crawled over frosted earth to meet boulders the ages had marbled with everything from pink quartz to gray granite. The days had grown colder. Even a New Yorker knew a winter-long freeze barreled toward the valley, but today she could detect water running not far from the trail. At first, pine trees camouflaged their exact location, but as they climbed, the cover thinned until she could see for what seemed like forever.

Wilderness had always meant "lack of city" to Lissa—a beach cabana, a golf resort, even a European ski chalet or her family's well-maintained country home. She realized now that hedges trimmed to look like Rodin's *The Thinker* didn't constitute nature, and the utter freedom in escaping every living soul on the planet could define a religion unto itself.

The weight on her shoulders shifted when she tripped over a rock, staggered, and struggled to lift everything higher and keep walking. Before she could put things to rights, Cole turned and marched in her direction. His mouth was an unyielding slash, not at all softened by the golden stubble covering his jaw.

"Such grace." He stopped close. For a fleeting moment, she thought he might touch her. For half of that, she wanted him to, at least until she noted the flat, disinterested look in his eyes, the one that said he wouldn't touch her *like that* for all of Solomon's gold.

Reaching out, he lifted both the tripod and the bag before she could react with either indignation or thanks. "Don't think I'll do this every time," he warned. "Today the dragging is getting on my nerves." Then he spun and headed up the path in the direction of several rocky peaks that looked *days* away.

Sweat slicked her skin by the time they stopped *hours* later. She rasped oxygen through clenched teeth. The air at his house had been pea soup compared to this. When he handed over an energy bar and a water bottle—supplies she hadn't even considered—she inhaled everything on offer.

After ten long seconds under his watchful eye, he said, "You're fine."

What she was, was dying. For a third time now, he'd tried to kill her.

"No nausea," he continued. "Your color's high, and I *know* you'd be whining if you had a headache."

"And I *know* you'd be gloating if you had a point."

"No altitude sickness. Seems we let you acclimate at the house long enough, or did you think I was twiddling my thumbs to log extra time in close quarters with you?"

Her lips locked like a bank safe. *Don't tell him you thought he was being an asshole.* "And here I thought you were merely being an asshole."

He contemplated her with a look of theatrical horror. "Aww. Is Lissa not feeling liked? Not getting her way?"

A pithy response shot to the tip of her tongue. Unfortunately, all the blood in her brain chose that particular moment to drain to her toes, and she rocked on her heels with a sudden gust of wind.

"Is dizzy an altitude—"

Hard fingers wrapped around her bare upper arm. No matter the chill, the physical climb had forced her to shed clothes.

"Sit," he commanded. "Right here. That's right. Close your eyes and let your body sink."

"Not good," she whispered, swallowing hard, not even lamenting her inability to give him hell.

He cupped her cheek with a cool palm. "It'll pass. I promise."

When she opened her eyes, he was crouched on his haunches in front of her with another aluminum water bottle. The calculated analysis he'd displayed earlier had faded to concern. He pressed the cool metal to her collarbone before sliding it into her hand. "See? You're already better."

She nodded, hating how he always seemed to be right. Whenever she thought he'd slipped and made a mistake, a buzzer went off shortly thereafter. *Wrong! Planned that one, Ms. Blanc.*

Leaning back against her hands, she heaved a mental sigh. They'd left the breathtaking, but closeted, valley below. Above the tree line, she saw nothing but rock chips varying in size from baseballs to BMWs, as if her dad's fleet of dump trucks had deposited layer after layer of shale over the mountain. In the distance, she swore she could see Wichita. Where they sat? Nothing to paint.

Seeming to read her confusion, Cole asked, "Do you know why we're here?"

"A test," she said wearily, "always a test."

He stood and toed the easel he'd laid at her feet. "More like a start. Of course, if the start goes badly…"

"As in worse than the one we've already had?"

"That doesn't count. You weren't *working.*"

How charitable of him. "What do you want me to focus on?" The question had to be asked even though she knew her every effort would scream "tired" and "get me the hell off Kilimanjaro."

"Stay put for now."

Happy to oblige, she slumped forward against her bent knees while Cole got busy. First he pulled a camp chair from his bag and arranged it in the rocks about ten feet away. When she thought he'd offer her the chair, or at least sit in it himself, he dug out a smaller, zippered bag, from which he extracted a serious-looking camera. Then he started snapping careful photos *of the chair*.

Cole moved with a grace that spoke of many miles trudged over uneven terrain, all tackled through the limited vision of a dice-sized viewfinder. A careless stumble would have been too mundane, too predictable. He flowed over the rock like water, first inward for close-ups and then moving far up the path for a wider perspective.

Several shots later, she couldn't resist. "*Why* are you taking pictures of a camp stool?"

Eye to the camera, he said, "This is today's subject." Then he prowled around the thing, clicking every few feet. A wind gust knocked the seat over, and he calmly set it back up, piling rocks around each leg to prevent another crash.

"You marched me up here to paint a chair you brought from home." She didn't pose it as a question because *of fucking course he did.*

He spoke without bothering to stop circling. "India won't be raindrops on kittens and whiskers on roses. Or *whatever*. There'll be no comfortable studio and no winging it in your head. You'll pay your dues for each and every scene. A portable chair is presumably not an object of great emotive power, even for you, meaning you might actually paint the damn thing as is."

Unused to anyone dictating her participation in useless activities, Lissa bit back a biting retort and managed to respond with some semblance of calm. "My paintings aren't the result of how I feel about my subjects. They're designed—purposefully, you understand—to convey whatever emotions I decide appropriate for the particular work. Occasionally, those emotions happen to reflect what I'm feeling at the time."

"Occasionally?"

"Often," she admitted, but only because there was no way around that glaring truth.

"I didn't come up here to compromise," Cole said. "Today you'll paint the chair." He tapped the seat with his boot. "An exact replica."

He was being unfair in forbidding her to contribute the only way she knew how. The man wanted Lissa because his fallen wife had appreciated her imagination. Yet he demanded she check that imagination at the door. Grappling with her fury, Lissa felt the small muscles in her face twitch. "Your way won't get the job done. Who wants to look at replicas? There's nothing interesting in my creating identical copies of your work."

"We're comparing *mediums*," he seethed, showing his own frustration in the bunching of his broad shoulders. "Regardless, we had a deal, Lissa, from day one. If you can't, or won't, keep your end of the bargain, you can catch a flight home tomorrow."

"I'll change your mind," she told him grimly. "Watch."

CHAPTER 8

Lissa heaved to her feet, easel in hand. Adjusting the legs low to the ground, she built one of Cole's rock towers around each pole, anchoring the tripod to the mountain. Her canvas was as small as the trek had been long, and she pulled it from her bag along with a travel paint kit she'd configured from a CD case. Within the circular indent, she'd stored fifteen streaks of color, each labeled in permanent marker. She'd lined the clear cover with thin white paper for use in blending. Next came several brushes and a sealed jar of water to clean them.

Cole eyed her setup with unconcealed surprise. Part of his "test" had obviously been to highlight her unpreparedness. Hike-wise he'd succeeded, but she'd come artistically equipped. "Prepare to be amazed," she murmured under her breath.

Using a dark colored pencil, Lissa drew a faint outline of the chair's basics in the middle of her canvas. Then she set to work with paint.

The "boss" had grown roots directly behind her hunched position. His quiet judgment grew so deafening she broke the silence. "No need to monitor my every move."

He didn't budge. "But there *is*."

With cold, precise movements, she methodically smeared forest-green and then black paint across the bottom of the canvas. The need to prove Cole wrong thrummed through her fingers, but she stifled the sensation. While this painting would convey deep feeling, she wanted the sentiment to be *his*, not hers. More, she had to make the overall impression positive, speaking to emotions he would welcome rather than repel.

No more broken hearts.

His hand fell to her shoulder. "There's no *green* in sight, Lissa."

A warning. One she didn't miss but couldn't heed. "Color can be tricky. What you see now might not be the endgame." She streaked rivulets of orange upward from the dark base, careful to avoid the center where she'd sketched the chair.

Next her brush found a yellow so pale it looked almost white, another color the obtuse man behind her wouldn't detect between the navy chair and the grey stone. "Take another hike." She rocked back on her haunches, brush in the air. "I'm not into creepy artistic voyeurism."

When he didn't budge, she added, "Face it. You and I are similar." He couldn't tear himself away, after all. They shared *dedication.*

"We're *vastly* different." His dry tone translated what the words left out: "different" as in she sucked and he didn't.

"Not so opposite we can't meet in the middle."

"Yeah?" Are you painting the 'middle' right now?" he asked. "Planning to bring me to heel without actually complying with our agreement?"

Tricky, tricky partner, but why not tell the truth? "Yes." Bringing the yellow into contact with the painting's periphery, she asked, "Are you worried we'll fail?" They would without a compromise. She could think of little else.

A short pause. "I'm worried *you'll* fail."

Lissa supposed the arrogance ought to irritate her, but she knew defense when she heard it. "Except if I fail, you follow." Cole's quiet inactivity in the year preceding Project Impossible hadn't bothered Lissa when she'd initially accepted the gig. In her mind, an artist lived a life of ebb and flow. At times she'd painted prolifically. At others she'd eaten a lot of Ben & Jerry's and watched reality TV.

Instinct said Cole's hiatus hadn't been a simple creative drought. Whipping around, she aimed her brush up at him like a weapon. "You *had* been making a name for yourself. I recalled your successes when you approached me with this proposal back in New York." Maybe she should say that again. "When *you* asked *me* to come aboard, I accepted based on your reputation. You'd become a slightly stale star, mind you, but hey"— she shrugged—"I gave a guy a break."

Turning back to the easel and the chair beyond, Lissa continued to apply the yellow in broad strokes, starting from the dark lines of the chair and tracing outward. "I spent much of yesterday digging deep into your last year." Deeper, even, than her initial research. Cole hadn't passed the time entirely holed up at Melina, eating ice cream and pandering to his grief like she'd assumed. "The fact that you were working wasn't a big surprise. You've come a long way, and not in the 'Congratulations, you're a badass' sense." Nope, Cole had transitioned from documenting active volcanos from the skies of Iceland and piranha feeding frenzies from the waters of Brazil to something else entirely.

"Tell me your former glory was merely buildup to interviewing aging hookers in dingy hotel rooms," she cooed. "'Jewel,' was it? Your other projects were equally impressive—drag-racing cars in Denver, even some pictures of a prized steer at the National Western Stock Show."

Long moments faded away after she lapsed into silence. Eventually, she thought he'd refuse to respond. Then he said, "Her name was *Ms.* Jewel."

Lissa's lips curled at that, only because he couldn't see the concession. "By all means, let's maintain formalities." Anything if he'd admit she was right. "But you see? We're not so different, after all. *You need me as badly as I need you.*"

She worked like a fiend but only saw dividends when she gave in and let her family help. Cole had been moving up, but he'd fallen out of play after Kate's death. The man had been working for the past year with *nothing* to show for it, and he could only skate on his aging rep for so long.

In other words, she wasn't the only semi-loser on the mountainside.

"Tedious pictures of tiresome things aren't going to save either of us." Lissa was the half of their duo who could spice things up. If he'd concede to each of them doing their individual best—Cole documenting the world as he saw it, with her giving his reality a little spin—they could be truly great.

The last color to grace the canvas was a bright white she used to trace the chair's skeleton in thick, almost textural lines that ran together. The final effect brought a watery sunrise rising from a dark, desperate pit. Light opposed shadow and implied a hard-won freedom. Not American-flag or death-to-Al-Qaeda-type freedom, but freedom from self-inflicted limitations, from "I can't" and "I won't" and "You can't make me."

Still, the "middle" she'd promise hadn't been forgotten. If Cole looked closely and used some imagination, he would see that his silly camp chair formed the sun. He would know that he could provide the inspiration, even pick the subjects, but he couldn't—and he shouldn't—hem her in.

Because Lissa had long-ago learned that fences were easily jumped.

She grabbed the edges of the painting and stood. Slowly she turned, ready for judgment, hoping like hell he'd see reason.

Or at least recognize his chair.

On sight, Cole's eyes flared, then narrowed to sharp pinpricks of blue—like lasers he'd summoned to burn holes through her work. He took a step, edging forward until they stood chest to chest with the canvas pressed between them.

He glanced down, eyes swirling and ominous. "You're pushing me, trying to see if I'll break."

"N-no. That's the last—"

"In the past, I was gentle and caring, always giving more, never taking too much. Now I'm jaded enough to know better. Go ahead and fuck with me, Lissa"—he stroked a finger over her lower lip—"but expect me to *fuck back.*"

Oh, God, please do. A flash of want branded her frontal lobe. Attraction had been seething beneath the surface, but she'd snubbed the signs, calling the twinges and pulses nothing more than a rampant desire to see the project succeed.

Complications were piling up on top of his artistic quirks... and now this. *Expect me to fuck back.* At least she'd gotten the rampant desire part right.

He leaned in, to where his lips grazed hers when he spoke. "Wouldn't that be interesting? The woman who doesn't admit to having any demons falls under the *thumb* of the king of them." Pulling away, he met her eyes. She could take a guess, but she'd never truly know what made him suddenly step to the side in a quick reversal of the last few minutes. Lips parted, he started to talk. "Don't..." His mouth worked for a moment, and his gaze fell to the painting pressed between their bodies. Finally he bit out, "Drivel, like all the rest."

With that, he scooped up his camera case and started down the mountain. Refusing to watch him go, Lissa flipped the painting to face her, manipulating the canvas in measured degrees, dreading what she'd see. Sure enough, the colors had been spread and smeared into a nonsensical mess instead of the careful message she'd crafted. Surely a matching imprint— and one he'd purposefully taken—stood out on the front of Cole's shirt.

This was a gauntlet, pure and simple. Her drive to finally be accepted as an artist in her own right insisted she meekly trail behind Cole and proceed to follow his instructions to the tee. That same need said the respect she'd earn imitating another wouldn't be worth a damn. The rich kid who'd been found undeserving by her peers had grown into a woman who received unmerited hype as the daughter of an overly generous—and supremely connected—industrialist. If she yielded to Cole, she'd become the cheater who crested on another's coattails, content to receive accolades despite a distinct lack of vision.

Smoke from burning dreams curled at her feet, and in the hidden recesses of her psyche, where she was allowed sadness and fear, she screamed in anguish. Years ago, when her peers' taunts had escalated to physical abuse, she'd *known* the problem hadn't been rich versus poor, but *different* versus *the same*. Recognizing a remedy for her torment had cracked her resolve, and a quest to fit in had taken over—cheap clothes donned in the convenience-store bathroom before first period, lies told to prevent the drop-offs at school, a quiet day face that concealed her charmed homelife, and an opposing boisterousness at home that masked her daily shame from old private-school friends like Scarlet and, most of all, family.

Her parents had transferred her to public school in good faith, hoping the bout of financial insecurity might ultimately strengthen her character. Lissa had changed all right. She'd *lied* to ease her way by pretending to be like the others. But the guise hadn't worked then, just like changing to meet Cole's ideals wouldn't work now.

Never sell out again.

Privilege doesn't obviate talent.

Despite the mental pep talk, defeat laced her fatigue, teasing her with visions of changing Cole's mind with her superior logic, but mostly reminding her of the subtle differences between stalwart and stupid. The former would move her forward. The latter would move her back to New York and another gallery where her dad bought all her paintings while the "real" artists laughed behind their hands.

She pushed out a weary breath, gathering her supplies with shaky movements. *An ounce of self-preservation, Lissa, not a pound.*

The dose of reality, however small, gave her the guts to plaster a fake smile on her face. Staring at Cole's retreating figure, she studied the long, stubborn strides of a man who obviously meant to get his way, by fair means or foul.

Tsk, tsk, she thought. Never issue a challenge you don't want me to accept.

"How about a wager?" she bellowed after him. A friendly bet she *wanted* to lose.

******

Cole halted his wavering descent down the mountain. He might have continued to the bottom, but her yell gave him an excuse to wait.

A racket sounded behind him, and he looked over his shoulder to see her clipping along with that dilapidated equipment bag, her easel, and the wet canvas. She'd left his chair behind.

Not surprisingly, Lissa didn't wait to start talking. "You want me to paint what I see, exactly as I see it?"

He acknowledged the non-question with a slight nod. They could only revisit the requirements so many times. He'd laid them out in the beginning and repeated them practically every five minutes since.

"Well," she said tartly, "I want our works to *mean* something, not to simply *show* something."

They *would*. "Funny how you think I care."

"Testy, testy." She caught up to him and gruffly thrust the painting that now looked a lot like the front of his shirt into his hands. "I have a solution." A pause. "For both of us. Call it a bet or a wager or a dare—whatever you want. Each time you manage the challenge, I'll paint exactly what you photograph. No deviations."

He'd believe *that* the day Sasha stopped craving bacon. "Continue."

She reached down for a chunk of rocky debris, a remnant of retreating glaciers. Holding it up, she aligned the rock with the sinking sun. "Had the light been lower, the ground darker—maybe dotted with moss or wet leaves—and the chair more precisely positioned, the picture you took today would have looked a lot like the one I painted."

Keeping her arm extended, she slinked to his side, still holding the rock chip high in the air. Inch by inch, she moved the stone into the path between the two of them and the sinking afternoon sun. For one second when the rock moved through the perfect arc, light fractured around its edges in a bright flare. "Had you waited until the sun was in *this* position and then angled your shot to catch the rays as they backlit the chair and obscured its lines, we would have produced similar images."

The tang of peppermint rose up from beneath her shirt collar, and Cole checked the urge to lean down and nuzzle into her neck. "Clearly you're reaching—"

"Not so, pho-tog. *Clearly* I've come up with an answer."

With that, she shot him an aha! look, and his resistance wilted. *Keep looking at me like that.* He knew Lissa assumed he'd purposefully ruined today's painting. In reality, the instant her breasts had brushed against his chest, his mind had blanked and he'd blindly pressed into the sensation until he'd mashed the canvas *and* those delectable curves between them. In that moment, only one thing had come to mind.

Fucking back.

Her eyes had nearly swallowed her face, and he'd gotten the impression that no matter how deft her verbal thrusts and parries, she *liked* the idea. That quick flare of invitation had made his situation so much worse. Rather than ignore a fantasy, he now had to resist a *possibility*.

A daunting task since he was harder than the granite she held in her elegant hand.

Pitching his voice low, he sought a distraction. "Details, Lissa. So far you've faked a solar eclipse with a piece of rock."

She beamed. "Just the beginning."

"Of what?"

"So glad you asked." The stone dropped to the ground and bounced. "We'll do more of these... exercises. I"—she clamped her mouth shut, then started again—"make that *you*, will come up with an idea for a scene to play on something ordinary or, if not that, at least familiar. Today would have been a chair, the sky, and a mountain. Using your start, I'll consider ways we can twist the backdrop to convey a more powerful message, and I'll instruct you regarding the staging, taking into account your input regarding photography logistics, of course. Then when you take your pictures, they'll reflect exactly what the two of us see, though what we see will actually be a skewed reality."

When he didn't immediately oppose the plan—he was working up to it—she rushed on. "Sometimes we'll work side-by-side, but in instances where the ability to get the scene right is fleeting, like today with the light, I'll work from your pictures offline. Each time you come up with a meaningful subject—and by that I mean sufficient fodder for interesting, emotive images that keep people guessing—I'll paint *exactly* what you photograph."

"And if I don't?"

"Then," she said, "and because you obviously require *inducement*, I'll paint what I want."

Talk about circular logic to circumvent his plan on a technicality. Kate, too, had been a master. Since he'd never been interested in timid women, he'd found his wife's clever schemes sexy. How the hell else had he ended up with a plantation home in the Rocky Mountains? Christ, tracked-in snow constantly threatened the parquet floors, and he had to keep a humidifier near the fragile mahogany banisters to keep them from cracking in the dry air. "Who decides if I've provided 'sufficient fodder'?"

"Me."

Her confident answer reverberated down the length of his erection. That would be a "check" on the enduring allure of clever scheming. "An example?"

Lissa arched both brows and looked around, as if to say, *I'm waiting… yup, stiiiill waiting.*

He frowned, refusing to reveal his intrigue. "All right, how about the firehouse in Nederland?" Not exactly the Taj Mahal, but it was the first thing to come to mind.

Her breath skated over his sternum, warm in the cutting fall air, reminding him she hadn't stepped away after her pet rock demonstration. "Wow, you *are* a wild one. First a camp chair, and now this."

Definitely the firehouse.

"Feeling any particularly strong emotion?"

Lust. "Frustration."

"Funny," she shot back immediately, slapping a hand to her forehead. "Frustration comes to my mind as well. Deal?"

He eyed the pulse pounding at the base of her throat, wondering if he'd given himself away so clearly when telling the same lie. "Yes, Lissa, you have a bargain."

CHAPTER 9

After a week of earnest effort, Lissa laid her fork on her plate and eyed Kent across the dining room table. He'd come knocking with more frozen food, this time with Trevor and Trevor's striking red-headed wife in tow. The defrosted meatloaf tasted like toasted paper shavings, and Lissa swallowed against the smell of roasted animal fat, forcing tiny bites in an effort to appear engaged.

After ten days at Melina, seven of them spent experimenting with her *bargain* and ways to fend off Cole's dry, flammable temper, she was ready to do violence. Tie-him-to-the-bed-and-take-it-out-on-his-body-until-he-begged-for-Jesus-or-mommy violence.

The only thing keeping her from exacting her sensual revenge was the fact that she hated his guts. And she had principals. And she didn't want to ruin her career reboot by BDSMing a grieving widower into a coma. Plus, she'd never actually tied anyone to a bed or done anything remotely sexually dominant.

Oh, and while he seemed to know exactly how much she wanted him— "You plainly can't wait to paint *me*," he'd taunted—he demonstrated a keen ability to resist. Too much brooding and too little ogling.

Tonight Cole hadn't seen fit to grace Melina's guests with his presence. In fact, Lissa hadn't seen Cole since they'd completed a scene featuring his deer feeder earlier that morning. Sexy stuff, those deer feeders.

She wondered where Cole went when he disappeared. *Taking pictures.* What did he photograph on his epic walkabouts, and how did he employ the results?

Though Lissa found the meatloaf revolting, Kent appeared to have it worse. He dug into a plate of lettuce with a marked lack of gusto. Fork poised over the pile, he reached for a basket of bread sitting in front of Trevor. The butter came next.

53

"Saw that," Trevor said the moment the butter left the table.

"Just a little." Kent's whine came dangerously close to sounding like Gollum out for his Precious. At least he didn't *pet* the butter.

Without looking up, Trevor calmly took the plate from his uncle's grasp and set it in front of Rhea, out of reach. "No butter."

Rhea snorted but stayed quiet. Her green eyes rested casually on each diner in turn, but she'd yet to utter a word. Even Trevor's introduction had prompted only a nod. Lissa found it hard not to stare. Tall and broad shouldered for a chick, Rhea was model beautiful and marathon fit. She wore workout clothes and hardly any jewelry. A woman like that didn't need diamonds or platinum. The flashing red hair curling around her shoulders set off pale skin and bright eyes, providing adornment aplenty.

Kent cast Rhea an assessing look, but he didn't give up. "My cholesterol is *barely* high."

"No butter," Trevor added implacably before biting into a slice of thickly slathered bread.

Resembling a naughty child who'd had his cake taken away only to ask for a brownie and actually expect to get one, Kent began to slowly slide the salt and pepper shakers his way.

Lissa was smiling long before Trevor intercepted. "No salt."

Kent's eyes shot wide in mock surprise. "It's *lettuce*," he groaned, drawing out the last plaintively.

"Spoken like a sixty-year-old man waving hello to his second heart attack."

A scowl tried to form on Kent's swarthy face, but he was too good-natured to pull it off. "You used to threaten me, you know, telling me I'd better buy you a bike or football cleats—with Cole it was always another camera—because you'd be picking my old-folks home."

Trevor chuckled. "Count yourself lucky, then. Those nursing-home people would be Nazis about salt."

Rhea ignored the back-and-forth but finally opened her mouth. "Kent raised the boys," she explained absently around a bite of bread. No butter for her either, presumably by choice. "When they were young, their father suffered a massive heart attack. Mommy dearest was a passenger in the car when it happened. Kent took over from there."

Trevor's look issued a warning, but all he said was, "Without Kent, it would have been foster care for both of us."

So Uncle Kent had a habit of stepping in after a tragedy.

"Don't you worry, m'dears." Kent patted the front pocket of his shirt, where Lissa could detect a round outline—probably a pill case—pressed against the fabric. "I'm armed."

"Always," Rhea replied, her voice sickly sweet.

Trevor's jaw bulged, but he let the discussion drop. A wise choice—

when Kent didn't get any more flack, he dug into his salad like the scuffle had never happened. Lissa soon learned why.

"Since Cole is so rudely avoiding dinner, Lissa, why don't you tell us about yourself?" Kent took another bite and chewed expectantly.

It begins.

"Let's see," she said, pondering what to share. "I'm a painter from New York City. I started when—"

"What do you think of Cole?" Kent's interruption said it all. A run-down on her life would be *blah, blah, blah* to these people. They had *expectations*. No doubt they hoped she and her host would make more than art.

Should she squash the dream now?

Rhea alone seemed unconcerned with Lissa's impression of her brother-in-law. She inhabited her chair with the confidence of an athlete, slightly turned out as though she might bail any second if not sufficiently entertained. The sun was setting outside, and the shifting light caused the chandelier to reflect the sheen of her second-skin shirt. The fabric looked high-tech—part reflective, part mesh, a bunch of pockets around the waist for mini water bottles. Lissa half wondered if Rhea planned to jog back to Boulder.

Before Lissa could craft a hedging response to Kent's question, the redhead filled in her own blanks. "You think he's crazy." The observation might have been keen, but it was delivered with a bored drawl that felt more contrived than disengaged.

A placating "no" wouldn't do the conversation any good. "His grief's too raw." Lissa sensed in Cole the kind of pain that couldn't help but bruise others. Already he'd made her face hang-ups she'd thought long buried in order to force compromises that felt one-sided.

Rhea threw a sidelong glance at Trevor, then shifted her gaze to Lissa and held. "Cole's ready."

Only if "ready" meant dictating unacceptable terms for Lissa to blindly follow. "You don't believe that any more than I do."

"Let me clarify." Rhea's expression remained bland, but the way she sat forward in her seat continued to betray a deeper level of engagement. "Cole was at the top of his game when Kate died. He fell far and fast. But now it's time to return to normal. A man like that can't sideline his gifts forever."

He *could*, Lissa silently disagreed, if he continued to let Kate's death hold those gifts hostage.

Kent eyed Rhea in mild reproach, shaking his head. "Easy when you say it fast, isn't it?"

Lissa had been round and round the issue in her head. Losing Kate kept floating to the top. It was the only explanation for Cole's über-strict adherence to realist ideals. Though Lissa didn't doubt the link between

Kate, Cole, and what she less-than-affectionately called Cole's artistic "stuntedness," she hadn't been able to piece together a coherent explanation.

Grappling anew, Lissa opted to ignore the elk-loaf and focus on her Sangiovese, swirling the vine-ripened courage around her glass. "Cole told me she—"

"Committed suicide?" Rhea finished. Lissa couldn't pinpoint why, but the woman's demeanor felt too casual for the s-word.

"And?" There had to be a story. "From what I can tell, Kate was a lovely, prosperous woman in the prime of her life, with an obviously doting husband and everything going for her." The kill-yourself angle didn't compute.

Rhea fell silent at the frank assessment. Trevor's attention passed between his wife and his uncle in darting glances, but those two had busied themselves with forks and knives like the food had taken first place at the state fair.

"There's little to tell," Trevor said finally, his expression closed, harsh even, making him look more like the sexy axe murderer she'd originally pegged him for.

Liar. There's little you will tell. If all the cards were on the table like Cole's relatives implied, they'd be more forthcoming. These three danced around their secrets.

Pushing her plate aside, Lissa sat back against her chair, cradling her wine glass and openly studying Trevor. Where Cole was all lean muscle and crackling anger, a mountaineer who looked like he could handle any obstacle life threw his way, Trevor was the actual mountain. At least thirty pounds of extra power packed Trevor's towering frame. On one hand, he reminded Lissa of Sasha—large and loving and perhaps overly aware of his appeal. Scratch behind the ears and he'd probably roll over. On the other, he went disturbingly quiet when pushed, pulsing in understated menace. Get too close and the fire inside the mountain might erupt.

Meh. She'd take the risk.

Despite Lissa's irritating tendency to incinerate from the inside whenever Cole came near, she wasn't some pushover to back down at a withering look.

Never sell out again.

She'd been dragged into a minefield. Accepting Cole's offer—finally stomping on the status quo—had been a huge risk that deserved more than a cheap excuse. *Aw shucks, suicidal wife,* didn't cut it.

Lissa launched her offensive. "Drugs or alcohol? Money laundering? Did Kate give her car to the Salvation Army the week before?"

Chairs creaked like chirping crickets as all three of them shifted in their seats.

"Was she ill? Had she ever tried to hurt herself? Lost her job? Gotten arrested—?"

"Nothing like that," Kent interrupted.

"Then 'like' what?"

Kent's shoulders hunched. "Kate had her moments. I noticed weight loss a few weeks before but chalked it up to a fad diet. My wife was always trying to live on cabbage-and-vinegar soup."

No wonder they feed Cole with such dogged resolve. Lissa sighed and re-reached for her plate, cutting the loaf into tiny pieces in an effort to be a good eater like Kent seemed to favor. "Moments?" Could be promising.

"Nothing much," Rhea said, now staring at the ceiling. "Kate kept to herself."

"How well did you know her?"

Rhea straightened and faced Trevor, not Lissa, when she said, "Obviously not well enough." A tremor worked its way across those toned shoulders before she added, "We were friends once." She sounded disgusted.

Lissa stilled her knife mid-stroke. "But no longer."

Rhea's attention snapped from Trevor back to Lissa. "She's dead, so obviously not."

First crickets and now hissing kitties. Quite the symphony. "*Pardonne-moi*," Lissa apologized with a flourish. "You *were* no longer friends."

"*Oui*," Rhea snapped.

"Why?" Lissa mouth clamped shut at her overstep. "Never min—"

"No," Kent cut in with an upheld hand. "I wouldn't mind hearing the answer."

Through gritted teeth, Rhea spoke, never turning in Kent's direction. "You *know* the answer."

"Yes," came Kent's light reply, "I suppose I do." The sly up-tick at the edge of his mouth suggested his "knowledge" didn't quite mirror Rhea's.

Lissa's head whirled with the implications of these people's problems. Accidentally stumbling into a family feud was one type of complication she *couldn't* afford. "Anyway, about Kate?"

Rhea piped up, her dislike increasingly clear. "Kate was kind of an introverted extrovert. Proper, composed, self-aware. She was *that* woman—"

"Yes, a perfect specimen with *moments*," Lissa finished. "What if her fall was an accident? Why would anyone think she killed herself?"

She shouldn't have bothered to ask. The most put together are often the closest to falling apart.

An abrupt slam sounded from the kitchen, and Lissa muttered a curse. Cole was back in residence, but she couldn't say whether the noise signified his recent return from parts unknown or his reaction to hearing her interrogate his family. With the exception of Lissa, voracious eating commenced all around.

Cole strolled in, dusty and wind-swept from a night—not that she'd noticed—and day spent god-knew-where. He cradled a camera with a foot-long lens and smiled at the group in a way he kept on lockdown with her alone. "Illustrious gathering we have this evening."

A glimpse of affectionate humor lurked in Trevor's answering gaze. "It *was*."

An extra place had been set next to Lissa. Cole paused behind her on the way to his seat. Before she could guess his intent, he plunked the camera to the table and swept her hair aside. She'd worn it down to conceal the healing wound on her neck.

The collar of her shirt covered the old scar at her nape. Like the "dog bite" beneath her chin, no one—not even her family—knew the origin of the mark. Not until a week ago.

Not until Cole.

Right in her ear, he asked, "When did you remove the bandage?"

"This morning."

"No swelling," he observed.

"No."

"Pain?"

"*No.*"

"Good." He brushed her hair back into place and stalked to his chair, ignoring the collective gaping silence of their visitors.

Awareness rippled through each of Lissa's senses—the spiced scent of her wine, the renewed weight of her hair brushing against her neck, the slow scrape of Cole's chair as he slid it from the table.

He'd been so close, practically sweeping his lips over her sensitive outer ear while his family watched in rapt fascination. The feel of his hands, of his hot breath skating over her sensitive skin, left her both heated and embarrassed.

Expect me to fuck back.

But the moment didn't last. Once seated, Cole struck without preamble. "I never said Kate *fell*." Posture rigid and eyes defiant, he elaborated, "I said she *flung* herself. We know because of the trajectory of her body. She landed too far from the face of the rock." Abruptly, he crashed his palm to the table. "There was *momentum*."

Cole *had* overheard her questioning his family. A hand fluttered to her throat. "Where were you?"

"Texas." Cole fisted a fork and stabbed an innocent chunk of meatloaf. "On a shoot."

"I'm—"

He didn't let her finish. "Yes, there was an investigation," he said, adding, "however shoddy," under his breath. "No, there wasn't foul play." With each blow, his voice descended. "She jumped, sailed, took a flying leap, whatever you—"

"I was going to say, 'I'm sorry.'"

The tirade stalled. Her empathy had shut Cole's mouth, but his furious gaze still blazed, beginning with her and then leveling on each guest in due time. One would think the messy hair and golden stubble would make him look him less intimidating. They didn't. The lack of polish implied he cared little about anything other than grinding his adversaries to a bloody, protesting pulp.

Some advice, Cole whispered with his eyes. *Leave me be.*

Kent stared blithely back, his regard bouncing between Lissa and Cole with gleeful optimism. Trevor cocked his head, respectful but persistent. If Cole wanted his thoughtful, patient brother to let the subject drop, he'd have to do more than glare through the tension that thickened the air between the two men.

Of them all, Rhea managed to be the most interesting. She withered against her seat, losing the bulk of her earlier bluster in the face of Cole's silent reprimand. Finally breaking eye contact, she returned her attention to the cooling meat on her plate.

Trevor's hand covered Rhea's with a squeeze, and Lissa examined the link. Mere physical closeness could never mimic the unspoken support Trevor passed to his wife through those entwined fingers. A responsive pang wrenched Lissa's gut with an unexpected twist. Thus far, her time at Melina had focused on a loss that hinted at great love.

The type of love she'd never had to lose.

At last sighting, her ex-boyfriend had grown a pair of ironic mutton chops. Right now the man no doubt trolled some little-known burlesque show in the East Village, looking for a girlfriend in a statement T-shirt who took lunch hour tai chi classes and got hives at the mention of a chain restaurant. The child-woman would have to be an original, even in her vapidity, right down to an insistence on mono-bloom honey produced by itinerant beekeepers in central Turkey.

Lissa's replacement would be an artist, of course, but an ego-boosting variant who created "cute" but non-threatening pieces no one took seriously.

Someone completely unlike Lissa, with her fire and her family. If the former escaped notice, the latter rose up, which meant Lissa had shared her lover's struggle but never his starving until her every success had been called undeserved.

Lissa chewed on her lower lip. The bond between Trevor and Rhea reminded her she needed a hand to hold when the reviews ate her alive, not one to slap her on the back of the head and chide her for reaching too high in the first place.

Giving and receiving that kind of no-strings support sounded like a fine idea until Rhea shattered the reverie by slipping Trevor's hold. A blatant flick of her wrist untwined her husband's fingers. Gaze locked on the food, Rhea finally reached for the contraband butter with her now-free hand.

Slick, if one were, say, trying to escape freaky Cousin Herb at Thanksgiving Dinner, but her sexy-as-fuck husband? The one who was trying to take her side?

No. Just... *no.*

Cole took charge before suffering a single bite. He stood and leaned across the table, resting his torso on splayed fingers and straining arms. Flicking his chin toward the door, he said "Go. Please."

The family began a slow scatter, technically not obeying but at least condescending to clear the table.

Lissa shot to her feet. After all her questions, she still had insufficient answers. If Kent and Rhea and Trevor withdrew, she'd be left with the man most determined to keep her in the dark.

The one she'd most like to see join her there.

Cole's expression tightened. "Don't even try it."

Now what? "You mean doing what you say?" Lissa batted her lashes with feigned innocence. "I wouldn't dream of it."

Kent had disappeared into the kitchen, but Trevor and Rhea were making a snail look speedy.

Ignoring their continued presence, Cole said, "I've had enough of this."

"Good." Lissa couldn't agree more. "You've spared yourself another 'scene,' and we can get back to the original plan. You photograph what you see, and I'll paint what *I*—"

"Not that." Cole's hand slashed through the air. "I mean the incessant questions. You're alone with my family for half a meal, and I arrive not to jokes and toasts, but to an interrogation."

They started it.

"Consider it payback for five days ago when I asked you to select an indoor subject, and you picked a roll of toilet paper."

"You got your revenge," he grated, "when you snickered about it being an 'apt choice' given that my 'work is shit.'"

She stacked Cole's full plate on top of her own uneaten food, shaking her head. "That was for the day before, when you let Sasha into my room at five in the morning. He tried to jump onto the bed but only managed to ram the side of my mattress over and over again like a drunken sheep. Eventually I settled him down into a roaring snore that rattled up from the rug for the next three hours."

"It's a sign that he likes you." The animal in question sprawled out at the end of the table and rolled onto his side with a groan.

"And a sign that *you* don't."

"Or a message that I'll retaliate when you eat every Skittle in the house and leave all the empty bags piled on the kitchen counter."

He'd noticed. "You know what? Maybe I asked your family about you"— she slid a glance toward Trevor and Rhea, both frozen in mid-step, backs to the action—"because I know you haven't been honest, and even though I'm sleeping with him, your dog hasn't spilled the goods."

Cole pulled the plates from her grip and set them on the table a bit too carefully. Then he crowded her against the chair that threatened the wobbly joints at the backs of her knees. "And *they're* going to remedy the oversight? You think Rhea here"—the redhead flinched, keeping her head averted but making no move to disappear—"will roll over and lay me out like a Facebook timeline?"

"You know what they say. 'If door number one disappoints because it hides a moody, uncooperative ass, check behind door number two.'"

"Right." He ground his molars together with a cringe-worthy crunch. "And you know what I say."

Yes, she did. Her eyes flew to his, but not in time to change what was about to happen.

Expect me to fuck back.

That furious mouth crashed into hers.

******

Her lips felt like satin fresh off a hot iron, the top a smidge fuller than the bottom, a perfect pout. At her startled gasp, he licked into her mouth. Deep. Then *deeper*.

"Like that?" he heard himself ask against her skin. He didn't need an answer. Her body pressed against his, breath coming in rolling pants that sped faster and faster. *Of course she did.*

"No." She gasped, then sank her teeth into his lower lip. The pinch wasn't nearly enough. He needed—

Sensation shorted with a sudden and unwelcome realization. Slinging an arm around Lissa's waist, he pinned her in the vee between her chair and the table. When he turned his head, he confirmed that his brother and Rhea still stood by, eyes peeled in what could only be called *rapt* fascination.

His family meant well. They *did*. Yet a clinging resentment overshadowed his appreciation for their interference. The invasions of his privacy had to stop. He finally wanted the freedom to be indiscreet, and he couldn't with his family enjoying free reign over his house and grounds, their watchful eyes guarding him like *he'd* been the one to battle bouts of clinical depression.

Moments, Kent had told Lissa.

"I said *leave*." His voice was soft, too soft, and Trevor reluctantly heeded the desperation he no doubt detected in the borderline plea. His brother grabbed Rhea by the wrist and pulled her into the kitchen, letting the swinging door flap in their wake.

A smooth pull dragged Lissa forward. She looked surprised—after all, Cole had given in to his need with no sign of second thought—but a hint of challenge shadowed her expressive eyes. The defiance of five minutes ago faded to speculative seduction.

Her voice took on a fine-with-me tone when she whispered, "Can't prevail at sparring, so you're taking it out on my *neeeedy*, little body?"

Maybe. Her breathy quip rushed along his cock, and he lost track of his agenda.

Oh, yeah. Lick her into submission.

She felt so soft and small and willing against his chest, he could hardly believe the same woman regularly flayed him alive with that pink tongue that, right now, licked the front of her teeth, the physical equivalent of sharpening knives.

Time to flay back. He trailed open-mouth kisses up the side of her throat, gently nibbling each time she made a noise. Their guests surely hadn't retreated farther than the other side of the closed door.

Heady scent infused the air around them—always a different embodiment. The woman went for variety in her soaps and lotions. So far he'd separately detected flowers and fruit and then spicy peppermint. The best *had* been last Tuesday—coconut—but today's almond was even better.

Of course he favored the edibles. *Just one taste.* Each night he imagined whether she could possibly deliver on the succulent promise of her milky skin. If she didn't, he could walk away.

He brushed his tongue over the pulse that fluttered below her jaw. Flicking back and forth, her taste hit—a jolting buzz in the back of his throat—along with a sweet little moan that escaped her lips.

"Were you planning to fight me every step of the way?" he murmured silkily. "Nothing has seemed to work, but I see pleasure subdues you."

"Not fair," she breathed.

He looked down and saw the hem of her sweater bunched in his shaking fist. Deny it all he wanted, but his body was ready for another glimpse of the high breasts he'd seen dripping on his carpet days ago, and he welcomed the hands that scrabbled for purchase against his taut stomach.

"Do you want me to lift this shirt, touch your pretty little breasts?" he growled against her ear. "Because I will. I *want* to." Despite himself, he so fucking wanted to.

When her answer came out a mewling, unintelligible rasp, he moved his hand to cup her between the legs. Through her jeans, he rubbed along the seam, pressing a little harder on the upstroke.

Above, he moved to her lips. Her mouth was hot and welcoming when he slipped inside. She batted his tongue with hers, tangling against him in wet strokes that ripped a groan from deep within his core.

"Do you, Lissa?" he grated against her open mouth. "Say the word."

With a wrenching cry, her hand landed on his forearm. "No."

No?

"*You* don't want this," she added weakly.

Incorrect. He'd never wanted *anything* more, never been strung so tight—

A rough shove against the table flung him away, not because she was right, but because she wasn't. He wanted and wanted and wanted her some more, which made him *wrong* in a whole different way. The two of them faced off, heaving but still fully clothed, separated from their spectators by a thin wall. He'd never been so turned on in his life.

He wouldn't have stopped. If Lissa had let him, he'd have pounded her into the table within a minute, letting her long, graceful body steal the memory of the only perfect thing he'd ever had.

And lost.

Lissa had been the one to see reason, the only one in the room who'd proven worthy of his wife's memory.

Motherfucker.

Cole pulled both hands through his hair, squeezing his scalp on each pass. The movements calmed him to the point of speech. "I told you to keep us above the belt. And then I—"

"I'm sorry," he said in a whoosh of emotion, then fled before he broke down and finished what he'd started.

CHAPTER 10

Shock hit Lissa in breaking waves, the lust Cole had fired along every nerve ending refusing to abate. Sucking air, she flattened her palms against the table crowding her ass and closed her eyes, grappling for simple things—like physical mastery over her quivering thighs.

"Goddamn," she muttered under her breath. *Focus.* "Spontaneous orgasm isn't even a real thing."

In front of her, Lissa caught the telltale swish of the kitchen door swinging shut.

"From the looks of it, you're about to debunk the theory." Rhea didn't sound particularly apologetic for the intrusion.

Summoning the insolent glare she pictured in her mind, Lissa blinked her eyes open to see all three of Cole's overzealous caretakers staring back at her. "Jesus Christ, you people never quit."

"Apparently, neither do you," Rhea quipped, and Lissa detected a subtle chastisement behind the calculating gleam in the other woman's eyes.

"Why would I?" The previous week—up to and including the last half-hour—had brought several realities to light.

First, Cole possessed a diamond-hard head, but also a brilliant talent. She *would* be standing next to him when the world took notice.

Second, all roads led to Kate. Unravel the Kate hang-up, and Lissa would have the key to Cole's malfunctioning creativity.

Third, Cole withdrew when Lissa probed *him*, but he went mental when she turned her questions on *others*.

The lesson? Probe others early, and probe them often. In the end, she'd either get her answers or push Cole off a second sensual cliff.

Win-win.

Clamping down on the heat still simmering in her veins, Lissa used her outside voice. "I want to know everything. Who was Kate Rathlen? What did she hold dear in this life? Most importantly, what changed to make such a beautiful, successful, well-loved woman kill herself, and why would Cole decide his penance must come in the form of hiring Kate's favorite artist but completely stifling his own artistic expression?"

All three of them looked shocked at her outburst. If they'd believed Cole's mouth-to-mouth reprimand would send her running, they had much to learn. Lissa had backed down in her past. She had learned never to run again. Or to hide. Or to change. Or to give in.

Lissa merely cocked her head, seizing the deafening silence to listen for Cole's return in the face of her purposefully loud string of queries.

The house was quiet. Cole wasn't racing across the upper floor in a bid to shut her up.

Eventually Cole's guests settled into a kind of collective acceptance, with Kent leading the way. He slowly crossed his arms over his chest and *winked*. The approving expression passed unnoticed by the others, a private congratulation.

Rhea stood between Kent and Trevor, hands fisted at her sides, jaw ticking. The woman couldn't hide her frustration, and for a moment, Lissa felt like a trespasser, one who didn't belong and shouldn't butt into family business.

But she sucked it up. The questions might be nosy, even irritating, but they shouldn't engender true anger. With her future livelihood hanging in the balance, these people *owed* her answers.

Rhea had yet to loosen through the shoulders when she addressed Lissa's litany of queries with three clipped words. "We. Don't. Know."

The unrealistic denial triggered Lissa's inner alarms. "Yeah, and Bill Clinton 'did not have sexual relations with that woman, Miss Lewinsky,'" she drawled. "I know you have a hunch."

A drawn-out exhale blew Rhea's bangs from her face, and Lissa suddenly sensed the other woman's budding need to share. *Yeah, girlfriend, let's chat.* Red played at outrage with her bristling posture and terse evasions, but deep down, Trevor's wife *wanted* to talk.

Her kind always did.

Which was *sweet* because Lissa wanted to listen. "I know you loved her like family," Lissa coaxed, meeting Rhea's gaze and holding. "And that you want to respect Cole's privacy. But I can't make this work unless I understand his motivations. Kate's death was heartbreaking—a misfortune you want and deserve to forget—but it's also the key to how and why Cole clings to antiquated and uninteresting artistic ideals."

Rhea jerked, then narrowed her eyes in a look of universal contempt.

Jackpot, Lissa silently gloated.

"Earlier you called Kate a 'perfect specimen,'" Rhea began. "Now you presume I 'loved her like family.'" A slug could have deciphered the undertone: *You don't know shit.*

Next to Rhea, Trevor went completely still. Not even the twitch of an eyelid gave him away. Lissa had never seen that kind of purposeful, rigid control.

Yet Rhea went on, either not noticing, or not caring, that her husband had gone dark. "Most people did." Her stare slid sideways, pinning Trevor. "Love her like family, that is. But Kate wasn't perfect. She taught Cole all about—"

"Check the basement," Trevor interrupted, his voice low and smooth. The man might have been ordering a cocktail rather than engaging in subtle verbal warfare with his wife. "That's where Cole archives his work—old portfolios, magazine shoots, personal albums, the works."

Lissa nodded. Cole's past might hint at his present. Lissa would pursue the lead, but she didn't speak, didn't thank him or even nod in a way that might distract Rhea from her musings. Gut churning with the knowledge that Cole's sister-in-law teetered on the cusp of a critical admission, Lissa willed Rhea to finish what she'd started.

"—Betrayal." The harsh word flew from Rhea's mouth like a lash. "Kate's pretty face and fractured mind hid a wandering eye. If only she'd strayed further afield."

CHAPTER 11

Trevor gripped the steering wheel and turned right onto Highway 72. Low-hanging clouds dimmed the usually brilliant night sky so that the road ahead disappeared into blackness beyond the reach of the headlights. Focusing on the edges of the pavement, Trevor tried to appear impassive.

"You shouldn't have come," he began evenly.

More and more, Rhea joined his visits to Cole's. Tonight she'd wanted a glimpse of Lissa. The curiosity had coincided with a scheduling conflict of Kent's. Instead of carpooling from Boulder, Kent had driven to Cole's alone, a good and bad change of pace. *Good,* because Kent's absence on the return trip meant Trevor and Rhea could privately pick over the evening. *Bad,* for the exact same reason.

"*You* shouldn't have wanted your brother's wife," Rhea said with equal calm, leaning forward to turn down the radio.

He *hadn't.* Kate had been a friend. Trevor's nails bit into the hard rubber of the steering wheel. Nothing would come of rising to Rhea's bait.

After her jibe had settled into anticlimactic silence, Trevor asked, "Betrayal, huh? What do you suppose Lissa will do with that kind of cliffhanger?"

Trevor didn't need to know Lissa well to understand the woman would prove *persistent.* Before, he'd been happy to see her digging at Cole, daring his brother to evaluate his choices. In opposing each of Lissa's keen observations and witty accusations, Cole took another baby step out of the abyss he'd been courting for months.

Whether Lissa knew it or not, her psychology was simple. She wanted to know why Cole was being such a pussy about his photography. Call a man a pussy enough times, and he'd eventually prove you wrong.

Even better? Lissa didn't appear to be playing mind games. She'd simply happened upon certain facts in her bid to secure Cole's cooperation, and she wasn't the type to internalize. It was shock-therapy problem solving he had to respect.

Instead of derailing the search, Rhea's flippant comment had highlighted the already-suspect connection between Kate's death and Cole's artistic rigidity. The second the word "betrayal" had fallen from Rhea's lips, both of Lissa's brows had shot up her forehead in unabashed interest. Now Lissa would be all the more curious.

All the more *dangerous* to Cole's attempts to forget.

Rhea shifted in her heated seat. "For starters, Lissa might ditch the hero worship for 'Kate of the tragic death.'"

"Who cares?" His question fell cold and flat. Once, Kate and Rhea had been close. After their bond had fractured, there'd been no fixing it. It didn't help that while Rhea was a stunning woman, Trevor suspected his tall, athletic wife had forever felt ungainly around the softer, more petite Kate. "Now Lissa will chase your juicy tidbit. She'll do nothing but remind Cole he hurt his wife—"

"After his wife fucked him over," Rhea said mildly, "with *you.*"

He saw her watching him carefully out of the corner of his eye, but this time he didn't bother to engage, unwilling to let an imaginary affair take up one more inch of space in their lives. Cole's mistake, though innocent, had cost one life and too many portions of others. What Trevor wouldn't give to extinguish the myth that, over time, had grown roots of truth in his wife's malleable mind.

Watching fall's first snowflakes bombard the black pavement that wound downward toward home, Trevor steeled himself for an equally cold reality. The Rathlen family saga, marred with wounds both real and imagined, all bone deep and barely healed, was primed for a new episode.

CHAPTER 12

A thin seam of light shone beneath Lissa's bedroom door. Cole crept up the main staircase, careful to avoid the two steps that creaked year-round. Other than Lissa's dim beacon, he couldn't see a thing. The night was completely black, without a hint of moonlight slipping through the high windows of the foyer.

The dark didn't matter. Cole knew every centimeter of the house—each corner, piece of furniture, wall hanging, and knickknack. He'd gone downstairs to sweep and scrub and polish after Lissa's noisy clash with his slow-to-leave relatives. Certain aspects of his life had suffered neglect after Kate's death. Melina wasn't one of them. With the help of a weekly cleaner and a compulsive need to maintain Kate's brainchild, he practically kept the place spit shined.

Lissa's final face-off against Kent, Trevor, and Rhea had been short, but revealing. When she'd raised her voice to a dull roar, he'd *known* she wanted to draw him out. A nicer man might have relented and gone downstairs to answer her not-wholly-unreasonable questions. His instinct had been to stay put.

Listening. Piecing her mind together.

Lissa had obviously linked his current views on artistic realism to the loss of his wife. Now she wanted to know everything about Kate's death and what Cole had been like before. If he were inclined to make bets, he'd say Lissa aimed to connect all the pre-and-post-Kate dots so she could better plan the trajectory of her eraser.

Make him forget, so he'd give in to her whims.

Frustration tugged at him, but he shoved it aside. Lissa had been onboard for less than two weeks, not enough time to understand he was the boss. Tonight that would *change*.

At her door, he reached forward to rap out a demanding, "*Let me in, or else.*" The woman barred her room like she couldn't stomach a chance encounter, probably because she knew he wanted her, simultaneously *on* his body and *off* his property.

Kissing her had been the kind of mistake he couldn't make just once.

Right before his fist crashed into her door, he heard voices. *Plural.* Snapping his hand back, he leaned in to listen.

"Yes, *now*," he heard Lissa say. "It's been a lick it, slam it, suck it kind of day."

A response followed, but the voice sounded garbled, an indistinct jumble that made Lissa chuckle under her breath. Intent on hearing more, Cole pressed his ear flat against the wood and tried to play dead with his shallow breathing.

"You better do a whole one, too," Lissa ordered. "Last week I *know* you went halfsies."

This time he heard a high, but muted, "Did not!" The volume grew. "Stop questioning my ABV or drink alone."

What the hell?

"Mmmhmm, I believe you," said Lissa. An unspoken "not" punctuated her reassurance. "By the way, I'm shooting vodka instead of tequila. From what I could find in the kitchen, Cole's solely devoted to distilled potatoes in his hard liquor."

Impossible. Lissa couldn't be in there shooting his booze with some chick. For fuck's sake, who?

"Look, Scarlet, call me back. You're cutting out."

On speaker with Scarlet. For shots.

Not normal. Or fun. Or sexy. Or like an activity he'd trade his best zoom lens to be a part of.

Figuring it wasn't possible to encroach in his own house, Cole stayed for the teleparty, ears peeled and feet shifting. Once Lissa and her friend scavenged a better connection—cell coverage was generally fine in the house, but there were occasional mountain glitches—he eavesdropped with ease.

"Was this week any better," Scarlet asked, "or are you still struggling?"

Cole tensed.

"Struggling," Lissa replied dryly, "with the delusion of not wanting him to bone me into next week."

An indelicate snort muffled through the phone.

"Even if I knew my own mind," Lissa continued, "he'll never be able to deliver, not artistically and definitely not romantically. One minute he's aloof. The next I have to stop him from giving me a raging orgasm on the kitchen table while his family stands by listening for a telltale squeal. In a word—*hang-ups.*"

Peals of laughter interrupted Lissa's tirade. His little guest hadn't slurred, but she was getting to the *honest* part of the drunk. True to form, Lissa compensated for Scarlet's hilarity by talking louder, drowning her friend out. "Worse? Those hang-ups are *mine*. I really need this to work."

Suddenly Scarlet grew serious. "No, you don't."

A pause. Then a quiet, "You aren't supposed to agree with them, Scarlet."

"I don't agree with *them*. I love your work—true love—and you know it. But a permanent gallery is a hard thing to waste. Maybe that's the way to go. Take your dad up on the offer, and build it slow and steady. In a few years, you'll get there."

"Not on my own." Cole didn't like how her tone implied she *couldn't* succeed without help. He especially didn't like the hollowed out pinch in his gut that reminded him he'd played a part in cultivating that opinion.

"So?" Scarlet burst out. "Where are you getting with Cole, who won't let you *paint what you paint?*"

Lissa said nothing.

When Scarlet went on, Cole could detect her frustration through the phone *and* the door. "Dali didn't do impressionist paintings of lily pads," she insisted, "and Monet didn't take on bizarre surrealism. You paint in the abstract. Act like it. This deal you've made with Cole is a game that can't mine your best work. Why are you trying so hard?"

A harsh clank reverberated through the wood at his ear, rather like a shot glass slamming to a dresser. Guess Lissa had decided to drink alone.

"Thanks," Lissa said on a choking cough.

"I'm sorry—"

"No, I mean it. You stuck with me through the hard stuff. My other private-school friends faded to black when I shipped out to the figurative wrong side of the tracks. You came closer, loyal as ever."

Cole's head spun with the rapid-fire topic shift. What did Lissa mean by "hard stuff?" Did Scarlet know about the bullying?

"We made it," Lissa said, "through schools in different worlds, colleges on opposite ends of the country, and a decade of my failed attempts at artistic discovery. You've been my best friend. Most of the time you've been my only friend."

"But?" Scarlet asked.

Cole smiled in the dark. He'd only met Scarlet once in New York. Then and now, she'd proven herself a smart woman, one who knew a mouthful of compliments from Lissa Blanc was the hors d'oeuvre, not the main course.

"But Cole isn't a game." *Exactly.* "He's merely stubborn and fucked up and totally inflexible."

Let's not forget "sexy" and "bonable."

Cole stood completely still, pressing silent fingers into the doorjamb, unwilling to miss either a blessing or a curse from this woman who doled out plenty of both.

"My little bargain with him," Lissa continued, "doesn't have to be permanent. The point is to get us working together, communicating, compromising. Eventually he'll come to appreciate my point of view. He *has to* because I'm right."

Don't count on it.

"And I *do* need him," Lissa went on. "You know my last show in Manhattan, on opening night, when we both met Cole?" Her pragmatic cheer had dimmed considerably. Defeat charred the edges of her speech. "*Time Out NY* called my works 'glancing' and 'uneasy' with 'shortcuts designed to disguise limited skills.' Apparently I'm a 'hipster fuck-off' who 'barely passes muster as a painter.'"

Cole twitched, dragging his head along the door before he could tamp down the outrage that surfaced on Lissa's behalf. Her work might not appeal to him personally, but she had talent in spades. Who the hell were these people who attacked with such casual cruelty?

Me. The admission powered into his conscience against his will. He'd repeatedly cut at Lissa with comments that were only marginally more palatable.

Her voice low and wary, Scarlet waded in. "Lissa, *honey*, don't pay attention—"

"My father wouldn't be giving me a gallery, Scarlet. It would be a *museum* because I couldn't sell a single work with reviews like that. Dad means well, but the path of least resistance is killing my reputation. I can't balance on the Picasso pedestal he puts me on, so he's out. Yet I *do* need help, so Cole's in."

Did she? Lissa relegated herself to the land of the needy and incompetent with too much ease. Fuck the critics—again, like him—who'd been so convincing.

"Here?" Lissa continued. "Once upon a time, someone *here* liked my paintings. Maybe that person was Kate and not Cole, but I either resign myself to selling to the sycophants chasing after Robert Blanc—them and *only* them—or I break out with something completely different. Cole might be a repressed devil with a difficult past, an unforgiving set of expectations, and an irresistible tongue, but he can *help* me."

Stomach still churning, Cole acknowledged that Lissa might be grasping to stay positive, but she had no shortage of conviction. He'd preferred to think of her as a self-important, egotistical little trust funder. Unexpected compassion over the very real obstacles she'd faced gentled his judgment and tamed his plans for the altercation barreling their way.

"Bottoms up, Scar." Another cringe-worthy clank of glass against wood. "They say psychopaths are predisposed for career success. If that's true, here's to a man who can't possibly let me down."

The door flew open before Cole could beat an outraged retreat.

******

"*You*," Lissa spat, clutching at her satin robe in an effort to hide the fact that she'd given Cole enough credit to make his spying a surprise. The kind of surprise that found her wearing a short robe and even shorter nighty. Only a faint bumping at the door had tipped her off. The sound had come from much higher than Sasha's usual head-butted knocks.

"Speaking of psychopaths," she told Scarlet in her most cutting what-a-coincidence voice, "Gotta go."

Lissa hung up with a forceful finger-flick against her touchscreen, sorry she couldn't slam a weighty, old-school receiver into a cradle. Cole had stayed away when she'd been yelling her questions to the ceiling. Now he'd gotten a load of her private affairs and, if the way his blue eyes had darkened from the sea in morning to the sky at night meant anything, her less-than-demure and more-than-chilled nipples.

He crowded her backward into the bedroom, using his big body to herd her toward the bed. "Psychopath?" The low rumble couldn't be called pleased, but no matter. Cole forgot that *he*, not she, was in the wrong.

"Let me think." Lissa tapped her temple with an index finger. "Cunning. Manipulative. Someone who knows the difference between right and wrong, but dismisses it as applying to"—she cleared her throat—"*him*. Egocentric. Untruthful."

Thinking on it, she warmed to the idea. Cole wore faded jeans and a crisp, white undershirt. The unassuming clothing magnified the lean, rolling muscle prowling in her direction. Like so many times before, words became her defense. "I question whether you exhibit above-average intelligence or charm, but I'll concede you have, at least in the past, demonstrated an ability to love and feel guilt. All in all, so many factors tend toward—"

"Are you done?"

"Depends." On how fast and how hard he groveled. Or possibly the removal of his shirt. She couldn't say which.

She let a bright smile steal over her face, hopefully duping him into assuming the best. "Utter lack of shame. Antisocial behavior. And my personal favorite—a failure to accept the consequences, resulting…"

The backs of his fingers trailed along her jaw and then her bottom lip, killing the end of her brilliant insult. Before she could adjust to the touch, he softly pressed his lips to hers in a sweet, closed-mouth kiss. "I'm sorry," he breathed on the breakaway. "I was wrong. I shouldn't have stayed once I heard you talking. Yet I couldn't go."

Groveling accomplished. "Okay, only a mini-psychopath," she grumbled.

When he'd kissed her downstairs, she'd pitted her overwhelming need against the knowledge that he'd later regret getting close. Very little time had passed, but *this* touch, this kiss, didn't have the same vibe. The attraction had mutated into something more acceptable, driven by chemistry *and* curiosity, not simple fuck-on-the-table lust.

Which, frankly, was way scarier.

Cole didn't reach out again. He moseyed over to the nightstand where her—actually, *his*—bottle and shot glass awaited. "You're right. I like vodka."

Picking up the bottle, he poured a shot, first into the glass and then down his throat in a smooth, undulating swallow. He set the small tumbler back on the stand with precise movements before patting the rim. "That's how you place a glass on antique wood."

She couldn't resist. "Pathological egocentricity?"

"More like *being right.*"

Their banter had eased into flirtation, and Lissa wondered if she should press her advantage, Rhea's recent admissions buzzing in her head. *Moments. Betrayal.*

When she opened her mouth, Cole said, "Shhh. It's my turn. You've been asking questions since you landed on my front porch."

A heartbeat passed while he considered her quietly, head cocked, then, "Does Scarlet know you downplay everything bad about your life?"

Lissa could pretend to misunderstand, but Cole had *heard*, heard her thank Scarlet for being a friend without the slightest implication that the friendship had been her savior during the hardest of times. Combine that with what he already knew and…

"No."

"So when you recognized her for being there for you, you meant it in a general sense. Scarlet doesn't know what happened when you went off the rails via education-by-*tax-dollar* while she continued along with education-by-*tax-advantaged-savings-account.*"

The truth shrank Lissa's shoulders inward, but she straightened. "Scarlet had her own problems. She didn't need mine."

"You at least *knew* about hers," he said smoothly. "Why not spread the burden?"

Because feelings of worthlessness were hard to share, especially with extremely worthy people.

Shrugging it off, Lissa said, "I don't dwell in the past." She let a silent *like you* linger between them. "I focus on the *future.*" A prudent choice, since most found her past distinctly lacking. "Try it sometime."

Normally she'd have softened the demand with "please," or "maybe," but she'd noticed Cole reacted better to terse commands. Give him softness, and he exploited it like a manipulative kid wooing a helicopter parent.

He arched a tawny brow. "With you?"

"Anyone, anytime. Let go, Cole."

"Ah." He poured another shot. Drank it. Set the glass down with extreme care. "There is one thing I'd like to do in the *future*, as you say." He came forward to where she'd sat on the edge of the bed. Nudging between her knees, he bent low and said against her ear, "You called this a 'lick it, slam it, suck it' kind of day. So far I think we've left it at 'slam it.' In the future, I'd like to get on with the 'licking' and the 'sucking.'"

"Mmm." She almost moaned outright, barely managing to make the sound imitate mild intrigue.

"Lissa"—he whispered now, and the low sound vibrated against her throat—"it's the future."

His tongue traced along her collarbone. "There's a lick." Then he pulled that same wet heat along the vee of her robe. She barely noticed his hands untie the sash until the material fell away, firing the tips of her already throbbing breasts in its sweeping wake.

Deep, uneven breaths coaxed her through the flare of expertly-stoked sensation. All the while, she reminded herself that the pleasure he gave had started to fit a pattern—Cole distracted her with intimacy when he either felt strong, and generally negative, emotion or when he wanted to weaken her for some personal coup. The man used sex like she used words—a defense mechanism.

On the mountain, he'd talked of fucking when his frustration had won out. Downstairs, he gone round the smexy bend in an apparent venting of his spleen. In the hall right after her arrival, he'd spoken of his operational dick, but only to warn her away.

So she wasn't surprised when he started to talk.

"I didn't want to like you, Lissa, but these breasts defy dislike."

All right, she hadn't expected *that*. His mouth still worked along the bodice of her nightgown—if the wisp of cloth deserved such a distinguished title—while his hands moved to her knees. They circled round and round, never moving up or down, soothing the skittishness she pretended not to feel.

"But I wonder"—*yep, here comes the end run*—"why you seek to fix me, when you're equally broken."

She heard the question but couldn't formulate a response other than, "Ooooh," because he'd gone from using his mouth to enunciate the last syllable, slow and easy, to enveloping one of her achy nipples through the silken threads of her gown.

"There's a suck." He drew back, allowing the heat of his next words to wash over the sodden material. "Hmmm? Why must I get better while you refuse to acknowledge ever being hurt? Such a double standard."

The hands stroking her knees finally began to travel upward. Lissa's head whirled in the web Cole spun with his leading questions, the leisurely movements, the smell of the citrus shampoo that lingered in his ruffled hair, even the way his jeans scratched her inner thighs as his fingers made their way to the same skin.

"Not true," she managed on a ragged exhale. "I told you—"

The quiet cluck of his tongue halted her feeble excuse. "Yes, you did, didn't you?" Wet heat scorched her other nipple, again through her nightgown, before it was gone. "You said some revealing things."

A tickling sensation swept across her core. *Oh God, he'd arrived.* Outside her wispy panties, Cole walked his fingers back and forth with barely-detectable pressure. Up and down. Up. And. Down.

"I have a theory." He spoke into her chest in a rough, mesmerizing lilt. The tender strokes between her thighs stopped, but the back of his hand stayed put, now pressing inward and releasing in a rhythm that set her teeth on edge. "You went through hell after you transferred schools. There because your family had experienced a dip in income, you *still* had more than your classmates. Out of jealousy or immaturity or whatever fucking thing allows young people to reject others' differences, they drilled you— physically and mentally—with the idea that individual Lissa was useless and lacked practically all value."

Ten minutes ago, Lissa might have bet her Jackson Pollock that when faced with this kind of psychobabble, she'd have shrugged absently and spouted something scathing and evasive. Perhaps, "Does your obsession with me make you uncomfortable?" or "Wanna hear my equally plausible theory about how leprechauns are actually the *children*, not the chasers, of rainbows?"

But Cole's fingertips were apparently made of truth serum, so her witty comments only floated in the inaccessible recesses of her mind, refusing to get close enough to grasp. "Such a psychic"—*tongue*—"mind."

"There's more," he said.

I certainly hope so.

She grasped at his hips, pulling him in until he touched the bed, so close she dislodged his hand from her center. Scooting her butt closer to the edge, she brought their bodies into contact, urging the ridge of his zipper into her sweet spot.

Head thrown back, he groaned at the ceiling. "I *knew* you'd be like this—hot and needy and demanding."

Lissa whimpered, wanting to show him all about demanding in the most basic way imaginable.

He snapped his head upright and lowered to his knees by the bed. "How about I give you what I know you want"—he stopped and swallowed, seeming to collect himself—"if you respond in kind."

Somehow, Lissa knew in her bones that responding "in kind" would not involve going to her knees like him.

"Don't worry," he said, "I'll make it a fair trade. Now"—he grasped the edges of her panties and began a slow slide down her legs—"why have you accepted your parents' help when, clearly, you haven't wanted to?"

A crisp epithet rose to her lips but drowned when two of his fingers sank into that sleek spot that didn't care what he asked. "It's the only way..." she gasped.

"Your skin is like wet, grasping silk. It likes me more, I think, than you do." His caress settled into a pulsing stroke that mimicked his earlier touches to her panties. "The only way to what?" he prompted.

Her abdomen clenched, and she bit down on her cheeks, hard. Answering would be fine at this point, but she refused to release the wail that would accompany any kind of speech. He'd done exactly as she'd predicted—snuck behind her plot to snatch the keys to *his* past with questions about her own, and used his hands and mouth in devious ways to win.

Breath whistled through his teeth. "Lissa, don't make me hold back. I don't think I can." He pushed her torso onto the bed, but not before she spied the sweat beading on his upper lip. Staring overhead, she could only *feel* him move. Light touches along her folds went deeper and deeper until he stroked into her channel with two fingers, all the way to the hilt.

Instant fire tore through her. "Cole, please!" She bucked her pelvis into his hand, clenching so hard she felt him tug to withdraw.

"Relax," he coaxed. "Let me go. I'll return. I promise."

But he didn't. After forcing her traitorous muscles to loosen, Cole slid to the entrance of her body. There he circled, barely breaching the sensitive tissues with a knuckle, giving her only a hint of penetration. "You went to college in New York, right? Columbia?"

She nodded frantically, trapping needy sobs in the back of her throat with quick pants.

"During all that time, from sixteen on, you were painting. By college, though, your dad had completed several huge highway contracts all around New York and New Jersey. Finances would never be an issue again."

Enough. "Let me touch *you*, Cole."

His voice shook. "That's not the trade, babe." He leaned in and cinched the deal with one soft, teasing swirl of tongue.

She bowed off the bed.

Instantly, the steel band of his arm fanned across her abdomen. Patiently, he pressed her down and held. "You never told your family." A feathering streak of heat skated up one side of her cleft. "You never told anyone." Then down the other. "Forgetting proved impossible, especially when the money and those assumptions of worthlessness followed you into adulthood. Now you take your family's help because some success is better than none, which is what you think you'd have on your own. And"—*Jesus Christ, there was more?*—"you feel obligated to accept because otherwise you'd have to explain how taking the help had hurt you in the past, and you refuse to punish them with the truth."

His fingers joined the fray, delivering on his earlier promise to return deep. Between his strong hands, slow tongue, and stubbled chin, Lissa didn't have a chance against her release.

She came.

And came.

But she never answered.

Cole worked her through the clenching orgasm, never ceasing in his slow, unhurried seduction. When it was over, and Lissa lay limp against her comforter wondering where she was and what the hell had happened, he sat back on his haunches and finished his story in lurching chunks.

"Every time your father signs a check… and every time you're blasted for being nothing more than a rich girl with an expensive hobby, you're mentally back in that grubby hallway where someone kicked you in the head and said you were nothing. To spare your parents that truth, you don't balk at what they offer. Instead you've pegged me—this project—as your way out."

She sat up and looked at him crouched on the floor, forearms flung over knees and hair mussed, with a shining mouth that he finally wiped with a thick wrist.

May perfection have no shame. "Cole, for *God's sake*, not now." He read her like he'd *written* the book.

"Okay," he said, straightening to his full height and coming forward to bracket her body against the bed with both arms. "You win."

Then, with another soft, chaste kiss to the mouth, much like the one that had started his carnal cross-examination in the first place, Cole was gone.

Never had Lissa lost so well.

CHAPTER 13

The basement at Melina didn't look anything like Lissa had pictured. When Trevor had recommended the search, she'd imagined a well-lit space with wall-to-wall carpet and shelves of labeled records, a space as useful and inviting as every other she'd encountered in Cole's home.

Instead, she found spiders. Big ones. The kind a half a can of Raid didn't faze. No wonder Cole had sent her down here with a smile when she'd casually asked if she could take a peek to *familiarize herself* with his work. The deviant planned to incapacitate her via black widow.

A pity. She preferred his other, more hands-on methods.

Mustering her flagging courage, she sat down on the wooden stairs beneath a lonely incandescent light bulb hanging from an exposed rafter. Huffing dry, dusty air, she pulled on a pair of leather work gloves pilfered from the garage. They overlapped the cuff of her long-sleeved thermal, which covered every inch of skin from wrist to neck to hip, where the shirt met her jeans.

Wearing Cole's gloves felt like stolen intimacy. A bit large, the inside of the leather scratched lightly against her skin with each flex of the hand, much like the stroke of his calloused fingertips.

Simmer down, Nancy Drew. Gloves don't "stroke." To complete the bug riot gear, she hauled an orange ski mask over her head. Another garage find, the ratty weave screamed, "deer hunter, circa 1983." The rafters looked like prime spider havens, dusty and dark. None of those fuckers were coming down on her unprotected head.

In a last-ditch effort to de-creep the hunt, she propped her phone against the stairs. A mix of old-school favorites blared outward, not as loud as she'd like, but with enough force to let Kylie Minogue and Madonna break the dank quiet that otherwise suffocated Cole's basement.

A deep breath propelled her across the sloping cement floor to the farthest corner of the room. Most of the stacked boxes weren't labeled, so she planned to work her way around the perimeter, stack by stack, until she hit the jackpot or came full circle. If Trevor's hunch was correct, she'd find hints that Cole hadn't always been so rigid in his work. Perhaps he might, at least occasionally, have taken the same liberties with his camera as she took with her paintbrushes.

Little surfaced over the next hour other than Kate's wardrobe and five, luckily uninhabited, spider webs. Most of the boxes' contents went undisturbed, until she happened on one that held a digital camera nestled in the nylon of a bright yellow shirt, along with a small backpack, a water bottle, a pair of sunglasses, and a tube of sunscreen. Lissa was no expert, but she appeared to have stumbled upon Kate's hiking gear.

The black Nikon wasn't one of Cole's professional jobbies and seemed more manageable, with an on/off button, digital zoom, and auto flash—more point and shoot, less master's degree in photography.

Inspecting the camera, Lissa wondered if she should be practicing offline. In the several days since their *war kiss* on the dining room table and the totally uncharacteristic time spent in her room later that night, Cole had made inching efforts at keeping his end of their bargain.

He had *not* made efforts to touch her anywhere below the neck, proving that one of, if not *the*, most pleasurable interludes of her life had been a covert fact-finding mission.

Jerk.

Mostly Cole tossed out ideas, usually bad ones, about random not-so objets d'art like the couch in the garage or Sasha's food bin, then left her to stage meaningful scenes to be photographed and painted. Cole's marginal success in providing inspiration meant Lissa ended up replicating real life, or Cole's photos of the same, with increased frequency.

You asked for it.

Courtesy of her self-inflicted position, she now had to imagine an image of a finished painting and then move mountains to represent that image in the physical realm for later imitation. The plan was a complete departure from her usual MO—view the world and paint whatever her mind conjured in response. More than half the time, she couldn't rise to her own challenge. When she could, she had to put brush to canvas in a way that copied the natural world.

And she sucked at it.

Practice-wise, the digital on her phone would be more convenient. The good girl inside Lissa's head told her to put the camera back in the box and move on. The bad one found herself sinking to a cross-legged slouch and pressing the power button on the Nikon, unable to suppress her curiosity about the camera's owner.

Dead, of course. She ran upstairs for her laptop and a connecting cable.

Returning to her spot on the floor, she hitched the camera to the computer so it could pull a parasitic charge and power up.

At first, Lissa flipped through shots of boulders and trees and a dawning skyline. Yup, hiking. The pictures might have been taken near the trailhead that Cole had foisted on Lissa right after her arrival. One photo showed a redhead with a lean build peddling down a dirt road on the slim bones of a road bike. Scrawny patches of snow dotted the landscape, but mostly everything just looked frozen solid.

The cyclist's head was down. Even with the wonky angle and the rider's distance from the camera, Lissa recognized Cole's sister-in-law. The woman's shoulders and the titan hair escaping her bike helmet combined to form a regular neon sign. Rhea's treaded hiking boots looked clown-like against the tiny silver clip-in pedals on the bike.

A later frame on the Nikon depicted an obvious self-shot of Kate, taken with the camera stretched to arm's length. Lissa grinned at the blonde's plump, wind-flushed cheeks, brightened by the yellow neckline of her shirt. Pine trees stretched to the sky beyond her pony tail.

These weren't the first pictures of Kate and Rhea among the stacked boxes. The two had sipped margaritas and planted roses and dragged Sasha down the dirt driveway, always beaming like the best of friends. Lissa had tried not to read them, but she'd stumbled upon several cards of the thank-you and birthday and thinking-of-you variety. By all accounts, Rhea adored Cole's wife and vice versa. Or *had*, in another life and time.

"Having fun?"

Lissa whirled from her spot on the concrete. Cole stood on the stairs, wearing only flannel pajama bottoms that rode the curving muscles between his hips. His longish hair was pre-coffee tousled, and his eyes still held the sleepy softness of early morning.

Lissa pressed a fist into the hollow of her throat. "I'm tying bells to your ankles." Those naked feet moved too softly.

He yawned, then stretched through his bare chest. "You're welcome to try."

The poor lighting cast shadows across what seemed like miles of exposed skin, and her fingers tingled for a taste of the torso she'd only felt through his T-shirt. Of course Sasha chose that moment to edge his head around the open door at the top of the stairs. When he saw Lissa, he started a slow, plodding descent into the basement, nudging Cole out of the way on the fourth step of the freely-suspended staircase.

Tearing her gaze from the dog, she noticed Cole's expression had grown more aware. Now a smirk played about his lips. He looked to be trying to suppress laughter.

"What?" she demanded.

His head dipped. "Nice mask."

She glanced at the ceiling to ensure no creepies were in the process of repelling toward her head, then jerked the suffocating stocking to the crown of her skull, letting the loose end flop behind her ears. "Spiders," she said in a voice dripping with wry accusation. "You didn't tell me."

"I know." He followed Sasha down. When Cole hit the bottom, she wondered how anyone could take the freezing concrete against exposed skin. He ran hot, she knew, but the floor was an ice block.

Protected by mounds of fur, Sasha proved impervious to the cold and made a beeline for Lissa. At the last second, he veered for the open box at her knee, plunging his head inside with a low whine.

The laziness drained from Cole's limbs as though he'd suddenly remembered catching Lissa engaged in his least favorite of her pursuits—prying. He came forward warily, the whole time staring at the St. Bernard. "You'd think he'd forget." Cole stood a little straighter. "But he never does. He can smell her after almost two years."

Lissa would swear Cole's cheekbones grew sharper. Before her eyes, he morphed back into the closed-off enigma that didn't shuffle or prattle or rub at bleary eyes. That look she'd come to recognize fell into place, as if he found everything entertaining but nothing truly funny.

Closed.

Snide, hard-ass Cole had returned, and he was looking around in a frank assessment of her progress when his attention caught on the camera in her lap.

He stilled. "You *play* with my wife's property?"

Forcing a nonchalant nod, Lissa turned the camera off and disconnected the charger. "I found it in one of the boxes—one of the *wrong* boxes. You could at least point me in the direction of your work."

Tense seconds raced past, until Cole reached down with deliberate movements and scooped up the Nikon before crouching next to Sasha and the open box. Expecting him to shove the camera inside and demand she forget it, she lapsed into silence when he only flattened his free hand against the side of the cardboard. Eyes closed, he *touched*, rubbing in slow circles while he appeared to grapple with a threatening tide.

Never before had she seen the suppression of emotion as a *physical* act.

When Cole finally spoke, his voice held a note of resignation. "To the victor go the spoils." The camera landed in her lap.

******

Cole stood, thrusting the box from his mind. For too long, its contents had been the center of his universe, silent relics of past failures. The box held nothing new to find. The woman who'd found it, however, kept him guessing.

Most of the talking during last evening's orgasms-for-answers program had been his. Lissa had taken the pleasure but remained remarkably tight-lipped, at least in terms of her past. Yet each day she stripped *him* symbolically with every move. Skittle thievery reminded him he used to be playful. Her instant rapport with Sasha taught him that even a dog, the most loyal of animals, could move on. Her most mundane habits called him a liar, seeing how a man who'd seduced her as a mere statement wouldn't get hard at the sound of her shower.

And, oh, how he did.

Cole pointed to the opposite corner of the basement, where more stacks lay in wait. "Records are over there."

Lissa didn't deserve a bone, and he refused to examine why he felt inclined to throw her one. "Most of my newer work is stored electronically on flash drives, and those are backups. Initially everything gets archived, either on my local server or in the cloud. The older stuff is in hard copy or on a CD."

"The older, the better."

Bristling through the shoulders, he let himself wonder. "Explain." She'd researched his work before accepting his initial offer, and several days ago she'd mocked his lack of photographic prowess over the last year. He could hear her now. *You need me.* The minx didn't have what it took to paint and sell pictures of the Brooklyn Bridge to tourists, yet she sought his private collection—unpublished, unsold, and, preferably, old—in another of her attempts to prove a point.

And here he thought he'd aptly demonstrated how points were best proven.

"Let's just say"—she fidgeted with the camera clutched in her gloved hands before dropping it back in the box—"I'm interested in the freedom of your untamed youth."

Then she'd have to pay the toll. "Hunting for dirty pictures, are you?"

Her lips thinned, and delicate color overtook what little skin he could see above the close neck of her cotton shirt. The question had burst out without a thought.

"Hunting for *dirt*," he improvised. "On me. My former style." Would he ever quit baiting her just to watch her flush?

Most likely not.

Because the contrasts hit him in the gut every time—a dusky pink against the pale backdrop of her complexion and the surprising ability to get embarrassed over an off-color joke when she herself could be the crown princess of rude, crude, and socially unacceptable.

Never one to be taken off-guard for long, Lissa responded, "*Incriminating* pictures, not dirty ones."

The urge to roll his eyes welled, almost insuppressible. "Even better."

Eying the piles of boxes she'd yet to conquer, Lissa used Sasha's shoulders for leverage in pushing up from the floor. The dog had splayed out on his belly, resting his heavy head on curling paws in an immovable canine lotus pose.

After a quick pat, she pulled the ski mask in place and shuffled to a fresh stack of potential loot. "Shouldn't you be wearing a shirt?" she mumbled over her shoulder.

So business-like, especially when he knew she used the mask to hide the blush. "I've seen you in less," he pointed out quietly. "And I recall throwing you a compliment. Remember? I said you had—"

"*Pecs*," she conceded in a rush, giving a nod to his earlier jokes. "You have nice pecs, Cole, as you know." The mask stifled a suspicious choking sound. "Now get a shirt."

Her gritted command came off like an order to do the exact opposite, and her unconscious approval eased down his spine, coiling low and hot.

"Whoa," he told her, "easy now." Cole let his tone say he was slightly embarrassed for her but willing to accept her lack of grace. Then he gave her a break and left to dress.

Jeans, T-shirt, and a piece of burnt toast later, Cole returned to hall-monitor duty. He'd okayed her search, yes, but Lissa's timing hadn't escaped his notice. She'd been in the basement long before he'd stumbled out of bed. At dawn.

His houseguest wanted to snoop alone, which meant he'd be by her side through *every last pixel*.

Rummaging right where he'd left her, Lissa had buried her nose in a thick binder. Leave it to her to find his family albums first.

Before he could steer her in another direction, she caught his gaze, and again he marveled at the guileless honesty shining outward from the twin cutouts of her mask. He knew she tried to hide behind a layer of bluster. In fact, he'd bet she prided herself on a level of emotional incognito. Yeah, a level of *zero*. He always knew what she was thinking.

Right now she was digesting something neither unexpected nor particularly pleasant from the photo album.

"Your wife was *very* pretty."

The fact had left Cole eternally suspicious, always waiting for others to notice.

Turning back to the book, Lissa continued with a fatalistic sigh, this time muttering low and, evidently, to herself. "There aren't enough sandwiches in the world to give me those."

"Those?"

Her head snapped up and the album whipped shut. "What do you think? *Breastees*." She rhymed the word with *testes*. "Kate's practically jumped out of her shirts, no matter how demure."

Another truth. No amount of minimizing or sport bra-ing or turtle-necking had ever contained them.

He'd loved those things—touching, tweaking, burying his face where only he was welcome—but as he looked over Lissa's shoulder at the now closed scrapbook, he couldn't picture Kate's assets in his mind.

"Show me," he whispered.

The album fell open to the page Lissa had marked with a thumb, and Cole saw Kate standing in front of a stone fireplace in a tight sweater. Once glimpse, and his wife came rushing in like the opening act of a private Broadway show. Curling blond hair. Heart-shaped lips glossed cranberry red. Fleshy cleavage and, at least on this particular day, her trademark grin.

The sense of being hollowed out—the one that felt like Kate's ghost had taken an ice cream scoop to his chest—failed to make an appearance.

Which, of course, left Cole with a reflexive urge to *miss* the sadness. Grasping, he rocked his chest compulsively against Lissa's shoulder in reaching motions. He wasn't reaching for Kate. He flailed about, searching for the gloom that had shrouded him in a protective coating long enough to become his security blanket.

Guilt. An emotion as old as grief and, if anything, harder to beat. Cole was supposed to get over Kate. He wasn't supposed to be relieved to feel her hold slip away.

The reaction felt like a milk commercial gone wrong. *Got pain?* No, dammit. Where had the pain gone, and how could he get it back?

"Incriminating enough for you?" he choked.

"Not quite." Lissa turned the page, then another. The first year of his marriage sped by—a honeymoon in Paris, plans for the house and the day they'd broken ground, cycling in the Indian Peaks down the road, on-shoot at a South-African diamond mine, and after, their inaugural trip to India.

The last picture flipped into view, but Lissa didn't shut the album and reach for another. Her shoulder tensed beneath his chin. "What's this?"

Cole took one look at the photo plastered to the back cover and knew Lissa had him. Definitely *incriminating.* "Label says desert." He spoke with the disinterest of a casual observer.

"Convincing enough," Lissa breathed, "but if that's a desert, I'm a double-D."

Cole reached around Lissa and flicked the end-cover closed. "We were in the Sahara."

"So? There's sand in that picture, Cole, but we both know the dirt's not the focus." She drew out the word "dirt" like a victory lap. "More like a garnish."

Sometimes he hated her way with words, of stripping back the hard chocolate coating for the creamy nougat beneath in five syllables or less. Breathing into her neck, he let the zesty scent of spiced lemon cool him down. More and more Lissa opted to smell like food instead of flowers, like she knew exactly how badly he wanted to savor the secrets of her skin. If he licked along her neck right now, would she taste like merengue?

The glossy edges of the album slipped against his fingertips when she pulled the book to her chest and turned in his accidental embrace. Looking up, she repeated, "*Garnish.*"

They were supposed to be having a disagreement about the picture, duking out whether she'd actually discovered him for a fraud. But with Lissa pressed against him, staring earnestly into his face and smelling like pie, he lost track of winning. Maintaining the artistic status quo felt far away, insignificant.

"It's Kate," he admitted. "She's *in* the desert, but I angled the camera to make her body—her hip, a rounded shoulder, the nip in her waist—blend with the sweep of the dunes behind her."

"You're telling me you styled an erotic photo of your wife to look like something it wasn't? Skin meets desert desolation?"

He let his head fall back against his shoulders in mock-focus on the network of abandoned webs in the rafters. "Yes."

"Why? What intrigued you?"

"During that first year of our marriage, there was this mystery"—*magic*—"about life." We knew each other so well, yet each day I learned something new. The trick fit. Here was my wife, who'd become totally familiar and yet remained unknowable, very like the shifting sands I'd photographed over and over... what?"

Satisfaction sparked in her eyes. "I think you *know.*" When he refused to bite, she went on. "You used your wife and a bunch of sand dunes as props to show something completely different—a feeling of mystery rising from the familiar. You did exactly what I do when I paint. You used your camera to capture a *sensation.*"

Her finger stabbed him in the chest. "Viewers don't *see* that photograph, Cole. They don't think, '*What a beautiful woman*' or '*Nice landscape.*' They *feel* your point."

Cole brought his palms to her shoulders. He knew exactly what she meant. He'd rebuked her for looking at a house and conveying sadness and grief or looking at a folding chair and painting the promise of a new beginning. Yet in the past he'd played with the same tactics. He couldn't block the irony from his tone when he said, "Busted."

Far from static, his creative process changed from project to project. Kate in the dunes provided one example of a nebulous take on reality, but there were others, easy fodder for Lissa's gloating smile. *Keep those to yourself.* In Northern Italy he'd staged a midnight icefall as a lunar runway. In Turkey he'd set a table with an endless array of exotic foods—köfte, dolma, thick yeasty flatbread, kebabs, baklava, cheese, olives, and pots and pots of tea. Instead of shooting the feast in sharp focus, he'd allowed the camera to wander close and the angle that light entered the lens to skew. The result had been a spread of vaguely recognizable shapes that reminded the mind of a life of plenty, but not all or even any of the foods waiting to be enjoyed.

Lissa's gaze stayed with him, eerily clear behind the ridiculous cutouts of the mask, like she was privy to the movie playing inside his head. "I'm sorry."

"For what?" Being right all the time? More like she wanted to rub it in and apologizing kept the conversation in full swing.

Lissa tugged the mask off and let it drop to the floor. "I'm sorry you can't look at the world with unblemished eyes anymore, that the beauty of seeing all the unseeable things was taken from you." Candor rang in her voice and raised a lump in his throat.

She doesn't know my imagination was cursed.

He'd mentally painted his devoted wife a jade. A look had become a clandestine invitation, a hug the prelude to a quickie over the washing machine.

All of it real, if only in his head.

No more.

"Don't be. I'll *never* regress to that." The words were sharper than necessary, and Lissa flinched. The challenge that had faded to sorrow now morphed into bitter regret.

Slipping between his arms, she withdrew with a curt nod that made him wish he could retract the insult. The album landed in its box, and she closed the lid with careful movements that only emphasized her desire to escape.

Damn her for making him feel guilty over the deserved harshness. He'd been nothing but honest about his expectations. *She* had overstepped. *She* had frustrated a done deal.

Breath came in increasingly shallow gulps. Each wheeze ushered in a more fully realized awareness. *She* was the woman he saw when he tried to picture his wife.

CHAPTER 14

"Look," Cole began, not with full-on desperation, but definitely plausible urgency, "I said that wrong."

Already halfway up the basement stairs, she snapped, "You say very little right." But defeat simmered beneath her bravado. Worse, now he knew why. Every time he challenged her work, she took a hit to her worth.

Throat stinging, he said, "I don't mean to upset you." Even so, he couldn't let lust override logic.

"Really?" she asked, slowing her pounding steps. "I try to show you our approaches aren't so distant. When proven beyond any conceivable doubt, you claim doing things my way—which we now know is also your way—would be an unacceptable *regression.*"

He held his hands up in surrender. "Lissa, I didn't mean—"

"You *did.*" Before, Lissa had reacted to his reserve with her own brand of breezy insolence, acting like the two of them staged a comedy of errors that would work out in the end. Now her voice flared raw with hurt.

Averting her face, she began to talk. "You guessed right the other night. My younger self was reviled for being lucky. I thought I deserved the hassle because I *was*… lucky, that is. When school ended, I figured I'd survived intact. Yet for years, I've been told my successes aren't my own, that they're the result of sucking the silver spoon. Critics say I'm as good as my parents' last dollar. Friends, and even lovers—unless they're on the hunt for a sugar mama—tire of trailing behind somebody they've pegged as inferior."

Lissa didn't need to add, "*Like you,*" for him to hear the accusation.

Expelling a deep breath, she plunged ahead. "I'll say this again"—she held up an index finger—"*one* more time. *You asked me here,* knowing full well how I create. I could give a shit about your rules or your hang-ups. I've had unique opportunities and made the most of them. How the hell do you think your wife came to love my work? *Because it's fucking good, Cole.* Instead of using my presence as a pretense, a fake shout out to Kate, why don't you respect her opinion by respecting me?"

Cole hesitated, a thousand reactions jostling for the chance to be said. "I realize," he hedged, "that your approach isn't inferior—"

"Could've fooled me."

"—but different." Strangely, he believed what he said. "'Regress' only relates to me, my situation. I don't mean to apply the term universally to *any* shift from my way to yours."

Moving forward, he cupped the back of her calf from the side of the stairs. Her position above put her lower legs at eye level, and he hoped an earnest touch might convey the truth. Smooth muscle tensed beneath the softness of her jeans, and he massaged into the tightness, drawing her strain into his palm.

"I fucked up with Kate."

The cloth under his hand moved, and he realized Lissa was turning. She lowered herself to the steps, elbows to knees, chin in hand. "Why do I feel like we're finally getting somewhere?"

Because you've bent me over, and I've finally grabbed my ankles, wanting you more than I should. "I loved her."

"I know."

"I suffocated her with it."

"Figuratively," Lissa prompted dryly.

"Yes." He licked his lips, stalling for time to explain how he could have caused such damage. "Like you said, Kate was a beautiful woman." Though not as beautiful as Lissa. "That's not an excuse. Actually, I don't think it played a part, but her looks always come up when I think about what happened."

Sometime during the speech, Lissa's hand swept down the length of her shin and caught his. She squeezed, an unspoken, *"Yes, about what happened…"*

Cole said, "Kent told you Kate had 'moments.' He meant depression. Kate was the sweetest thing imaginable, but she had her own inner demons. She used exercise and sleep and sometimes medication to keep the worst at bay. Despite those struggles, or maybe because of a will to overcome them, she made friends easily. I think people who grapple with depression often present the happiest front."

"She got particularly close with another man, and I assigned every gesture a double meaning. If they spoke at dinner, I fumed over being left out. If they touched casually—and I mean overlapping fingers in passing the salad dressing or a head-on collision through the swinging kitchen door—I imagined they did more behind my back."

Cole tried to tell the story objectively, but the facts, even without the seething anger that had accompanied them, sounded ugly to his ears. "The way they horsed around—playful slaps and faux karate chops—felt too familiar. There was a knowledge, almost a muscle memory about their movements that said they'd had their hands on each other in a different way."

"How'd she know him?" Lissa asked.

The truth was too damning. No one else would have suspected what he had. "Through me."

"Even harder."

It shouldn't have been. "On a random Tuesday, Kate parked her car outside the St. Julien hotel in Boulder. An aging ding in the bumper left no doubt. I pulled into the parking garage, thinking we'd have a drink after she finished what I assumed was a late business lunch. Parking was sparse that day, so my brother's truck stood out. Supposedly he was traveling back from a business meeting, but in that moment I knew—*knew* with a certainty that pushed all critical thinking aside—that he was in that fucking hotel with my wife."

More like in that hotel fucking my wife. There, he'd said it. His brother.

"How did you know the truck—"

"Corporate logo in the back window." Cole tried valiantly not to cringe at Lissa's pitying look. She thought him the injured party, but he was the culprit. "I lost my mind. That night I told my wife—my very *vulnerable* wife—that if she wanted him, she could have him. Her tears spurred me on. Two weeks before Kate jumped from that cliff, I accused her of being unfaithful."

"God, Cole, I'm so sorry."

"I almost," he rasped, "*almost* wish I'd been right."

Cole swallowed, hoping he'd said enough. He couldn't go beyond the sure and the solid and the seen. Imagining more had cost his wife's life.

******

A heavy thump sounded from somewhere overhead, breaking through Cole's confession like an axe to a sickened tree.

Lissa recognized Cole's words for exactly what they were—the *answer* she'd been searching for. Cole had accused his wife of fooling around and been wrong. When Kate had reacted drastically, he'd assumed all fault. Now the man didn't imagine. Anything. Ever. Not even for the sake of art.

The house had been quiet, but the commotion unfolding above proved she and Cole weren't alone. Lissa let her hand tighten on Cole's as she looked warily over a shoulder to the door at the top of the stairs.

The low growl from Sasha, surprisingly menacing, proved they might not welcome the company.

The stairs spit them out in the far corner of the kitchen. At first Lissa didn't see anything amiss, only Rhea standing behind the granite island, looking pale and shocked against a fuchsia wind breaker. Lissa wouldn't have guessed someone as beautiful as Rhea could look like a clown, but the bright pink did little for the woman's bloodshot hair, like the jacket had a vendetta against its owner.

A collection of Rubbermaid containers spread over the counter. Lissa and Cole had happened upon a morning food drop.

"He collapsed," Rhea whispered, worrying the edge of a dish with shaking hands. "No warning."

Cole didn't ask who. He simply rounded the island on a harsh curse and dropped out of sight. The vicious demand that followed brought the situation into stark focus. "Call 911 for fuck's sake!"

Rhea didn't budge. Fear and indecision froze her face into slack lines, so Lissa scrambled to the basement and snagged the phone she'd propped on the stairs. Back in the kitchen, she charged around the granite blockade to see Kent leaning against a cupboard, one hand clutching his chest. Labored breaths sawed in and out of his throat, but he managed a muted request. "Nitroglycerin pills," he said, lifting his eyes to Rhea. Their gazes held for a single heartbeat before Kent's jaw went slack, and his torso slumped forward.

Ruddy color faded too fast from Kent's cheeks. Dear God, was he dead? He didn't make a sound. No movement, only that horrible, lifeless slouch.

Cole let out a feral growl and dove for his uncle, stretching Kent's unconscious form flat on the floor and patting the front of his polo shirt. All of Cole's focus remained on Kent when he spoke. "His pills?"

Rhea's response was immediate. "I don't know." Fluttering hands rose against her throat in a faintly protective maneuver. "Not in his front pocket?"

"No." The rest of Cole's exasperated reply faded behind the voice of the emergency operator who answered Lissa's call.

"Ambulance," Lissa urged. She fumbled through the story of an unconscious man who'd probably gone into cardiac arrest. In the meantime, Cole took a deep breath and looked up at the ceiling, neither lost nor searching. His face bore a mixture of resolve and acceptance, the kind of look that said he dreaded death, but knew all too well that death didn't care.

Lissa laid a palm on Cole's shoulder. "Ready?"

Calm certainty broke through after a moment of silent commiseration, and Cole nodded. Without any coaxing, he bent close to Kent's face, ear to mouth, obviously listening for breath. Shaking his head, Cole trailed two fingers down Kent's throat, resting at the pulse point beneath the chin.

Sasha approached Kent with somber knowledge in his brown eyes. The dog usually lumbered along, never in a hurry. Somehow the encumbered movements never interfered with him looking perfectly pleased with himself and the world. Not today. This time when Sasha dropped to the floor with his favorite kill-the-elbows dive, he made the same noise that had leaked out in the basement beside Kate's box—a mournful, beyond-his-dog-years whine. Sniffing at Kent's foot, Sasha occasionally licked the man's Denver Bronco's sock, doing his part without interfering.

Unable to help in any other way, Lissa gave the operator the address and a play-by-play of events, while Cole felt for a pulse with increasing urgency, upping the pressure in circular motions along Kent's neck. After several spots, Cole whipped his hands away with a muttered curse. He stacked his palms over the center of Kent's chest, and then over and over in a rapid beat, Cole pumped his uncle's heart. Every thirty compressions or so, Cole tilted Kent's head and pinched his nose, blowing into Kent's mouth with enough force to visibly inflate the man's chest.

Once. Twice. Then back to that steady pressing.

The work lifted the veins flowing along Cole's forearms. With each pump, his healthy arteries seemed to beat a unique brand of encouragement to Kent. *This is how you do it*, they said.

When Cole looked up at Lissa, his eyes were swirling and dark, his usual sea breeze suddenly a hurricane coming ashore. The stark change reminded Lissa that even through their most antagonistic encounters, Cole had retained a level of boyishly crumpled appeal. No matter how dry or how cutting he'd become, those tangled blond curls and Caribbean irises had lightened the mood. At first she'd think, *He's pissed*, but then she'd graduate to, *How serious can one be and still look like a Coppertone commercial?*

The answer crouched on the floor, radiating equal parts resolve, desperation, and helpless rage. Shoulders bunched and face ghostly beneath his usually-swarthy tan, Cole looked ready to kill the very concept of heart failure.

Keeping his eyes on Lissa, Cole snapped, "Find the nitro, Rhea. He *always* has the pills." The sharp command pulled Rhea from her stupor, and Cole's sister-in-law joined him on the hardwood. Feeling her way, she checked the pockets of Kent's khakis, one by one.

Nothing.

The woman on the line calmly explained that the nearest hospital was Boulder Community, over forty minutes away. Numb, Lissa stared at Cole's systematic pressing and Rhea's frantic pat down. "Should we drive to meet the ambulance?"

"No, ma'am," came a polite reply. "If at all possible, continue CPR until help arrives. You can try to cool him down to reduce his metabolic rate and oxygen requirements, but *don't* get him wet." She explained that moisture on the skin would make shocking the heart extremely risky due to the possibility of electrical arcing.

"Cole," Lissa began, her voice steadier than she'd expected, "the

ART-CROSSED LOVE

ambulance is on the way." *Keep going.* No need to emphasize a wait that felt like a lifetime.

"Rhea," she went on, "we need ice packs, frozen vegetables, whatever. Wrap them in towels and pile them on. *Don't* dampen his skin."

Trevor's wife looked up slowly, posture loose, gape vacant and aimless. Initially Lissa thought the woman had misunderstood, but suddenly Rhea lurched upward and spun toward the freezer.

Lissa remained on the line. The dispatcher didn't have a magical solution—only stay the course and keep oxygen flowing through Kent's body—but Lissa felt more useful with the phone against her ear.

The screen door leading to the back veranda slammed with a haphazard bang. Trevor joined the mess in the kitchen, immediately surveying his wife at the fridge and his brother and uncle on the floor. A pair of hedge clippers dangled drunkenly from Trevor's right hand. His left raked roughly through short, spiky hair, probably pulling in an effort to clear a vision he didn't want to see. "What the...?"

Bewilderment only lasted a second. Then Trevor looked to Lissa and the phone she clutched to her ear. "Ambulance?"

Lissa nodded, and Trevor immediately fell alongside Cole. "Nitro tab under his tongue?"

These men knew their uncle well. Lissa doubted she could be so cool if a loved one were to collapse to the kitchen floor at seven o'clock in the morning. Today she could keep it together because Kent was more of an acquaintance, though the burn in her chest said the man had a way of worming himself into the heart.

"Can't find them," Cole gritted between compressions.

At first Trevor didn't reply. Then, "He *always* has the pills."

So we've heard.

"Except today." Self-blame laced Cole's disavowal. He might as well have added, *When Kent had a heart attack while looking after me in BFE.*

Trevor's massive shoulders rose to his ears in a wall of solid indignation. "Don't start. Some things don't get to be your fault." When Cole released Kent's chest to begin the breath portion of the cycle, Trevor swatted him away. "You pump, I'll blow. We switch off if necessary."

With that, the two men fell into a rhythm, not an easy one, but one Lissa prayed could keep Kent alive until the paramedics arrived with their shockers and nitrates. Even she knew that poor flow of blood and oxygen meant brain damage. Fast. And help was coming from the far side of the county.

Blood rushed in her ears, drowning out the soothing voice of the operator, so Lissa focused through a murky tunnel on the activity buzzing on the floor. Cole pumped and Trevor puffed and Rhea packed towel-covered frozen meals around Kent's sides. If the situation weren't so dire,

Lissa might have laughed. At least all those refined carbohydrates and processed "cheese products" were being put to good use. Save the day they would not, but Lissa supposed an icy tuna casserole to the groin couldn't hurt.

Having a concrete job had snapped Rhea out of her immobilizing shock, but while the anxiety sat well on her shoulders, obligation did not. Unhurried hands wrapped each plastic container in a tea towel before placing it against one of Kent's extremities. Lissa understood why Rhea couldn't put the cold packs on *top* of Kent—they'd only slide off with the next chest compression—but she couldn't help but notice the redhead's lack of strategy.

Or that Rhea, in all her robust athleticism, moved like an old woman competing in a bingo tournament. Sluggish. Robotic.

Hesitant.

Sirens finally bounced off the front of the house, and Lissa ran to escort the medics to the kitchen. Within seconds, Rhea's cooling packs had been scattered, Kent's shirt cut off, and the pads of a portable defibrillator adhered to Kent's chest. After a warning to stay back, Kent's torso jumped off the tile like he'd taken the blunt end of a cattle prodder. Then again.

And again.

Cole and Trevor had never looked more like brothers. Glassy eyed, they shuffled away with a visible hesitance to stand aside, as though afraid to turn Kent's care over to anyone who didn't love him enough to pour soul into the beating of his heart.

Little was said. Instead, Kent's family was forced to look on in hopeful, but uninformed, horror. The EMTs loaded the once-jolly Kent onto a stretcher and wheeled him out, only his gray and aging face peeking above a tan blanket.

Lissa looked skyward.

Thank you.

So long as they didn't *cover* Kent's face, no matter how limp and colorless, he lived.

******

Lissa's shoulder trembled against one of Melina's front pillars. She didn't belong at the hospital. Not yet. The touch and go waiting at Boulder Community should be reserved for family, and she wasn't among those exalted ranks.

Cole climbed into the ambulance behind the stretcher while Trevor and Rhea barreled to Trevor's truck. Before the red-and-white doors slammed shut, Cole turned with a guarded look. He didn't beckon her to join him, didn't motion for her to jump in with Trevor. He lifted his hand, pinky and thumb extended, and shook it next to his head. He'd call. When his arm dropped, he mouthed, "Thanks."

"You're welcome," she whispered, knowing he couldn't hear.

The medical caravan took off as fast as the gravel would allow, and Lissa sank to the top step, dizzy with worry and fatigue. Her decision to rise at 3:30 am to search Cole's basement had left her drained in the aftermath of the morning's events. She vaguely welcomed a fuzzy nudge from Sasha that enveloped her in stale bacon breath. His soft panting whirled around her head like it came from all directions.

Trevor's corporate logo grew blurrier and blurrier until his truck dropped out of sight with the fading wail of the ambulance. Lissa made out a computer, a brain, and a padlock in the shape of a white triangle, seeming to suggest computer security of some kind. "Rathlen Cyber," said the tagline. "Be sure."

The distinctive symbol *did* render the truck unmistakable, and the sight caught her off guard. No matter how heinous the last forty-five minutes, Lissa's brain automatically rewound to the basement and Cole's latest revelation.

Remembering injected life back into her limbs.

Bingo. In one gut-wrenching sentence, Cole had revealed the link she'd been searching for. *I almost wish I'd been right.*

Cole had accused his wife of adultery. And hell, why stop there? He'd marked her for sleeping with his only sibling, apparently realizing his lunacy too late.

Continuing to stroke Sasha's glossy fur, Lissa eased backward until she lay belly up on the veranda, staring at the ceiling formed by the second story porch. She checked her phone for no good reason.

Surprise, surprise—no news yet.

Knowledge was *supposed* to be power. *Stupid cliché.* The tawdry story that had sent Kate over a cliff had arrived with all the surprise of Kent's heart attack. Neither had been outside the realm of possibility, given Lissa's campaign to understand Cole's backstory and Kent's history with coronary disease, yet both had been unexpected.

Complicated and complicat*ing.*

When Lissa hadn't known the extent of the fear driving Cole's blind inflexibility, she'd held firm in the idea of him as a self-righteous, closed-minded ass in need of her infinite wisdom.

There went that luxury.

Now she saw a stubborn, self-flagellating man whom fate continuously sought to lay low with blows to the people he loved. He saved the ones he could, and mourned the ones he couldn't, all with the same acerbic severity.

Lissa glanced at her phone again, then blew out a breath she couldn't stop holding.

Down periods, even stints of despair in Lissa's life had been the result of passing external forces rather than an internal darkness pulling her under. Never having faced depression, Lissa couldn't empathize with Kate. A misunderstanding had left the woman without options. In Kate's shoes, Lissa would have brained Cole over the head with a Birkin bag charged to *his* credit card until he'd straightened out. Kate hadn't been able to do that and had settled on an irreversible retreat. She must have felt hopeless and powerless and unable to cope.

Especially since the accusation that had alienated Cole had taken Rhea, too. One savage blow had divested her of a better half and a BFF.

Yet the chemical makeup of Kate's brain had *lied* to her, told her to leave it all behind. Now Cole lied to himself. He believed his active imagination had killed his wife when a *disease* had taken Kate, an insidious force that had crept between husband and wife through no fault of their own.

A headache started behind Lissa's eyes, joining the concern that churned in her stomach. She rolled up off the wooden planks, leaning her torso against Sasha's side. He, of course, leaned in. They met in the middle, balanced, both of them staring down the tree-lined driveway in morose silence.

The game had changed. A week ago her strain might have been born of concern for the project and how another brush with death might affect Cole's attitude, her career, and the ongoing efforts to persuade Cole to relent.

Now Lissa worried about the grim recognition in Cole's eyes when his uncle had collapsed. She worried about the fervency with which Cole had worked to save him. Most of all, she worried about the flat acceptance in Cole's voice when he'd called Kate's death *his* fault.

Today she worried about the man.

Years of channeling emotion into her work had rendered the two inseparable. So it didn't surprise Lissa when, almost as if in a dream, she found herself in her room, paintbrush in hand. This time she let herself ignore the bargain with Cole and simply create. She didn't worry about making a painting that would please or impress or convince an onlooker she'd changed her ways. The sadness poured out like the telling of a story to an old friend.

A blurred background took immediate shape. Black faded to blue and then back to black in inconsistent patterns that shrouded the canvas in gloom. She chose a lighter shade, still blue but more electric, to highlight a shape off the center of the painting. Symmetry would be too perfect, the opposite of what she sought to convey.

Out of the shadows grew a wavering form, an amalgamation of head, heart, and Casper the Friendly Ghost. In the center of the figure, she added faint, unstructured highlights as a reminder that light could shine on the worst disappointments.

This wasn't a painting she would share, at least not with Cole. Her previous abstract efforts at Melina had been real, but they'd also been designed to provoke. *Shock and awe*, as Trevor had suggested on her very first day in Colorado.

She didn't want that anymore. If Cole directly associated her brand of imaginative exercise with the death of someone he'd loved, asking him to embrace it felt wrong, cruel even.

Blunt force trauma was out. Gradual acceptance, in.

The path was clear.

Lissa would help Cole heal after all.

CHAPTER 15

Hospitals smelled of death. To Cole, that's all they'd ever brought. After his parents' accident, they'd been rushed to this very facility.

Only to die shortly thereafter.

Kate, too, had spent nearly an hour in the familiar intensive care unit down the hall.

Before succumbing to head injuries.

Not this time. Twelve hours ago, the doctors had performed emergency angioplasty surgery and placed a stent in one of Kent's coronary arteries. The way Cole understood it, they'd used a tiny balloon to inflate the blocked blood vessel and then propped the thing open with a mesh tube to guard against a repeat closure.

Kent would never consume saturated fat again, even if Cole had to tie him to the chair and feed him three squares a day. Standing by the bed and staring down, Cole mentally apologized to his frail, unconscious uncle for all the deprivation easing down the pipeline.

On the other side of Kent's beeping contraption of a bed, Trevor shifted on a hard-backed couch that must have been designed to discourage overnight visitors. No pillows cushioned the L-shaped slabs, and yet Trevor appeared right at home. "You saved him," said his brother.

Their uncle would live.

"No," Cole replied. Trevor always assumed the best of Cole, never vilifying him, offering unconditional care when Cole had proven himself incapable of the same. "I performed CPR. So did you. Let's hope Kent remembers us when he wakes."

"You moved fast"—Trevor sat forward, draping beefy forearms over his knees—"so at least we have hope."

Suddenly Kent blinked. Bruised rings circled each eye, and his lips were as pale as the surrounding skin. Dry and waxen. His heavy gaze roamed the

98

room without focus. "Boys," he whispered on an inhale, and Cole's pulse jumped. "Where the hell am I?"

Trevor bent chin to chest and murmured, "That answers a couple of questions."

"The hospital"—Cole tried to inject humor into his tone to diffuse Kent's worry—"where all the butter addicts go."

"*Former* butter addicts," Trevor clarified.

"What happened?" Kent sounded bewildered, almost afraid to hear the answer.

Cole and Trevor started in unison. "You—" "We—"

With a nod, Trevor dropped off.

"We found you on the kitchen floor," Cole explained. "You'd been loading the freezer with Rhea and went down without warning. The doctors performed surgery successfully." Those details could come later. "You'll be all right."

Kent's eyes drooped wearily, and Cole suspected the conversation would be short lived and soon forgotten. "Whose freezer?" Kent finally asked. The words leaked out painfully, a shameful admission of his lack of recollection.

"Mine." Cole answered as though Kent had asked the most normal of questions.

"Why?" Kent's pitch was rising. The doctor had called the mind "unpredictable." Some of Kent's memories would return soon. Some later. Some never. They were to treat the lapses with kindness and patience, pretending all was right with a complete blank about one's recent whereabouts.

Trevor jumped in. "You're a male version of a mother hen, that's why. Plus Cole's got a beautiful painter nestled away in the spare bedroom. Naturally, you've had us up there constantly." He crossed his arms over his chest and whistled to the ceiling. "Can't imagine why."

A smile ghosted across Kent's lips. "That's hopeful." Then he drifted off again, looking worse than he had two minutes ago. Cole had long viewed this moment as inevitable. Kent had a genetically weak heart, high cholesterol, high blood pressure, and a penchant for the finer things in life.

His uncle had earned his lamb chops, but that didn't mean they wouldn't kill him. Beta blockers could only do so much. Like Kate before him, Kent had a disease. His kind hardened the arteries, while hers had softened the mind. Yet the two sicknesses stole through the body with equal treachery.

Underhanded and fatal and hard to fight.

Cole wondered about a world where you could protect people from the dangers that might befall them, a foolish thought that didn't bear contemplation. Striving for that kind of divine control only called forth a terrible darkness in him, the locked-away part that knew any efforts in that direction were doomed to fail. So he silenced those yearnings, or at least covered them with rules and sarcasm and denial.

"Cole." Trevor's patient prodding cut through the musings. "You should call. She'll want to know Kent's all right."

Trevor didn't have to explain whom.

"You think she's beautiful." Good thing Rhea had gone long before her husband's offhanded comment.

"Just like you do." Trevor shrugged. Grinned. "I'm allowed. We've established I'm a monument of restraint, remember?"

That they had. The hard way. Cole had been late to catch his mistake about Trevor and Kate, but Rhea *still* clung to the belief that her husband had been unfaithful. Yet she stayed, periodically hoarding the past over Trevor with a biting reminder he wasn't to be trusted.

Another log on the flaming wreckage at Cole's feet.

"I don't think about how she looks." He *obsessed.* The truth might not be so unacceptable if that were all—if he didn't dream of her smelling like peaches or almonds or coconuts, and tasting like all three. If he didn't secretly bait her because he liked to watch her mouth move, especially when she was angry enough to talk fast and certain with that telltale flush sweeping down her neck and over the breasts he *needed*—any other emotion implied choice—to see.

A choked sound spewed from Trevor.

"That's funny?"

"You're the worst kind of liar—a bad one."

And Trevor was the worst kind of brother—a right one. Cole rolled his shoulders in a smooth, indifferent shrug. "Fine."

Looking unconvinced by Cole's easy capitulation, Trevor threw an ankle over the opposite thigh and flopped back against the rigid couch. "I've known you for thirty-six years. I gave you your first bloody nose, taught you to drive, and bought a pregnancy test for your panicked high-school girlfriend. I *felt* the relief on your face when the results came up negative. I taught you calculus and how to use a compass. When Mom and Dad died, I worried over you more than I did them. I carried your wife's casket and have bought your favorite candies every week since she died, all on the heels of your breach of trust. Because I know you and why you believed the worst. Of me. Of her. *Just like I know your back teeth are throbbing with want for Lissa Blanc.*"

Cole's fingers curled around Kent's bedrail. The need to turn inward might have been an instinctive rejection of Trevor's insight, but... no. The solid grip really represented what Cole wanted to do with Lissa. Touch. Not let go. Give.

Take.

Maybe for a little while. Maybe forever.

"Go home, little brother." Truck keys sailed through the air, forcing Cole to pry his white knuckles from his uncle's unforgiving bed rail. With the snap of a wrist, Cole snatched the keys from their flight path before they landed on Kent's stomach.

"Come back once you've gotten her off your... chest." Trevor paused, not bothering to mask the speculative gleam in his eyes, the one that gave away the other things Cole would get Lissa off of. "And bring her with you. This is where she should be."

******

Lissa's room sat dark and still and quiet. No signifying lump rose beneath her comforter. Sasha didn't lounge on her floor. An unexpected chill wandered over Cole's shoulders. He shouldn't have been surprised now that October had given way to November. At this altitude, November passed for winter.

Cole dropped in front of Lissa's hearth and arranged logs in the grate. Next came the crumpled newspapers kept at the ready in a wicker basket beside the mantle. Flame crawled from a lit match, through the paper and over the bark clinging to the bottom log.

And then there was fire.

Now he had crackling flames and a raging hard-on without the willing woman. Cole considered waiting her out, but with Lissa that could take all night. He was halfway to the still-open door when the firelight caught the blue winking from her easel.

His Lissa had been busy.

No matter where photography had taken him—the poverty in the children or the pollution in the water—he could *almost* always find a patch of sky to appreciate. Blue had been his favorite.

Her painting morphed that fondness into mourning. If Lissa stood next to him, she'd ask her favorite question: *What do you feel when you look at it?* For once, their answers might match. Despite his well-worn affinity for the color, a burn flared behind his ribs—the trickling drain of unavoidable loss layered beneath a rush of expectation. Fittingly, he saw more of the former than the latter on the canvas, but the slight hint of better prospects, of Lissa's hope that greatness awaited, couldn't be ignored.

One got to understand a person when living and working together, especially when all that living and working occurred primarily one-on-one. Show Lissa the stars, and she'd fly to the moon to collect the future lying in its dust, no matter how difficult, impossible, or grim.

He ran his knuckles lightly over a corner of the murky background, testing the paint. The dryness of the smooth surface told him she'd begun before Kent's ambulance had fully departed the front drive.

The woman *thought* in paint. She worried in paint, rejoiced in paint, grieved in paint, and used paint to talk to the world. Her brush was an extension of her mind. Her mouth. *Her heart.*

Cole could only wish for that kind of connection with his craft.

He lifted the work from its resting place, slipping it safely under his arm. He wouldn't negligently destroy Lissa's art again. From the hall, he checked his own room first. A man could hope. Maybe he wasn't alone in tonight's epiphanies.

Unfortunately, his king bed looked as lonely as ever. He kept moving, room by room. First he exhausted the upstairs, then ruled out the couch and a rug she favored in front of the fireplace in the living room. The dining room and kitchen were clear.

He found her in the basement, hunched in the corner they'd invaded together that very morning, the remnants of his twenty years with a camera spread in a semi-circle around her folded legs. The ski mask was back, along with the suffocating clothing that covered every single inch of the skin he'd gotten so desperate to see. Sasha stretched out amid the chaos, snoring in a chuffing, inconsistent rumble. She'd let the dog make a nest of glossy eight-by-tens.

Figures.

The location made perfect sense. Lissa Blanc still searched for her rocket ship to the moon. She never gave up, not even on the worst of days.

How come the poor-little-rich-girl haters clamoring after her hadn't figured that one out?

She didn't look up from her laptop. Every two seconds or so, she jabbed the keyboard, obviously trolling through electronic photos. "He's okay?"

Cole shrugged. "For the next while. They cleared the blockage." *We'll see how long that can last.*

She set the computer aside and considered him at length, chin resting on bare, steepled fingers. She had fine-boned hands. Artist's hands, some would say, the kind with delicate joints and tapered nails. He'd noticed her lack of polish and attributed the simplicity to her profession. Removing stray paint from her skin would likely strip the heartiest polish.

"*You* okay?" she asked.

"Yes," he answered simply. He stayed on the stairs under that one glaring light bulb, letting her look her fill. The eyes examining him were shadowed. She'd been waiting.

Where did he start? How did he ask?

Tell her.

Before he could wade in, Lissa turned speculative. Her eyes pinched in the direction of the painting he held, and her lips turned up mildly, only half amused, as if she doubted what she saw and tried to reserve judgment until she *knew*.

"If you've sabotaged that painting," she said in a voice that could freeze boiling oil, "I'd call you a slow, slow learner."

******

Triste—the French part of her mutt heritage liked the alliteration—had been a private exercise. Now Cole clutched the painting in a trigger hold, steady, but hesitant, as though he wasn't sure whether he'd made the right choice. If his choice had been to damage more of her work, she'd let Sasha do more than *sleep* on Cole's prized photographs.

Slow words rolled over his tongue, each one individually enunciated. "You're driving me *crazy*. Literally, I think."

The twists of his logic never failed to surprise. She'd anticipated some snide comment about her skill but got an admission of a sluggish decline into madness. "You were crazy already, *I* think." Which was fine because Lissa liked the unexpected. Predictable meant boring.

He smiled at that, a bitter twist of lips and gleaming teeth. "I knew myself before. I knew I'd made mistakes that required amends. You make me wonder whether I'm willing to pay."

"Good." Someday, she'd be that introspective. She would worry about the people she'd wronged and drive herself nuts wanting to make it right. *Or not.* For now, she wanted to lift every ounce of self-reflection from Cole's shoulders and fling them to the rafters for the spiders to devour. "You've nothing to pay for."

Cole took a step and kept coming. He didn't stop until he loomed over her, separated only by the albums and photos and disks she'd piled around the floor. The meat of *Triste* remained concealed in his long shadow. She couldn't tell what he'd done to her latest work.

Attitude generally coated Cole in a thin veil of *tread carefully*. Even when he'd reached out with toe-curling intimacy, she'd sensed his internal mastery. Tonight his bruised presence felt lighter, like he prepared to ask instead of tell. But for what?

Dangle a carrot.

Reaching beneath her, she lifted a dog-eared *Travel + Leisure* magazine opened to a marked page with Cole's name printed in tiny letters along the bottom edge. "I've never been to Machu Picchu." She made the comment idly, like the subject wasn't completely random. "Seems like a place certain kinds of photographers are expected to cut their teeth. I bet it's been the subject of a million talents. Yet all the pictures I've seen—years and years' worth—look the same. The camera points downward to a cliff-side ruin with a sharp, rocky mountain rising in the backdrop. That same photograph, taken by hordes of professionals, has made that lost city one of the most recognizable in the world." The satin pages quivered in her grip. "Cookie-cutter greatness."

Cole stilled, waiting, but not particularly expectant. No surprise there. They didn't share a history of compliments. He was preparing for the worst.

"Yours is better," she admitted, now holding the open magazine with one hand and tracing the outline of stone terraces with the other. "So good I want to think the clouds are computer generated. They cradle the city too perfectly, holding it up to the eye, creating depth, contrasting color—"

"They're real."

"Of course they are. You're you."

He bared his teeth without a sound, then toed a pile of DVDs out of the way and sat close. The intensity he never quite shirked settled into the space between them, charging the air with whatever Cole planned to say.

He delayed, which meant Lissa killed time enjoying the view. Across from her, his sharp, gorgeous face was serious. Unkempt hair fell over his forehead, almost blocking those suspicious eyes, eyes that mocked and caressed all at once.

"So?" she asked, ignoring the warmth spreading to her limbs. If she was going to give him a compliment, he could damn well work for it.

Cole leaned back against his palms in a smooth glide, looking too collected for their face-off. His grin was so fast she nearly missed the message, a flash of sun on steel and then gone again. "I went back at sunrise, four days in a row. Weather had settled in. The shot became a matter of timing."

Neither the innocuous words nor the quick smile diffused the tension. That alone said he merely humored her with his answer. Whatever he really wanted to say would come later, after he disposed of her untimely fixation on the photos.

"Not the tiniest bit of digital manipulation?" She knew the answer, but felt it best to build him up, just in case she had to tear him down.

"None."

Honesty surged on her tongue. "Congratulations," she whispered. The sentiment cost her. Who knew how Cole would react to her sincere admiration? He might use it as the wrong kind of fuel. Those in the know believed constructive criticism should follow positive feedback. She'd started out right, but if he attacked, if he showed any inclination to use her compliment as a concession, she'd fall back on the stack of examples sitting behind her. One photo after another proved he'd never been totally devoted to what-you-see-is-what-you-get. He, of all people, knew that waiting in one place for four days to capture a fleeting reality wasn't the *only* way.

Naked Kate in the desert had been the smallest start.

Triumph kindled in the subtle incline of Cole's head. Were he standing, she suspected he'd take a bow. "You're learning," he said.

So close. Her fingers skated over one of her "gotcha" photos. This one looked like tropical fish swimming in a glass-encased aquarium. A closer look—mainly at the caption—proved the picture had been taken underwater through a huge metal frame meant to impart a staid, safe impression. The fish were Amazonian piranhas in their natural habitat. The picture lied, and it was magnificent. "Listen, genius, I just reached across the aisle. You might try—"

Cole flipped her canvas out from behind him. One moment she'd faced her recalcitrant partner, the next the blue swirls of *Triste*. He might not take up the space of his brother, but Cole possessed whipcord strength and fluid movement and the decisive speed of a released slingshot—tense and still one moment, loose and still the next, something profound and easily missed in between.

Unexpected relief relaxed her ribcage. The painting was pristine. Cole hadn't done any harm. She released the picture of the swimming fish, keeping it hidden for the moment. Observing her own work, she said, "I know—*good*, right?"

"No." After a tick, he added softly, "Great."

Elation whirled in an expanding ball beneath Lissa's ribs, and she couldn't stop her grin. Cole was instantly forgiven for invading her space. Thank God some unexplained initiative had led him to the one painting she'd decided to keep to herself.

Because her quest to belong had morphed. General acceptance—a few pats on the back or a handful of willing buyers—would no longer do. She'd take them, of course, but she wanted—needed—*Cole's* respect. *No more talk of drivel.*

Now...

Lissa stilled. The moment she'd worked for with such fervor should have arrived with more fanfare. Cole wasn't eating crow with the proper enthusiasm. "And?"

You're sorry you mocked my work? My profession? My existence? You were wrong all along?

Expectation threatened to break through her sardonic façade. She shook it off, refusing to show how deeply she cared. Because she didn't. *Not at all.*

"Go ahead," he said, "ask me."

Oh, she would. Couldn't wait. But ask him what?

His head tilted when she didn't jump at the invitation. "Ask me what I fee—"

Her breath caught in dawning understanding, and she rushed to get the question out. "What do you feel when you look at it?"

Feel. An industrious word. Cole sat close enough to touch. If she were to reach out, her fingertips could trail down—

"When I first saw it, I was hit with equal parts sadness and disappointment."

Yes, when he'd been rummaging alone in her room in the middle of the night. *Maybe going through my underwear drawer.* One never knew when the landlord would retaliate for past transgressions. For that, she'd piled her sexiest thongs on top. Staring at Cole's private possessions scattered around her knees, Lissa admitted most would have invaded her room far sooner.

"Then what?" Her voice was husky. She should stop focusing on Cole's possible proximity to her lingerie and seize her progress against his closed-minded views. Concentration was a hard thing, though, when he sat inches away, looking rigidly aloof.

About to break. Or give in.

He surged to his feet, tension roiling visibly beneath his skin, and she knew her face reflected pure feminine appreciation. Scooting back against the boxes at her rear, she settled in to watch him pace.

Cole wasted little time. He crossed the room to the far corner she'd searched that morning. "I'll show you *what*," he muttered, presumably to himself. Without pausing to examine any contents, he bent at the knees and lifted a stack of four boxes, depositing them front and center. Before she could do much wondering, he pulled the top box down and set it on the floor in front of the other three, forming an L-shape.

When he reached for *Triste*, she understood. He'd constructed a makeshift easel at her height on the floor.

Careful hands set the base of her painting on the front box, then tilted it back for viewing. "Here"—his finger stabbed at the murky highlighting in *Triste's* center—"you didn't stop at sad or disappointed. You, *like you always do*, kept going."

Her ears perked. Perhaps she should have given Cole more credit. Telling herself he didn't "get" her work had been a consolation prize. "I do that because there's always more to show." Like right now. She didn't feel mere surprise and satisfaction. She also wondered at Cole's game and whether his praise stemmed from an honest change of heart or a drive to officially push the boundaries of their relationship. "We've been over this. You see emotion in black and white. I see cream and heather gray." *And pink and purple and persimmon.*

"Right." His chest heaved.

Poor man. "What does the white mean, Cole? If more complex than sad and disappointed, then what?"

"*You.*" His shout echoed off the concrete walls, ripped from his throat like a vile insult. "Always *you.*"

Lissa swallowed against the instinct to lash out. Cole's outburst didn't bring an iota of clarity. He sounded so angry. Yet he'd obviously come to the basement bearing an olive branch.

He stretched his arms back, clasping those big hands behind his head, breathing hard against whatever speech he wouldn't let himself make.

Lissa blinked, then let her eyes drift shut. "I don't understand. Tell me."

"All this time I couldn't tap the veins running through your work. The paintings hinted at meaning that proved elusive. I blamed you, told myself a real artist ought to be able to reach even me."

As he talked, his rasping breath tapered to a manageable rhythm. "You never could."

Bullshit. "I *did.*" She'd touched a nerve the size of the Grand Canyon.

"When I see that halo floating in the gloom of blue, I get the surrounding despair, so I'm improving. Other than that, I can only guess at what *you* must have felt and try to grasp it. Hope, I suppose. Hope I don't understand or share."

Her eyes snapped open. "But you want to."

"Pay attention." He scowled. "I want *you.*"

CHAPTER 16

"What, exactly," Lissa choked, "is that supposed to mean?"

"You know, exactly." Cole abandoned the painting and surged across the chilled concrete on lead feet. Lissa might think he'd accepted her as a partner. Or that he intended to amass more of her work. Both were true. But her parted lips and shallow pants told him otherwise. She knew he meant *her*, as in legs wrapped around his waist as he glided through soft, clutching tissues. As in sucking kisses to the back of her neck while she begged him to move lower.

Which he would. Because he planned to give her what she wanted, and like it or not, Lissa returned his sentiment.

He crouched in front of her, hands on her calves, stroking.

She didn't move away. If anything, she leaned in. "Your presumptions know no bounds."

"Really? That must have been what you were thinking a week ago when you screamed 'please' and came on my tongue."

She swallowed.

"You came in a rush, and it was the sweetest thing I've ever tasted. Beautiful." Another truth. In every other way, she'd fought against his control, ignoring his dictates, outsmarting him at each turn. He should have guessed her warm, wet welcome would be unusually gratifying. Physically, at least, she couldn't resist. Like him. "I can't stop thinking about your response. Don't even want to."

More convulsive swallowing and her eyes grew huge behind the silly mask. Then, "Jesus, Cole, is *this* what you've been hiding behind that tower in your head?"

In a word, "Yes." Maybe he couldn't embrace the emotion, at least not easily, but he'd always gotten along with the sex.

"Give me that." He rolled the stocking gently over her lips, then pulled it free and dropped it to the floor. Without the mask, she was still swathed in clothes. He hadn't seen her truly naked since that second morning in the hall. Yards of cotton and denim did little to mute the picture he carried in his mind.

Perfection.

Peeling away the jeans would reveal slim hips and a smooth, pert ass. Divesting her of the heavy thermal top would expose efficient little breasts that stood high without support. Nipples that puckered at the slightest provocation. His mouth watered with the urge to nuzzle through the shirt.

But not here, not in the cold and damp, a place she felt the need to cover up.

His hand found hers. "Come." With him for now. Later, around him.

His Lissa—he couldn't place when he'd begun to think of her that way—followed without a fight. Sasha snorted when their steps hit the stairs. Leaving the breathing throw rug behind, Cole led Lissa to the kitchen and through the dark house. Her heat coated his back all the way up the front stairs and into her bedroom.

Lissa would be warm. He wanted her free and giving and, as he knew she could be, *greedy*.

"You started a fire," she observed, cozying toward the warmth and reaching delicate hands to dying embers. He waited for her to elaborate, but when she swiveled her head to look at him, an arched brow said it all. She suspected he hadn't come looking for canvas and color. Her gaze flicked to her dresser and back, looking sly. Next time he dropped by uninvited, he'd see what waited in those drawers.

Cole chuckled, feeling true mirth for the first time in what felt like forever. "You don't approve?"

"I do… of both your motives and your methods."

The last word faded away when he approached from behind and pressed his lips to her nape. His erection had grown painful, and he cursed the cock that was three steps ahead of the action and damn unwilling to wait up now that he'd taken the plunge. "Speaking of methods—"

"Cole?" she interrupted, sounding lazy, and yet determined.

He licked the spot he'd kissed. Blew. "Shhh." They could talk later.

"Cole?"

The vulnerability she injected into his name said the question couldn't wait. He knew that tone. They'd talk now or fuck never. Either option might kill him.

He caved. "Hmm?"

"Can you handle this?"

I hope so. "Not sure I have a choice." His body had taken the decision out of his hands.

"Once we start this—*if* we start this—we still have to make a go at the project."

He nipped her bare earlobe. "You smell like gingerbread."

A nod brought her head back to rest on his shoulder. "Holiday scents came out at Halloween, and I'm really talented with online shopping."

For a rich girl, she minimized when it came to jewelry. Her ears and neck and fingers were bare in blatant invitation—*kiss me, touch me, suck me.* But the body products? *Jesus Christ.* The most tantalizing woman in the world smelled like cookies.

She whimpered when he mouthed her throat. "Can we have both?" she asked.

Cole knew what she meant—could they successfully be colleagues with benefits?—and chose his words carefully. He wasn't offering a white dress or a picket fence. But with that question, neither was she. "We'll compartmentalize." Granted, the last two years hadn't been a great example of his ability to separate. Work had been tied to tidal waves of emotional bombardment, far from his specialty. This could be simple. Elemental. Necessary.

He didn't hurry when he wrapped both arms around her middle, waiting patiently for her answer, but also not letting her escape. Concern barely overrode his desire. It shouldn't have. There were other women.

Not that you want. The others didn't tell him to fuck off when he needed a set down. The others didn't have silken chestnut hair, not quite brown, not quite red. The others didn't smell like dessert.

She nodded after way too long. "I trust you."

Anything but that. His arms spasmed, giving Lissa an involuntary squeeze. Not trust. She could hand over lust and anger, heap on the frustration, but she shouldn't put her wellbeing in his hands. No one should. "Trust," he repeated, his rasp a scrape along his protesting conscience. "Trust me to what?"

Her head rolled on his shoulder, and he felt her smile into his neck. "To make me feel good."

Relief came in a rush. She talked of tonight, not tomorrow morning. Women—especially this one—were never so simple, which meant she lied to herself, if not to him. But they could pretend.

Make her feel good? The woman had no idea.

******

Lissa kept her lips against Cole's throat. The unexpectedness of each run-in with the man was outdone only by the next, and the next. Why should tonight be any different?

He needed a sign around his neck: *Safety not assured.*

She needed one too: *To hell with safety.*

A gasp caught in her throat when he lifted her from behind. With a heavy flick, he sent her tumbling onto the mattress, sprawled out like a less-than-virginal sacrifice. He followed on all fours, then straddled her hips.

Leaning forward, he paused at the junction of neck and collarbone. Her best guess said he was… breathing her in.

"Your scent," he whispered, burrowing in further, "is so sweet. Like candy and chocolate, with breasts. You do it on purpose."

"No"—she gulped when his fingers began to draw wide circles around her nipples—"I never—I—maybe." Not to attract, certainly, but she loved the way a delicate layering of scent stayed with her through the day, revealing itself as the hours passed. Chocolate and vanilla comforted more than French musk. Instead of pretentious armor, they were lingering friends.

With his fingers still circling ever inward, Cole licked up the side of her neck. "Last week wasn't enough. I need to taste more."

Proving it, he ran his tongue back down, across her collarbone, and up the other side to her ear. He bit, rolling the sensitive lobe between his teeth. "Sample every last inch."

"Start here." She pressed his face between her hands and met his mouth with hers, ready to devour all he was willing to give. He talked of *her* taste, but it was Cole who turned out to be irresistible. Her lips parted, and he slipped inside, then again. Soon he licked at her in a rocking, carnal slide that mimicked their driving hips.

Lissa ached. She hurt where he touched her and more where he didn't. Wonder shivered through her limbs. The men from her past had been just that—adults of the male variety. Not lovers. They'd never made her feel like stopping would bring unimaginable pain. Instead, they'd been caricatures of the sitcom boyfriend—"Innnn." *Sweat.* "Good?" *Pant.* "Wow, babe, great sex." *Smoke.* "So when do I meet your dad?"

Cole wasn't even *in* and already she'd surpassed *wow*.

All of a sudden, he sat straight, looking pained. *At least I'm not alone.* Like her ski mask in the basement, he began to roll her thermal upward, his mouth trailing behind. Patient at first until he rumbled, "Fuck this," and jerked the shirt over her head. Ten seconds later, he'd dragged her jeans from her hips, pulled them free, and shucked his own clothes.

Then—*molten steel*—he stretched his body over hers. She hadn't bothered with a bra to peruse the basement, so only a wispy black thong kept her from his hard, searching length.

She arched every possible inch into him, loving the feel of his chest as it abraded her nipples. This first time, she expected madness, a frenetic pace to match the fever raging beneath her skin. But he tempered her movement, winding his arms over hers and stretching their hands over her head. Rumbled curses sounded in her ear. Then a promise. "Need to slow down. *Savor.*"

With a firm press, he tethered her hands to the mattress. *"Be still."* Then he rose up, high enough for her to track those blue eyes as they roamed over every peak and valley, like he'd waited too long and was literally starved for her.

She quivered. Forget *savor*, she needed him to touch fast and hard. Now.

Cole finally dusted his knuckles beneath the curves of breasts, over her belly, leisurely exploring her secrets. He shifted his hips back to sit lower on her thighs, revealing the scrap of lace that barely covered the junction in between.

The slow discovery continued, here and there and just short of maddening, until desperate gasps sliced from her lips.

"Easy, easy." He was whispering now, his fingers petting through the drenched cloth.

Heat sank through to her skin, and Lissa's hands jerked. Almost with a will of their own, her arms raised, and she sank her fingers into his silky hair, pulling him down. She didn't care how or where... "Cole"—her touch drifted down his bunched torso to graze the smooth head of his cock—"I need you."

He shook his head. "Not yet." He moved aside and tore her panties down her legs, muscles tense, body rigid. Once steeped in awe, his gaze now burned with *resolve*. Cole had a plan.

Grasping her knees, he guided her thighs apart. Teasing fingers instantly stroked through her lush wetness. "Hard to be gentle," he gritted, turning that flare of intent on her sex.

Moaning, Lissa bucked into his hand. "Be gentle later."

Pleasure roiling, building.

His mouth found her nipple, dousing the sensitive peak in liquid fire at the same time he worked a finger inside her. Then another, all while the heel of his palm pulsed against her clitoris.

Unbidden, blinding pleasure had her clutching his head to her breast. *So giving.* He broke away and stared at her face, still thrusting deep in an unhurried stir, petting her on the inside. Only the lip he chewed between his teeth and the wild intensity in his eyes betrayed the effort he put into those languid movements that were softly, gently winding her tight.

"Come," he instructed with a harder drive that made her whimper, "and I'll fuck you."

The sharp promise ramped her up, higher... wetter... totally open. And in the next second, totally free.

******

A harsh groan tore from Cole's chest when her tight passage cinched around his fingers. Her flesh was warm and silken in his clasp, telling him she'd be heaven around his cock. All of his self-control poured into each second he spent on the wrong side of her hot little sheath.

But he was determined to make her need this. He hadn't known whether Lissa would want to be with him. Until the last second, when she'd declared her trust that he could make her feel good, he'd wondered whether she might pull away.

Not today. And he planned to make his Lissa *crave* him through a zillion tomorrows.

At least sexually.

Once the spasms died away, he slipped free and knelt between her thighs. Her slick heat beckoned, and for a second, all he could do was *look*. From the crown of her glossy head to her pink, glistening core, this woman had him in a vice. The more she opened for him, the harder the bars clamped down.

Reaching out, he toyed with the subtle indention between her hip bones. "Soft and sweet," he murmured. Lissa was slim in the way of a satin ribbon. Some women took it too far, until they achieved the cut physique of an athlete. *Or a man.* He imagined taking that to bed would be like sleeping with a bag of gristle, whereas Lissa flowed over him with the grace of running water.

She surged off the bed in an impatient rustle, her color deepening. "You promised," she breathed, practically sobbing.

Couldn't have that. "I did, didn't I?" Quick like, he slid off the bed and grabbed his wallet, then the condom he'd stashed inside at the Seven-Eleven on the way home from the hospital. *Another push he'd thank his brother for.* Somewhat sheepishly, he looked over at Lissa with a shrug, acknowledging his preparedness. She'd already called him presumptuous, and this proved the hell out of that theory. "As if we could have gone *any* other way."

She didn't argue. Like before, her gaze shot dark sparks in the direction the dresser.

Cole's attention followed her path. "I'm going to find out what's so intriguing about that drawer."

"Perhaps you weren't the only one with plans."

Niiice. Cryptic and obvious at the same time, the comment assuaged some of the guilt he felt at showing up ready for sex. Rushing to settle between her legs, he discovered he was shaking so badly he could hardly hold the foil wrapper. "You do it," he said, handing over the condom. "You... just... do this." *For me. For us.*

Lissa grabbed the shiny package and ripped through the perforated line at the top. She extracted a condom that was thin and lubricated. Crazy, but he didn't care that he had to wear the barrier if it meant *she'd* be outfitting him.

Her hands were soft and sure as they flitted over his sex, first exploring the heavy sac below and then moving up the length of his shaft. *Hurry, please, hurry—*

She squeezed the head. *Hard.* Then her thumb started slow circles through the wetness he hadn't been able to hold back. With each pass, his erection kicked against her fingers.

Tingling pressure whirled at the base of his cock, and he jacked his hips in her grip. *Don't be too demanding. Nice and easy and gentlemanly.* But fuck that—it had been years. Now he was skin to skin with a dream, and she was fisting the end of his dick like it was a balloon and she couldn't let the air out. The condom went on now or he—

Lubed latex hit the tip and rolled down. He exhaled, the groan escaping his lips as though it were flying shrapnel. Who would have guessed a rubber could be a relief?

Palming his cock, he ran the blunt head over her glistening folds. With each pass, she let out a little mewl and surged toward him when he reached the most vulnerable spot. He could *smell* her arousal.

Finally, he wedged the tip of his penis inside. She clamped down.

"Oh, Jesus. *Fuck.* Please, Lissa, let up on me. That's it, baby, let me in."

The passage he attempted to breach had been tight on his fingers. It was a goddamn tourniquet on his cock, if tourniquets were hot and wet and poised to rip off his favorite limb.

At his plea, he felt her channel ease off, just enough for him to push forward a fraction without losing his sanity. Lissa's breath hitched, and her breasts jerked with each catch, but she never looked away from his face. "Too close?" she asked. "Too tight?"

"*Never.*" Cole pivoted his torso forward. With an elbow planted on either side of her head, he settled his lips against her neck, licking at a pulsing blue vein while he slowly, incrementally inched himself deep. "Easy now. Relax, baby. Open up. Ah, yeah, sink right into the bed."

More licking. She was delicious. Better than dessert. Better than eating real food ever again.

He pulled out, not all the way, but almost, then surged forward. The two connections—at her neck and below—weren't enough. He wanted to rub his whole body over her like water creeping up a beach, no grain of sand left unexplored. Pressing close, he rocked slowly inside her, tip to base, feeling his own pelvis grow wet and slippery. He tightened, pleasure climbing up his shaft. Unable to hold back, he thrust hard on a guttural moan. When she responded with a heavy gasp of her own, he ratcheted up the force. Again and again, he drove into her with relentless purpose, sliding against her swollen clitoris on every stroke.

The sudden constriction of her flesh broke over him, along with a cry that relayed pure, shining ecstasy. Hearing the joy of it, Cole wanted her pleasure to last forever. Rising on his arms high enough to glance between their bodies, he watched her take him in, watched his cock piston through the pulses that called forth a responsive throb of his own.

No chance now. Lifting his head, he saw the pleasure work across Lissa's flushed face.

And he joined her, coming in a flood of warmth that made his vision go fuzzy.

Buried in Lissa's welcoming body, a frenzy bubbling in his veins, he felt only the two of them. The demons he usually carried like a mantle were far at bay, finally quiet enough for him to notice their absence.

That's when he panicked.

CHAPTER 17

Kent split his eyelids and faced the dark, the tang of ammonia tingling in his nostrils. A spear of moonlight broke through a gap between the blinds to bathe the sterile room in enough light to make out vague shapes. He could see metal railings encasing his bed. Snores billowed from a sturdy couch beneath the window.

One of his nephews had stayed on for the night.

He vaguely remembered his first round of consciousness, what must have been hours before. Both Cole and Trevor had been standing by, self-designated ventricular sentinels. They'd talked, probably. He couldn't recall much beyond the slightly chiding tone of the conversation.

Initially he'd been so disoriented life had seemed an unrecognizable blur. Already this had changed. He was Kent Rathlen, a family patriarch who couldn't keel over because his dead brother's clod-headed sons needed him.

For very different reasons. One needed to blow through a past that begged to be overcome. The other needed to burn through a present that begged to be left in the past. At least Kent *thought* that was the case.

Part of Cole's story came easy. Sporadic chunks of family history streamed by like the replay of a familiar movie. Kent remembered he'd literally been feeding the guy, making sure his nephew took care of himself in the wake of a tragedy. But there was more, and Kent struggled to grasp details through a haze of drugs on top of a set of barriers his mind had erected all on its own. "*Stop,*" they silently scolded. "*Turn back.*"

Kent might not be able to recite what he'd eaten for breakfast, but he still knew himself to be more stubborn than a tree-climbing goat. There'd be no shying away from the memories trying to break through.

Heart attacks were hard work. Throat parched, Kent reached for a remote sitting on his rolling bedside table. He punched the green button and held, hoping the thing would move his bed upright so he could reach

116

the water sitting on the far side of the same tray.

Of course the TV blared on.

A massive slumbering form scrambled upright, kicking the end of the couch with a wayward size thirteen. Guess that told him which brother had stayed over.

Trevor grumbled, "What the hell—"

"Sorry!" Kent made his best contrite face, though he doubted Trevor would recognize the masterpiece in the dark. "Maybe you could nudge me that glass." He pointed at the water with his pinky.

"Somebody's feeling better." Trevor rolled off the sofa and had the water in Kent's hands pronto. Then the light flicked on. "You need a straw? Some ice?"

Kent merely shook his head, marveling at the differences between the two people he loved most in the world. Trevor had been instantly solicitous. Cole would have shoved the water at him and demanded he drink it all immediately because dehydration would not be tolerated. Then he would have refilled the glass and watched Kent obediently drink the liquid down again. Forget niceties like straws and ice. Cole favored utility.

"You want food?" Trevor asked. Cole would have hunted down a bowl of high-fiber cereal for force feeding.

Yet, for all the brass, Kent couldn't shake the feeling Cole was the bigger concern.

"Cole has a woman..." Kent knew this, though the details had refused to gel when he'd asked his brain nicely.

"Yup." Trevor grinned in a way that said he didn't want his uncle to guess at his concern over the memory loss. "Lissa the abstract painter appears to be giving him hell, and he's secretly being a pain in the ass, in my humble opinion, to make her dig a deeper pit. The guy *likes* it."

The man's smile grew so wide Kent wondered if it might split Trevor's lip.

"I sent him home to sleep with her," Trevor admitted conspiratorially.

Kent choked on his sip of water, wheezing through Trevor's "gentle" hammers on the back. "What?"

"I sent our boy home to get her out of his system. That, or realize this particular woman is in the system to stay. I figure he'll know by morning."

When Trevor said the name—Liiiiissa with a strong "L" and a lazy "i"— Kent could almost picture her, but not quite. Even so, he had a warm feeling for the trying. He decided to trust the functioning gray matter up top and go with the idea that Lissa was on the right team. A re-meet of Cole's painter might be paramount.

Squinting up at Trevor's protective bulk, the gray matter whispered something else, something not quite so bright or shiny. Recovering and restless, his swirling brain cells didn't speak to him of facts he knew. Instead they dredged up urges, familiar curiosities regarding things he *wanted* to know.

About what?

Kent set the empty cup on the tray and eased back against the stiff mattress. Waking up after a near-death experience led to trust issues. With himself. Was he to believe his oxygen-deprived brain when it hinted at a hunt for information he'd yet to find?

Fast, rather like his baffling assumption that Cole had gotten involved, an urgent question pushed to the top of Kent's mental mush. He didn't know how the answer mattered to the missing pieces his mind still held hostage, but he figured a man ought to take his own instructions, however inexplicable.

"Trevor," Kent started in, figuring the powers that had spared his life might intervene if he started to say something really stupid. "Where's your wife?"

CHAPTER 18

In a daze, Lissa felt herself lifted and turned. A pillow fell in place beneath her head as she was laid gently under warm sheets. A dry kiss landed on her brow. The hands manipulating her position did so with great care, but the touch felt impersonal, completely devoid of sensual promise. She might have been subject to the ministrations of a competent nurse or a concerned parent.

She opened her eyes.

Above her, Cole was quiet with no outward expression of regret. He didn't spring from the bed or sprint for the door. The truth surfaced in the elevens notched between his brows. Unlike a moment ago, when Cole had scrambled her insides with his brand of slow and loose and then rough and wild, they weren't alone in the bed any longer. Despite the care he took in tucking her in, she noted he didn't join her under the covers. A peek over the pile of high thread count would likely reveal one of his feet covertly planted on the floor, poised for flight.

Intimacy with a man like Cole held inherent risk.

She had known.

That he might not be ready. That he might never be ready.

"You were…" He cradled her cheek even though a ravine had cracked between them and continued to spread. "That was—"

"Shh." She laid a finger lightly over his mouth. "We don't have to speak." If he'd hurled accusations or scrambled away like she had the plague, she could have responded with anger. Too bad, really. Fighting was so much easier than forgiveness.

He'd stolen her easy escape the moment he'd internalized the blame, silently recognizing that she'd *asked*—albeit in the roar of the moment—if he could handle such a step. Every reverent touch belied the self-hatred swirling his eyes, leaching away the final remnants of *ohfucksogoodsogoodsogood*

119

till only the *OHFUCK* remained.

Hard to blame him, too. First off, the sex had gone beyond physical. For her, the situation had approached chest level last week, when he'd trapped her between his thighs at the dining room table. Hiding those feelings under the guise of rampant dislike over artistic differences had veered toward impossible when he'd pilfered *Triste* tonight and called it *great*.

Those firm lips had barely rolled through, "*I want you*," before she'd opened with a lot more than physical welcome.

Shrinking into the bedding on her side, Lissa shrugged off Cole's caress and curled inward. She landed in a defensive position she wouldn't need, at least not bodily. Pitching her tone light and wry, as was appropriate for all double entendres, she said, "I'll never doubt your skills again."

Cole stalled mid-shift in his trek to the guest side of the bed, and she gave him credit for the sacrifice. Pretending he belonged at her side, at least for the moment, was a decent thing to do. When he looked her way, she saw she'd surprised him with her casual comment. Then the shock flickered out, replaced with relief. She met both with a kittenish smile, a silent lie.

I'm fun. No pressure. Take your time.

The ultimate cooooool girl.

Except she wasn't and never had been that person. Lissa wanted to spoon, ass to chest till the sun rose in the east. Saving Cole from the want and need and concern crawling through her psyche was her gift to him, one she hoped he might one day appreciate. For now, she settled for his relief and bit back the rest of the words threatening to jump off her tongue.

"Wore me out," she mumbled, letting her lids grow heavy and eventually close. Then Lissa Blanc—self-styled dragoness, a woman who didn't scoff at drawing blood in a fight—faked sleep so the man she'd given too much could sneak away in peace.

CHAPTER 19

He'd loved her and left her.

Cole had barely dragged his ass far enough from his own bed to sniff the side of a milk carton pilfered from the fridge. Yesterday. Overlooked in the mess the morning before, the carton had sat on the counter for twenty-four hours. From the looks of it, Lissa had avoided the kitchen entirely during Cole's foray to the hospital. Soggy bags of peas littered the tile where Sasha napped in the sun pouring through the back windows. Every few seconds the dog blinked a brown eye, scanning the room for signs of edible castoffs.

The sweet smell of rot wouldn't seep through the waxed cardboard, but Cole had zero interest in twisting the lid and starting the day with a full-frontal of sour milk. He already had to deal with himself. Tossing the whole thing in the trash, he went for the fridge. The eggs appeared safe, at least in their natural state.

Who knew what would happen when he tried to cook them.

Since cereal was out, and the growling from his midsection gave a decent reminder that killer sex made a guy hungry, he'd have to try.

Because the hollowed-out emptiness was so *not* the result of stomach-gnawing guilt. Over leaving Lissa alone. Over having the fucking sex in the first place.

Touching Lissa had been a self-inflicted wound from a knife tipped with heroine. Inside her he'd been euphoric. The aftereffects had left him wounded and raw, yet fighting a corrosive hunger for more.

Because Lissa had been so back-clawing, ass-clenching, vision-winking good.

And he knew she would be again.

Sex with Kate had been sweet and... rare. He'd lived to make love to his wife and then hold her afterward. Kate had always said coming wasn't her goal, closeness was. Now he knew neither of them should have settled for one or the other.

Upstairs, in that moment when Lissa's orgasm had squeezed his cock like a slamming door, he'd felt closer to her than any other woman, any other person, in his life. Apparently grief took smoke breaks when its owner was getting ultra-laid.

So he'd skipped the holding afterward and expected the sacrifice to make his betrayal all better.

Doing half only made him a dick to *both* women.

Cole cranked the gas burner to high and coated the pan with the non-stick spray that was supposed to save breakfast. After a couple minutes, he began cracking eggs. Surely Lissa would show in the middle of this farce—her absence this late in the morning didn't help the constriction in his chest—so he cracked a couple for her, too. The eggs fell like gelatinous blobs, one on top of the other, into the pan.

All the yellow and white immediately ran together, so Cole hammered at the yolks with a spatula, figuring he could forcibly subdivide the uni-egg when it came time to flip. These wouldn't be the pretty, sunny-side-up kind of eggs featured in Denny's commercials.

They'd be the kind to show Lissa firsthand why his family had been delivering prepared meals.

At least Lissa had no cause for complaint about last night, or the first part of it anyway. All the wariness and hostility of the last few weeks had melted into soft entreaties against bare skin. His dry spell had left him wary on all kinds of levels, but not that one. The woman had enjoyed herself immensely.

He hadn't even made her beg.

Smoke suddenly poured off the food. Instinctively, Cole used the tip of the spatula to slice the egg sheet into individual squares. Then he flipped each piece, only to find the opposite sides partially congealed with strange, almost transparent crusts weaving around the edges.

Uneven heat, maybe? Turning the dial on another burner, gas flared in a wider circle that would cover the entire bottom of the pan. As he moved the smoking food to its new home, he figured the additional heat would at least fire the pieces until he couldn't contract salmonella. He wasn't taking chances on vegetables—dicing was a cringe-worthy affair that typically ended in blood and Band-Aids—but he could probably handle cheese.

He fished a grater from the drawer in the island and a pound of Kraft's finest from the fridge. The grater stood on its own, a six-inch protrusion with a handle sprouting out the top. Each side of the rectangle featured a different pattern. He went with the least intricate. Their cheese didn't need to be delicate or pretty.

With one eye trained on the eggs sizzling next to him, he raked the yellow bar back and forth over coarse metal slats, sure to press the handle so the whole project didn't fly across the room.

The monotony of the motion guided his mind back to Lissa's bed, as though he could only distract himself with bad cooking for so long. He'd known the sex would be good. She was too passionate and honest and, frankly, *real* for it to be anything else. The reality had been a gassed rag to a blowtorch.

And damn him for being the bastard who bailed after the heat died down. After his breathing had returned to normal by sheer dint of will, he'd gotten Lissa situated against the sheets. And *bam*. He'd only been able to see the woman who'd picked out the bed. Not her face—he had the hardest time picturing Kate's face these days—but her essence. A phantom to heckle him for wanting and doing the wicked thing his wife had not.

Cheating. Giving himself over to another. A crime he could hardly wait to re-commit.

Certainly people who needed to lose twenty pounds didn't *want* to eat that next cheeseburger, yet in a weak moment, they might enjoy the hell out of one. A gambling addict didn't *want* to bet on an unknown horse in the dead of night, but he might not be able hold the urge in check.

Resisting Lissa's siren call required willpower. *Control.* And he was fresh out, swimming alone in a sea of buyer's remorse with a smear of unadulterated hunger floating across the top—

Searing pain sliced into his knuckles. "Holy... ooowwww," he moaned. Blood oozed down his hand, soiling the pile of tasty he'd been building on the counter. He dumped the grater into the sink and thrust his hand under running water. Scratch the cheese, too.

Breathing deep against the sting, he made a plan to toss half the eggs to Sasha, eat the other half, and never tell Lissa he'd tried to cook her a really crappy breakfast in addition to the other poor choices he'd made within the last twelve hours.

MEEP! MEEP! MEEP!

The blare of the fire alarm mocked the eggs that were still on the burner undergoing a veritable nuclear meltdown. The appliances had finally decided, much like the rest of his family, that the only thing Cole was allowed to do in the kitchen was eat.

******

Shrill ringing at her bedside woke Lissa from a recurring dream, the one where all her paintings were piled in a gothic-looking town square, burning. No one else was around to help, so her life's work went up in smoke while she watched without a fire extinguisher. The dream neither ended nor progressed. The paintings simply smoldered, curling into themselves and barring rescue with the acrid scent of burning hope, until she jerked awake, each and every time.

Lissa scrambled into a sitting position, happy to be released from the subconscious struggle. Before she went for the phone, she chanced a glance.

The opposite side of her bed was empty, as expected. In fact, the covers lay completely undisturbed. Cole had escaped fast.

Distracted by the unwritten memo forged across those smooth sheets, she swept her hand out, blindly feeling for the phone... and toppled half a bottle of vodka. Jerking to attention with a low curse, she righted the bottle at the same time she thrust her legs from beneath the covers and used her two big toes to reach for her discarded robe, dropping the otherwise useless garment on the puddle to soak up the eighty-proof mess.

A picture of her father puffing a fat cigar flashed across the mobile sitting right next to the disrupted mini bar. Two more beats of "Stand by Me" would end the call, and she dove. "Hi, Dad." He'd caught her oversleeping on a Thursday, so she injected some cheerleader into her drowsy. No use confirming she was a parasite failing on too many levels to count. Her dad could at least be spared the question as to why she lazed in bed until ten on a weekday morning.

Oh, you know, Cole and I had a groundbreaking discovery, followed by a medical emergency, which preceded a couple more breakthroughs, a few life-altering orgasms, and finally, I gave up and decided to wallow in an itsy-bitsy abandonment issue.

Robert Blanc cleared his throat and said cheerfully, "Hi, hon, it's me."

Air siphoned out of her in slow increments as Lissa shifted against the pillows, searching for a more comfortable position. "I know." She forced a teasing tone. "You and your Cubans"—her dad didn't have anything against a little contraband in his smoke—"show up every time you call. Reminds me you're a rebel."

He chuckled in his deep dad voice. "Capitalism ought not be stifled by any government, not even ours and not even for a good cause." Robert Blanc believed in voluntary do-gooding, but he didn't sit for any form of government regulation of commerce. To him, free trade *was* fair.

Somehow he reconciled all that pull-yourself-up-by-the-bootstraps fiscal conservatism with a seriously socialistic streak when it came to family affairs.

"How are things in the Wild West?" he asked.

Lissa hugged her knees to her chest with her free hand. Admitting her stumbles with Cole would only prompt a well-intentioned bail-out talk. And, hell, maybe bailing didn't need to be in the cards. Last night had been a fuck-all move, but at least she'd had the fortitude to bring up the project before she'd passed into sensual lockdown.

Cole had said they'd *compartmentalize*. Apparently—she glanced at the comforter, still straight and pristine next to her thigh—he knew what he was talking about.

"Lissa?"

"Yeah?"

"Are you all right?"

They said if one looked good while talking on the phone, one would sound good on the other end. Too many artist friends had been forced to join the rat race when commissions ran dry. Lissa had always recommended wearing a suit for telephone interviews. Remembering her own advice, she called forth a broad smile, even though her farther couldn't see it. "Sure. We've just been really busy, and yesterday was nuts. Cole's uncle had a heart attack. *He's okay*," she clarified quickly, "but it was touch and go for a while."

"Wow," her dad said after a moment, like he was thinking of possible implications. "Is this going delay the project? Do you need anything?"

The worry in his tone squeezed in her chest. Robert Blanc's "anything" held distinct and unavoidable meaning. He might as well have said, "Do I need to write a check? Make a call? Donate a wing to the hospital? All three?"

Can you stop a man from leaving my bed before the sheets go cold?

"Thank you, *really*, but no. I'm good. *Great*. We'll take a few days to—"

Her dad's tone grew stern. "I know when my daughter's great, and now's not it." Then he pulled back, cajoling. "You don't have to do this if it makes you miserable, honey."

Yes, I do. "Of course not. I know that, without a doubt. Okay, maybe I'm not perfect or even great, but I *am* fine. The project is moving forward, and Cole's starting to appreciate my work." Before she could control the reaction, panic hardened the refusal that rose in her throat. "Dad, *no* help. *None.*"

She held her breath when he didn't answer. As the silence stretched from Colorado to New York, she berated herself for chastising her most ardent ally. She'd sworn to never ostracize her family for offering everything they had—unconditional love and support in the form of advice and influence and, most of all, affluence. Her dad, especially.

"I'm sorry," she rushed. "I only meant—"

She cut herself off, not sure how to make him understand her appreciation for what he offered without accepting it. The choice had always come down to this, and she'd taken the help. Years of acquiescing nods and docile thanks had won her nothing but shallow, reluctant praise delivered from behind fluttering hands.

Half-hearted bias based on her last name forged the wrong kind of legacy.

This gig with Cole might be curdled, but she didn't know that yet, not for sure.

Tinges of foul-smelling smoke curled under her nose. Sliding from the bed, she cracked her door and peeked out. Visually, the upstairs appeared its perfectly-ordered self—sun lit the landing, and vacuum lines marred the hallway runner. Whatever was burning, it wasn't the house... smelled too much like food. Closing the door again, she refocused on her father, who'd been talking in the margin of her thoughts.

"...hope you know I would never want to suffocate you. You can set boundaries. I... all of us... we'll respect them."

"What?" Her fingers stilled in the act of pulling a pair of jeans from the dresser.

Her dad fell silent again. Then, "I hate that my own daughter is surprised I respect her wishes. Lissa, we only want the best for you."

Barely anything left her dad feeling incompetent. In fact, she couldn't name a single trigger, and she refused to be the person who left him tasting failure. "Nothing could be more obvious to me—"

"And if 'best for you' means doing less, then we'll step back."

This time, despite the increasingly toxic air flowing under her door, her phone smile was genuine. How had she gotten so lucky? "I suppose I don't mean *nothing*, Dad. I've officially no plans to move out of the brownstone into a cardboard box under a bridge."

He sighed. "My promise to ease up would never extend that far."

Of course not. She squeezed the phone between her shoulder and cheek and shimmied into her jeans. The shirt would have to wait.

Grumbling over the line said her dad was clearing his throat, again. It seemed to be the way he began and ended touchy calls. "Honey?"

"Yeah?"

Now he'd inform her of his deadline, after which he'd move to "secure" Cole's cooperation, checkbook a-blazin'.

"I love you," he said instead. She heard rustling in the background and then a muffled whisper. She should have known her mom had been there with him the entire time. "And for what it's worth, we both know you can do this."

The sudden screech of the fire alarm mangled her heartfelt thanks.

******

A gentle tap slid across his shoulder, and Cole almost groaned in defeat.

Lissa's voice followed, calm and mockingly grave. "Morning, Wolfgang Puck."

Busy watching his knuckles bleed in red, gushing starbursts, Cole didn't turn from the sink. "I can pour milk over cereal, make a ham sandwich, burn bacon, and open a bag of Skittles—not necessarily in that order."

She reached around him and turned off the water. Before he could protest, she dabbed a clean dishtowel over the cuts and let go, leaving him to rinse and repeat. "Press hard." Face averted, she inclined her head toward the tall island stools. "Take a seat. If all else fails, we can thaw some balsamic-glazed salmon filets in the microwave."

Cole glanced between the bloody cheese and the ruined eggs and sat. "The only thing I hate more than salmon is that goddamned microwave." *Years* of sustenance had come out of that thing by now. Moving to Boulder was a tantalizing prospect—meals could shift from warmed-up to taken-out.

Lissa worked quickly to clear away the cheese. Before Sasha could drag his butt off the floor to claim the egg goo, she scraped the black remnants into the disposal and set the pan and spatula to soak. When she turned to face Cole, he saw why she'd tucked her chin and gone to work without much of a jab. Shadows swam beneath her wide-set eyes, drawing her face into an ethereal replica of its usually lively self. At the same time, cool amusement lurked in the depths of her gaze. Lissa thought he was an idiot, all right, and it was a sad day when she didn't have the energy for a proper belly laugh at his expense.

Her fatigue hit him in the gut he still hadn't managed to feed. Lissa's lack of sleep was his fault, but he didn't have any magic words. Somehow he figured, *I'll try to stay away from you, but if I can't—and maybe I can't—then I'll at least cuddle after*, wouldn't work.

Which meant he had to successfully keep his distance. At least in *that* way.

For now.

Lissa spoke up. "Point me to that first-aid kit of yours."

"Bathroom," he answered quietly. "Mine. Under the sink."

The kit slapped the counter in front of him not a minute later. "Hand," she said, her tone dull.

"I'll handle this." They were still in the kitchen, after all, where he was cleared for anything but cooking. Doctoring his mangled knuckles definitely would do. "You make food."

That earned him a smirk. She held up jar, about half the size of his Skippy. "I busted out the reserves." The jar slid across the counter into his uninjured hand. *Nutella*.

"Yeah, I travel with chocolate spread," she admitted. "Never know when you'll have an emergency, and since I was headed for the sticks…"

Saliva poured into his mouth. "I have peanut butter." Which might be useful if she could manage edible toast. Cole always ended up with random patterns of charring, kind of like those people who claimed deities channeled themselves through the toaster to leave Jesus-shaped imprints on their bread.

"I know you're grateful"—Lissa's hands lifted in a flippant "just stop" motion in front of her chest—"but, no, really. I can't marry you and have your babies over a little hazelnut butter."

The sarcasm fell hard between them, not quite a throw down, but also not a free pass to kiss and run in the future.

Before he could respond, her demeanor changed. She snatched the Nutella back, and her joke met an abrupt end. "What I *can* do is pack my ass up—Nutella and all—if you don't promise me last night won't destroy this job. Prove that to me, Cole. Fast."

All righty then. Cole shifted on the stool. While his brain pitted relief against frustration at her single-minded determination, his body reacted with pure appreciation. Cole knew, *knew*, the night had left them both reeling. As hard as it was to admit, he'd never experienced that kind of lights-out, blow-the-grid connection.

Ever.

Yet she managed to talk shop over a plastic jar of nut butter, a subtle reminder that he couldn't, wouldn't, shouldn't underestimate Lissa Blanc.

Cole thought on his reply, using the time to extract antiseptic cream and bandages from the portable kit. A slow squeeze covered his knuckles in clear ointment, and the smell of menthol cut through the lingering stench of smoke and scorched egg. For what it was worth, he blurted, "It won't."

"Excuse me?"

"I don't know how to prove anything to you"—*other than how bad I wish we were still upstairs and that you were breakfast*—"but last night won't destroy our working relationship. I'll give you India, Lissa."

Even if I can't give you me.

CHAPTER 20

Lissa stared at the kitchen ceiling. Cole had no idea what it cost her to play indifferent. Hopefully he never would. Project Impossible existed to usher in a new era of artistic development, not a new man.

So keep your head on straight and your pants on… period.

She found the toaster moldering in a corner of the cupboard below the island. She'd seen Cole eat toast before. From his demonstration this morning, he'd probably cooked it with tongs over an open flame on a gas burner. She dropped bread into the slots and asked, "When?"

His head snapped up. Cole knew she wanted to know when he'd be *giving her*—as if the country were his to bestow—the ever-elusive India. "When we're ready," he said.

"Fine. *Great.*" She punched the lever to sink the bread. "Maybe you could elaborate on your special definition of 'ready.'"

Earlier Cole had carried a look of faint shame. That and his attempt at breakfast had been an obvious peace offering. All his bashful and apologetic fled with her demand, and he hardened into the familiar task master who wouldn't be swayed. Not by a first-aid kit. Not by a spoonful of Nutella. Definitely not by the memory of coming inside her.

"When we can work in tandem without wasting our time, and thus our trip."

The simple answer was disquieting. Lissa couldn't bounce back with a pithy "we've trained long enough" when Cole's logic offered no place to hide. He'd complimented her latest painting and she his photographs. *One time each.* While a better place than "drivel" and "boring as hell," a single nod did not a long-term partnership make.

The toaster popped, and she laid two pieces on a plate in front of Cole, along with her Nutella and his peanut butter. "Here's to tandem."

Cole carefully heaped toppings on his bread, then placed both pieces side-by-side on the plate and looked up, like he wouldn't eat the food until they had an understanding, a real honest-to-God meeting of the minds. "I also can't leave until I have a sense of Kent's health."

The acknowledgement reminded her of her dad's offer, of the shifts of nurses he'd hire for around-the-clock care for Kent if it meant she and Cole might progress the way Lissa wanted. "I know."

With that, Cole took a bite. Chewed. "Trevor called this morning. Kent's doing well. He'll probably be released within a day or two, basically on his own recognizance. The doctors slapped him with additional drugs and a strict diet. Trevor's calling it the NoLo diet—either no or low everything. Egg whites and Greek yogurt from here on out."

Lissa dripped honey over her Nutella-Skippy magic, feeling for Kent with every lazy swirl.

"His memory is vacationing." Cole let out a jerky laugh, as if his breath had caught in the trip down his throat. "Short term is horrible, as in he doesn't recall whether he brushed his teeth five minutes ago. Long term has holes, but seems to be coming back in bits and pieces."

Only a nod was possible, unless she wanted to make an unholy honey-chocolate-peanut-butter mess.

"Yet he remembers *you*," Cole drawled. "He expects us both to visit today."

Well, there was a newsflash worth choking over. Lissa struggled to get the mass of carbs and sugar past her tonsils. Then she did exactly what she'd promised herself she wouldn't. She threw their incendiary night in his face in a way that definitely wasn't business.

"For *some*"—she drew out the word—"I'm hard to forget."

******

Cole informed Lissa that Kent wanted to see Rhea, too, as they flew over Melina's gravel drive in Trevor's Chevy, vibrating like the spin cycle of a ghetto washing machine.

At first Lissa didn't understand Cole's reason for sharing the request. A motive only occurred to her later as Cole silently navigated Boulder's tree-lined streets in that exceedingly un-Boulder-like truck, dodging road cyclists and runners and even skateboarders Lissa would never have guessed could fit in so well. Maybe Cole linked Lissa to Rhea in an effort to trade the distance he'd demanded in the night for a replica of closeness during the day, implying an almost familial connection.

Almost like he cared.

Cold, flat sheets warned her not to get caught up in that line of reasoning, so Lissa did the next best thing. She studied her driver from the corner of her eye, drinking in the granite profile that didn't appear capable of softening. Only bandaged knuckles hinted that Cole, too, might be out of sorts.

Despite the invulnerable visage, Lissa regretted the thoughtless comment she'd hurled at Cole in his kitchen. The taunt had been instinctive, never intended to engender guilt. Yet now, Cole overcompensated with meaningless nods to an importance that didn't involve either paintbrushes or pleasure when there was no need.

Big girls don't cry over undented pillows.

Without warning they stopped in front of a charming bungalow, not ten feet from a statuesque maple tree in the process of molting over the fading grass. Shed leaves whipped in the sharp, nearly-winter air. It was then that Cole proved, again, that his brainwaves ran on a different frequency that hers. "Trevor stayed at the hospital," he explained. "We need to pick Rhea up."

Refusing to betray her senseless imaginings, Lissa slid—more like *jumped*—from the truck with sealed lips. The front door to the house was wide open in a decent rendition of invitation. Naturally, Lissa responded by stepping over Trevor and Rhea's Boulder threshold, waiting a second or two, and then yelling Rhea's name.

When Rhea didn't answer her call, Lissa left Cole at the curb and ventured further into the house. Arching wood—the type of heavy, built-in gateway germane to early twentieth-century homes—separated an updated kitchen from a short hall leading to what looked like a sitting area beyond yet another arch.

Distressed oak floorboards protested each step with a faint creek, and Lissa found herself moving softly, slowly, more like a cat burglar than the pickup crew. "Rhea?"

Peering into the kitchen, Lissa noted a coffee cup next to the sink but little else of interest. A newspaper sat on a table for two tucked into the corner. Other than that, the nook was neat and tidy and empty.

Light footfalls carried her into the equally empty living room. Like the kitchen, the space was tasteful and clean, with a compact beige couch and matching reading chair, no television, and an anonymous rug fresh from IKEA or some other big-box warehouse. Even the *Better Home & Garden* magazines had been gathered into a basket lying on the floor. Lissa detected a trace of rose potpourri with a chemical aftertaste that advertised its origin—not actual flowers or spices, but a plug-in freshener that spat eau de rose into the air at regular intervals.

While every inch of Melina spoke of *care*, every inch of Trevor and Rhea's home imparted *correct*. Despite the gorgeous, hand-crafted architectural features that came standard in a house of that vintage, the place might as well have been staged to sell—no bright walls or fabrics, no knickknacks to advertise the couple's hobbies or tastes, no books to hint at their priorities or politics, no dust. Frankly, no evidence of life or love.

Perhaps that's why Lissa's painting stood out.

Sisters was the other piece Lissa had expected to find at Cole's. According to her business records, both *Redemption*, currently hanging in Lissa's room at Melina, and *Sisters* had been purchased with Cole Rathlen's credit card. Yet here Lissa found *Sisters* on the floor in Trevor and Rhea's living room. Splashes of bold color barely peeked from behind the tan couch. If Lissa were to hazard a guess, she'd call even that amount of visibility unintentional.

The work—the very title—speaks of closeness. Most certainly the painting had been a gift from Kate to Rhea.

Since Rhea had made her hostility toward Kate clear, emphasizing a rift incurable by even the forgiveness-inducing bonds of death, Lissa wasn't surprised to find *Sisters* in a state of neglect behind the furniture.

Lissa knelt next to the couch, knowing she ought to ignore the coincidence and keep hollering for Trevor's wife. Sliding the print free also dislodged a shelf of dust, notable in a dustless home. The particles that didn't float to the floor stuck to the face of the frame in a smear of oily grime that called for more than a feather duster.

From the looks of it, *Sisters* had never seen the light of day. Two sets of heavily fringed feminine eyes peered outward through mingling streaks of primary color, which had been there from the start, and accumulated filth, which hadn't. One gaze gleamed chocolate, twinkling as though the mind behind it got an inside joke. The other flared a steady blue—*almost Cole's blue*—and looked outward in level, determined concentration. The stares unmistakably—at least to Lissa—represented Scarlet and herself. Lissa had painted *Sisters* in her early twenties, a time of change for both of them. Lissa had learned to wield humor against a judgmental world while Scarlet had undergone a shattering of all her sheltered ideals. They'd relied on each other more than ever.

A sound near the kitchen caught her attention, and Lissa gave a guilty little jump. "Rhea?" slipped from her lips before she could shove the print back where it belonged. "You home?"

"Guess I'll find out," came Cole's even reply, "since you've been *diverted*."

By now he stood over her shoulder, no doubt examining her discovery. "Don't let this go to your head. Despite the two-for-two record, you *won't* find a Blanc in every Boulder home."

"Such wit," Lissa said, studying the picture. "Did you know your credit card paid for this?"

"I'm not surprised. Kate and I shared a Visa account."

"Why would it be stuck behind the couch? And if you say 'drivel—'"

"Drivel," Cole finished, his tone *too* smug. "I can only assume Rhea disagreed with Kate regarding its merit. Many did." He didn't bother to point out he'd been first in line.

For nearly a minute, the only sound in the room came from a clock ticking above the window. With each flick of the second hand, Lissa relaxed her bunched shoulders away from her ears and considered a response—take him down or blow him off, sucker punch him in the nads or laugh in his face.

His chuckle beat her to a choice. When she turned and looked up from her place on the floor, she saw sly humor lingering in the corners of his eyes, almost matching the mysterious hilarity she'd given herself in the painting. With a wink and shrug, Cole dared her to go ballistic.

The fucker had been kidding.

And just like that, she was disarmed by his slow, melting grin. Those golden good looks had gotten more dangerous overnight. Yesterday she'd seen subterfuge in that sea-bearing gaze. Cole's lean, sharp muscles and sly smile had only looked like a really, *really* good time. Inside—she'd told herself—he was about force of will and iron resistance, a mental rocket launcher. Now she knew he was *both*.

How did one put that kind of temptation back in the box?

"A better question," he said, "examines why *you're* practically stuck behind the couch. I thought your need to pry pertained to me exclusively. I see the tendency is universal."

"It's *my* painting!"

He cupped her jaw gently, sliding his thumb across her bottom lip. "Not anymore, Lissa."

Heat boiled into her cheeks at the correct assessment. She jerked around and slid the painting into place. Then, using the blades of her hands, she carefully swept the dust into a pile. "Rhea's not here. We should go."

"She is," he corrected, his voice retreating with each syllable. "Listen."

Lissa went still. At first she heard nothing. Then, sinking into the rhythm of the house, she detected a low whir coming from below. The sound was reminiscent of the methods she'd used to drown out dorm-room chaos—nothing like a dishpan full of silverware at the base of a vibrating fan to morph a cacophony into white noise.

"I take it that's not the furnace?" she asked.

"That'd be Rhea getting even fitter." Cole stomped heavily in the entryway, looking down as though he could see his sister-in-law through the floor. "You'll have to drag her from the basement. Stairs are behind the back side of the fridge." With that he strolled out the open door toward the truck.

Only a prolonged, rhythmic buzzing greeted Lissa's shout from the top of the stairs. With each step down, she descended another foot into what sounded like an underground wind tunnel. At the bottom, she saw why.

Rhea pedaled away on a stationary bike. Kind of. On closer inspection, Lissa saw the woman rode a real bike with the back wheel tethered to a steel stand. The green neon frame looked familiar—thin tires, fluorescent metal, black grips. The same cycle had carried Rhea toward Kate in the amateur hiking photographs Lissa had found in Cole's basement.

Earbuds added a nice touch to Rhea's spandex—dare Lissa say unitard?—ensemble. At this range, the whole ride-my-bike-inside operation escalated to raze-the-basement loud since the bike stand relied on an attached resistance fan. Every pump of Rhea's strong calves translated enough power to give the fan another whirling jolt.

In a final effort, Lissa jumped off the last step and flailed her arms, screaming, "Hello!" and "Jesus Christ, why aren't you ready to go?"

Rhea's head jerked from its slump over the handlebars. The infernal buzz wound down like a broken toy the second she kicked her feet from the locking pedals. "What a pleasant surprise."

Always, Lissa mentally snarked. How silly to assume Cole had called ahead. "Kent is asking for you."

One day Rhea might have to spruce up her poker face. The guarded gleam that entered her eyes did a poor job of conveying concern over Kent's near-death experience or joy over his desire to see her now that he was awake.

"Why?" Rhea asked, grudgingly canting her sweaty limbs to the side and sliding off the bike.

Lissa shrugged. Obviously he's bereft without your lively wit and caring personality. "He's asking for me, too. For us both."

"Figures." Rhea wiped her brow and tossed the rag into a basket near the wall. The movement drew Lissa's attention to the whole of the room. Here, finally, was a reflection of the bungalow's inhabitants. Perfectly spaced exercise equipment filled the floor, corner to corner. Beyond Rhea's green road bike and stand, two mountain bikes and another road bike huddled near the far wall. Between Lissa and those bikes were free weights and benches, a treadmill, a stair stepper, hanging jump ropes, yoga mats, and a contraption that looked like a medieval torture rack.

"Pilates reformer." Rhea mumbled the title as she brushed by Lissa for the stairs. "Good for lengthening muscles."

Lissa turned around and watched Rhea's unitard stretch over some damn perfect muscles with each upward step. Most women would kill for Rhea's rear view—supple and fluid, obviously strong but never bulky. Kate had been the Marilyn Monroe to Rhea's Tina Turner.

Sometimes Lissa couldn't open the spaghetti sauce. Most of the time, she left the push-up padding in her bras. Next to those two, Lissa felt flat and scrawny and weak.

Swallowing a useless sigh, Lissa trailed behind sleek, taut calves, marveling at the bike riding, weight lifting, and Pilot-oga regimen that had ushered them into to being.

Rhea's trek across the house came to an abrupt halt in the living room. "You moved it." She immediately knelt over the end of the couch and tugged *Sisters* a fraction of an inch further into view.

Not quite unintentional, then. "You noticed," Lissa acknowledged with a biting smile. Who was this woman who pretended not to care? "I couldn't resist."

The admission seemed to shake something loose. Rhea stared at the revealed sliver of *Sisters* and shrugged. "Neither could I."

Meaning what, exactly?

The inference sank in, bit by bit, while Lissa studied the unnatural reaction of her kind-of-boss's sister-in-law. A smarter woman would have ditched the whole scene, but not Lissa. She took in the tense lines of Rhea's throat and the way Rhea's fingers began to curl inward and then relax, as though she knew any stress reaction might logically be assigned deeper meaning.

An inkling hit without warning. "You're *pretending*." Lissa shouldered Rhea aside—lightly lest those well-formed muscles retaliate—and jerked the painting free from its hiding place. Propping the dust-greasy canvas on the couch, Lissa let her suspicions fly. "You act the injured party, even though everyone around you acknowledges Kate never touched your husband. I've been wondering why you persist, but I've been asking the wrong question, haven't I? You damn well *know* Trevor was faithful. Some other reason prevents you from betraying any tenderness for your sister-in-law. What, Rhea? Why the arbitrary disgust?"

"Nothing," Rhea seethed, "about my feelings for Kate are, or ever were, *arbitrary*."

I know. That's the point. "Then why relegate the heartfelt gift of a dead woman to a crevice behind the couch?"

Rhea spun on her heel, striding for yet another wooden arch that likely led to bedrooms. When she returned, the unitard had been replaced with a pair of capris, a breathable T-shirt, and comfort-first clogs. REI all around.

"I don't like you, Lissa." Rhea wore a serene look she'd no doubt wrestled into place while getting dressed. Yet despite her smooth features and clean, picnic-ready outfit, anger radiated outward from the woman in waves, stressing the meager control she'd garnered during her absence.

"You don't like anyone, Rhea."

That did it, Lissa could see. Rhea's mouth opened and closed like a snapping rubber band. Over and over she tried to speak, but each time, she swallowed the words.

"Isn't that right?" Lissa pressed. "From what I can tell, you don't think highly of Cole or Kent. You especially enjoy baiting your own husband.

And of course you *hated* Kate—poor, innocent, *dead* Kate who somehow deserves your eternal vitriol."

Rhea lurched forward, agitated but clearly fighting the hell out of it. She stopped just short of too close. "Interesting," the redhead murmured, almost in Lissa's ear, "somebody doesn't like it when her paintings aren't given pride of place."

The accusation hit hard and squirmed through Lissa's conscience. Like the crescendo pitch of an operatic high note, she rejected the noise, even though she knew it might have merit. "How'd you two jump from sunrise hikes and sunset margaritas to 'I don't care if you're dead' in the space of one man's mistake?"

Rhea slammed the painting back behind the couch with a look that said *as if.* "The *day* I'd hike with that woman."

The discarded Nikon in Cole's basement begged to differ. "You—"

"Hate was your word." Rhea stepped away and yanked at her ponytail. "I simply told you that most, excluding me, *'loved her like family.'* The last thing I ever wanted was Kate for a sister."

"A shame, then"—Cole's restrained hiss blew in with the wind through the open doorway—"that in the end you got your wish."

CHAPTER 21

Lissa's next few weeks passed in a blur. After Rhea's vicious admission, Cole "invited" his sister-in-law to stay the hell away from Melina indefinitely. Lissa explained Rhea's baffling reaction to seeing *Sisters* moved a fraction of an inch—a part of the conversation Cole had missed—and argued that Kate must have meant something for Rhea to be so in tune with Kate's gift.

To Lissa, a woman who didn't care also didn't notice.

Cole remained incensed. To him, rejecting Kate as a sibling was tantamount to treason. Rhea didn't deserve even the most peripheral place in the Rathlen clan.

Of course, the initial trip to the hospital was a disaster. Cole and Rhea prowled around each other like wild animals, while Trevor and Kent looked on in confusion. Kent threw question after question at Lissa. A few showed a clear effort to regain memories that dangled out of reach—things like the date of Lissa's arrival at Melina and the details of each time he'd visited— but most betrayed a salacious interest in the state of affairs between Lissa and her grudging landlord. The third time Kent slyly asked whether Lissa had slept well the night before, she knew he'd not forgotten her two previous yeses.

With Rhea, Kent showed more finesse. Veiled inquiries implied—or at least guessed—at convoluted connections between members of the Rathlen clan. Lissa didn't know whether Kent's insinuations were purposefully vague or whether the grasping frustration in Kent's eyes meant the man himself didn't quite understand his own drive for certain answers. He admitted that the morning of his heart attack had fallen to the murkiness of oxygen deprivation, but later, after Trevor and Rhea had taken themselves home, Kent owned up to feeling a strong, and yet vaguely inexplicable, urge to interrogate.

Rhea deflected Kent's onslaught with fuzzy evasions, relying mostly on the standard defense that Kate hadn't been the woman she'd seemed. Cole's flinched at the implication. "How the hell would you know?" he accused.

Rhea didn't seem to grasp that the more she clung to her irrational anger over a non-existent affair between her faithful husband and Cole's faithful wife, the less trust the Rathlens could extend.

When Cole finally gritted, "My wife never fucked anyone but me, Rhea, *ever*," Rhea grew superior.

"Why is it," she asked in a voice throbbing with the authority of secret knowledge, "that all anyone cares about is what Kate did, rather than what she *wanted* to do?"

Symbols.

Jeopardy theme.

"Let's say Kate's imagined transgressions were forgiven"—Trevor cleared his throat—"about the time she introduced herself to the wrong side of the nearest cliff."

"Of course," Rhea answered stiffly, "forever the martyr."

The observation offered an irresistible invitation. Go ahead. Prove otherwise. Say you'd feel the same had Kate lived, that you'd still see her as a victimized angel.

Cole's shoulders bunched beneath a cheek that twitched spasmodically, antagonism in every beat. "Interesting word choice—'Martyr.' What cause did she die for? What belief won the day?" When Rhea didn't answer, he added, "Because I don't think 'martyr' means a woman who snapped under the weight of retracted accusations and extended anti-depressants."

Rhea clamped her mouth shut and crossed her arms. "You get the point."

Cole blinked. "I *get* nothing." And with the flip of a switch, he turned the hot seat on his uncle. For fifteen minutes, he gilled the man—meds, release, diet, exercise, further tests. By the time Cole stopped, Kent looked plenty leery about his future lifestyle at the hands of two overprotective nephews.

With a terse nod, Cole sought the door. On the threshold, he stopped. "I'll be over to clear the fridge." Another step. "And the cupboards."

Then he was gone, leaving Lissa to chase after her ride.

The hospital released Kent two days later, and it wasn't long before his mad cap of white hair hit Melina with bags full of groceries like nothing had happened. Cole balked and called the service unnecessary—secretly Lissa begged to differ—though Cole didn't press overly hard. By now Lissa knew if Cole truly wanted to stop the deliveries, they would end. When she caught Cole emptying a container of soupy three-bean chili down the disposal before sitting down to a ham sandwich, it occurred to her that Kent wasn't the only one who took care of this family.

Cole was simply more judicious and *sneaky*. Kent felt useful bringing the food, so the drops would continue. Apparently whether Cole actually consumed the bounty wasn't something Kent ever needed to know.

Trevor resumed his visits, too, but Rhea stayed away. The arrangement seemed to suit everyone, even Trevor, just fine.

At least three times a week Lissa and Cole staged a scene. Gradually their focus shifted from staging an abstract reality that could be painted and photographed to picking a subject and each doing their level best to bring their respective visions to life. Lissa relied on Cole to produce lifelike renditions—beautiful, sometimes haunting, always faithful. Admittedly, Cole had the tougher job of gauging Lissa's more unpredictable results.

And then there was the sex. Or, more accurately, the lack thereof. Strained resistance grew as Cole and Lissa held out, sidling around each other like a pair of opposing magnets. One little flip, Lissa knew, and their simmering attraction would boil over.

The ground shifted the moment the flip—make that the triple-axel front-tuck Lutz—debuted in the form of yet another artistic difference of opinion.

Lissa stood in front of her easel, shivering, clutching her paintbrush through fingerless gloves. The winter's first snow had prompted an attempt at the Flatirons that skirted the eastern slope of the mountain overlooking Boulder, an image so famous it had become the City's iconic symbol, the equivalent of Paris's Eiffel Tower or Dover's white cliffs.

A wool hat muffled her ears, and she fought to keep a steady hand despite the little hopping dance that kept her equally snuggled feet from freezing into solid blocks.

Cole had chosen black and white and had finished an hour ago, flaunting images that transformed a landscape Lissa had previously associated with sunshine above and wild flowers below into a mass of glinting, mean slabs of rock, each tripping over the next in a bid for domination.

In pre-dawn December, Lissa realized, that's exactly what the cliffs were.

After his last shuttering click, Cole resorted to pacing while Lissa put the final touches on her painting. The frigid air slowed her progress, and truth be told, the last wavering lines were a product of her trembling defenses against hypothermia, not any inspired creative interpretation.

She was learning that city cold differed from country cold. At home, the very streets steamed. Long columns of vapor rose from the pavement in churning clouds, billowing through the ambient light. If that weren't enough to distract a person from the damp chill, then the cumulative effect of millions of laundry vents and restaurant kitchens and rooftop chimneys certainly was. Throngs of bodies moving in unison never hurt.

Middle-of-fucking-nowhere cold chewed on Lissa's bones. Standing on a rolling plane and staring up at the Flatirons, Lissa's breath became the only source of heat. Even that floated away in puffs of frozen fog.

Art became her weapon against the chill. Standing before her easel, she breathed softly, feeling an overwhelming need to have this painting be *the one*. She closed her eyes and let a single word drift between her ears—*drivel*. Instead of an insult, she let the slur take on other meanings, like an inability to express joy, like a fear of moving forward, like a mask for things *too* appreciated. Knowing what she did now, Lissa realized Cole's criticism had covered the positive things he couldn't accept with the negative things he could.

How to pardon a tortured soul? How to show him he'd done nothing wrong?

She had to send the message the only way she knew—by using a paintbrush to bring joy to ordinary things.

As Cole made his way toward her, then retreated to start over again, Lissa fringed each jutting cliff with bright fuchsia—just a little and just enough—because the color made her feel warmer. Instead of gray, Lissa etched the rocky slabs from stark, uncompromising white. The lines resembled the slopes in front of her, so much so that a bystander would no doubt spot the marked resemblance. Yet Lissa's rocky faces were more crowded, more jagged, and, with the white and pink aura, more rock 'n' roll. Her Flatirons would be at home against a leopard-print background.

Her Flatirons lent her coldest day in Colorado a little New York.

Lissa didn't hurry. The final streaks of color appeared with a will of their own. She wanted to push Cole hard, barely shy of too much. So she took her sweet time. Let him pace. Wonder. Worry. Even he showed signs of being ready, ready for a future she couldn't predict and he couldn't avoid.

Yesterday they'd visited a different formation, this one called Elephant Rock a couple hours north. Cole had adjusted his angle, his distance—as in he'd driven miles back and forth over the encroaching road—until he'd proven himself the master of the perfect shot. Each picture showed the viewer exactly why Elephant Rock had such a descriptive name. Each screamed understated talent that might be that lucky shot in a million, but wasn't.

Lissa had strung together a series of multi-colored blotches that, when viewed in her frame of mind, totally formed an elephant.

"Why"—Cole had sucked a deep breath—"why can't you"—another pause, this time to scowl with, unfortunately for him, little effect because Lissa *liked* it when he boiled over—"*calm the fuck down?*"

Oh yeah, they were completely ready.

India, here we come.

Now Cole ventured her way... again. This time he kept coming. His easy grace, even when he grew impatient, reminded her of the tricks she played for the sole purpose of goading him.

Teasing him.

Except not today.

His down jacket ended at his waist and emphasized broad shoulders and narrow, loose hips. He arrived as she signed her name with unsteady, numb fingers. *Lissa Blanc*, another tour de force. A title had come to mind fully formed—*Turning*. Of the seasons, of her life, of a miserable day into something almost warm and inviting.

Looking up from the wet paint, she saw a liquid-blue gaze that defied the bitter cold. It clashed with hers for a heartbeat, then slid to the canvas.

Silence drew out. First long. Then *too* long.

Lissa saw a flare kindle in his averted irises and admitted, silently, that hot-pink mountains might have been a mistake. So she offered the only thing she could. "They remind us that even harsh and lonely has a purpose, that we have to brave those terrors to reach the bright and shining on the other side. Cole," she whispered, "help me believe that sometimes black edges have a pink ending."

Cole didn't reply. Instead he stroked the side of her canvas and slowly turned his head to gaze at her. Suddenly the dry, cold air cackled between them. They'd been here before, but this felt different. In the past, Lissa had detected a need in Cole to pounce, controlled sexual heat fringed with undeniable ulterior motives.

This time, his hands gently gripped her shoulders like he wanted to soothe. The smell of lemon soap and wind swirled in her senses when he leaned in, sharing the warmth he seemed to collect in his long, lean body.

Focusing on the vee of exposed skin at his throat, Lissa didn't realize his initial intention when he held her still, pressing generous lips to the woolen material covering her forehead. She jerked into the sweetness of the innocent kiss, letting a deep, pulling longing melt into the little pockets of rigidness that kept her upright.

Flip.

A rush of Lissa's own heat swept through her limbs, bringing chilled muscle and bone back to life. With the added motor skills came possibility. She *could* push him away, *could* stay the course, *could* keep the focus on whether he'd offer his stamp of approval.

But she wouldn't.

Somewhere along the line, Lissa had decided Cole couldn't be had *only once*. Steady progress on the project was no longer enough. Getting along and working cohesively wouldn't do. Some would call her choice true to form, and in this instance, it was at least true—Lissa wanted it all.

More than that, if she couldn't have Cole *and* success, she wanted Cole *then* success. The shift in priorities had crept up on her, wrestling to break her from aging chains while threatening her distrustful heart.

Not since a band of cruel children had decided Lissa Blanc would never amount to anything but *that one guy's daughter* had she allowed a measure of patience in her quest for achievement. Patience was dangerous, though, a scant inch from the complacence others placed at her door.

Yet the treacherous order of her priorities didn't budge, not with Cole's lips pressed against her forehead, and definitely not when he grazed his cheek down the side of her face until they quietly breathed the same air. Stark elation broke open in her chest, pinching too near the center. The ache demanded she sideline her quest for a special exhibition at the Guggenheim and brake for blue eyes and ridged abs and a sly smile that rarely came to play.

Obviously sensing her acquiescence, Cole reached up and flicked her stocking cap into the snow at their feet, shoved his big hand into her hair at the roots, and dragged her forward against his long, hard body. This time his intent was evident.

Lissa stayed put, melting when he let out a little growl.

"Perfect," he said, right before his head bent to hers.

CHAPTER 22

Cole finally admitted he wasn't in control and never had been. After weeks of fighting off the constant ache of an insistent erection in favor of the growing, and grudging, respect he felt for his short-time partner, he gave up. Who gave a shit if he couldn't resist? He no longer cared, and the hot, searching lips that grazed his neck said Lissa didn't either.

All she wanted was a rosy ending. His Lissa deserved that. He did, too.

Their blazing interludes from weeks ago had merely whetted his appetite. She felt as good as he remembered, maybe better for the wait. Her sweet, welcoming heat invited him to gorge.

He intended to.

But then he remembered how he'd left after their only night together, how she'd let him. Lissa had feigned sleep—he knew that, of course—while he'd faded into the night as if sliding inside her had been a dirty secret. Afterward, she'd reverted to business and kept her distance, proving that his forced isolation had hurt. Yet she hadn't compromised her ideals. Every day Lissa painted like a wild thing and smiled like a drunken idiot when he gritted his teeth. Succeed or fail, she'd make it on her own terms. Nothing—not his influence over her struggling career, not his vocal disapproval, not even a chance at fulfilling the desire he knew she hid—had bent her to his will.

His Lissa painted hot-pink mountains, then speared him with an equally hot gaze that invited him to pound sand if he didn't like her interpretation.

The thought gentled his hands. Pulling back, he slid off a glove and traced one of her dark, arching brows before slipping lower to cup her cheek. Her skin felt cold and smooth, as though he caressed frosted glass.

"Why can't I stop?" he wondered aloud, shaking his head even as he explored the curve of her upper lip. "I don't *want* to want—"

Lissa's eyes went glassy, and she nipped his drifting finger. "Me either," she admitted. "You, with your judgment and superiority, and don't get me started on your *issues*. Plus—"

"I think I get the point." Cole forced his tone to go as dry as a seven-year drought, a difficult task under the circumstances. With her body so close and his so hard, he didn't care if she maligned his character with every breath, just as long as she did so while the honeyed vee of her legs straddled his thigh.

Without another word, he shifted, pressing his leg up and into the one place he knew she defied the cold. "You can't"—he rocked forward and back, gritting his teeth—"stand me." *Right.* Her lies were nearly as big as his.

Lissa's mouth immediately closed around the finger she'd bit, tongue circling. Then she pulled away, letting the wind bite the flesh she'd warmed so sweetly. "But none of that seems to matter," she continued. "I get within five feet of you and I…"

Cole's detached curiosity evaporated. "*Want*," he finished. *Believe me, I know.*

Layers and layers of wool and fleece and Gor-Tex shielded the softness Cole desperately wanted to touch. He wrenched the zipper of her outer shell and reached inside, only to feel her trembling violently.

"You're cold." Too cold for what he had in mind. Real warmth couldn't be had, but he could scrounge up a windbreak and plenty of body heat.

Tell her.

Lips compressed against encroaching words, Cole entwined their fingers and tugged her toward the truck.

"My easel," she protested halfheartedly. "My painting. That's the one."

Goddammit, tell her.

He couldn't. Lissa was ready. India loomed in her very near future, but that had nothing to do with how badly he wanted to shred her clothing and fall on miles of soft, fragrant skin. Telling her now would inextricably link sex with approval. He wouldn't let her think his decision hinged on the orgasms she was about to receive.

"Later," he said, tugging on her hand. They ran across the meadow and onto the gravel bike path that led to the truck. There, he propped her against the side of the vehicle. *Damn*, warmth waited inside, but he had to get his mouth on at least part of her. *Now.*

When he kissed her, he couldn't hold back the groan that escaped against her parted lips. Cradling her face in his palms, Cole flicked inward, giving her a preview of what he saw in her future.

Only lower and wetter and, if possible, even more decadent than the satiny depths of her mouth.

Tiny fists rose to clutch at his hips, urging him on. But then she pulled away, glancing up without making an effort to mask her need.

"My Lissa wants more than a kiss?" He'd been thinking of what that might entail for *weeks*, couldn't wait to give it to her.

She nodded, letting the impassioned flare in her eyes say what she, for once, could not. No worries, though, he got the message, if not from the look, then from the yearning stamped in every hitch of her breath and inviting contour of her body.

"In you go, then." Cole eased Lissa to the side and jumped in the truck, where he revved the engine, threw the manual transmission into neutral, and set the emergency brake. Both ends of the bench seat had internal warmers, and he cranked them to high.

Crawling out of the cab, Cole flattened his palms on either side of Lissa's shoulders and leaned in close. Not even the cold dispelled her sweet spice, like arousal-tinged apple cider. Lucky for him, he planned to do more than bite his own watering tongue. Nothing would do but another mouthful of this most infuriating, delicious woman.

But first he had to make sure she was with him, as in *all in*. "Have you ever made love to a tongue, Lissa? Been fucked by a tongue?"

She stared at him, mute with shock. God, he loved stealing this woman's words. The only thing more glorious than a ranting Lissa was a speechless one.

"From behind," he enunciated, pressing inward, "while you rock against the warmth. It's so soft, Lissa, not like a cock. It's forgiving and indulgent and, I'm told, mind-blowing."

"Jesus," she breathed, "even you—"

"No, not licked, baby. Not sucked. Fucked. In and out until you come from the smallest of invasions."

She squeaked. Actually *squeaked*, and he swallowed hard. *Yup, all in.* "Let's get you situated."

Recognizing the last few minutes had been a lot to take in, and that was without the sub-zero temps for a decidedly indoor girl, Cole turned her slowly, so that his driver's seat met her ribcage. "You all right?"

Please, please be with me on this.

Her head moved, more a jerk than a nod, but the message was clear.

"That's my girl." He lifted her hips upward, higher and higher until she could easily crawl forward on the seat and into the path of the hot air streaming from the vents.

"Feels good already, doesn't it?" he crooned behind her. "In a minute, I'll get this door shut, and we'll get some of those clothes off. I bet you'll like the warm air on your nipples. Are they cold?"

"Cole," she sobbed. "I—I'm not sure what I'm doing."

Of course she was confused. They'd been avoiding the unavoidable like professionals. "No, baby, shhh. Just relax. Get warm. It's time." *For so many things.* "Now stay still." He climbed in behind her and slammed the door.

Balancing on his knees to hover over her, he reached around to her front. With infinite care, Cole spread her outer shell, then the fleece jacket beneath. Tapping her left wrist, he ordered, "Lift."

After stripping the two coats from one side, he moved to the other. In no time, Lissa wore only her sweater up top.

"Sit back for a second," he said, pulling on the knit and easing her shapely ass toward her thighs, just until he could slip the sweater over her head and off the arms that no longer supported any weight. "Now back up."

Her pert little breasts swung free. "The layers," she began, almost shyly, like she felt she owed an explanation for leaving the house sans undergarments, "they make a bra unnecessary."

"You do what you want with that," he rumbled. *Never wear one. Always bare. Always free.* Whetting his fingertips in his mouth, he reached around and circled each of her budded nipples, one after the other. Never touching directly, he stroked in a gentle ring that grew ever closer.

"Cole… Ooooh, the air. *The vents.*"

He'd imagined how her glistening nipples would pucker with the warm air rushing over them. "A good thing?"

She moaned, shimmying her shoulders in a tiny dance.

"You need to tell me yes, baby."

"Yes."

Again, then. This time when he reached round her front, he brought two fingers to *her* lips and pressed. "Suck for me," he bit out. His voice had dropped a register, and the command came out rougher than he'd intended.

She obeyed, and after seconds in her scorching heat, he forced himself to extract his fingers and circle the tips of her breasts again. This time when she started mewling softly, he rewarded her with slow, long tug to one peaked tip.

Chest bucking, she said again, "Yes."

Yes was exactly right. "I didn't ask anything, though." He teased her with a smile. Lissa didn't have to ask. Shit, yeah, he already knew what to provide.

Outside the flurries had intensified. Hissing bursts of windswept snow stung the windshield. Lissa didn't notice, but Cole's attention snapped to the hazy, barely discernable outline of her easel the moment it crashed to the ground.

Could he make her sacrifice a worthy one?

She whimpered beneath him, and he knew the answer was one she'd already given—*hell, yes*. He didn't have a choice.

Thankful for the truck's protection… and isolation, Cole reared back and pulled her jutting hips in line with his, her rear to his front. The snug jeans that molded to her elegant curves had become his favorites. He flicked the top button and stripped them away to the music of a splitting zipper and Lissa's surprised gasp. Almost desperate, he dragged the denim past her bent knees to bunch along sleek calves, riding the tops of her boots, just enough to let him part her thighs.

And zero in on an honest-to-God Christmas-tree thong.

"Jesus... Christ." Saliva pooled on his tongue as he traced the strap of red lace that circled her hips and plunged between the high, firm globes of her ass. A sprinkling of tiny green trees, complete with multi-colored twinkles he pegged for holiday lights, stood out against the red.

Cole thought back to the dresser in her room at Melina. The last time he'd had her practically nude and in his sights, she'd cast a quick look to its closed drawers. What other surprises would he find hidden inside?

Straying from the panties, Cole palmed her smooth skin. He ran his hands down the backs of her legs, brushing the indentions behind her bent knees. There he paused to gauge her reaction, making sure she was still with him. It only took a heartbeat before she shook that flawless behind in his direction, filling the cabin with her desperate pants.

"Seems we're still going with yes?" he rasped.

"Mmmhmm."

Her low murmur buzzed through his entire body, ending with a shot from up the length of his dick. *Easy, or you'll never get to that tongue-fucking you promised.* "Can you go to your forearms for me?" He wanted the perfect angle.

She did, and he carefully slid those saucy panties over her hips, caressing them downward until they met her jeans. Intact. He wanted to see them again.

"Now lean forward with your whole body... that's it." Bless the angle of the truck seat, the cant of her lithe body. The movement showed him everything he dreamed of, opening her up, especially the soft slit he sought. He could *see*... God, she was warm and wet and so fucking perfect.

Cole couldn't help it—he licked his lips. "I hope you're ready." Nothing but bodily restraint could stop him now.

"Cole, I need you. *Please*." An erotic sigh floated back to him, music to his ears.

He *lived* to serve. Stuffing his lower body to the floor by the gas pedal put him at a perfect, angled height. The way she scooted toward the edge of the seat, following him, was a sign that blared brighter than any green light in his history. As she arched her back to bring her hips a little higher, he caught another glimpse of the glistening core he sought.

And he surged forward and took her with his mouth, immediately penetrating the very center of her with his tongue.

Her scream layered over his groan, a discordant sexual symphony. He'd known. It wasn't like Lissa's flavor was completely new. But this was hotter.

Better.

Tastier.

Spiced cider could never compare to Lissa Blanc.

******

Lissa was sure she couldn't breathe. Air. *Air*. She needed it. With a whoosh, she drank in a breath that only came screaming out again as she cried Cole's name.

Gone were the tender questions and gentle positioning. Cole gripped her thighs hard. His mouth worked the entrance of her body even harder.

She hadn't believed this could feel so real. Like sex, as he'd said, only more sensual and more over the top. Clearly Cole offered a gift she couldn't find wrapped under a tree.

Behind her, he was a huge presence that controlled her pleasure with pistoning softness, not a heavy length of muscle and bone that held her down. With a slight forward rock, she could evade his touch just as easily as he'd slipped from her bed that first night. Easier, actually.

He was giving her that choice, along with his gift.

So, of course, Lissa pressed back.

"*Right*, Lissa, *move*," he growled. "On me, around me. Take from me."

Yes, please.

Establishing a rhythm, Lissa rocked against Cole's mouth. Each delicate slide of his soft, wet tongue upped her frenzy. It felt so damn good.

And that was before he began to alternate each penetration with a slow, thorough lap across the top of her sex. Every plunge went deeper, and every sinuous drag got harder, until the very heart of her unfurled, opening and relaxing in a way she'd never imagined possible.

There wasn't time to tense. Spasms already threatened from an epicenter deep within her core. "Cole? I'm—I'm going to—"

His answer was smug. "I *know*."

Two more cycles—plunge and drag, plunge and drag—and Lissa crumpled forward on the seat.

He followed her, keeping up as her channel seized and rippled, letting her body hold his mouth for ransom. Letting her demand everything.

The pleasure raged on. "Keeps coming." She gasped. "What the hell is happening to me? Holy… shit…"

Finally the outpouring ebbed. Lissa didn't move. She remained absolutely still, trying to control her heavy breathing. Cole's movements gentled and tapered away to soft licks and then what felt like a closed-mouth kiss. He rose behind her and pulled her torso upright so that she sat back on her knees and shins against his chest.

"Definitely mind-blowing," he said against her the curve of her ear.

That simple truth could have made her weep, mostly because she knew he meant for *him*, not her.

He had *no* idea.

Almost embarrassed by her naiveté, Lissa admitted, "I didn't know that could work—from the back? It really did feel like sex."

"Because it was."

True, she supposed. "I mean, I felt like you were absolutely inside me."

"Ah, baby," he sighed, stroking over her hair and down her bare arm, "I *was*."

Baby. The endearment melted whatever resistance she might have mustered to end this madness. He'd said it hard, then in desperation, and now soft and natural, as though calling her that were the most normal thing in the world.

"You're still wearing your coat, Cole." The restraint he'd exhibited...

Heavy arms tightened around her bare shoulders. "Yup."

"Your pants, too." Though not for long if she had her way.

"All of it, Lissa." His voice sounded reassuring, as though she might be asking out of concern that he'd strip.

Actually, she was counting on it. "Would you do me a favor?"

After a pause, "What did you have in mind?"

Was it her, or had his soothing manner grown a bit skeptical? Maybe a tad husky? *Hopeful*. "I thought maybe you could take them off."

Though she couldn't see him, she *felt* his mouth tighten against her neck. "Yeah"—he swallowed audibly—"that can be arranged."

Suddenly the hands bracketing her torso released, and she scuttled forward to spin on the seat. By the time she'd turned, an awkward move considering her bunched panties and jeans, Cole had lost his jacket, a fleece, and was in the process of peeling a tight black thermal over his head. The first two must have gone fast, but with the thermal, he took his sweet time. Each crawling inch upward revealed another band of muscle on his stomach, not to mention that golden strip of hair that made like runway lights, pointing her in the direction she planned to go.

"Mmm, Lissa," he groaned, reaching to caress the contours of her breasts with both hands. Testing each individually, his eyes drifted closed, and he rubbed over her nipples with extended thumbs. "Unzip me now. Take me out."

Utterly enthralled, Lissa eased his pants apart and pulled him free of both the low-slung jeans and the snug boxer briefs beneath. That light arrow of hair certainly didn't lead to disappointment.

He pulsed in her hand, the crown wide and straining, moisture whetting the slit. Veins traveled the length of his velvety shaft, beginning beneath the head and sinuously working their way to the base. Lissa fought a burst of elemental need, desperate to fondle and stroke and *give*.

She squeezed, then watched when his eyes flared with a look that *demanded* satisfaction. Earlier Cole had been careful, almost reverent. That patience had fled. "Ah, please"—his grip covered hers, upping the pressure and guiding her hand forward and back in a strong pump—"have a suck."

As if she responded to crass requests like that? Except, wait a minute, the rebellion only sounded nice in theory because—token as it was—she'd thought it too late, right before her mouth enveloped…

"Holy CHRIST." Above her, Cole thrashed, almost upsetting her balance.

…the head of his cock.

A smile stretched her lips around the tip. More moisture eased over the head. She lapped it up. Lissa had done this before, but not nearly as much as her smutty jokes implied. And never had she been overcome with a single thought—*more*. Of the feel. The clean, earthy smell. God, the *taste*.

Additional broad-tongued laps set Cole to shaking. She slipped her hand from his hold and inched it downward, cupping his heavy testicles. Not Cole, though. He maintained a strangled grip on his shaft, holding himself out to her. For her.

Let it not be said that Lissa Blanc didn't accept help when offered. She eased him into her mouth, taking him back until her tingling lips met his knuckles. She could take more. Needed to. In an effort to gain access, she licked against the edge of his hand. *Let go*, she silently pleaded. *Gimme, gimme, gimme.*

The message worked. That limiting hand disappeared, and Lissa surged forward in a rush, slipping toward his taut stomach until she truly couldn't go any farther.

"That is," he rasped, sounding smothered, "so… fucking… good."

His clear pleasure made her twitch for more of the same. Wrapping her much smaller hand tightly around his base, she began to move in tandem—fist to lips and away, over and over.

Random noises flew from Cole's throat. *Love that he adores this!* After less than a minute, the moans and indecipherable words changed, grinding lower and longer. A subtle ripple rose under her tongue, telling her Cole was fighting release.

Too soon.

He hadn't let her off so easily. Not in life and certainly not in love.

Favors like that had to be repaid.

******

An hour ago, Cole had been fighting his attraction. Now that Lissa had wrapped her swollen pink lips around his shaft, he realized he'd lost the skirmish, the battle, the war, and quite possibly the tenuous grip he had on his sanity.

She whimpered, and the smell of cloves and apples mingled with her heady arousal in the warm air blowing over her skin. His Lissa *liked* having her mouth on him.

When she prompted, pushing at his fist with her bossy tongue, he let go of his erection and gave her free reign. One hand plastered the rear truck window. The other fell to her nape with a will of its own. Not pushing, just stroking, assuring her she could do no wrong with that hot mouth and tight grip.

Cole tried to relax, but he loved this too much. Every second was an exercise in suppressing an explosion. Here was Lissa—beautiful and frustrating and iron-willed—eagerly suckling his cock like she might reach a hidden candy center.

She would. In five, four, three, two...

The pump of her hand added to the slide of her mouth, and he knew it was over. Never vocal before, he struggled to keep his mouth shut. "This is... I... the way you... FUCK!"

His orgasm was barreling upward. "Lissa, baby, you're making me come."

But she was easing off before he could finish the words. In the beat of a moment, her hand stopped, and her mouth deserted him. His seed hit a wall that left him moaning and mentally *begging*. For pity, mercy, a quick lick, *anything*.

Pleasure speared into disappointment, almost pain. *Let her be*. From the self-satisfied look on Lissa's face, she was eager to get back to him, but in her own sweet time.

Evil, but effective.

She found his sensitive slit with her wet little tongue, and he lost it. "Lissa! You're killing me."

"Ah, Cole." She sighed, mirroring his earlier tone, "I *know*." But then she we went to work with that blissful hand-to-mouth combo again. In seconds, he was shaking and sweating with the urge to ejaculate.

"Don't stop," he grated, panting. "Not now." *Not ever*.

A mumble drifted upward—flirtatious words moaned around his desperate cock—and he struggled to tell her time was short. "Baby, now, no stopping..."

Without a word, without the slightest lull in her rhythm, Lissa rolled her gaze skyward to meet his. Her shallow nod acquiesced in a way that was both content and *expectant*. Those huge brown eyes looked so happy, so sweet, that he came completely undone. Thrusting into her kiss, loving the nails that scored his ass to urge him on, Cole roared her name and let himself go in great, pulling surges.

The cataclysmic orgasm took all his energy and, with it, some of the bile that had clung to his bones for too long. He tapered his driving hips and gently, carefully, drew Lissa off his spent arousal, pulling her upward for a soft kiss. "I don't know what that was, but thank you."

He drew her into his arms and collapsed against the seat, both of them staring in dumb silence at the heavy snow now blanketing the truck.

Lissa gradually stiffened against him, and he couldn't help but notice her steady withdrawal, right up to the moment she broke the peace. "My easel," she said flatly, and Cole recalled seeing it fall.

Oh, shit.

Her beautiful painting of the Flatirons—the one to finally break him down—was gone.

******

Jeans and boots and panties still hugged Lissa's calves, a shameful reminder of how easily she'd abandoned her Cole fast. The cramped space left little room to restore her clothing, but Lissa was desperate to reach the spot where she'd abandoned her easel, so she made the most of the space, yanking and pulling until she was decent. A sinking feeling made her spin on Cole. He still sat in the seat, looking limp but gorgeous and slightly bemused.

She spoke around a developing lump in her throat. "Did you mean for this to happen?"

Did you actually use sex to destroy another of my paintings?

The mystified remnants of pleasure vanished from his face like so much smoke. "This?" Cole punctuated the question with a hard look and a flick of his thick wrist around the cabin.

"Us," she choked out, pointing at the seat, "in here." Unable to hold back, she let her knuckles rap a harsh crack against the passenger window. "My painting? Out there."

Later, he'd said, pulling her away from the drying paint.

Suddenly Lissa could hear his favorite word in her head again, only this time she wasn't dumb enough to give *drivel* any connotation except the obvious. Blinking back futile tears, Lissa tried to control a quaking that started deep inside and worked its way to the surface. Face it, Cole disliked her work to the extent he was willing to go to extremes. On multiple occasions he'd set events into motion that had harmed her paintings. Each time added another clenching finger to an invisible hand around Lissa's neck. Letting him in would strangle her self-esteem, her talent, her very value as a human being.

Over the past few weeks, Lissa had come to see Cole for what he really was—a gateway drug to independent living. Ready to lessen her reliance on her family, Lissa had transferred some of her dependence to Cole. *Like a blind, trusting fool.* In so doing, she'd pegged him as the final arbiter of her success, and he repeatedly rejected the entire notion that she might ever be successful.

Cole's answer struck, completely unequivocal, newly angry. "*Never* would I mean for this to happen."

Did he refer to her loss or his inability to force a limp dick when in close quarters? Theirs was a viscous cycle, certainly, but at least he'd been honest. Until now.

"Where's your camera?" she demanded weakly. "I bet it's not buried in the snow."

Cole's reply was calm, as minimalist and logical as ever. "I finished long before you, Lissa. When I did, I put it away."

He'd misled her with one word. When Cole had muttered, "Perfect," and kissed her amidst the early flurries, she'd thought he'd meant the painting currently swallowed by the developing storm. More, she'd wanted to believe he'd meant her. Now she knew he'd referred to something more sinister, like the perfect plan to seduce *and* drive a beleaguered point home.

Your work sucks, baby, but while I might be emotionally stunted, I sure wouldn't mind a quick fuck in the truck. Yeah?

And she'd *known*, known that Cole still didn't like her work and still really liked his deceased wife. He'd already demonstrated a capacity to get physical without inviting any form of emotional entanglement. The concepts of respect and intimacy and grief had tangled around her relationship with Cole, suffocating her ability to either separate or merge their professional and personal lives.

In a weak moment, she'd let him in again—maybe because she'd misunderstood and thought him safe, maybe because she didn't particularly care for safe and couldn't resist a few stolen moments. Either way, her stomach pitched in protest. The warmth from the vents and the shared heat of their bodies faded to a blank, meaningless cold, the kind of cold that didn't bite the skin, but siphoned heat from within.

Swiveling on the seat, she glanced through the back window and saw his equipment stacked neatly in the truck bed, safe beneath the camper shell.

Deep breathes weren't enough to suppress the hurt, and they had absolutely no impact on the anger. "This is the *third* of my paintings you've had a hand in destroying. To think you would use…"

She couldn't finish. Fumbling for the door handle, she let herself out and ran, coat free and exposed. A faint lump marked where her easel and canvas might be, not to mention her paints and brushes.

"Lissa, I didn't. I *swear* to you." Cole's voice faded as she pulled ahead.

Too much had been lost because she'd wanted to believe she and Cole had an unspoken agreement. They would meet in the middle of their artistic battleground, and meet on the *right* basis—art. Otherwise, how was she not using their attraction to sway his opinion? And how would that be any different than using her dad's wallet or some other tool that had nothing to do with her brain and her brush? Anything *other* than her talent confirmed her talent wasn't enough.

Cole had cheated.

Falling to her knees in the snow, Lissa brushed and scraped, letting whirls of white whip her face and ungloved hands. Moments of digging brought her to the doctored wooden leg of her easel. The sight of ineptly-applied duct tape only reminded her of the first time Cole had pulled a stunt when he hadn't liked the results of her efforts. She jerked the leg and flung the tripod to the top of the snow.

In the space left behind, she spied a sheen of hot pink in a state that made her see red.

Smeared. Not frozen. Oil paints demanded more than a snow day to freeze, but the sweep of rock that moments ago had jutted into an ominous sky now curved in weakened streaks to the ground. The flash of bright pink that had lent the collecting snow a majestic edge now appeared accidental, like her canvas had run up against a half-eaten pomegranate in the dumpster. The future didn't hold an edgy leopard-print matte like she'd imagined.

Her best work since setting foot in Colorado was destined for the dump.

CHAPTER 23

Kent shifted in his easy chair, stifling a pleasured sigh that told of a steak in lap and a beer in hand. What the boys and the doctors didn't know…

Besides, this was a medicinal beer, drunk for a specific purpose. He figured the next one would go down for the same cause, and, well, if he had to, he wasn't above a third in the name of family.

Usually he'd be watching reruns by this time in the evening, but not tonight. Tonight Kent was on a recollection mission of sorts. Happy and relaxed had to be the first step in revealing the most elusive of the shadows in his head, thus the fine meal, a fire burning on the nearby grate, and a table lamp to cast both him and his food in a warm, but decidedly low glow.

His short-term memory had returned, thankfully. At first, a steak would have been out of the question. Kent would have forgotten the meat sizzling on the grill mere minutes after putting it there. Now he might be more forgetful than before, but nothing beyond what he figured were the natural frustrations presented by the aging mind.

Setting the beer aside, he sliced into his steak with his sharpest knife. Cholesterol sucked. Not eating filet mignon sucked more. And the pulling need to understand what he'd forgotten could no longer be ignored.

Good old Uncle Kent was officially willing to *die* to remember.

Booze and red meat could be the final shovel of dirt on his waiting grave, or they could be the right tools for the task at hand. Good thing Kent had always been an optimistic sort.

Happily patting the small, round container of nitro pills in his breast pocket, Kent downed his first bite. Then he eased back into the cushions of the recliner and let his mind wander. Not *trying* to remember—Kent resisted the urge to force his brain to go places it remained hesitant to venture—but trying to create an environment conducive to remembering. The doctors said some of the months leading to the attack would return, which they had, and some would be forever lost. The more he struggled, they scolded, the more his brain would lock down.

So he chased his first perfect bite with a swig of beer and floated on a sea of endorphins, convinced that a person can never know the true pleasure of the life they enjoy until deprived of the very same. Traversing that little epiphany, he let his conscious mind cajole his subconscious one.

No pressure, nonfunctioning brain cells. I've got all the time in the world. In fact, the more you hold out, the more nights I'll have like this— juicy, delicious evenings of relaxing silence—so test me. Please.

Kent chuckled into the night. Hard not to laugh at a man who sat alone in the near dark, eating a slab of meat the size of a guinea pig while fostering a silent conversation between one part of his brain and another.

All necessary, though, because he'd been after something.

Before.

Now he grasped little more than a burning desire for answers to an unknown question. The same feeling had dogged him since coming around to beeping machines and two terrified nephews.

"What the hell are you doing?"

Speaking of...

Palpable irritation lacerated Kent's peace as his eldest nephew walked into view. "Do not *touch* this plate," he told Trevor with more ferocity than he'd imagined himself capable. "Don't even *think* about getting near this food."

Trevor sighed. "You've lost your mind."

Literally. "I am, in fact, working to get it back."

"By inviting another coronary *event*? Smart man."

Trevor reached an enormous arm out for the beer balanced on Kent's armrest, but Kent beat him to the bottle. "Don't touch that either."

Trevor reared back, surprise evident in every line of his huge body. "You're beyond forgetful. You're fucking crazy."

"I'm determined."

"To do what?"

"Fix my idiot relatives."

The flames behind Trevor hissed as though they'd chosen that moment to punctuate Kent's sentiment. Of course Trevor didn't notice. He grabbed the poker and stoked the logs. Threw another on the pile. Then, in a quiet voice filled with doubt and disappointment, he asked, "By dying?"

Some of Kent's righteous indignation dissipated, and he tried to explain why he couldn't follow the rules. "Boiled broccoli without salt has me so tense and pissed off I'll never recover my past. To get my health back, I have to torture my mind. To get my mind back, I have to be a little lax on my health. Guess what?" Trevor shrugged, and Kent finished around another bite of his cooling steak. "I choose my mind."

Looking troubled but resigned, Trevor disappeared into the kitchen and returned with his own long neck. "You win. *Today*."

Which Kent recognized as code for, *Don't be surprised when your fridge is miraculously free of animal fats and alcohol come morning.*

The veiled promise brought no shock. Trevor had always been the fixer. Even tempered and methodical, he dismantled life's emergencies the same way he decided what to wear each morning. Hack the CIA? Check. Build a thriving company based on said hacking? Check. Maintain a superhero body? Check. Look after his grieving brother, his ailing uncle, and his angry wife? Check, check, check.

Trevor needed to shake his preternatural calm the same way Kent needed to relax. Might as well start now. "How come Cole's so sure you never slept with Kate?"

The thick muscles banding Trevor's shoulders lurched.

"I mean," Kent drawled, "your brother went from incensed to accepting overnight. To this day he has zero reservations about your loyalty. Why is Cole so sure you never touched Kate, while Rhea remains positive you did?"

For a long time, Trevor stared at the sweating bottle in his hand, giving Kent the chance to devour a few more bites. Then, staring at the fire instead of Kent, Trevor said, "Cole believed me when I swore fidelity."

No one had to explain that Rhea believed the exact opposite. But why?

Kent shook his head. "Without any kind of proof?"

"No, I had proof, of a sort."

"Like what?"

"Cole had this rabid idea that I'd holed up with Kate at the St. Julien. A Southwest boarding pass put me at thirty-thousand feet about the time I was supposedly engaged in nefarious seduction. That pass didn't prove my complete innocence. I could have got my hands on Kate some other time, but I handed it to Cole and swore on Mom and Dad's grave that I'd die before touching my brother's wife. All he said was, 'Jesus, what have I done?'"

Trevor closed his eyes and went on. "I'll never get his realization out of my head. Cole knew he'd crossed a hard line, knew he and Kate would never recover. I still don't know how the first inklings of suspicion sprouted, and I'm not sure he does either. Two weeks later she was gone."

The hidey holes in Kent's head buzzed to life. *The St. Julien.* "Your promise wasn't enough for Rhea. All the world's boarding passes wouldn't have mattered."

"Exactly," Trevor conceded. "Yet she's the one who drove my truck that day. Of all people, she *knew* I never set foot in that damn hotel."

Again, the St. Julien.

There were no flashes of light, no searing pain. Kent didn't see stars or wince at the onslaught of new information. His transition from not knowing to knowing came gently.

An inaudible *click*.

"I *know*." The words flowed naturally, as though the knowledge had been there all the time, waiting. "Did this alleged rendezvous with Kate take place on the day Cole fired his initial adultery salvo?"

Trevor nodded.

"I saw Kate and Rhea together that day. At the St. Julien." Kate and Rhea had shared a late lunch at the hotel's swanky restaurant, Jill's. Out for his daily walk, Kent had seen the two of them through the window. After stopping on the sidewalk, intent on a wave, the details went fuzzy.

Kent recalled a vague sense of surprise, not at seeing the two women enjoying an afternoon together—that was common enough—but at the way... The information highway Kent had pried open slammed shut. Nearly seized memories slipped through his fingers, fading beyond a shrinking, unnavigable vortex.

A blurry visage moved into Kent's peripheral vision, and Kent hauled his attention back to the present—a winter's night full of unanswered questions. Trevor had knelt next to the chair, tense and attentive. "You *saw* Rhea and Kate together that day?"

"I guess I didn't attach the sighting any significance since they were together all the time. I was out for my walk."

"You talked to them?"

Kent bristled at the challenge but shook his head. "If I did, our conversation continues to elude me."

Trevor bared his teeth and stood, eyes narrowing on Kent. Suddenly he disappeared into the kitchen and returned with—what do you know?—a second round. He popped the caps with his keychain and handed over a fresh IPA, brewed and bottled just down the street.

When Kent sent him a questioning look, Trevor shrugged, as if to say, *A little beer never killed anybody.*

When Trevor finally spoke, his voice had dropped to a lurching growl. "All this time I thought Rhea had parked at the hotel. *Parked* and then walked elsewhere." Trevor drank deep. "Why didn't my own *wife* mention she'd been with the woman I was accused of having sex with at the exact time I was supposedly having sex with her?"

Kent flicked his eyes to the wedding ring Trevor never removed. A crippled frontal lobe was an impediment, but a capricious one. Certain details of Kent's past were white noise, while others had patches of clarity interspersed with gaping holes that couldn't be reasoned through. Yet his mind rolled the demise of Kate and Rhea's friendship like a movie. The two had crashed to Earth the day Cole had accused Kate of sleeping with Trevor. Ever since, Rhea had been a picture of the shocked, aggrieved wife.

The focus had always been on Kate and Cole, especially after Cole's accusations and Kate's quick death. But someone else had paid a price.

Trevor had lost Rhea on that first day, and he'd never gotten her back.

"I think," Kent said, "the bigger question lies in why your wife *pretends* to believe the sex happened in the first place."

CHAPTER 24

Lissa slept late the next day, determined to drowse away the black emotions Cole pulled from her psyche. After the stunt in his truck, he'd wanted to *talk*. Since she'd wanted to *stab*, she'd put him off until a semblance of reason could take hold.

She still felt optimistic about stabbing, so their talk couldn't occur just yet.

The late-to-rise strategy worked as far as avoidance went. By the time Lissa dressed and wandered downstairs and into the kitchen, only a snoring Sasha gave the house a voice.

Kneeling, she patted the dog's deep, vibrating chest. "Morning, darling." He didn't move through the stroking, but when she stood up, he jerked awake, sending one floppy ear askew. He saw Lissa above him and stretched his front and hind legs to a full six feet, yawning in a high-pitched whine that nearly unhinged his jaw. Suitably conscious, Sasha lurched himself off the floor and in the direction of his bowl.

Even Cole's dog knew a few underhanded tricks.

All these con artists under one roof.

The dog had eaten. Lissa knew that much. Yet every newcomer to the kitchen would get the same show. More than once she'd caught Kent or Trevor passing out a second breakfast. They knew, too, but who could hold out on two-hundred pounds of fur and soulful brown eyes the size of coasters?

And Sasha could have a full conversation with those eyes. *What?* he projected, loud and clear. *I haven't eaten today. Yesterday either! Look at me, wasting away like this.*

Lissa wouldn't double him up, but she wanted to. "I know he fed you, beast."

A cocked head. *You wound me with your distrust.*

"Not falling for it, beast."

A nudge of the bowl. *You like bacon?*

"That's it," she chided, "you're *fat*, not fluffy, and I will not fold."

All fat dogs go to heaven.

Shaking her head against the inevitable second feeding, Lissa went for the fridge to see about her own calories. Digging through piles of neatly labeled Tupperware and baggies of Sasha's crispy bacon—Cole couldn't boil water, but he had bacon microwaving down to a science—she dug out a yogurt and an apple.

"Lissa."

Lissa jolted and spun to face Rhea, who suddenly stood on the other side of the island. Apparently that revolving door to the dining room could be completely silent when warranted. Dressed in her favorite fluorescent jacket, Rhea held a spade and a tiny handheld rake. The grip to a mini broom peeked from under the crook of her arm.

Cole had asked Rhea to stay away. Now the woman stood in his kitchen with gardening tools. "Before you play lookout for my brother-in-law," Rhea started with a glance toward Sasha, who remained fixated on his empty bowl, "I know Cole's not here. When he heads out alone, he always tells Trevor where he's going. Trust me. Your man won't be back for a while."

Her man. Oh, the wit on this woman. Lissa's cheeks burned at the thought of her ruined painting upstairs, at how she'd willingly abandoned her project in lieu of a few moments of Cole's affection. The only parts of Cole that belonged to Lissa were his disdain and the various physical attributes he employed while expressing it.

Before Lissa could ask exactly where Cole had gone in order to more aptly plan her day of avoidance, Rhea cut her off. "Appears you drove him away."

A snort escaped through Lissa's compressed lips. "Unfortunately, I doubt it." Cole never hinted at cutting her loose. Perhaps he found the drivel game too much fun.

Seemingly pleased with the exchange, Rhea walked toward the back door like she belonged at Melina, almost like she owned the place.

"Excuse me?" Lissa took a juicy bite of her apple and purposefully spoke with a full mouth. "Where're you going?" She almost hated to help Cole with his Rhea ban, but apparently being a do-gooder died hard.

The other woman stopped but didn't turn around. "You've seen how we take care of the place."

"Correction. I've seen how you bring food to the place."

After a miniscule pause, "I manage the grave."

Lissa stopped chewing. "*You* care for Kate's grave?" How about that? Rhea, hater of all things Kate, had volunteered for perpetual Memorial-Day duty.

The world was full of surprises.

Rhea sighed like Lissa was the worst sort of simpleton. "Always have. Maybe Cole thinks the weeds pull themselves, and the snow simply blows away. I've never fielded any questions."

Probably because Cole believed Trevor or Kent took care of such things. Or perhaps he thought the grave was simply low maintenance. Lissa had taken a passing glimpse, and Cole hadn't lied in describing Kate's final resting place as a rock garden. To Lissa, a careful smattering of rocks didn't demand much.

"Fine," Lissa conceded, "but why *you?*"

"I own a nursery. For plants."

So Lissa had been told. "Not for rocks?"

Rhea turned around, and behind her stoic look, vulnerability wavered. For the briefest second, she looked lost before the roughness returned. "Why do you care? I help out. Cole's gone for the day. I saw my chance to remove the snow. Big deal."

Uh huh. Lissa put her hands in the air in the classic surrender pose. "Fine, go save the grave." *I'll be right behind you.*

Once Rhea had gone, grudgingly, as though she knew Lissa's questions hadn't run dry, Lissa allowed ten minutes of peace. Ten minutes for Rhea to think she'd be alone with Kate's consecrated ground.

Watching the clock, Lissa licked her spoon clean of a final dollop of strawberry Yoplait. "Time's up," she whispered.

Fetching a piece of bacon, she fed Sasha a distraction and slipped out the back door. The dog meant well, but he was more PA system than partner in stealth.

A worn and now familiar footpath meandered away from the back of the house. Fresh tracks marked the way. A few minutes' walk through pines heavily laden with snow and Lissa rounded a bend to find Rhea on her knees, surrounded by a smattering of rocks the size of Sasha. Cole's sister-in-law crouched in front of the largest, the one with an inscription. The words had taken up permanent residence in Lissa's psyche after her first glance several weeks ago: "Katherine Elaine Rathlen. Loved."

Loved.

Period.

Lissa got it. Kate had loved and been loved and was loved still. A more elaborate outpouring would simply diminish emotions both offered and received.

Cole had devised the tribute, Lissa knew. That kind of statement, the simple type that left zero doubt in the recipient's mind, was his trademark. He used the skill to convince, criticize, demoralize… tantalize.

Where Lissa commanded too many words to convey a point, Cole only required one. While Lissa looked to color and imagination to make a work of art, Cole relied on what was already there.

Good for him. *Really*.

But what would Cole think of this? Rhea sat so still she might have blended in if not for the bright jacket that interrupted the natural lines of Kate's tombstone. Well, not a tombstone exactly, more like a massive boulder cut straight from some faraway ground and deposited here. From the looks of it, Rhea had cleared the snow from all the rocks during her alone time. Wispy, trailing lines left by the miniature broom announced the redhead's movements through the harsh angles of the garden.

Blanketed in white, the summer and fall flowers long gone, Kate's cemetery-for-one looked cold, all rough edges that did little to blunt the blow of her passing. Rhea fit right in. It was the pink coat—usually blending into an endless supply of fluorescent workout gear—that looked out of place, like an inappropriate and unwelcome Band-Aid of cheer.

Rhea huddled within the bright material. She looked small, as though her focus on the grave marker had sapped her considerable strength. Then, from that bunched spot on the ground, she reached out and traced Kate's inscribed letters with a gloved fingertip.

L. O. V. E. D.

Lissa swallowed a gasp and took a quick step back, then another, and another. Rhea either didn't hear, or she refused to acknowledge a second presence.

Lissa faded back down the path, leaving Rhea to trace those soulful, painstaking letters over and over again. From now on, Rhea could spit gallons of distrust and dislike. She could snipe about betrayal and smile over Kate's death. She could get herself banned from Melina twenty times over and swear she couldn't understand how the dead woman engendered such loyalty. Rhea could grit her teeth and bemoan the number of people who'd loved Katherine Rathlen.

And Lissa would still know that Rhea had been one of them.

******

Nursing her discovery, Lissa made her way toward the house. She started at a sudden buzz in her pocket. Thankfully the sound muffled against her hip and probably wouldn't carry back to Rhea at the gravesite. When she saw who was calling, she debated the single swipe it would take to send the call to voice mail.

Cole.

If he'd *really* wanted to talk, he wouldn't have left in the first place. Yet, one more ring, and curiosity won. Resolving to confront the lingering sting of yesterday's outing, she picked up.

As in she employed technology to connect his phone to hers. Other than that, Cole didn't deserve a pleasant hello. "I'm told you're gone for the day." Her voice didn't sound properly flippant, filtered as it was through her hurt and resentment.

"Was," he said evenly. "Came back."

That piqued her interest. Had he seen? "So you know Rhea's on the property?"

"Even I can spot an extra car in the driveway." His tone gentled before he went on, almost sounding hesitant. "I got here, and you weren't in the house. I worried."

"That, what, I'd left?" She couldn't even if she wanted to. They'd returned her rental car during the first week, realizing the SUV would only sit at the house for a hefty price tag that neither the grant money, nor her newly frugal self, would cover.

"Yes."

On second thought, she could probably get into Nederland and then catch a bus to Boulder and on to the airport, but that would be too easy.

For him.

Despite the fact that Cole held a chunk of her heart in his hand and was currently squeezing the last of its blood, the project remained... too valuable. In general, Lissa sucked at personal preservation, always girding her loins a second too late. She'd become particularly careless in the face of—if Cole's obvious talent provided any indication—a near guarantee of success.

Guarantees were good. "I didn't leave. Been outside"—*creeping on your cracked sister-in-law*—"clearing my head."

"Will you come in?" The tentative, guttural edge in Cole's tone said he cared deeply about her agreement. If she said no, over six feet of pure life-force she had an abysmal track record of resisting would be in hot pursuit. "Can we talk?"

An answer might have been nice, but ultimately, it was unnecessary. She'd arrived. Lissa threw the back door open, figuratively stripped bare, ready to make demands that Cole would heed or... She stopped cold.

Scarlet Leore-almost-Blake of the New York Leores stood in front of her, wrapped in a cream Armani trench coat. The diamonds her friend rarely went without glittered at Scarlet's ears, and a warm smile curved a pair of perfect lips painted Dior red. As always, Scarlet looked slightly out of place—only the most gilded of surroundings let a style statement like hers blend naturally—and like the most natural thing in the world, all at the same time.

Lissa loosened all over. Previously tense muscles elongated, almost reaching out in physical welcome. Cole's unstable relatives and his tendencies for sabotage were immediately forgotten. To her, Scarlet looked like *home*.

Behind Scarlet's extravagant stillness, their mutual friend Brian—a lawyer colleague of Scarlet's who'd snarked his way into Lissa's graces long ago—paced back and forth with an eye to the ceiling as though he wanted to make sure the crown molding was up to snuff. He wore a pair of charcoal slacks and a black button-down with a smattering of purple stars on the chest. The sleeves had been rolled up, most likely to show off his seventeen-thousand-dollar watch.

"Nothing *too* excessive," Brian liked to say, "just a modest gift to myself as a reward for another year of three thousand billable hours."

As the scene came into sharp focus, Lissa's eyes lifted to Cole, who leaned against the inland counter opposite both Scarlet and Brian. Still technically on a call with her, he leisurely drew the phone from his ear and slipped it into a pocket.

"You?" she asked, inappropriately ignoring her best friends to ask a question with an obvious answer. Scarlet might have been able to hush a planned visit, but not Brian. Brian would have slipped, maybe in an e-mail asking about reunion champagne or whether she knew any good hair removal professionals in Boulder for his monthly chest wax. Brian didn't do subtle, and he preferred to remain ever ready for the next joke, the next drink, and most importantly, the next woman. No, Scarlet and Brian had abandoned Manhattan for a desolate stretch of land outside Neanderthal, Colorado on Cole's watch.

Lissa would bet they hadn't known they were coming until practically on the plane.

Cole threw out a curt chin jerk before flicking his eyes to her friends, silently admonishing Lissa for her bound-up greeting skills.

That was all she got. Yet the fraction of a second proved sufficient. Cole's eyes were guarded, yet imploring. They reminded her of a movie teaser, giving her a little while hinting at a thousand words left unsaid, piquing her interest and amplifying the connection she always felt when he turned those blue pools her way. Like a Trekkie to the opening of Star Trek 37, she'd be in line to hear the rest. No amount of suspicion could overcome that blind, all-consuming urge.

Cole had wanted this for her, had made it happen. *Why* would come later.

For now, she examined Cole, thinking, *Thank you*, but saying, "Nice save." Then she hurled herself into Scarlet's arms.

******

The kitchen erupted into peals of laughter, followed by, "My God, where did you get this coat?" If that didn't convince Cole he'd made the right choice, the tears did. When Lissa let go of her friend, moisture tracked unheeded down her cheeks.

Those tears reached out like pummeling fists to strike him in the chest. Through the unwelcome constriction, Cole recognized that Lissa looked insanely happy—no longer sad or angry or wounded. At least he'd given her relief.

Since you're the bastard who made her need it.

The morning had gone as planned, with Brian and Scarlet appearing with a pile of designer luggage outside the baggage claim at their appointed time. They'd come to play cleanup.

To say things Cole had forgotten how to say.

"Look"—Brian clapped his hands in sluggish, heavy beats—"Lissa's leaking." Then he winked at Cole and spoke in a stage whisper. "That's a good thing. *Rare*."

Cole bit his cheeks, gulping down the "Fuck you" that rose in his throat. The last time he'd caused a woman's tears hadn't ended well.

"I missed you," Lissa said quietly to Scarlet before looking at Brian. "You, too."

The blunt acknowledgments underscored the extent of Cole's damage. He'd lured this brave but secretly vulnerable woman from her home turf with a promise of respectability. Once here, far from the people and the life she could lean on, he'd held out, hinging his promise on his own subjective approval.

Which he'd withheld.

Yesterday, more than shadows had flitted across Lissa's delicate features. Once she'd recognized the loss of her painting—*another* painting—her look had held a horrible, jaded familiarity. She'd showed him a glimpse of pain he didn't want to see.

Did you mean for this to happen?

Hell, no. But neither had he offered praise and a plane ticket to the subcontinent. Instead, he'd lost the battle with how much he wanted her and orchestrated a botched seduction, one that had made it clear he could reach out and touch, but only to rub another ruined work of art in her face.

Clumsy. Cruel.

Cowardly.

Last night, after Lissa had mutely climbed the stairs to her room, Cole had staggered to his freezing truck. No amount of chill could chase away the warm, inviting scent with which she'd painted every inch of available space. Each surface held her imprint. The seat had supported her soft knees, her spread palms. The steering wheel had hammered him down to the exact height needed to make her scream. The rear window sported a smeared handprint. *His*. The makeshift crutch had kept him upright when her mouth had settled around him, offering pure, undiluted perfection.

Long after the sun had set, he'd picked up the phone. Scarlet had been one of Lissa's personal references, provided soon after he'd made contact about the project. The woman might regret her generosity after receiving his midnight call, especially since Cole had asked her to gather reinforcements and embark on a cross-country journey in less than eight hours.

But Lissa's friend had answered simply, her tone ripe with devotion. "I'll borrow my fiancé's plane." Maybe somewhere along the line, Lissa had applied her brand of clear-eyed thinking, of sheer enthusiasm, to a tangle of Scarlet's. Yes, Cole thought, Lissa liked the business of saving people. Look at how she'd tried to save him, at every turn adding color to gray and meaning to emptiness.

Without thinking, Cole reached for the glove box and pulled out a tattered, stained envelope. He didn't know why he kept it there. Maybe because people didn't search for secrets between the insurance card and vehicle registration. Maybe because careless placement implied innocuous meaning. More likely because this way, the letter would always travel with him.

There in the cold, refusing to shiver lest the night win, Cole reread Kate's last words. He reread the note the world didn't know she'd written.

If you're reading this, I've gone and done what, right now, I'm too afraid to do. Otherwise I'll have snatched this paper from your pillow long before you find it.

I know you believe me. Still, though I'd never be unfaithful, I don't feel worthy of your trust. Perhaps your suspicion means you know something about me that I'm finally learning.

Never could my choice be your fault. Yet, without you, I don't know how to make it.

Cole stared down at Kate's final thoughts, wondering how he'd allowed a mistake to hurt someone he loved. *She knew I believed her.* Yet they hadn't returned to normal.

Some mistakes, he'd learned, could be repaired with an apology. Others ripped hearts and shredded lives, leaving no path to backtrack.

"Hey, man"—a broad fist appeared in Cole's face, fingers snapping— "don't you have a little something to share? Maybe to *unwrap?*"

Cole surfaced from the night before, back to his kitchen and its expectant occupants. Lissa and Scarlet sat at the island in chairs they'd dragged apart to give Sasha room to sack out in between. Scarlet sent a flat box flying across the granite, and Lissa caught the flash of blue before it descended off the edge and into dog fodder.

Squinting, Cole made out the logo. *MarieBelle New York*.

"Edible art," Lissa explained, still rigid when she spoke to Cole. After slowly untying a brown ribbon with those elegant artist's hands, she lifted the lid to reveal rows of miniature paintings. "If all else fails, maybe I can paint chocolate." Each candy picture differed from the next, many with bright colors and illogical patterns that really could pose as a Blanc abstract.

Scarlet made a grab. "There could be no greater calling." When Lissa jerked the box out of reach, Scarlet pumped her fingers in an effort to snag the candy. "I get the two dudes worshiping the red shoe."

Lissa placed one chocolate in Scarlet's open palm. Sure enough, two men in pink tuxedos were on their knees, hands raised in praise for a car-sized, cherry-hued high heel. The image disappeared past Scarlet's matching lips.

"Jesus," Scarlet breathed, "cilantro chocolate made from the songs of sirens and kisses of angels. I want—"

Lissa screwed her face into tight lines as though the thought of cocoa and vegetables held little appeal, but she slapped her friend's seeking hand. "Mine."

Slinking away this time, Scarlet smirked. "It's your ass."

This time Lissa retaliated. "Like your legs, my ass stopped growing in the ninth grade." She bit down on a picture that looked like a shattered mirror, pieced back together and painted with blotches of yellow and red. "Frangelico," she marveled. "How *do* they do that?"

Rolling his eyes, Brian thumped Cole's chest, kinda friendly, kinda not. "See that? We brought *gifts* to the party." It was hard to believe a guy in a starry shirt could be threatening, but Brian's voice held the power of suggestion nonetheless.

Cole reached across the island. The center chocolate showed a blue-tinged man wrapped in a winter scarf. He held out a single red rose.

An offering. Cole picked up the sweet and lifted it toward Lissa, mute and hoping she took his meaning.

The chocolate disappeared into Brian's fist before reaching its intended destination. "N-n-n-noooo," Brian clucked. "When you told Scarlet you 'didn't excel' at this, you lied. You *suck* at this. And all good men know that not all sucking is created equal." He handed Lissa the confiscated chocolate with a murmured, "Here, darling," and then growled in Cole's face. "Try again, and this time, make it worth the favor I'm doing you because you can bet I'll collect."

A glossy manicure curled around the edge of Brian's arm from behind, and Cole registered Scarlet's soft admonishment. "Brian, let's give them some space—"

"No," Brian taunted, not turning to face the two people he obviously considered "his girls"—his to care for, his to laugh with, his to protect. Cole had had that once. He barely remembered the feeling, the security of knowing another's well-being rested safe in his capable hands.

Except it hadn't.

Brian inched forward, until he stood toe-to-toe with Cole. All the man's bristle blasted forward even though he spoke to the women behind him, like Cole wasn't worthy of the wasted breath. "You said he asked for help?" he asked loftily. "I'm rising to the *occasion*. That's what this is, after all."

"Lissa," Cole began, wanting to free the violence coiling in his chest and destroy something—anything—that Brian found indispensable. Like his legs. Or his teeth.

Or the happy fucking stars on his shirt.

"Lissa," Cole said again. This was the part where he opened up. In a blistering monologue, he'd admit that his head remained fucked, but that he'd never meant to demean her or make her feel like... less. He'd make her understand that pain, at least hers, had never been the plan. Wanting her was peeling the skin from his bones. Guilt from the wanting chewed on the leftovers.

Except he only said, "Get out."

Lissa froze. "Get out?" She fidgeted with the chocolate box, her voice suddenly small. "Of the kitchen? The house?"

"You"—he pointed at Starburst and his sidekick, clinging to one last filament of control—"Both of you. Out."

Scarlet slid off her seat, aiming a just-do-this look at Brian, and the two clamored through the swinging door. A thump sounded from the other side before a large cardboard box slid back into the kitchen, coming to a halt just beyond the door's reach. Muffled words drifted in behind the box. "What?" Brian asked, though the intervening wall subdued the question. "Ethan would have punched him. Your fiancé would consider it my sworn duty to fill in for him, and *that guy* deserves to be punched."

Ignoring the muted banter, Lissa stared at the box in bemused silence. Cole's *cue*.

CHAPTER 25

Cole went to his knees in front of the box and coaxed her softly. "Open it, Lissa."

The low plea crept along her spine, leaving tingles in its wake. But Lissa had exceeded her order-taking quota, a limit she'd reset over and over in dealing with Cole.

"Why?"

He lifted his gaze to hers and swallowed. "I want you to."

Boss-man wants. Lissa hadn't been sleeping well, and she second-guessed every waking moment in the name of Cole's wants. "*I* want you to give me"—she stopped herself from asking too much—"*my work* a chance."

They both excelled at wanting. Getting, however, required some progress.

"Open the package, Lissa."

Like before, Cole's quiet command pinched her insides like a vise, a warm squeeze of a stroke that made her yearn to defy him and devour him all at once.

The latter option had disappeared the moment he'd plotted to destroy *Turning*, not with a brutal hand, but with a slow, careless tongue.

Turning had been painted exactly right, except rather than occupying a soaring precipice above good things, she and Cole were locked in the abyss below. A devastating fall separated one from the other.

Stuck gripping the counter, Lissa argued with herself about whether she could do as he asked even one more time. Scarlet and Brian waited in the next room. One word, and she could be on a plane, ensconced between them, flying back to a life that presented so few demands.

Except now she wanted demands and recognized the need for external constraints on her work. No longer did Lissa mindlessly create what she felt, results be damned. She painted with a plan. Brush didn't hit canvas until she understood exactly how to make the viewer feel—or at least understand—what *she* felt. Cole had made her better.

Yet Cole's brand of help came with addiction.

And her parents' came with humiliation.

Cue the dramatic music—lose or *lose her soul.*

Closing her eyes, Lissa heard a faint pop and a laugh from beyond the door. Then came a slow whoosh… the window to the china sideboard. Two glasses clinked. This was no mimosa brunch. Brian and Scarlet were celebrating on the other side of that wall.

Probably because they knew she'd be going home with them. Cole had asked her friends to *fetch.*

Somber intent apparent in every line of his body, Cole moved to toe the box resting on the floor. "They know what's inside," he said, as if that explained all the happy in the next room.

A parting gift.

Lissa grabbed a knife from the butcher block at her elbow. The seals on the box had bubbled, like the tape had been opened and reapplied. With a shrug, she slit the top open in neat lines, then dug through a sea of Styrofoam peanuts before encountering a wooden rectangle. The familiar grain of lacquered ash popped against shadows cast by the cardboard walls.

A smile surfaced against her will. "A French easel."

Folded to the size of a sketch box, Lissa easily lifted the gift by the shoulder strap and placed it on the floor. A few pulls and snaps opened the contraption into a full, three-legged easel with telescoping legs. A sleek equipment drawer disappeared beneath the canvas support.

Lissa sat back on her heels. Top-end portable equipment meant she'd be painting life off the beaten path, maybe even in a faraway land. "Why?"

Cole wound his arms across his chest, his bearing stoic with the faintest hint of uncertainty. "You'll need it."

A heavy knock sounded on the swinging door. Scarlet sounded a mite tipsy when she yodeled, "Yoooo-hoo? Need some liquid courage?" When Lissa and Cole stayed quiet, she added, "Liquid forgiveness, maybe? Liquid sexy times? Liquid—"

"Come on, Scar," Brian interrupted. "Let's go call your man. See how much money he made today." Brian's voice grew faint as the two of them wandered away. Brian knew Scarlet's fiancé didn't have much use for him, yet he always seemed to encourage Scarlet to be in constant contact with Ethan when the two of them got together. Lissa couldn't decide whether Brian did it to keep Ethan reassured of Scarlet's devotion—probably to make Brian look less threatening—or reminded that Scarlet often chose to while away the hours with her exceedingly good-looking man friend.

Knowing Brian, the outwardly considerate gesture was a carefully constructed torture device for his one-time rival turned ally, if not friend.

Genius.

Refocusing on the easel, Lissa realized Cole had come to stand directly next to her. He put a hand over hers and guided their grip to the brass pull protruding from the equipment drawer. "You need this because yours is broken—"

"Right. You broke it." *Like an ass.*

Cole stilled. "The *wind* broke it." Cole took several breaths, and when she peeked up at him, she noted a clenched jaw and an unholy focus that speared the handle they both gripped too hard. "Know that I regret destroying your painting that day."

Huh? "So that's why you squashed the next one?" She could still see them standing chest-to-chest on a rocky mountainside, the earthy colors of her sunrise smeared across his shirt. *Expect me to fuck back*, he'd told her.

The statement had been less a play on words and more a *factual* threat.

He spoke against her ear, a gruff rumble that slid along her skin. "That next one was an accident." Strong fingers tightened over hers, and he began to ease the drawer outward. "I sent your initial painting—the broken-hearted house on that first morning—to hell on purpose. I couldn't help myself. With you, I rarely can. After that, I've never intentionally caused your work any harm. I've never intentionally caused *you* any harm."

So much for intent.

Heat flickered and spread from where his lips touched her ear… down her neck, across her chest. The drawer hit a back stop, and she felt the loss of his touch when he let go of her hand and reached inside.

"And yesterday?" she asked. "What was that?"

He tugged a foldable palette free of the drawer, revealing a number of divided compartments beneath. Cole had obviously taken note of her equipment needs. Instead of a bag of supplies and an unwieldy easel, she'd be able to carry everything in one neat package. French easels weren't new news, but she'd never considered carrying one. Most of her work happened in the studio, flowing more from an overactive imagination than any particular setting. Convenience hadn't been key. Until now.

Cole turned her from the new toy and gently lifted her chin until she looked him in the eye. "A miscalculation. Once my hands were on you"— his caress trailed down her throat, stopping over her heart—"I couldn't take them off. I should have. I saw the easel fall."

"And so you—"

"Went to my knees on the truck floor like chains were dragging me down."

Blood deserted her brain, pooling lower and screaming for attention. Lissa fought the wave of want. "Did you even *think* about a different option?"

He answered with a dry, "You underestimate your appeal."

"You underestimate the value of my paintings."

"Really?" he drawled darkly. "What would you have done, Lissa?" His palm fanned out from the center of her chest, roving in a wide circle down her side, then pausing on her quivering stomach. "If you had seen your easel fall while your sweet ass nuzzled my cock, my hand on your zipper, would you have bailed?"

Lissa's jaw wouldn't work. She wanted to tell him *of course* she would have. "I... of..."

"I didn't catch that." His thumb stroked her abdomen in small circles.

Not fair. Thought vaporized on the way to her mouth, again. He had her.

"Precisely," he whispered with a perceptive nod. That wandering thumb made its way to her bottom lip, tracing the curve. "Glad I'm not the only one susceptible to... distraction. But your painting? The Pink Cliffs of Boulder? If you wanted to convey, to make me *feel*, that hope is possible in the midst of glacial desolation, you succeeded."

Not an insult. A compliment. The kind of compliment she lived for.

"Maybe too well," Cole amended with a grin.

A real smile. Flashing white teeth that erased his shadows and made him look happy and carefree. Another rare occurrence that spun her world on its axis.

What the hell is going on?

Cole abandoned her lips and split the folded palette he held in his other hand. "Your style may never be my ideal, but your talent is as obvious as it is indisputable. Lissa, you're—"

Brian burst through the door with Scarlet tripping over his heels and juggling two bottles of Veuve Clicquot, one nearly empty.

Arms wide, Brian yelled, "Surprise! Thank Christ Mr. Dark and Ruminating got it right this time." He shrugged. "Sorry, we had to listen at the wall to get the timing right." Brian looked about as apologetic as an Olympian climbing the podium. "For a while I considered sliding a napkin under the door with a speech written in purple crayon to help our boy."

Heart clamoring to bang out of her chest, Lissa considered this new, alternate universe. Glancing down, she saw a piece of paper, unfolded and neatly stretched over the clean palette in Cole's hand—a printout from Qatar Airways.

Tunnel vision took over, blocking out everything but the fine print on the page. *Denver to Delhi, leaving in five days.* She choked on a gasp that was too big for her lungs.

"You're *ready*," Cole finished quietly, catching her chin so she'd see his confirming nod.

"No going home now, Lissa." Scarlet veered off her ladylike rails and swigged straight from the bottle. "We're the going away party."

Peeking again at Cole, Lissa saw an apology lurking behind the belief that he wouldn't be, maybe even shouldn't be, forgiven. That hesitance mingled with a host of other emotions—fear, embarrassment, *desire*, even hope.

Lissa would have taken a blunt, "I'm sorry," had it come with the plane ticket quivering in her hand. But now? Now she knew she hadn't been crazy to harbor a little hope of her own.

CHAPTER 26

January—New Delhi, Rajasthan State, Northern India

India hit Lissa like a sixth tequila sunrise, a roaring good time tinged with the promise of pain. Most international flights, including theirs, arrived in Delhi around three in the morning. After blearily slogging through immigration, baggage claim, customs, money exchange, and locating an ATM, Lissa found herself seated at a fully westernized Costa Coffee in the international arrivals hall. Cole fell in line behind a suit-wearing business type and a tiny, gray-haired grandmother wrapped in a cobalt sari, promising to return with espresso shots and a chicken curry sandwich.

Grandma's salt-and-pepper braid fell to her waist, and she wore a confused look, as though she didn't often do the job of ordering. She looked pleadingly to a beautiful woman seated with two children. The younger woman had skin like warm, polished toffee and wore a less-traditional outfit—an emerald tunic over a pair of loose-fitting black trousers. She spoke in crisp, rapid-fire English. "A coffee and two yogurts." When the older woman made a meek gesture, she added, "Just make the order and give them the money. These two are hungry."

Nice to see that mother-daughter relations never changed.

Soon Cole juggled two cups and one cellophane-wrapped baguette. The shrunken plastic table between them creaked when he folded his long frame beneath it, seeming to laugh at his attempt. "Train to town opens at 5:15," he said with relish, "so settle in."

Cole appeared eager to transition his reign of terror from the deserted mountains to the teaming city. Despite the fact that their twenty-three hour flight would stretch to a twenty-eight hour trip, including curb-side check-in at Denver and train hopping in Delhi, he'd developed a decided jaunt in his step.

"No cabs?" she muttered, remembering the throngs of people she'd seen waiting outside the double-doors that exited the airport. Even now, frenzied cries echoed off the high, barren ceiling every time the doors slipped apart. "Cab, cab?" "Ride, ride, cheap ride?" "Here, with me!" "Good price!"

Cole took a sip. "Exactly the opposite, actually."

"Holy shit, I'm stuck on the losing team of *The Amazing Race*."

"Five times I've flown into this airport. You don't want to mess with getting a cab outside those doors. You'll be eaten alive unless I break you in gently."

Five times? At least she accompanied a true enthusiast. "Leave out the 'in' and the 'gently' from that last part, and you're not such a liar. Maybe."

They finished their snack and tried to mill around, but the arrivals hall, with its smattering of processed food and faintly stale air, didn't encourage weary travelers to linger. "It's 5:17," Lissa announced. "Time for this to get real."

"You sure?" He glanced out the doors to the waiting masses of humanity. "The sun's not up."

"Good thing much of the trip is underground." Even she could read *Lonely Planet*.

At that she won a smile, a more frequently recurring phenomenon since they'd set a departure date. Cole picked up her heavy pack and waited for her to slip it over her arms. Once she'd strapped in, he gestured to the sliding doors with a mocking bow. "Your chariot awaits."

Outside the doors, heavy air slapped her in the face like the blow of a cold palm. Her exhales, each one a smattering of crystalized water droplets, joined the sickly pallor that lingered in the air, smelling of oil and plastic and wood. "Is there a fire?"

"There are thousands, maybe millions, of fires."

Lissa coughed against the smoke that bit into her throat. "What?"

Cole sighed. "It's worse in the winter. Most people think 'heat' when they think 'India,' but the Himalayas rise up about three hundred miles due northeast. New Delhi in January can be colder than Nederland during Frozen Dead Guy Days."

Lissa groaned, thinking of the billboard that had welcomed her to Cole's home. "What *is* that anyway?"

With a straight face, he said, "We keep a dead guy on dry ice in a shed. Once a year, there's a festival of sorts to celebrate his continued presence. We drink beer... jump naked into the thawing reservoir... that sort of thing."

There weren't words. "You do this?"

"I'm wearing the T-shirt right now."

Lissa considered Cole's wool sweater and heavy jacket. She might never know. "What do you mean by *millions* of fires?"

"Dung fires," he answered. "I'm sure you know cows are sacred to Hindus. That means cows sort of have free reign. An efficient way to utilize all the waste—if you can get over the pollution and the stench—is to dry it and burn it. Generally for heat. Sometimes for cooking."

Eyes already stinging and starting to water, she sputtered, "That gives new meaning to the term 'eat shit.'"

He took her hand and squeezed, a comforting gesture in a sea of unfamiliar. Then he ruined the effect. "Outrageous," he said, "how the majority of a population—now over 1.2 billion—has managed to survive without the help of stainless-steel Viking stoves."

As he talked, he led her away from the doors and down a long, sloping concrete ramp. Before they could reach the end, a group of cab drivers—at least she assumed they were hawking rides since she heard, "Five hundred rupees to town!" and "Nice car!" over and over—pressed them toward one of the banked concrete walls. Beyond the crush of bodies, a woman wailed, holding the hand of a grubby child with an even dirtier patch over his right eye. His exposed left eye wandered beneath a yellowing film, blind and searching, while his mother thrust her free hand forward, sobbing inconsolably.

Hotel runners darted between unsuspecting backpackers, asking if the newly landed had a place to stay and invariably bemoaning the fact that the chosen haven was "full" or "closed" and offering up a better option. A man meekly approached Lissa's side. He made it all the way to her shoulder, suddenly occupying the space vacated by a cabbie who'd given up for easier prey.

The man silently held out a handful of stone necklaces. They were stunning, each a different color. "Handmade," he said, showing a mouthful of teeth that shined bright white against his darker skin. When Lissa reared back, his hand followed, keeping the dangling rocks inches from her face.

"*Don't* ask how much," Cole instructed under his breath, "of *anyone*." Then he spoke in a firm yet friendly tone to the crowd, "Nahin! No!" before pulling her through the bodies blocking their way.

Further down the ramp, women had laid out blankets to display their wares. Voices rose in a cacophony of pleas as Lissa and Cole passed. "Table mats," one woman yelled, "made of banana leaf!" Another, this one weather-lined and shrunken to the point she could pass for the Mother of Time, rose from her perch on the concrete and limped forward. She carried a bright scarf with fringed edges. Before Lissa could react, the woman had wrapped her in the length of vibrant cloth. "All pashmina," said the woman. "*All.* See, you feel."

Cole jerked to a halt and speared Lissa with a look. "Don't *ask*." He threw the woman a respectful smile but still unwound the scarf from around Lissa's neck. Once free, he lifted it to the woman, patience in every move. "No," he chided her softly. "Take it back."

The woman stepped away, and Lissa sensed that half the power struggle had been lost the second the "pashmina" had touched her skin. "Very cheap," the woman hedged. This smile was toothless and rimmed with bleeding, discolored gums. "You buy for wife. *Pretty* wife."

Lissa couldn't take her plea. How expensive could the damn thing be? "Cole—"

He stopped her with a violent shake of his head. With another firm, "No," toward the woman, he dropped the scarf to the ground.

The second they entered the underground train terminal, Lissa bent at the waist. Hands splayed over knees, she sucked at thick, rancid air and tried to wipe the blind child from her mind. Intellectually, Lissa knew life wasn't fair. Emotionally, she balked at a world in which a tiny blind boy could be on the streets begging before sunrise.

"I know you've traveled." Cole's insolent decree cut through her valiant attempt to assimilate. "Don't tell me you're surprised."

"To France," she snapped, "and England and Monaco and Hawaii." And the Virgin Islands, Norway, Japan, and just about every other first-world destination deemed appropriate by wealthy parents, protective older brothers, and shopaholic friends.

When he didn't answer, just looked at her with the full force of judgment that said she must not care a thing for the world or the problems of its inhabitants, she put her head in her hands. "I *do* care." A truth she put mildly, considering how her mind couldn't navigate away from the hungry child with the eye patch or the woman with blackened gums. She might see those initial images forever. "I'm just momentarily surprised. Tomorrow I won't be surprised anymore."

But, Jesus, tonight I need a get-out-of-jail-free pass.

Studying her, Cole pressed a thousand-rupee bill into her hand. "Go over there to the counter"—he motioned to a glass-encased ticket stand— "and buy two tickets to New Delhi Station."

When she came back, he counted the change, jaw hardening with the flick of each bill. "Go ask where your other two-hundred rupees are."

Lissa grudgingly counted the change Cole handed back, tempted let him remedy the problem himself. Sure enough, she was short.

To think they'd trained for *art* when they should have trained for *India*.

Lissa spun on her heel, finally feeling angry rather than fascinated or heartbroken or afraid. She marched back to the man behind the glass. "I gave you a thousand. You owe me seven hundred in change." She slammed the five hundred he'd given her onto the counter and lifted two fingers. "Two hundred more."

Without so much a twitching a brow, the clerk reached down, not into the cash drawer, but somewhere below. Soon several additional coins slid through the slot in the window—four fifty-rupee pieces.

"Thank—" The words cramped on her tongue. Never would she thank a man for grudgingly amending his attempt at train-way robbery.

Stepping away from the counter, her anger drained away as exhaustion tugged her limbs downward. "Let's go, Inspector Rathlen," she said, heading for the waiting train.

A soft tap on her shoulder halted her progress. From behind, Cole spoke with the conviction of long-held belief. "Lissa, some of India will be dirty, some even monstrous. More will be interesting. A little will hold the most amazing things you have ever, or will ever, see. *All* will be hard."

Lissa nodded. Cole had brought her to a place as provocative and unpredictable as him. "If only a country could be a kindred spirit."

Yellow markings divided the train platform into sections, the first marked "women only." Matching arrows on the pavement pointed to a first car that held three women, all covered from neck to toe in swaths of bright cloth. Men packed the second car. Most faced forward, staring through the glass separating them from the women, open and unabashed. Too many of the stares went beyond curiosity or boredom. These men looked on with a gleam of ownership, as though the women were on display for their enjoyment.

Her feet refused another step. "Am I safe here?"

Cole had her by the shoulders and facing him in a single, painless move. "Yes," he promised, gritty and intense. "Absolutely and unequivocally, *yes*."

******

Cole herded Lissa into the second car. Before the train eased away from the platform, he had her pressed against the far wall, legs bracketing her hips, an arm on either side of her wary face. Vile oaths pinged around inside his head. He'd mangled Lissa's first moments. Wanting to immerse her in beauty, he'd forgotten that beauty is sometimes difficult to see.

How many times had she taught *him* that? Pushing his Town-Car girl onto a Chester-the-molester-van train hadn't been the right start.

Beneath him, Lissa's delicate features had washed white. Her eyes darted from side to side, and when he tore his gaze away from her face, he noted what she obviously saw—their fellow travelers were looking their fill.

"The papers," she whispered, and he barely heard over the chug of the train. "There've been attacks. On tourists, even. I guess I assumed those happened in rough areas. You know, back alleys and dark wharfs. Jesus, Cole, this is the train from the airport. In the capital."

"Hush." He tucked an errant lock of hair behind her ear. "They're only looking because we're different."

If possible, her voice grew more strained, rising to the loose edge of panic. "I don't *like* being different."

Of course not. Being different to Lissa meant being ostracized. Hurt. *Punished.* "Baby, you were born that way. You'll never spend a day in your life cloaked in normality." *Perfection stands out.*

"I have to be normal here. Cole, I *have* to."

God, the whole scene was taking her back. *His fault.* He stroked a thumb in slow, comforting circles over the side of her cheek. "All you have to do is paint. And look at the world like you naturally do, with an eye toward the truth as you, Lissa Blanc, see it. Make me *feel* India, Lissa." *Like I used to.* "Bring me pink mountains."

She stilled, and he trailed his hand over her clammy skin, down to her heart, feeling the heavy thump against his palm.

He went on, speaking low and steady. "I'll show the world what we see. *Exactly* what we see. You'll show them what's actually there."

She closed her eyes on a hesitant nod, and he sensed a Herculean battle for strength taking place behind those whisper-thin lids.

One that, before he knew it, she won. Opening her eyes, she said, "Cole Rathlen sounds like he trusts me, almost like he needs me."

"That's because," Cole answered gravely, "he does."

CHAPTER 27

They changed trains at two more underground stations. To Lissa's relief, Cole purchased their new tickets. Long, frenetic security lines separated the airport train from the day-to-day metro, as in bag scanners and a full frisk with separate lines for men and women. Lissa stood dazed on a rickety box tucked behind a half-closed curtain while a young woman patted between her breasts. The guard slowed, poking again and again at the rigid underwire in Lissa's bra, and Lissa wondered *why?* Was courthouse security really necessary?

What were these people afraid of?

"A precaution," Cole explained on the other side. "After the '08 terror attacks in Mumbai, security tightened all over the country. Some fair, like here in the metro, where every schmuck gets the same treatment. Some not, like at high-end hotels where you'll waltz right in because that porcelain skin of yours screams *safe.*" Cole grabbed her hand. "Do you want to ride in the women's car?"

"With you?"

"I can't. No men, no exceptions. But I'd be one car back with you always in my sight."

Lissa cringed, remembering the scrutiny placed on the women in the last train and wondered which option made her more conspicuous. "No, I'll stay with you."

The city loomed dark and quiet when they resurfaced at Patel Nagar, and suddenly Lissa missed the dueling cabbies and hawkers and beggars outside the airport. The map Cole had printed from their guest-house website promised only a few minutes' walk, yet they faced an uncertain path. No signage to say which exit they'd used to escape the tunnels. No outdoor lighting. No street signs. No cars. Orienting themselves became nearly impossible.

So they walked.

Around piles of brick and dirt. Over hedges of long-set concrete, forgotten rebar thrusting upward. Through soot and exhaust lingering from the previous night. And past the fires Cole had promised. Tiny dots of flame skirted the street in sporadic outcroppings of warmth, each hosting a circle of silent people huddled on the ground beneath thick, coarse blankets. Breathing through the scratch of smoke in her throat, Lissa could barely make out shapes. She saw only orange flickers in the whites of eyes, eyes trained on her.

Safely tucked into Cole's grip, Lissa looked more closely. Most of the gazes glinted with curiosity rather than hostility. Locals were right to question the audacity of foreigners on a freezing morning, before dawn, walking the street with no obvious place to go.

Frankly, Lissa did, too. "We shouldn't have raced the sun."

"Correct," he said, without reminding her that waiting had been his plan and leaving, hers. They'd come to an enormous traffic circle beneath what appeared to be an elevated byway. Cole examined the map with a flashlight he'd pulled from a daypack slung across the front of his chest.

Peering through the first shafts of light, Lissa stated the obvious. "Still no street signs."

Cole chuckled. "I can count on my hands the number of street signs I've *ever* seen in India."

"How do we get around?"

He leaned down and pressed his lips to the space in front of her ear. "Carefully."

Coughing discreetly into her opposite shoulder, Lissa nudged him for more.

Cole straightened. "My phone's an international one. I can get online and upgrade the plan for mapping and GPS here in India. First we'll gauge how stupid it would be to flash a five-hundred dollar phone. Blending issues, you know."

Lissa looked to the nearest fire circle and confirmed that all eyes remained on them. "I do."

Alternatives dwindled, and Lissa realized they were lost and, for all intents and purposes, alone in the middle of a metropolis of over twenty million people. Perhaps they should disappear into the metro for an hour or two, riding in circles until the city woke up. If they couldn't navigate post-sunrise, hordes of cabs would be back and at their disposal.

Just as she opened her mouth to suggest backtracking, a rickshaw wobbled out of the haze. At first the driver didn't spot them, but once Lissa slid a reluctant foot into the empty street, he jerked his head and pedaled doggedly their way.

The driver had paired a faded button-down with a long, once-white sarong that wrapped around this waist. The cotton crushed upward where it hit the bicycle seat, shortening the garment to around knee length. Only rubber sandals protected his feet from the dusty street. The man was bone thin in a wiry, capable sort of way, and Lissa supposed only the most committed, or the most desperate, trolled the streets at this hour. He had to be the first out for the day.

Rolling to a stop in front of them, the driver spoke rapidly, likely in a dialect of Hindi. The language rolled over her ears, unintelligible but lilting, the sound like new music.

"English?" Cole asked.

The man shook his head, so Cole stepped forward with the map and pointed to their destination. Lissa stifled a yawn that threatened to dislocate her jaw, hoping like hell that finding a rickshaw on this particular corner meant the driver knew his way around the immediate vicinity. If she didn't find a bed soon, she might join one of the campfires for a power nap.

The driver turned the map in circles, mumbling to himself before motioning for them to jump into the seat balanced on his rear wheels. Lissa stumbled back onto the dirt that wasn't quite a sidewalk. This man obviously had no idea where the guesthouse was. She'd rather take her chances with tired feet and a back that bowed under the weight of clothing and supplies.

She should have followed Cole's instructions to pack "like every pair of underwear equaled the weight of an Indian elephant" since he "would *not* be lugging her junk."

"No, Cole"—she swayed heavily—"no way. He doesn't know where to go."

Two things happened at once. First, the weight of her pack drifted from her shoulders as if by magic. When she turned loosely, surprised at the relief, she saw that Cole had slung the straps over a vascular forearm. Second, beyond that forearm she could navel-gaze for the duration of their trip, she spied something far less pleasant.

******

Like the rickshaw, the men emerged in crawling degrees, seeming to grow out of the abyss beyond. Cole counted five in total.

"Shit," Lissa whispered beside him. Like him, she ignored the rickshaw driver's confusion. Instead, her eyes searched farther, to the approaching band of tool-wielding men. One held a sledge hammer, another what looked to be a shovel.

"Stay low-key, Lissa," he said with a calm bred of fear more important than for himself, "self-assured, confident, and *casual.*"

Only her ragged breathing answered him, but her head bobbed. When she gripped his arm, he could feel tremors radiate through her slender fingers. Angling his body between her and the rickshaw, with the approaching men on the other side, he pushed her hard behind him. The move masked her smaller frame with the combined bulk of his body and the packs he carried.

How to play this? Though it wasn't the India he knew, Lissa had been right about the news reports. The last year had been a devastating one for women in India. Stories of brutal sexual assaults, often perpetrated by groups of several men, had incensed the globe. The calls for increased protections and consequences thundered through his head.

He could have started the protecting by not bringing his Lissa here, not like this. With Kate, there'd been private drivers and five-star hotels. He'd never questioned anything less. Why had he done different with the woman now shaking behind him?

Because she's stronger, a voice whispered in his head. Cole knew he imagined what he wanted to hear, but the sentiment translated with the force of external knowledge rather than internal hope—a truth the universe would finally force him to accept. *She doesn't want the gilded cage, is ever trying to escape it.*

The armed group threaded closer, heading their direction with quiet purpose. Cole should hear taunts by now—whistles, questions, the soon-to-be ubiquitous comment that his wife was *pretty*.

Too-fucking-pretty Lissa Blanc, with the smart mouth and fragile body he refused to break.

Déjà vu couldn't be that cruel.

Behind him, Lissa beat on his pack. "Get in the rickshaw."

"Too slow." *Walking* was faster. Instead of climbing aboard, Cole threw Lissa's pack on the seat and talked to the driver in a language he knew the man would understand. Pointing to the star on the map like he hadn't a care in the world, Cole enunciated clearly. "Thirty rupees."

Lost or not, the driver perked up. Before, he'd seemed unsure of the destination. When Cole offered several times what the ride should cost, the man abandoned the plight of the directionally-challenged.

The driver's greed played on Lissa's fear, totally worth it if one of those emotions swept her off the street.

Because the numbers weren't in his favor. With a quick glance at the incoming group, Cole realized if he couldn't beat them, he would distract them.

Gladly.

"*You* get in," Cole demanded. Sickness swam in his stomach at the possibility that his plan wouldn't work. "I'll meet you at the guest house."

"I will *not* leave you," came Lissa's implacable reply.

Cole eyed the driver, keeping him talking until he could all but shove

Lissa onto the rickshaw. "Fifty rupees." *Or twenty-five thousand. Didn't matter.*

With a quick jerk, Cole dragged Lissa around to his front. Lifting her bodily, he dropped her on the seat next to her bag. "Go." The demand came out more like a prayer. *Please go. Be gone. Be safe.* But the driver didn't move. Instead he sat perfectly still, eyes darting from side to side, head facing rigidly forward. Finally, the little guy had noticed they were about to have company.

Cole amended the thought—more like *did* have company.

The men clustered around the back of the rickshaw. Up close, Cole realized the five were a construction crew. The tallest one in a yellow hard hat broke out the Queen's English. "Where do you go?"

Cole wanted to buy the friendly angle, but he couldn't, not with Lissa sitting, pale but mutinous, on the back of a trumped-up bike that had a fat kid's chance in a candy shop of serving as a getaway car. Snatching the map from the driver, Cole pushed it forward toward the hard hat and faked oblivious. "A guesthouse," he explained evenly, "very close by." In the same breath, he beat the driver on the back and stepped away to make room for the rickshaw to blast forward.

Nothing happened.

The worker took the map. His four comrades bent forward to peer at the paper, which had, in the last fifteen minutes, been folded and rolled and manhandled until the lines were faint. The men lapsed into Hindi, muttering amongst themselves. Every few seconds, one of them pointed in a different direction, obviously making a case for the way to go.

The sun chose that moment to crest the ridge of city rising above them. Shafts of gray light filtered through the smoke, immediately lifting the taint of danger surrounding the group. A car blew by, followed by a motor bike. The uncharacteristic silence of new morning gave way to raised voices and the staccato flare of honking horns.

The men kept bickering amongst themselves.

Cole almost laughed when the hard hat broke away and hammered out terse instructions to the rickshaw driver, who nodded enthusiastically. How quickly relief shifted to embarrassment. Indians did things differently, with a whole-body, whole-brain passion the rest of the world not only lacked, but couldn't begin to understand. Cole knew better than to assume the worst.

These men had come to help.

Hard hat handed the map back to Cole and said, "Very close. Ten rupees to him. No more. *Ten.*"

"Ten only," Cole agreed. "And thanks."

Hard hat smiled and held up both hands. "Ten."

The driver meandered a while, long enough for even Cole's unfamiliar eye to see the same hotel—of course not theirs—pass by several times.

When they finally pulled up in front of their home-away-from-home, the driver held out his hand.

"Fifty rupees," he said, snapping his fingers at Lissa's reproachful snort.

This time Cole did laugh. They were off to a great start.

CHAPTER 28

Lissa blinked open bleary eyes. Judging from the shadows creeping across the water stains on the ceiling, she'd slept much of the day. Probably not the brightest jet-lag plan, but by the time they'd checked in and tripped up the rickety stairs to their room—the *single* room Cole had failed to mention around booking time—she hadn't had the energy to brush her teeth at the rusted sink.

Her comments about the flypaper hanging in the shower, or at least the corner of the bathroom with a spigot and a drain, had been met with amusement. "Our grant budget is fresh out of white marble bathtubs," Cole had informed her.

"Is it also out of toilet paper? Because we don't have any."

Cole had flopped onto his twin bed with a look that said no matter how tired, he'd always enjoy seeing her bristle. "Don't drink from the tap."

Before she could inform him she wasn't *stupid*, he was deep asleep.

Now Cole shifted, slapping his footboard with a long leg not meant for his tiny single bed. Looking at him, she noted Cole wasn't one of those people who softened at rest. The planes of his face appeared just as severe, and just as beautiful, in slumber.

She tilted her head against the mattress, memories of her own dysfunctional nap flooding in. The dreams had sifted through past months, cresting on one restless scene before the next. First, she'd seen the blaze in Cole's eyes on their first morning, when he'd destroyed her painting of Melina and told her life was about to get hard. He'd been the hard one in the next moment, beating back questions about his family and his past with a searing kiss against his dining room table. The kiss had thrown them on a one-way, no-exit conveyor belt to *complications*. Suddenly, she'd seen him over her, felt him inside her, a feeling so real she'd jerked awake with his name trapped behind sealed lips.

187

Waking hadn't helped, not when her wild eyes immediately swept from the ceiling to the clothes slung over their shared nightstand and to the bare, lean slabs of muscle rising and falling within arm's reach.

Lissa shuttered her traitorous gaze and forced herself under a second time. Again the dreams came, equally tumultuous, exceedingly haunting. Instead of the slow pump of Cole's hips, she sensed the drag of her heart the morning after, when she'd awakened alone, but unsurprised.

And then her imagination jumped the rails. Instead of her own perceptions, her mind superimposed *Cole's* point of view over their hardest day. All her chattering mental interjections faded, replaced with his cold, clean need. He had to get her into the truck. Now. *Yesterday.*

"Have you ever made love to a tongue, Lissa?" His well-founded arrogance sounded in her head. *Probably not one like his, deep and thorough. Motivated.* "Been fucked by a tongue?"

Lissa *felt* how intent he was on her response. He inhaled, and his pleasure washed over her. Cole loved her scent. She reminded him of candy, and he wouldn't quit without a taste.

"From behind," Cole went on, and Lissa detected the control he called upon to tamp down the urge to dominate, "while you rock against the warmth. It's so soft..."

Dream Lissa panted over a mere glimpse into Cole's world. She would have snapped, yet he mastered his body's demands, focusing on *her* mindset and what *she* needed most. "Let's get you situated... You all right? That's my girl," he said. Admirable, given how badly he craved the pleasure on offer.

The dream delivered every detail. Cole swelled tight, hot and needy behind his jeans as he dipped his fingers into her mouth and then raked them over her breasts. Through his eyes, she peered through the iced windshield and saw her easel fall. A flash of instinct demanded he stop, his need to prove his respect nigh overwhelming.

A thready whimper escaped Lissa's throat, and he clenched. He could make the loss worth her while. Soon he'd be licking her, hungry and eager.

Game fucking over.

Reality intruded again as Cole's mouth sank over her warm, warm center. Lissa jerked upright, searching for the noise that had sent her crashing back to earth. She found it in the space heater clamoring between their matching beds, a contraption Lissa had already predicted would kill them in their sleep, either death by electrical fire or noise-induced aneurism. Hours ago she'd piled all the room's knick-knacks—a bottle-glass ashtray, a vase sans flowers, and a partially-used air freshener—on top of the heater in an effort to stop the rattling. Mostly the technique worked, but every so often, the shaking escalated to the level of a Mazda Miata driving seventy miles per hour over a washboard road.

Lissa swung a heel down and repeatedly jammed the top of the box, wanting desperately to return to the dream. What she saw there implied Cole had joined her in purgatory, that he walked the same edge of want and need, of acceptance and denial.

He'd told her as much. Until now, when her subconscious had taken matters into its own hands, she hadn't believed.

The heater died under her violent onslaught. Relieved, Lissa inched away.

"Perfect." Cole cut through the quiet. "Now the only noise in the room will come from you."

The urge to look at him was overwhelming.

"Close your eyes, Lissa Blanc." Cole's lips curved into the hypnotic smile of a Cheshire Cat. "I like how you dream."

He knew. "How long have you been awake?"

The grin didn't budge. "Long enough to hear you *moan your own name.*" Flinging aside a blanket that strangely resembled a ratty beach towel, Cole joined Lissa on her bed, legs bent over the edge. His palm found her quivering stomach.

"Who was in the dream with you?"

Oh no, not gonna happen. Never would she tell. You were there, but I was you and you were crazed with lust.

His hand began to circle, ever wider until each pass swept over the top of her pubic bone. "You weren't alone," he reasoned, "unless you commonly pleasure yourself in the third person."

Heat flooded Lissa from the chest up and the waist down. She could only look out the smeared window and try to ignore his roving caress.

"Someone else was in that dream." He pressed a spot that made her gasp. "I think he was me." *Jaysus*, he pressed again, longer this time. "I think your beautiful mind played a trick. Minds tend to do that, you know."

Lissa couldn't stop the soft cry that crawled from her throat when he trailed the pressure lower.

"Tell me, Lissa, did you get inside me in that dream? When you called your own name, were you feeling me with you? Did I like it?"

Lissa's hips lifted with a will of their own, but she bit down on her cheeks, refusing to admit he was right.

One long finger slipped beneath the satin between her legs, rubbing. "You're wet. I'm either right, or you wish I was." The strokes slowed. As always, Cole meant to use his glorious hands to coax forth the words he wanted to hear.

"If you *did* dream you were me," he continued, "then I know the answer. I *loved* it."

He kept talking, slowly building her up. Cole always seemed more talkative in intimate situations. Most of the time he guarded himself, clipped and closed. Get him aroused, and he went all erotic poet.

Lissa swallowed a giggle. *I'm holed up with a sex ninja.*

She stopped laughing when he didn't give her what she wanted. Swirling two knuckles over her core, Cole didn't offer a hint of satisfaction. She wanted his fingers to slide deep. He drew gentle figure eights around her clitoris, nice and easy. She wanted him to ditch the boxer briefs and slam home. He used the back of his hand in driving pulses against her open sex, light on the friction.

At least he talked. "Yeah, if you saw me touch you through my eyes, you know I can barely breathe." His face flushed, eyes going glassy. "You know I get restless and single-minded."

"Cole," she began, but he stopped her protest.

"You smell like *cinnamon*"—a long inhale left him looking crazed—"like your whole body's been dusted."

Probably because it had been. Nothing like a little spicy cinnamon body powder to take the edge off a long flight. "You like?" When he didn't answer, Lissa amped up the urging, ready to get explicit. "Could we—"

"Too late, baby. We can't go back."

As if she wanted to. But she knew he didn't mean this particular encounter. Cole had resisted every part of her for so long. Now he admitted the futility of his efforts, letting his sensual monologue ride in on soft touches, relaxing her, opening her. Driving her nuts.

"Cole," she said again, only this time she meant something different.

"At least you're saying the right name." His fingers barely glided over her skin. "I know. You want harder, deeper, faster. This is what *I* want."

Torture ensued, like he'd injected warm massage oil into her veins. Her body grew languid and sluggish. The need to come was ever present without being overwhelming. Once her hips rolled toward him in a lazy grind, she felt an unhurried push into the center of her being. Lissa boiled over. Rather than a fiery burst, she melted in a leisurely rush of warmth.

"Ooooooh, Cole." She moaned his name too many times to count, and all the while he kept his finger inside her body, perfectly still.

When she opened her eyes, she saw a man on the brink of either violence or madness. Shoulders taut, lips rolled inward over teeth, he'd thrown his head back to stare at the ceiling. Cole held himself in check by the thinnest of threads.

"I picked you, and I picked India in *tribute*. You were to clear my conscience."

The words flash-froze her pleasure even though she'd suspected as much all along. Lissa jerked upright and scooted away, wishing she'd misheard, sure she hadn't.

He pinned her with his clear blue gaze. "But all that matters now," he said, his tone low and dark, "is making sure you say my name when you come. And when you wake. And when you sleep. When you're afraid. When you're happy. Or sad. Or bored. Or lonely."

A chill crept over her exposed skin, and she wished she'd been gentler with the space heater. Cole had wooed her with the tough love of a harsh critic. His tendency to push her away before dragging her close had somehow made him the center of her world and, she now knew, her the center of his.

That truth should make her ecstatic, erase the pain of their inauspicious start, yet it felt irrelevant. The tone of Cole's confession, the strain evident in every line of his body, told her the more Cole let himself love another, the more he hated himself.

CHAPTER 29

She'd said, "*You're welcome.*"

Here he'd admitted to overshooting his goals to the level of betraying his ideals, and all she'd mustered up was *you're fucking welcome.*

"For what?" he couldn't help but ask.

By now she was off the bed, shimmying those long, smooth legs into a fresh pair of jeans. "You haven't found absolution, but wanting me—dare I say, *needing* me, even *caring* for me—has delivered a hell of a lot of closure."

She zipped her pants and stared at him, pained, obviously waiting for a string of denials about how he felt.

Denials that didn't come. If a woman haunted his dreams and preoccupied his mind, that woman was no longer his wife. That woman had morphed into an attitude with long legs and glossy auburn hair.

Closure. he supposed.

"Always so confident," he said, mostly to fill the empty, expectant space with sound.

"More like observant." She pulled a down jacket over the tiny T-shirt she'd slept in. "Remember, I'm the one who looks behind the veneer. In you, I see a man clutching a rule book telling him how life should be lived. Like a dieter who eats when he's not hungry, you seek comfort in routine, somehow finding pleasure in the guilt of self-sabotage. Because if you feel bad, you can credit yourself with at least *respecting* the rules, even though you no longer *obey* them."

When she reached for the strap of her portable easel, Cole grabbed for his own clothes.

"As much as that pisses me off," she spat, "I call it progress."

The muscles in Cole's throat worked convulsively. "You don't know what you're talking about."

"Yeah?" Lissa bent to tie a shoe. "When we met, you were involved with a dead woman and felt guilty about me. Now you're involved with me and *still* feel guilty about me. Get the difference?" The lecture died away, but Cole easily made out one last word—silent and exaggerated—that Lissa mouthed in his direction.

Progress.

His lips stiffened, preparing to lie. "I'm not involved—"

"Why do you care whose name I say?" Lissa grabbed the doorknob just as Cole jammed stiff arms into the sleeves of his own coat. "I'm saying it now, *Cole*. Why do you care?"

The rest of the lie dove down his throat, abandoning him to the truth. "When you say my name, I hear you. I don't hear her in my head anymore. She left me. I hear *you*, see *you*, feel *you*. And it's a relief."

Fuck a relief, more like a miracle.

"Then hear me say this. I'll only let you deny us for so long. I can't be a dirty secret, not even one you only keep from yourself."

The door didn't slam in her wake, which lent her solemn vow all the more power. Cole grabbed his lightest camera and eased into the hall behind her, keeping his distance. Her instinct might tell her she needed space, but his said she'd roam the streets of New Delhi alone about the time Indians embraced carpool lanes.

Outside the guesthouse, the city teemed with the schizophrenic business of survival. Trailing a few feet back, Cole followed Lissa along a narrow street. Sidewalk free, they joined the throng of people walking in the eight inches of road separating the parked cars from the moving ones. Crowded apartments loomed above, and Cole smiled inwardly at the sound of chattering housewives who hung laundry and beat Persian rugs over sagging balconies.

A haze of engine exhaust bloated the air, and Cole saw Lissa cough into an elbow every few minutes. Pollution hit people differently, burning in the eyes and the nose, even the throat. For an unlucky few, all three. With multiple motorbikes for every car, two-stroke smoke became more than an ambient irritant. It was a steady part of a balanced diet.

Lissa skirted around a stray dog doing its business in the limited walking lane, and then she stopped. Looking past her frozen shoulder, Cole saw her attention land on a child. A little girl, probably around four years old, clung to the back of motorcycle like a seasoned pro. The driver paid her little mind as he surged in and out of stopped traffic.

Catching up, Cole spoke to her back. "They have *slightly* less stringent car seat regulations."

"She's a *baby*," Lissa breathed.

"This is *India*." Cole replied. "That's baby's a seasoned pro." Her sanitized vision of humanity would die a quick death. He hoped it could be painless.

She turned, and he saw the remnants of their fight in her eyes, now cauldrons of fatigue and cynicism. Usually so merry, those dark, beautiful pools swirled with indecision.

"Don't give up yet." A grimace stretched his lips. "You've come too far." Frankly, Cole didn't care to examine whether he meant for her to hold out for India, or for him.

Remaining somber, she whispered, "Ditto," and kept walking.

Right into a goat. The animal had been pawing at the base of an overloaded utility pole and reared back for a running start about the time Lissa attempted to pass. The two collided. This time Lissa didn't bother to stop. Slim shoulders merely lifted in a shrug as she moved on.

A few blocks landed them in the traffic circle they'd discovered that morning. The street fires had long smoldered, not to return until the night brought bitter cold. Lissa stopped at the edge of the street, and Cole sped up. Crossing an Indian road took brass balls and gold-medal technique. The trick was to wade through slowly—forget waiting for a break in the flow—and let the traffic diverge around you, rather like walking through a school of fish.

Too many times Cole had witnessed failed attempts to dart through the chaos. Those people ended up dragged aside by other pedestrians, bleeding or dead.

Before he could reach her, Lissa withdrew. Her hand went to the shoulder strap on her easel and, navigating the waves of people and animals like she was born to it, she retreated to the edge of the nearest building. The whole time her gaze remained trained on the traffic circle itself.

Like before, Cole positioned himself at a respectable distance, one that gave him a feel for her target. Homing in didn't take long. A chain-link fence enclosed an elevated patch of dirt in the center of the circle. Beyond the fence, Cole spied a makeshift tent formed of ragged sheets and blankets. A woman sat on a pallet outside the dwelling.

She was breastfeeding an infant.

Around her, children played as though thousands of cars didn't wiz by hourly. For all the attention they paid, those children might have been playing pirate ship in his isolated backyard in Nederland, Colorado. One small boy appeared particularly afflicted. He fumbled in the dirt with the others but moved on all fours, belly up. From knee to mid-shin, a shiny fixture protruded from his leg, as though a brass comb had sprouted from the bone.

Lissa must have practiced with her easel. By the time Cole tore his attention from the fishbowl in the street, she'd set up, pencil in one hand, brush in the other.

The camera around his neck itched for action. Since Lissa was an attention magnet with her looks and equipment, he kept one eye on the viewfinder and another on the shoulders she arched over her canvas. The urge to immerse herself in work whenever life proved challenging said Lissa treated paint like he did pictures—therapy first, job second.

The first taker was a man in a suit. At home, he might have been a real estate agent. Cole heard him welcome Lissa to India and inquire, "Where are you from?"

Don't go there. Don't. Don't...

"US," Lissa replied.

"Aaah," said the suit, blooming with an ecstatic smile. "I love America!"

Lissa kept sketching. She also kept nodding.

Which meant the suit began an impressive wind-up pitch. "How long will you stay in our beautiful country?"

"Not sure yet," Lissa answered. When suit's face fell, she added, "But so far? Fabulous."

"Good, yes?" the guy replied, regaining steam. "Have you wish to purchase fine things in India?"

There it is.

"Maybe a rupee or two worth."

Cole grunted. A letter had arrived in the mail as he and Lissa had driven out for the airport. He wondered at the amount of "emergency money" Lissa's dad had loaded on the prepaid VISA inside. Suffice to say, she was likely equipped to purchase one of India's nuclear weapons, if she'd like.

"I have car," said suit. "*Very* nice car. I take you to best markets."

Lissa finally looked leery. "Thanks, but—"

"No, no, madam! No obligation to buy. None at all. You come?"

"Uh"—Lissa gave her easel a long look and finally swiveled her head around to find Cole—"kinda busy."

"My car very nice. Get to best shopping very, very fast." His "very, very" sounded like "betty, betty."

Cole cringed. The guy was safe, just a hustler looking to feed his family. But if Lissa didn't learn early, she'd go through this exercise often. Plus, unlike Cole's, Lissa's art required her to remain stationary. She couldn't evade touts by walking away on a string of "No thank yous."

In an overabundance of enthusiasm, the suit moved to help Lissa pack her things so she could go to a very nice market in his very nice car. When Lissa moved closer to her easel in evasion, the guy's palm *almost* landed on her arm.

"Hands off." Cole's voice sounded colder than he'd planned. When the suit spared him a glance, Cole tried to look casual but saw his failed effort in the way the tout subtly jumped away. Letting Lissa find her path among strangers in a strange land was one thing. Letting them *touch* her... quite another.

For a moment, Cole thought the man might press. Instead, he bobbled his head from side to side before melding into the passing crowd.

After that, Cole had expected Lissa to recoil with every new approach, not look *him* up and down as though unimpressed and then calmly put brush to canvas. Over the next couple of hours her painting took shape along with her ability to handle interruptions with warm efficiency. Cole watched her politely avoid offers to buy flowers, have her shoes shined, visit a textile factory of "best quality" ceramics, ride an elephant tethered to a stop sign two blocks away, and take a guided tour of the state of Rajasthan—private car, again *betty, betty* nice.

Some she chatted up, in the end refusing whatever was on offer. Others she waved on immediately. She laughed hysterically when a teenaged boy offered to clean her ears with a handful of medieval instruments for a hundred rupees.

Cole strived to leave her be, passing the time with his own photos of the happenings in and around the traffic circle. Fitting that no matter how he tried, all his photos appeared bleak and stricken, a wasteland of poverty porn. None highlighted the fact that these people were, by and large, joyful and content. By shirking the chains of great wealth, so many Indians seemed truly free.

Lissa's quick acclimatization surprised him. Thrown into a world that couldn't be further from her pampered existence and, within a day, she embraced the change. Thinking on it, Cole realized she'd done the same in Colorado. He'd never given her credit for "going rural" when life in Nederland had to have been a shock. Cole had seen firsthand how perfectly Lissa filled the role she'd been born to play, that of a young, beautiful socialite preordained for impressive feats. Yet she'd smoothly replaced gallery hobnobbing with frozen dinners and morning battles over a tree swing.

Without really knowing his goal, he circled back to check her progress. One look over her shoulder, and the din of the street receded.

Meaning crawled, layer by layer, up her canvas. On the bottom, Cole detected the dull gleam of a metal fence. Nothing stood beyond, leaving him with the sense of entrapment without reason. A thick diagonal slash segued to a separate scene above, showing a tangle of arms and legs and an occasional disembodied grin. Another slash led to the impression of dark, watchful eyes. The hint of an intent stare could have belonged to the breastfeeding mother or, just as easily, the passersby who tried not to look on in overt fascination.

The top fragment of canvas to fall to Lissa's brush held a number of gauzy ovals, each in a different muted color and with a string trailing in its wake. On first pass, Cole didn't get the significance. He plunged into the old abyss of Lissa's work, the one where he felt like he'd missed a joke the whole world found hilarious.

Man out.

But the next color to land in broad swaths broke through his familiar frustration. Around the vague circles, Lissa streaked a grayish blue that puffed here and there into anemic clouds. Immediately Cole recognized the potential of a polluted sky. The withered circles had to be balloons—floating on the bloom of unspent youth but faded and shrunken to the point of hardship.

No matter how abstract, misunderstanding wasn't an option. She painted, and he *felt*.

Simple as that.

In two hours Lissa had captured both the turmoil and tenacity on every Indian street corner. She hadn't whitewashed the poverty. Neither had she ignored the promise.

"I get it," he murmured against her neck, craving the cinnamon spice that wafted from beneath the warmth of her jacket.

"The painting or the fact that I'm the master of the universe?"

Both.

Under his chin, her shoulder jerked, suppressing a cough. The sharpness that escaped her lips cut through the blare of a passing motorbike. Overhead, the real clouds she'd painted so aptly hung like a blanket of noxious fumes her body obviously sought to reject. "That's coming from your chest." Not her throat. Her throat would be better.

She scanned the sky. "A tickle. The body must adjust somehow."

Not like that. Before he could press, she tapped the side of the canvas with the wooden handle of her brush and said, "You know the drill, Cole. What do you feel when you look at this?"

Love.

The realization materialized slowly, lighting up protesting nerves, as surprising as it was unfair. If love were water, he'd used his ration. No one, especially not his Lissa, should shoulder the burden of his dehydrated soul.

"I *feel*"—his voice took on an edge—"you'll do."

Her anemic, "Bullshit," only prompted more nonsense.

"I already told you I picked you for absolution. Well, thanks, because this"—he pointed at the drying balloons—"at last is good enough to give it to me."

******

"Sure, sure, Cole," Lissa said to herself, trekking up the long, stone steps to the main entrance of India's largest mosque with her new driver-slash-shadow, Sonu, in tow, "I can do Delhi solo." For two days now, she'd proven it.

Her first adventure had taken her to the outskirts of the city on the banks of the river Yamuna. There, she and Sonu had toured an amazing cultural complex with an air of a Hindu Disneyland. They'd explored acres of pink sandstone and white marble monuments, darting through ornate gates and past carved statues. Lissa hadn't been able to take her easel into the facility, but after a boat ride through ten-thousand years of Indian heritage and culture, she'd sat upon a lush lawn, finally staring at a clear blue sky amid perfumed air, and dreamed up the perfect tribute.

If she was in India to clear Cole's conscience, she had no problem riding his relief straight to the top. He'd get his clean slate. She'd get hers.

Leaning on her family hadn't resulted in true success. The idea of relying on Cole to propel her to new heights had been a farce from the beginning. She'd spent three months blind to that futility, but in the process, she'd learned an important lesson.

Lissa didn't *need* anyone else.

Despite the crash course in Colorado, Lissa had made a convert of Cole, at least artistically. Patience and persistence had paid off because lord knew he hadn't condescended to embark on India out of charity. All on her own she'd forced him to see value in their differences. Now when he viewed her work, appreciation gleamed behind what had formerly been a mask of distaste.

If she could reach Cole, a man predisposed to subliminally connect her paintings with loss and despair, she could reach anyone. Sitting there with her driver, soaking in one of India's cultural masterpieces, she'd realized that plus or minus one Cole Rathlen, she would reach everyone.

Sonu had proven himself a diligent and reflective companion, and she could see why Cole sought him out over and over. The man had answered her questions, but otherwise left her to her own devices, seeming quietly impressed with her growing enthusiasm. At the end of the day, he'd escorted her to the guesthouse door before promising to return the next morning. When she'd tried to tip, he'd stepped away from her outstretched money. "We have many days. At the end, if you're happy, you pay."

Lissa had rushed the stairs to break her confident revelation to Cole, only to find him gone. A note told her he was out shooting night shots.

Don't wait up.

The second day, she'd set the alarm for six in the morning only to find Cole had risen earlier. Like in Colorado, the man had a way of ghosting out the door before Lissa's head left the pillow.

Lissa had endeavored to orchestrate a chance run in, be it five in the morning or ten at night. Cole proved elusive. While Sonu was attentive to her every need, he remained hesitant to cross the boundary between hired help and friendship. India suddenly felt not only new and overwhelming, but incredibly lonely.

At the top of the mosque's steps—had they been steeper than they'd looked?—Lissa bent against a gust of cold wind and gave in to a coughing fit. Other than the occasional outburst, she felt decent. Before she could straighten and contemplate the awe-inspiring behemoth in front of her, a pair of fuzzy slippers were shoved her face. "Fifty rupees," came a shout from above.

Motioning for Sonu to wait at the car, Lissa straightened and traded rupees for slippers, leaving her shoes under the watchful gaze of an attendant. A teenager ran forward with a ticket. "Two-hundred rupees."

She paid.

As she walked through an arch into the open-air platform of the Jama Masjid mosque, a bright silken robe landed on her shoulders, and another teen with an official-looking badge fell in step. "One hundred rupees," he said. When she looked confused, he pointed to the robe.

She paid.

The guide led her over alternating strips of red sandstone and white marble flanked by towering minarets standing guard over Old Delhi. He explained where the prayer rugs went and how the mosque had been constructed. The view from the elevated floor stretched over miles and miles of seething city.

On the streets, Delhi overwhelmed. From her perch high above them, it amazed. The sight nudged a balking voice in the back of her mind. Like a city that seemed as impenetrable and inaccessible as a bank vault, Cole lied. Delhi wanted to be dirty and dangerous, yet the soot hid an artistic heart of temples and monuments and mausoleums. Rumors of violence masked a people who offered help to strangers in the dark and watched over visitors' shoes while they toured the city's treasures.

Cole had never disliked her work more than when he'd been fighting its hold over him. When he'd wanted to take her to bed, he'd warned her away in the crudest manner possible. Now, when he feared liking her too much, he acknowledged their attraction but swore she was nothing but a means to an end, a balm to soothe a guilty conscience.

Hands on hips, she clucked her tongue and surveyed the pandemonium below. Delhi did dusty and despicable in the same way Cole did derogatory and detached—extremely convincing but misleading all the same.

Shame on Cole for thinking her so easily fooled.

Shame on her for nearly proving him right.

When her guide led her back to the shoe pile and demanded five-hundred rupees for his services, services she'd had no idea weren't included in the price of the ticket or the slippers or the robe, she swallowed and wiped away beads of sweat that dotted her brow despite the chill.

And she paid.

When the man watching over her shoes stuck out his palm and grunted about twenty rupees more, she grinned despite the increasing pressure in her chest.

But she paid.

Because five questionable fees to see one house of worship was one of Delhi's harmless quirks. Pay too much mind and she'd risk her enjoyment of an entire city.

Patience and persistence. Sometimes good really did sprout from bad, making the good all the sweeter.

Lissa couldn't wait for the sugar shock of Cole falling at her feet.

CHAPTER 30

Kent stopped on the sidewalk outside the St. Julien hotel, peering through the windows into Jill's restaurant. Sasha—who was baching it with Kent while Cole worked in India—meandered to the end of his flexi-lead, admiring his own reflection. Before Kent could reel the dog in, Sasha's huge head bonked the glass, leaving a smear of slobber behind to commemorate the failed attempt to lick his likeness.

Kent could see the table where Rhea and Kate had dined on that fateful afternoon Cole had accused his wife of adultery. No takers today. The two-top sat empty, its tasteful, upholstered chairs blurring behind the waves of winter sun buffeting the window.

The details of that faded day had started a slow creep into Kent's current reality. Similar weather—sunny but frigid in the middle of one of the coldest, driest winters on Colorado record—had lent the windows the same glare.

Kent knew he'd been curious, at least before his heart attack, about what he'd seen beyond the glass. He'd actually filled in quite a few blanks over his a nightly "relaxation" beer, a developing tradition neither nephew had successfully snuffed. Still, daily walks led him to the St. Julien, as though something important lay in wait.

Today the past yawned behind him, blank as ever.

Turning to leave, Kent stopped for one last glance. A young couple now sat at "Kate's" table. The woman wore a sweater and slacks and appeared surprised, while the man looked unsettled, apologetic even, in a three-piece suit. At first Kent assumed the two were having a genteel business disagreement of some sort, but by the time couple's drinks arrived—stiff drinks by the looks of it—the hairs on the back of Kent's neck vibrated with the frequency of a tuning fork.

A newspaper vending machine beckoned from the curb. Lugging Sasha in retreat, Kent fiddled in his pocket for change and took his time purchasing a paper, all while observing the showdown in the window. Opening the front page, he leaned against the machine and pretended to be engrossed, eyes wandering beneath his sunglasses.

The scene played out like a silent movie. Some words he recognized.

"*I'm sorry.*" From him.

"*Why?*" Her.

"Not your fault." Him.

"Don't do this." Her.

Other parts of the conversation piggybacked on a live wire of emotion strung between the two participants. When the woman reached for the man's hand, Kent ceased to see two strangers. Suddenly it was Kate who recoiled from Rhea's searching grasp. Though unwilling to make physical contact, Kate shook her head in obvious sadness. She didn't rebuff Rhea lightly.

The physical rejection brought an abrupt halt to Rhea's cajoling. Even from a distance, Kent saw the seeking desperation of her earlier appeals drain away, leaving a brittle shell.

Accepting, but probably not respecting, Kate's wishes, Rhea stood and backed away from the table. A parting shot—"*Wrong choice*"—left Kate staring after Rhea's retreating back.

Kent charged for the door. Halfway across the sidewalk, he jerked to the end of Sasha's lead and realized the dog had wrapped himself around the base of the newspaper vendor and fallen asleep. The sight cleared the vision, leaving him alone outside a restaurant, spying on two strangers. He wouldn't interrupt their moment any more than he had Kate and Rhea's two years ago, when he'd noted the tension and faded into the background, determined to learn more.

Which explained how his curiosity had survived partial amnesia.

Kent had witnessed more than a casual lunch between his two nieces-in-law. If forced to guess, he'd say he'd watched two people, intimate if not in love, part ways.

CHAPTER 31

Cole woke in the night to Lissa's suppressed coughing. The creaking bed made more noise than she did, but he could still make out the wet squeeze of her lungs with each muffled burst.

Today they'd headed south with Sonu and their compact car for Agra and the awaiting Taj Mahal. The hundred-and-forty-mile trip had taken hours, with Sonu calmly charging around everything from meandering cows, to an ancient tractor dangling a wrecked tuk-tuk, to what Cole would always believe had been a dead body. Sonu claimed prostrate forms bordering the road were a common trick—first play dead and then play on a motorist's sympathies—but the facedown form had been too diminished for miraculous resuscitation.

Before vacating Delhi, Cole had been leaving Lissa to her own devices during the day, hoping she'd explore and create solo. In turn, he'd been trying to follow suit under the guise that his head—not his cock and definitely not the empty organ between his ribs—ran the show.

Trying and failing.

At night, when she'd been deep asleep in the single bed next to his, he'd looked his fill. Lissa reminded him of a flawless wind-up doll. No matter the draining frustrations of the day, she slept like a rock and headed out again the next morning, armed with a handful of brushes and a mindset that no one and nothing could stop her.

All of *his* pictures, on the other hand, screamed sophomore photography student. Plus, he still wanted every part of Lissa, from the top of her head to the tips of her blue-painted toes. He also wanted to talk to her, even if only to pretend to ignore her theories about him needing her and not the other way around.

Ignoring her let him pretend she wasn't right.

Strangely, leaching off Lissa's essence during the wee hours of the morning hadn't resulted in a shared of vision of depth and insight.

Now Cole winced at each weak cough that drifted from her bed. He tugged on a pair of nylon pants and trekked across the teak flooring to the second bedroom of their new suite. After making her rough the cold water and freezing floors in Delhi, he'd upgraded about a hundred notches in Agra. Few could call the Oberoi Amarvilas, literally six-hundred meters from the Taj Mahal itself, anything but perfection. The private balconies where they could work—all commercial activity had been banned on the Taj's official grounds—were alone worth the personal expenditure.

Lissa's murmured, "Thank you baby Jesus and Shiva, too," when she'd spied the colossal pedestal tub crouching before a Taj-facing wall-o-windows had sealed the deal.

He nudged into a spot next to her hip, stroking the ribbons of dark hair that spread over the pillow. "Baby, I know you're awake. I can hear you."

"Sorry," she croaked.

"Do you want water?"

He felt her nod beneath his hand. A minute later, she was propped up in bed, sipping from a bottle of Indian-equivalent Evian. She looked pale in the lamplight, wan even. Lissa wasn't supposed to look vulnerable. Despite her delicate build, he trusted her to be hearty enough to be difficult.

He counted on it.

Difficult he could fight. Needy he could only hope to fix. Whenever Kate had been down, struggling against the darkness that had so often tried to suck her under, he'd been overcome with a need to make things better. Bringing a smile to Kate's face had made him feel worthy. Knowing he'd held the proverbial gun to her last grin had killed his desire to try with anyone else.

Yet he would. "Roll over," he instructed Lissa, slipping the water bottle from her grasp. "You'll recover if you can go awhile without agitating those pissed-off lungs. When the sun comes up, I'll find codeine." Or something even better. "For now, you have to relax."

"Relaaaax," Lissa repeated lazily before more wracking coughs cut her off.

Her skin radiated heat, and he began to massage her shoulders and back, hoping the slow pressure would lull her to sleep. When she quieted, he reached around her front to rub along her throat in soothing circles.

Just when he thought she was out, she curled a slender hand around his. "I have a plan for us."

A ball of barbed wire knotted in his stomach. "Do you?"

"We work *together*. Or nothing."

Of course Lissa hadn't appreciated his defense mechanisms. Who the hell would enjoy being hauled across the world and then dumped with a driver?

"By together," she went on, "I mean mixed media. We share a base—a canvas, photo paper… whatever—and build from the bottom up."

"Details?"

"Pretty obvious, I'd think. You do your thing. I do mine. We make the two mesh in the same piece of artwork."

"Like, what, I take a picture of the Taj Mahal and you paint the trees surrounding it?"

"No, *I* paint the Taj Mahal."

She wheezed in a shallow breath, and he returned to rubbing along her spine. "Big aspirations, baby."

"No more separate, Cole. Else I'll withhold my valuable contributions and leave you to compare one exact reproduction of the Taj to another."

Was that a threat or a promise? Despite the warmth coming off Lissa's body, she shivered against him. He began gathering her up, hating the sound of her lungs and the chills simmering in her limbs. Thank God he'd traded up to the gilded version of India. The thought of her sick in a cold, dingy room made his gut roil. "You need steam." *And a doctor.*

Lifting her up, covers and all, Cole carried Lissa into the palatial bathroom, where he propped her against the edge of the tub and then wrenched the glass-encased shower to scalding.

Returning, he ditched the blankets and set her inside the porcelain basin in her panties and bra, willing to soak any barrier to blast the congestion in her chest. All the pollution had gone to battle with her airways. "Sit back. Like I said, relax."

Between the streaming shower and tub, the bathroom practically flash heated. With each degree, Lissa sank further into the water. "We probably ought to plan."

"You probably ought to breathe." The way she gasped in sudden, searching eruptions had him worried. "Deep. Over and over."

"I've been reading up on the Taj." Lissa should have gone limp in the water and focused on her protesting chest cavity, but she chattered like she wasn't a hair's breadth away from a midnight hospital run. "It's seen as one of the world's great symbols of love, but I don't think many people—at least not that many women—know this emperor Shah Jahan had other wives. Mumtaz Muhal was merely his 'favorite.' If that's not enough to impugn the 'greatest love of all,' how about the fact that poor Mumtaz died while giving birth to Jahan's *fourteenth* child. That would be *one, four.* I do *not* hear a Whitney Houston track in the background on this one."

Leave it to Lissa to boil things down. "This *was* the early seventeenth century."

"I bet he didn't breed his *dogs* that hard—"

"He wasn't a modern man. Polygamy was accepted—*expected*—of his rule. More male children meant a secure line of succession, and the other

205

women were simple procreation placeholders. Plus it wasn't like the Empress could go out and get a quick IUD."

Lissa snorted through thick lungs. "Yeah, yeah, the suffragettes weren't exactly marching on the lawn."

"Right," Cole agreed, swallowing hard. Water had crawled past Lissa's thighs, dousing her tiny lace panties and ratcheting inviting up to irresistible. "The story is at least an interesting one." Cole waited for her to interrupt. For once, she didn't. Thank God for pre-pneumonia. "Two people fell in love, despite living in a time when marriage was an institution devoted to the political and the practical. That Mumtaz Mahal died in tragic circumstances and Shah Jahan devoted himself to her memory only adds to the mystic."

Quiet enveloped the steaming room. Then, "If he loved her, why did he hurt her?" Whether earnest or inflammatory, Cole couldn't tell, but Lissa's dry question boiled through two years of doubt.

The bathroom washed pitch black. Cole threw his hands in the air, backing away from the threat in the tub. "Why?" He braced himself against the shower glass, sucking in hot, wet air. "*Because* he loved her, was by all accounts completely enthralled, besotted... *obsessed*. She meant everything— confidant to lover. His inescapable need to have her, killed her." *As it so often does.* "So he went fucking crazy and spent a year in seclusion. Then, white-haired and bent, he built one of the world's most beautiful monuments in her name and spent the remainder of his pathetic life alone."

Opening his eyes, he saw Lissa had braced her chin on the outer curve of the tub, pillowed by soft, slick arms. Those arms invited his touch, but an inch up, her mouth stretched in a sneer. "You aren't an ancient Mughal emperor," she said, her voice surprisingly smooth and stern as steel. "You didn't kill your wife. You're not crazy. And you don't have to build a legacy to her name before withering away to nothing."

He deserved this, with all his talk of Lissa and India and absolution. Yet she drew parallels where none existed. The man who'd built the mausoleum Cole could see shining in faint lines through the bathroom window had done nothing wrong.

Natural causes were a fickle bitch that stole loving spouses right and left.

The man in the mirror, however, had made huge mistakes, blunders that couldn't be rectified by something as simple as a piece of art by his wife's favorite artist in his wife's favorite land. That man deserved to be alone, flipping through years of pictures of brash prostitutes offering up freebies. Cole had known that all along.

Still, knowing and *doing*—pun intended—remained two different things.

What had started as a nice but futile idea to get his game back had evolved into a disguised passion the moment he'd strolled into The Gray Halls gallery in New York City and found his Lissa in a blood-red corset.

Desire had been instantaneous, but he hadn't expected his unwelcome hard-on to graduate into respect and then... *this*.

"*Correct*," he said, pitching his voice low and brutal, relishing that while she slumped naked and ill in the bath, he stood in fighting form, clothed, and towering above her. Closer with each second. "Unlike Shah Jahan's, my wife *wanted* to leave me. I'm fresh out of white marble. And I think I've already proven that I don't intend to while away my life in a state of celibate atonement. Should I prove it again?"

"One more step"—Lissa wagged her index finger feebly in front of her face—"and I'll do the proving. Your eyes have that gleam they get when you want me, but taking what you want is the mental equivalent of flogging yourself with a butcher knife."

Porcelain hit his thighs, halting his march straight into her bath. "Right now you're too weak to prove two plus two equals four."

"I warned you."

Before Cole could react, she stood up.

******

With all the doubt in her life, Lissa didn't know a great many inalienable truths. But like every other woman on the planet, she sensed with complete and utter confidence when a man neared the edge.

The second she'd risen from the barrier of the bathtub, Cole had jumped off it.

Sugar shock.

Purposefully, face taut and eyes glittering with undisguised lust, his scrutiny traveled the length of her body. "Jesus," he rasped, "you have no mercy."

Suddenly Lissa felt completely bare, which she supposed she was, wearing nothing but sopping silk and lace. He laughed, and the husky sound rippled over her damp skin, raising patches of goose bumps. Yet she was so hot. Giddy pleasure at the close-up of his striated torso warred with a rising frailty she couldn't ignore.

"Mercy is for fools and children." Cole didn't happen to be either.

"We *can't* do this." Yet the crazed look on his face made it clear that if pushed, he might do it over and over again. "You're sick."

"Mmm," she half-acknowledged, lifting shaking hands to his shoulders. "Emperor Cole has deemed me off limits." *What else is new?* The taunt drained her remaining strength. Exhaustion washed over her, and she closed her eyes and swayed into his chest. So much for her devious plan. *He* was supposed to fall at *her* feet, not the other way around, and preferably not literally.

Dazed, she felt herself lifted and set gently on a towel he'd already spread over the tile. When she opened her eyes and looked at him, he shook his head. "No."

"Yes." Lying back, she rubbed at the droplets clinging to her skin with the oversized cloth beneath her. Horizontal felt better. The dizziness abated, and Cole had been right about the steam. Her lungs no longer seized with every breath. "Haven't you wanted this? I swear if I see your perfect ass walk away one more time…"

Instantly he was hovering over her in push-up position, arms tight. A warm strip of moisture meandered up the side of her neck. *His tongue.* "Damn you. I'm not the one who sleeps in a scrap of lace. Or the one with a coughing problem that jiggles my magnificent breasts on every exhale."

Almost in a trance, she gripped his sides and rocked upward into the hardness he held out of reach. "You've deserved it." But enough play. This was serious. "Every time we've been intimate"—not often enough in her estimation—"the pleasure's gone down on your terms."

Proving her theory, he graced her with a dip of his corded hips, and she chuckled up at the ceiling. Instead of falling at her feet, she thought with fuzzy abandon, he could fall onto her clitoris.

Flexibility had always been one of her finest qualities.

Thorough swirls of his tongue traced to her collarbone in a steady, fiery tease. But then Cole spoke and ruined the effect. "Something wrong with my terms?" His breath roughened as he bore her to the floor, stretched out and straining, lips never leaving her skin.

"Only the fact that they're yours," she said. He'd pleasured her for secrets, for a distraction, even to gain reluctant admissions Lissa had preferred to hold close, but never upon request. "Time for *mine.*"

Without a word, he eased himself into the cradle of her body. Then, like a man half starved, Cole threaded his hands through her hair and tugged her face to his. The kiss that followed was obviously intended to punish, a lesson against making demands. He'd kissed her like that once before, after catching her probe his family for answers. Then, his aggression had been tinged with anger. Now she tasted desperation.

Lissa welcomed the rough thrust of his tongue. Instead of shying away, she met him in an all-out struggle for dominance.

With an abrupt twist, he tore his mouth away. "And your terms involve getting fucked on the bathroom floor while you're ill?" He met her gaze with speculative fervor. "One more move, and I'll accommodate you in a way we'll both regret."

Lissa gasped. Only if regret sounded like, *Yes, sir. Thank you, sir. Again, sir!* "Please"—*air,* she needed more of it—"have me. But only if I'll find you where I know you want to be in the morning… in *my* bed."

No more running. That was her term.

She bucked under him, trembling with the memory of the pleasure he'd given her before. "In *my* bed, where I'll proceed to have *you*"—she writhed beneath him, convinced her lower half was melting—"before we work together, the team we're supposed to be."

In the fight between all and nothing, *all* had to win.

A wicked roar sounded from Cole's throat. With one hand, he jerked his workout pants down and her panties to the side. He sank into her softness, demanding she receive him. No gentle prodding. No coaxing words. The ruthless thrust stretched her wide from the sensitive nerves at her entrance to the mouth of her womb.

Nothing had *ever* felt so good. Nothing would rival the feeling again.

"Enough?" His voice was strained to the point of sounding inhuman.

Once, in the days when she hadn't had the strength to take control, one of her adolescent tormentors had bent her thumb back in the hall near her locker. He'd wanted fifty bucks, which had been a ton of money between high school kids. "*Mercy?*" he'd taunted. When she'd shaken her head, breathing deep, he'd bent the digit farther. "*Mercy, Lissa?*" She hadn't had fifty dollars on her. In the end, she'd given him a garnet and gold ring—not a priceless gem but certainly worth more than fifty.

Cole said *enough* the same way that jerk had said *mercy*, only Cole wanted her to give in to save herself... from the rough sex he thought would make her sicker, from attachment to a man off limits... basically, from him.

"No," she breathed, mired in the shock of sensory overload but stubborn to the end. *Never enough.*

"Lissa, goddammit." The muscles of his arms strained at her sides. "I need you so much." He started to shake. "I can't stop." Yet he slowed way down, his frenzied entrance fading to a slow, tender rocking she couldn't have expected.

"Love the feel of you," he whispered, sliding deep. "Won't hurt you."

As if.

"Relax," he crooned against her throat. "You're so tight around me. Just feel. That's all you need to do, sweet girl. Mmmm... like that."

She'd heard of women having orgasms from penetration alone. Hadn't believed it, personally. But now? Cole had her arms pinned above her head, and every time he eased through her swollen tissues, a prickling awareness sparked. The sensation both wound her up and laid her open, more open than she'd ever been.

"Cole," she said in wonder, "I'll come from this?" Not a question, really, but proper intonation was hard to come by under the circumstances.

"*Yes* you'll come from this—"

The contractions started before he could finish. While the feeling of clenching around his thick shaft was familiar and oh, so welcome, this time her body pulled harder. Spasmed longer.

He worked her madly, drawing the pleasure along a stunning, wet slide.

"It's so strong," he growled. *"You're sucking me under, baby. God, keep coming."*

She did. On and on, like her muscles were hooked to jumper cables. She was still twitching when he stiffened and flooded her body with warmth, gritting a firm, "Always like this, like *you*," in her ear.

Drunk on adrenaline and slowly-receding pleasure, fatigue instantly replaced the sexual high. Lissa lay stunned, slack as a wet ribbon, though anything but regretful.

They hadn't used protection.

"I'm on the pill." She wanted to get the info out in the open, before she descended into the tunnel calling her name.

He pulled her against his chest, preparing to lift her from the floor. "I know," he said quietly. Of course he did. They'd lived together for months. She'd even taken one of the tiny blue pills on the plane between Qatar and Delhi to get the timing right with the twelve hour shift.

"A deal's a deal," he said, standing with her cuddled against his pecs. "Sleep. I'll see you when you wake."

A beat of silence descended before he added, "In *your* bed."

CHAPTER 32

Ten percent humidity at fifty-four-hundred feet sucked a Christmas tree dry long before Santa came to call. Trevor had put off the inevitable needle spray that would come with removing the scorched pine for much longer than that. He circled the tree, eyeing the single string of white lights and the two Target ornaments. He and Rhea managed the minimums, but no one would accuse their house of being a home.

That would change once he hauled out the lumber now masquerading as a holiday. Lissa's painting would soon grace the wall behind the crispy tree, whether his wife liked it or not.

And she did *not*.

Even so, Rhea's resistance mocked the bear hug she gave the canvas in question. So did the hand that idly stroked the suspension wire slung across its back.

To Trevor, hanging the damn thing was a no brainer. Their living room had been decorated with "wall art" from Bed Bath & Beyond while a Lissa Blanc original lived behind their couch. No time like the New Year to spruce up the house and force Rhea to confront leftover... conflictions.

Because Trevor was done with them.

Setting both ornaments aside, Trevor decided the lights could join the tree in the dump.

Rhea sat on the arm of the couch, still clutching the painting. "I'm not ready to hang a gift from your mistress."

"Bummer." Especially since he knew that *she* knew there had never *been* a mistress. Rhea could move on. Or not.

"You're asking too much," she reiterated. Rhea wouldn't beg or plead. That would require heart.

Trevor shrugged and lifted the tree off the ground, stand and all. Instituting his plan while she watched, seemingly from the other side of a thick pane of glass, left him with a curious sense of detachment, an emotional disengagement that brought only relief.

"As they say, shit happens."

He made it around the corner to the hall before he saw Sasha. Behind Cole's dog, Kent rocked from side to side, shifting from one foot to the other in the doorway.

Excellent. *Useful* company had arrived. "Hold the door for a sec?"

Kent ignored him. His uncle looked around the bulk of Trevor and the tree into the living room. His attention landed on Rhea. "I remembered," Kent said.

Trevor let the tree touch the floor. New memories were always welcome. Kent deserved to possess *all* of his past. "Yeah? What came up this time?"

"You," Kent answered, his gaze still locked on Rhea. "And Kate. Having lunch at the St. Julien on *that* day. I saw you through the window on my walk. I've remembered *all* of it."

Kent's explanation held *expectation*. Whatever he'd recalled, he believed telling Rhea would garner a reaction.

Trevor swung around, keen to see what she'd do.

The impenetrable confidence Rhea wore like a shield wavered in the uncertain, almost protective way she tightened her hold on *Sisters*. "We were friends. There were lots and lots of lunches."

Kent's muffled snort sifted through the tree branches. "Not like that one, I'm guessing." Without waiting for another response, Kent pressed. "Now I know why I was so curious before. I wanted to know what exactly happened at that lunch. Because, honestly, if I had to guess, I'd say Kate broke up—"

The tension shattered when Rhea exploded off the couch. Before Kent could finish, she tore through the hall, jostling past Trevor, the tree, a disgruntled Sasha, and a squinting Kent to reach the door.

Lissa's painting never left her arms.

Her shove set the Christmas tree off-kilter. Trevor steadied the wobbling but didn't have time to secure the coat tree flanking the door. The iron rack crashed to the floor, sending Sasha backpedaling into the kitchen.

Within moments, Rhea's car roared to life.

"Jesus," Trevor muttered.

Kent held the door wide so Trevor could at least chuck the tree into the yard. Turning back, Trevor saw that Kent had gone to one knee. His uncle reached out for something on the floor. Item in hand, he froze.

"What?" Trevor lifted the rack and set it in place. Then he retrieved the only jacket that had been hanging—Rhea's hot pink windbreaker.

Instead of standing, Kent lowered himself fully to the floor, shoulders to the wall, like he bore the weight of a hundred years. After a string of taut silence, he looked up at Trevor. Kent had arrived with life in his eyes, bursting with the euphoria of another recollection. The man on the ground had lost that spark. He looked haunted, a dead man still breathing.

Trevor beat back a tide of panic, dropping to his haunches. "Chest pains? Should I call 911?"

Kent held out his palm. "I'm sorry."

With one look at Kent's hand, the heart pounding in Trevor's chest cleaved in two. One side, the forgiving side, fell to sadness. The other dipped into a blazing anger that threatened to burn him from the inside out. His marriage had been crumbling. His wife tended toward the illogical. But this?

Kent held a shallow, circular container. A pill container. The kind of pill container Kent always kept in his breast pocket for emergencies.

The kind missing from Kent's pocket when his heart had called a time-out.

Trevor closed his eyes. When he opened them, he looked at Kent pleadingly, asking the only way he could if he really saw what he thought he did.

Kent nodded solemnly.

They'd found the missing nitroglycerin tabs, and the only place they could have come from was Rhea's pink jacket.

CHAPTER 33

The sheets stretched wide and empty the next morning. Lissa squinted through a dull, beating pain in her skull, but a deep inhale—more like a test breath—proved her lungs were on the up and up.

Lucky, she'd need all her energy for the tricky, lying bastard who hadn't fulfilled his end of their bargain.

She'd like to think Cole had gotten antsy and gone on a coffee run. She knew better.

Nope, he'd steam-cleaned her lungs, railed her silly, and then tucked her into bed before slinking off to nurse his never-ending guilt complex.

In the meantime, she'd dreamt in murky scenes where she'd grown sicker instead of better. A doctor had appeared at her side, and, of course, Cole had featured prominently as the attentive but forceful nurse in Calvin Klein boxer briefs.

Weeks ago, the thought of giving him time had seemed like a mandatory concession to his grief. Days ago, she'd chided herself about patience and given herself a pep talk about accepting the good and releasing the bad that came her way. Hours ago, a two-minute vaginal orgasm courtesy of an out-of-control Cole had equaled good.

This very second, why wasn't it enough?

Testing the waters, she curled into the fetal position and rolled onto her knees, noting that sometime between the bath and this moment, she'd managed to dress herself in a pair of yoga pants and an "Incredible India" tank top. Nothing else. When she could breathe somewhat normally, she unfurled until she sat upright on her shins.

And met Cole's worried stare.

He'd been reading from a tattered piece of paper. Notably, he wore black boxer briefs and tired eyes. Numerous bottles crowded the dresser at his side. Bottles of drugs. The kind a doctor might provide.

Squinting didn't help. The labels were written in Hindi. To her, the text looked like swooping curly-cues connected via a ruler-straight line.

Trying not to furrow her brow in obvious confusion, Lissa considered the bottles, then Cole, then the bottles again.

"Good afternoon," came Cole's deep welcome.

Afternoon? Logic intervened—*Calvins* plus *meds* plus *afternoon* added up to an empty bed that told the wrong story.

"What happened?"

******

Cole pinched the paper between his fingers. Defying logic, Kate's last words always chilled him out when he sensed a loss coming on. Comparatively speaking, nothing could get as bad as her choice to leave, so reminiscing gave him a sick sense of relief about the future.

"Technically," he said, "the air pollution gradually caused a serious case of acute bronchitis. The smoke and exhaust—apparently you don't get enough of that up by Central Park—irritated the air passages in your lungs until they swelled and caused all sorts of excitement. Probably pneumonia, in the end, but I wouldn't let them drag you off for an x-ray."

He'd had a hunch. So of course he'd had sex with her on the floor instead of seeking help. When he'd awakened hours later to Lissa's desperate, flailing attempts to breathe, he'd panicked, meaning if either of them got sick again, they'd need to do it in a different hotel. The doctor currently on call would probably be cowering under his desk for a while.

Unless Lissa had an immediate relapse, then the little man could damn well deal with Cole and the threats of mayhem that came out of his mouth when riddled with worry and regret.

Lissa settled back against the mountain of pillows he'd used to prop her up and ease her breathing. "How did you get me to take the drugs?"

She didn't know? "Amazing how persuasive I can be, and how accommodating you can be, when I play my cards right."

In fact, a relapse—so long as he was assured of a favorable outcome—wouldn't be so bad. His Lissa made a soft, endearing patient when completely out of her mind. "*Thank you,*" she'd murmured. "*Need you, Cole.*"

The day had passed in rounds—an antibiotic, then a cough syrup. When she'd winced in her sleep, he'd gone in with the pain killer. A steroid had topped off the cocktail, along with one of those birth control pills she'd made sure to mention. Each time he'd coaxed her to open her pretty lips, she'd obeyed with an abandon he suspected hadn't surfaced since infancy.

Lissa had swallowed her meds, both vulnerable and incoherent, and then burrowed against him for to sleep. "*Don't go, Cole.*" He hadn't. Only after she'd slumped into oblivion had he allowed himself to leave the bed, and then only to a bedside chair to watch her sleep.

And to read.

Far from recovered and probably still slightly dazed, she murmured to herself, "I *do* like persuasive." Then, her head stretched forward from her shoulders, straining toward his letter. "Whatcha reading?"

There goes the reprieve.

He folded Kate's letter along worn lines, returning his wife's parting words to an innocuous, portable square. "Nothing important." *At least to you.*

"Looks old."

"Not at all." *Two years is practically new. Carrying it around for that long is totally normal.*

Life hit new lows when a man didn't believe his own thoughts.

Lissa's fingers crawled forward across the bed. "Can I see this not-that-old piece of non-importance?"

Too bad underwear didn't have pockets. That one lame fact left him with nowhere to stash the evidence.

******

Lissa couldn't pinpoint exactly why, but she wanted to read Cole's secret letter. Badly. Probably because of the wary defensiveness that flickered across his features before fading away to nothingness. Now he sank into lounging insolence, but it would take a better actor to disguise the fact that the tattered sheet had meaning he'd prefer not to share.

A decision loomed. She owed him for a few trivials, like seeing her through the night, fetching a doctor, and coaxing her through dose after dose of drugs. Memories were popping up one after another. Cole had cocooned her in the bed. Each and every dose, down to the last pill and tablespoon, had gone down with his body stretched around hers... sitting her up, handing over the water chaser, whispering that he knew she'd feel better if she took one more swallow for him.

And sure enough, she could breathe again. Her chest pulled tight, and her body ached with the physical memory of the night's strain, but she could breathe. Funny how first worlders, with their overabundance of doctors and pharmacies and a 911 system that actually worked, took things like "not dying from bronchitis" for granted. Here, waking up and realizing you could only access a limited amount of air deserved the DEFCON 5 treatment.

The Cole treatment.

Not to say that Nurse Betty in his chair should get to lie. He hadn't fibbed about sleeping in the same bed, but he wasn't telling the truth right now. Sick or not—better because of him, or not—those days when she gave him a hall pass had met their end.

Moving sluggishly against her lingering malaise, she crawled toward the edge of the bed, closer to Cole and his sentinel spot. "You saved me from—"

"It's bronchitis, Lissa, not lung cancer."

Cole used bored and superior like a bulletproof vest. He seemed to think nothing could get past him so long as he had his smug shored up. "Regardless," she replied, not sparing a glance at the note clutched in his fist or the distinct ab muscles that clenched behind it, "a woman needs oxygen, and I wasn't getting any. So, thank you."

She got a nod for her trouble. A grudging one, but discernible all the same. Seemed like as good a time as any—

Lissa sprang forward. He hadn't seen *that* coming from Sicky MaGee. Before he could jerk back—or up or to the side or even pull the note out of reach—she snatched the paper right out of his hand.

Back on the bed, she scrambled to the headboard, sure he'd be on her tail. Balled up in the furthest corner of the mattress, with the note tucked against her tummy, she knew he either wouldn't get to the thing or the getting would be entertaining… in a "go ahead, stretch my limbs wide and go for my tender underside *I dare you*," kind of way.

A few seconds passed. Then a minute. Then two without a sound or even a dent in the mattress. Cole was letting her get away. Still wondering at his game, she craned her head around and took a look. He sat in the chair, gravestone still, with his arms crossed over his pecs. Long, muscular legs spread wide in front of him, a GQ pose that didn't work with the steam rising from the top of his head.

When he didn't make a move, relief slackened her taut muscles, letting her straighten to the position she'd woken up in a few minutes before. She lifted the note in front of her face and let it dangle. "I *will* read this," she promised meaningfully. *Last chance.*

He made no move to stop the inevitable.

Slowly, with all the purpose of a woman who'd invaded another's privacy and thought doing so boldly might somehow heal the transgression, she unfolded the paper.

And she started to read.

If you're reading this… I know you believe me.

The writing curled in a flowery, feminine script. Lissa's heart decelerated, dragging with the kind of beat that predicts what's coming and tries to stop the train wreck by slowing the fuck down. Only one woman in the world could have written Cole a letter that he'd be reading at another woman's bedside thousands of miles from home.

Cole cut in, caustic and challenging. "You see, Kate wrote that my believing her didn't matter. She felt the fact that I'd asked the question in the first place had destroyed her. Had destroyed us."

Lissa suspended her disbelief that this was actually happening and read on.

Perhaps your suspicion means you know something about me that I'm finally learning.

Stomach cramping and afraid, literally scared to absorb the next and final line, Lissa looked up. Cole hadn't moved. Now he challenged her with his calm. "Don't stop now, not when you worked so hard for the privilege."

Right, the privilege of reading her first suicide note. Why couldn't Lissa, for once, have left him alone? Dreading the onslaught of knowledge she needed but desperately didn't want, Lissa returned to the page.

"I'll help," Cole interrupted again. "She wrote that without my trust, she couldn't go on. And here you wanted to know how I *know* I killed her."

Never could my choice be your fault. Yet, without you, I don't know how to make it.

Not what Lissa had expected. "How good was Kate with grammar?"

"*What?* Fuck you, Lissa, to ask that at a time like this."

Lissa braced herself against Cole's oppressive fury. She hadn't been joking. "Was she an astute writer? Because if so, this letter is *not* what you think—"

A wave of coughing overtook Lissa's revelation, and Cole shot to her side with a brown bottle of syrup. "Open up."

She obeyed, and within seconds another shot of codeine careened through her system.

"This last sentence"—Lissa held the note out to Cole—"clarifies the previous one. When she says she doesn't know how to 'make it,' she's referring to making the choice she faced, not an inability to 'make it' amongst the living."

Cole grabbed the letter and crushed it against his chest. "Hair splitting."

"If that's what you call reading two related sentences and assigning them the meaning they were intended." *Stupid man. Stupid, injured man.*

The letter acknowledged Cole's fading suspicions. Kate had known the raging waters had subsided, yet to her, his initial fears meant he'd known something important about *her*, a secret Kate herself had been figuring out.

Air hovered beneath Lissa's nose, at her lips. She could hardly force it down, and this time the breathing difficulty had nothing to do with infected lungs. "Cole, why did you accuse Kate in the first place?"

He jerked back, taking the note with him when he left the room. Probably for the best. Kate's words were forever branded on Lissa's brain, and Cole only grew agitated when he saw the thing in her hands. He could withhold his letter but not his answers.

She dogged him across the suite and into his room, almost relieved when he pulled on his loose-fitting nylon pants and a sweatshirt. *Almost.*

"Why," she said again, "did two parked cars at the same hotel—an occurrence with a million legitimate excuses—make you question your wife's fidelity? You had *another* reason."

He approached the window and looked out at the Taj Mahal, which fought an ongoing fight for supremacy against a shroud of brownish-gray clouds, keeping his shoulders to the room like he could kill the conversation with rigid posture. "I had *every* reason."

"So narrow them down."

"No."

Make that stubborn, *stupid, injured man.* "That letter says you knew something about Kate that left her with a choice. Seems like she thought you might blame yourself for her decision, and I don't think that decision boiled down to 'jump' or 'live life to the fullest.'"

Never could my choice be your fault. Yet, without you, I don't know how to make it.

"She wanted your input. Last time I checked, one generally doesn't *ask* her spouse if she should hurl herself into a ravine. That can't be what she was debating."

Quiet stole over the room. Then, fraction by fraction, the tension in Cole's body released. He turned, and for the first time since she and Cole had met, he appeared... confused, blue eyes gone vague and searching.

If only Lissa had answers to her endless string of questions. "Your wife was *torn*—learning herself and fighting herself and hoping you could make it better. What was she torn about?"

"*Me,*" Cole answered, his voice hoarse and final.

Lissa tapped her toes. Cole didn't elaborate.

"And?" she prompted.

Dark, flinty emotion bled into his stare. "The things you want from me, in *sickness* and in health, she... avoided." A bitter traction took hold with each additional word. "She didn't beg me to fuck her on the bathroom floor. She never let me go down on her in the cab of my truck. The bathroom was for bathing, the truck for driving, and the bed for sleeping."

The rough descriptions should have put Lissa off, but she leaned forward for more. "A lame sex life—one more thing I *don't* generally equate with suicide."

"No, only with infidelity."

"Ah." This time it was Lissa who sank into a bedside chair. "If not from you, then sex must have come from elsewhere. Right?" Sarcasm leached into the question, but how could the man be so dense?

Cole shook his head. "At first I thought it a normal slow down. But the longer we went—months—the more I suspected her depression. We treated that, and she seemed to be doing better. She planted flowers and cooked dinners. Her clientele in Boulder grew beyond her capacity. She spent time with friends. But her sex drive? Nothing. When I accused her of being with Trevor, she unraveled."

"Because you were wrong."

Cole scrubbed a hand through his shaggy curls. "Can we stop? You've heard it all… from the root of our problems to the fact that they were irrevocably, pretty much inhumanely, my fault."

Lissa contemplated an intricate rug beneath her feet. Interlocking patterns swirled into a mix that, taken separately, made a mess, yet as a whole, made a museum-worthy work of art. She closed her eyes, still seeing the blues and greens dance against the backs of her eyelids. A knocking had started in her skull about the time she'd read Kate's first word. Not a headache signaling a shutdown before she let too much in, but an insistence that she gather more, that she pay attention.

That internal thump, thump, thump grew louder. She'd saved Cole from his slavery to realism with his own pictures. She'd save him from his guilt with his own words. "Who gave Kate my painting?"

"I did. You know that."

Nice try. "Not *Redemption.*" The pretty one. "*Revenge.*" The dark one hidden beneath the bed.

"Can't you guess?"

If not, she could search her records. For now, Lissa focused on connecting the dots pounding away in her head. They spelled out an answer that fluttered beyond her reach, a blinking neon sign with a few too many missing bulbs.

Opening her eyes, Lissa reasoned out loud. "I suppose one person might have found *Revenge* an apt gift."

Cole half-nodded, half-shrugged. "Yeah—"

"The only other person who felt betrayed by Kate and Trevor's supposed affair." *Who still feels betrayed.*

"Getting warmer—"

"Rhea."

The knocking went quiet.

******

"Exactly." Cole watched a stealthy smile spread across Lissa's lips and bit down on his own. What good would all this do? He'd let Lissa see the note to *end* her craving for answers but had gotten the opposite result. The woman must lead a double life as a conspiracy theorist.

"So the two of them dueled in code?" she asked. Then, under her breath, "Rhea doesn't hate like normal people."

"There's a right way?" If so, he wouldn't mind perfecting his methods.

Lissa shrugged. "After Kate presented Rhea with *Sisters*, Rhea set the work aside and responded with a cryptic gift of her own—*Revenge*—which stopped just shy of a threat." She stood and worked on wearing a track in the rug. "I'm guessing Kate gave Rhea *Sisters* during happier times. After you burst the bubble with your theory about cross-pollination between the two marriages, Rhea retaliated with a painting that told Kate the last thing she wanted was a lying, cheating sister."

All true. After losing her husband's trust, Kate's best friend had gone next.

Lissa paced faster and faster, hands wringing at her side.

"Lissa," Cole murmured, inching away from the window toward her progressing flame-out.

She spun around. "Don't patronize me. You have to accept that Rhea *plays* at the hate feeding your prickling conscious. All the cryptic messages? The latent hostility? They're empty because she knows Kate did nothing wrong. When I told Rhea I suspected her of faking, she didn't deny it, not outright."

Suddenly, Lissa lifted a shaky hand to her forehead, and Cole lunged forward, wrapping her against his chest. "I shouldn't have showed you the letter."

"They're related," she insisted, sounding too thready to be convincing. "Not-so-coincidentally, Rhea's erratic behavior makes as little sense as Kate's note. Whatever Kate was trying to decide has to have caused, or have been caused by, Rhea's withdrawal."

A hesitant knock sounded on the door.

Lissa's gaze shot to his. She looked feverish and frantic. "Don't answer. Not now. We can figure this out."

The madness of her plea yanked a thread of logic that had gone dormant. After their first awful morning in Colorado had planted nagging seeds of doubt, Cole had attributed her schemes to manipulations, to poorly-played attempts to snag herself a project puppet. Now, looking down at the desperation in her flushed face, he realized Lissa only wanted to release his guilt and grief. Managing him hadn't been the goal, not for a long while, maybe not ever.

His chest ached beneath her resting chin. This beautiful, infuriating woman tried to solve a nonexistent puzzle because she cared, powering through enough hydrocodone to tranq a horse in an attempt convince him he'd had nothing to do with his wife's death.

The selflessness, misguided but unrelenting, destroyed him.

No more letting her crusade on his behalf. Cradling Lissa's cheeks, he hardened his tone, "Lie down. You're exhausted. Drugged."

For you, I'm letting go.

He clenched. Beside her upturned face, he saw the tattered edges of Kate's letter—ground zero of his eventual spiral—wedged between his index and middle fingers.

The knocking on the door sounded again, more forceful.

Cole stepped back and snapped, "I'm coming." Before Lissa could utter one more syllable, he shredded the paper, leaving nothing but confetti to drift to the floor. The act left him feeling light, suddenly free to share the feelings formerly trapped in Kate's words.

A discrete clearing of a throat sounded through the wood. "It's Sonu, sir."

Cole flashed a dark glance at the door. "A minute!" He wasn't moving an inch until Lissa was flat on her back. Breathing harshly, he returned a perceptive stare to the woman barely able to stand in front of him. He waited, tapping a foot like he had all day. When she stood her ground, he growled, "Bed. *Now.*"

"Lissa closed her mouth, sucking her teeth in a way that said any silence might be brief. But she plodded to his four poster and climbed aboard. Lying back, she pulled the covers to her chin and rolled until Cole stared at her curving profile from the rear.

"Thank you." *For once.*

At the door, Sonu held out a cell phone, appearing slightly shaken but conscientious as ever. "Your brother calls the hotel again and again." Made sense. Cole had silenced his and Lissa's electronics so she could sleep.

His long-time driver went on, looking at the floor while he spoke. "Sir, your brother's wife…"

Not this again. "What?"

"She's, well, she's tried to kill your uncle."

The gasp that flew over Cole's shoulder said Lissa's rest would be short-lived.

CHAPTER 34

By the time Cole hung up, Lissa had packed her bag. He found her in her bedroom, stuffing medications into a carry-on. Dark lashes lifted from her pale cheeks as she met his gaze, pupils dilated with uncanny knowledge. Determination burned through the weariness he'd seen before. "You can explain what 'tried to kill' means on the way," she whispered. "We're going home."

Somehow he knew "home" meant Colorado.

Reaching out, Cole passed a hand over her shoulder. She trembled beneath his touch—not so recovered after all. Her distress reached him where her earlier logic had not. "Why do you care so much? India and I are your golden tickets, remember?"

She zipped her backpack with a yank and turned to face him head on. "You have to ask?"

He couldn't take his hand from shoulder. She shook, violently now. The initial tremors might have been weakness left over from the long night. This was anger. "I don't understand, baby. You *need* what we're building here." More like *he* needed her to need it, giving him a purpose more noble than the lies he'd told about assuaging his guilt.

Moisture obscured the intense look in her eyes before her lashes again drifted downward. "That's not true anymore."

His stomach clenched with two years' worth of fear. "What isn't?"

"I don't need *this*." She threw her arms wide, as though she could embrace an entire country with two slender hands. "I relied on my family, too much and then some. To escape the dependence, I leveraged *your* name. You were the nicotine patch to their three packs a day."

Lissa slowly opened her eyes. She'd gotten control, gaze bleary but tearless. "I don't need either. I'll trust my talent. Give it time."

"Like you did with me." Lissa had challenged his judgment with each refusal to compromise. The tactic had worked. She had a new fan.

He sucked in a long, painful breath. Lissa *didn't* need him. And she wanted to leave.

"Home" hadn't meant Colorado after all.

"Of course." He looked away. The fear of losing her—or at least his chance to have her—gave way to the searing knowledge that he'd already lost. *Time's up. I cared too late.* "Sonu will get us to the airport."

Hoping like hell the numbness he'd conquered would rise again and take over, Cole started across the suite with long, measured strides.

"You idiot!"

Her maniacal shout stopped him at the halfway point. Cole turned back. Color had swamped the parchment of Lissa's cheeks. Without thinking, he pictured the first time he'd made her flush with emotion. He'd loved the look of her then.

He loved *her* now.

A smack in the chest brought him out of the quick reverie. Lissa stood in front of him, heaving, *enraged*. "You think I want to leave so I can flutter away and sell pretty pictures? That I got what I wanted and now I'm done?"

Never particularly wise, Cole at least had the foresight to let the questions pass. With her hands almost around his neck, he took advantage. Grabbing her hips, he pulled her whole body flush with his. Even drug-logged and recently bedridden, his armful of pissed-off smelled like *cake*.

She kept yelling.

"I don't need your *name*, Cole, to succeed. Or your *help*. What I need is a bit more basic."

Relief poured into his veins like a soothing balm. Fuck numbness. Numb couldn't handle Lissa's velocity, the fact that she sped from injured to accusatory faster than she switched from smelling like raspberries to frosting.

Gripping her tight, he gathered his presence of mind. Curse her for being a perfect, perfect fool. His Lissa planned to throw away his help in favor of helping him.

"Cole, I need *you*." Her volume leveled out, and his chest tightened at the uncertainty masked within the bold statement, as though she worried her feelings might be unrequited. "*All* of you," she asserted, softly now, "not just the part here with me here in India. I can lose this project." She paused. "I *can*. But I can't lose you to a past that's already half eaten you alive. We have to go back to stop the feast."

No, no, *no*. Cole gently shackled her biceps and pushed her to arm's length, searching her earnest face. Such irony—Lissa offered a sacrifice she could ill afford at the exact time he realized he didn't need it. Kate had gone away, the how and why now reduced to nothing more than an intellectual puzzle. For too long he'd clung to the imagined perfection of a deeply flawed marriage with no place in his future. That image had joined Kate's annihilated letter on his bedroom floor, in pieces ready to be swept away.

But Lissa couldn't know that. Nor would she take his word after overhearing Sonu's announcement about the happenings in Colorado. Returning wouldn't change a thing, not for him, but maybe it would prove to Lissa exactly how much everything had changed for *them*.

A slight tug brought her back to his chest, and he pressed his lips to the roots of her hair. "Of course," he said, repeating his earlier answer but with whole new meaning. "Sonu will get us to the airport."

CHAPTER 35

January—Boulder, Colorado

"What do you mean, 'She's still gone?'" Cole lowered himself to Trevor's kitchen table, leaning toward the pill case resting at its center. A hired car, two planes, a bus, a cab, and thirty-nine hours had reduced India to a distant memory.

Snow fell beyond the kitchen window in a steadily growing blanket that clung to the side of the house. A radio on the counter squawked about flight cancellations and a crawling morning commute. He and Lissa had landed just in time.

Cole took a deep breath. He'd make this up to her.

For now, something is rotten in Boulder.

Trevor hunched over the opposite corner of the table, impossibly still. The heft of the man's broad shoulders looked strangely diminished, like he'd shed twenty pounds overnight. Charm had abandoned his sunbaked features, and he spoke only when spoken to.

Cole got the feeling Trevor battled a seething fury he wasn't conditioned to manage, not after a life spent tempering the edges of his brutal size and looks with a core of decentness. If Rhea had purposefully compromised their uncle, the bars coming her way might be the only barrier that could save her from a husband more than ready to get back to what nature had originally intended.

"I *mean*," Trevor eventually answered, "the bitch bolted when Kent arrived with his epiphany."

Grimacing at Trevor's harshness, Kent cut in with a comparatively glossed accounting—at least next to Trevor's telling over the phone—of what Kent had started calling the "trouble with the Christmas tree." He spoke of the memory of the lunch he'd cultivated for so long, his unannounced arrival at the bungalow, and Rhea's abrupt departure. Unsure whether the nitro tabs would've helped, Kent made it clear he could forgive and forget for the sake of keeping the peace, ending with, "Rhea doesn't even know about the pills." The silent rider, "*And she never has to,*" reverberated off the kitchen walls.

"*No.*" Trevor surged upright in his chair. "She doesn't know *we* know about the pills." The reproach in his tone warned them to give his wife the benefit of the doubt at their own peril.

Lissa had hoisted herself onto the kitchen counter, legs dangling. Throughout the long explanations, she stayed unnaturally quiet. The meds had helped her condition, but the traveling hadn't.

As Kent and Trevor added logs to the fire of uncertainty surrounding Rhea's possible desire to hasten Kent's demise, Lissa never revealed Kate's suicide note or how Lissa had mentally linked Kate's decision to take her own life with Rhea's obsessive hostility.

She let Cole keep his secrets.

After forty hours and counting, they were left with little choice but to assume the worst of Rhea's disappearance. Cole stood and dug through a kitchen drawer until he found a sandwich bag. He scooped up the pill case with a Kleenex and dropped it in the plastic pouch. "Do we call the police or lie in wait?"

Trevor and Kent spoke in unison.

"We call—"

"We'll wait—"

Lissa hopped off the counter and left the room, reappearing with her coat and gloves. She didn't vote for either of the passive alternatives on offer. Instead, she said the one thing guaranteed to get action.

"I know where Rhea is."

*****

Both highways leading to Melina remained open. Lissa didn't doubt the physical ability to drive west, but the practicality of doing so thinned the air in Trevor's truck. Blowing snow pelted the windshield. Ice overtook the glass at a rate that challenged the defroster, leaving only small half-circles of visibility in front of Trevor at the wheel and Kent in shotgun.

Cole and Lissa flanked Sasha between them, riding blind in the backseat.

Tense and silent, Trevor navigated with one sure hand on the steering wheel and another balanced on the stick shift. He whipped the four-wheel drive around the curves of Boulder Canyon, almost daring the cliffs rising to their right or the plunge into Boulder Creek falling to their left to smite him. "We will *ski* in if we have to."

Lissa opened her mouth to suggest they delay pursuing her hunch about

Rhea's whereabouts. They could do this later. Maybe next week. Before she could utter a word, a tight squeeze imprinted high on her thigh. Cole merely shook his head at her responsive eye daggers.

Quiet, he daggered back.

Perhaps she should have voiced her intuitions more eloquently. She could have said, "I *might* know where Rhea is," or "It makes sense—to me at least, but what the hell do I know—that Rhea could be at Melina."

Instead, she'd injected her words with the certainty of an inspirational quote from the Dalai Lama. And, what do you know? The four of them were hugging a race track pregnant with black ice and horizontal snow on their way to Lissa's proposed destination.

An hour after vacating the bungalow, Trevor killed the truck in Melina's circular drive. A relieved sigh escaped Lissa's compressed lips, its purpose twofold. First, they were alive. Second, they'd parked next to Rhea's vehicle.

Inside, the house sat still. Lissa didn't detect a television show or any music. Not even an indoor bike-a-thon disturbed the quiet. Despite the lull in activity, two plates bordered the kitchen sink. One held the remnants of a sandwich, the other only crumbs. Fitness magazines littered the counter, and a throw blanket hung drunkenly over one of the stools. Sasha found his sealed food bin and rested a massive head on the lid.

The evidence of habitation, minus one specific inhabitant, made the constriction left over from the trip up the canyon cinch tighter in her chest.

Lissa hadn't wanted to be right.

She opened the back door and examined the expanse of white spreading to the trees bordering Cole's property. No footprints, but she supposed the snow fell too hard to expect a dead giveaway. Angling her head toward the trail she couldn't see, Lissa considered their options.

"I don't know who should go first," she said absently. "Rhea might have harmed Kent directly, so there's a vote for him. She's your wife, Trevor, so you're fully invested. And then there's Cole." Rounding on the man in question, Lissa said something she knew the others wouldn't understand. "Once married to the woman who brought Rhea here in the first place."

Their eyes met in a clash that changed everything. Tenderness bled into the set of Cole's mouth, releasing the tension that habitually gathered at his eyes and in the set of his jaw. He took a slow step closer, shutting his relatives out. A curt shake of his head told her that, *no*, he wouldn't be first in line for whatever she had in mind.

His refusal to cooperate was nothing new. Yet *this* time the reticence came from a different place. Somewhere between the look that said she could have whatever she wanted except his desertion in favor of his sister-in-law and his close proximity that swept across her nerves like a physical stroke, Lissa realized *why* he wouldn't follow along.

Cole hadn't come to Colorado or Melina for himself. He'd come because Lissa had asked him to. And he wouldn't be leaving her behind.

With an impatient chuff, Trevor lifted Lissa by the shoulders and set her away from the door, whirling her around so she stood back-to-chest against Cole. Then, peering between her face and the empty yard, Trevor scrutinized the direction of her automatic attention. "You think my wife is sitting at Kate's grave," he growled, his disbelief apparent. "On a Wednesday morning. In the middle of a blizzard."

Lissa swallowed, hesitant to meet Trevor's stare. "I know she is."

******

In the end, Cole sent his uncle and his brother out together. He stayed behind with Lissa, who stood at the screen door tapping a finger to her lips, head cocked. He didn't blame her trepidation. If Lissa's theory held, Rhea had commandeered another woman's grave, and she'd soon confront the wrath of a man she may or may not have nudged toward death's door and a husband none too happy with her deceit.

Trevor and Kent disappeared around the last visible bend into the trees, dressed for a coming of the next ice age like native Boulderites—North Face from the top down, convertible gloves, ear-flap hats, rubber boots good for January ice fishing or a muddy spring thaw. The layers might be their only insulation against an ugly awakening waiting around that corner.

Lissa rubbed at the back of her neck. "You should go along."

Studying her, Cole found her expression too carefully neutral. He reminded himself that she too bore the weight of their search, perhaps more than any of them since this wasn't her fight. "Why?"

"We came thousands of miles for answers. At least take the last few steps."

The easy lie doubled as a dare, implying he couldn't bear to hear news that might involve Kate. The trick pricked his temper. "I think you know I didn't come for answers." *I came for you.*

She nodded. "But I did, and certainly not to get them for myself." Right. She wanted them for him. What a pair they were.

Lissa abandoned the view in favor of stacking the magazines Rhea had left on the counter. Next she folded the throw. Still ignoring him, she attacked the dishes. Bit by bit, order reclaimed the kitchen with only the occasional searching look flicked his direction. Towel and dish in hand, he swore Lissa's gaze darted briefly to the latched door above the basement, but in a flash, her focus returned to the drying of Rhea's cast-off plates.

She was waiting him out.

Cole stepped in and took the dish, then the towel. No matter what happened at that grave, he'd be solid. "Lissa, I don't need—"

"Shhh," she said quietly, bringing her finger to his lips. She drew even closer, as though her message could only be said against his neck. "They haven't returned, which means she's there." Warm lips landed on his jaw. "Go." A nuzzle. "Don't ask me why. This one last time, please just do it."

Well, when she asked like that...

He ruffled Sasha's fur and grabbed his coat off a kitchen chair. Voices rang out as he neared Kate's garden. With the knowledge of impending closure, the burdens of guilt and amends lifted, floating into the ether like the snowflakes swirling in his wake.

Hidden agenda or not, Lissa was onto something—facing demons became worthwhile when the act of facing them set them free.

The scene in the trees stopped Cole short about fifteen feet from his wife's headstone. The rock garden had been cleared of snow. Neatly shoveled paths darted around each boulder, and crimson poinsettias flanked the walkways, stark against the white. A few of the surrounding trees sparkled with slim ribbons of garland.

Time and thought—likely a great deal of both—had gone into transforming Kate's spartan resting place into a winter wonderland.

Why?

Rhea knelt before Kate's engraving, her profile bleached as white as the ground. Tendrils of flaming hair whipped above shivering shoulders that swam inside an old coat taken from Cole's mud room.

Trevor crouched at her side, dangling the bagged pill case in midair. Kent stood a distance away, leaning on a rock and nodding to himself. "I was right," he muttered.

Cole stepped into the clearing. "About what?"

Rhea's head jerked to Cole with such force he wondered how she didn't snap her neck. "About Kate."

Patience. "Let's go with a little less cryptic."

Seemingly blind to Cole's arrival, Trevor stared at Rhea with eyes soaked in intelligence and pain. He brought to mind an injured predator, fiercely loyal yet capable of lashing out when over-provoked. "Tell him," Trevor demanded.

Defeat settled over Rhea's shoulders, and she slumped fully to the ground. Finally, after a few taut moments of reflection, she reached for Trevor, who stiffened but let her hold his free hand. A moment of visible understanding passed between the couple before Rhea's voice, thick with dread, sliced through the wind. "It was me." She swallowed. "The day you pegged Trevor and Kate at the hotel? *I* met Kate that day. Kent saw us. At first I didn't know he'd been there, but over time he began asking questions, leading questions I couldn't answer."

"Why would you care?" Cole wondered aloud.

She ignored him, lost to the story. "I put him off with increasing... enthusiasm. But the fewer answers I provided, the more questions he asked.

The morning of his heart attack"—she sent Kent a pleading glance—"we were loading the fridge as usual. He laid out a theory and threatened to tell you both."

The slow slide of panic inched up Cole's throat. "What did he guess?"

Blind to Cole's rising sense of urgency, Rhea kept talking. "I *couldn't* let you know. Then everything would have been for nothing."

Rhea plays at the hate, Lissa had said.

"What were you hiding?" Cole's whisper barely rose above the accusations swimming in his head.

"When Kent fell—I swear I didn't cause his attack—I panicked, went for his pills. That's all. Nothing else."

"That's all?" Kent echoed faintly.

Looking right at Kent, Rhea promised, "I never wanted you to die. I just didn't want you to talk. Instinct won."

Cole almost doubled over. Hell of an instinct. "Tell me what you knew about my wife."

Rhea flashed Cole a scathing look, but the bravado didn't mask her regret. Or her fear. She let go of Trevor's slack hand and stood, stroking Kate's headstone as though it were the most familiar act in the world. "Kent saw your wife refuse me." She snatched her hand away. "Kate said she couldn't leave you, that how she—how *we* felt—had to be extinguished."

A ragged sob wrenched out of Rhea's throat, and Trevor shot up. Never able to watch suffering without wanting to help, he pulled his wife into a loose embrace. "Rhea, don't do this—"

Lancelot to the end.

"Kent had to forget," Rhea whispered, so low Cole strained to hear. "He knew how we felt. He knew I loved her."

"Then why"—Lissa emerged from the trees, an all-too-familiar box clutched high against her chest—"did you kill her?"

CHAPTER 36

Lissa had known her claim would be a bomb. She hadn't realized it would also be a test. As soon as the inflammatory words left her lips, the men whipped to attention, horror drawn in tight, disbelieving lines bracketing chilled faces. Similarities Lissa hadn't noticed jumped out. Cole might be the lean version of his brother's bulk, but when clenched, the two shared a jawline as harsh as any of the jagged rocks in the clearing. All three shared their imposing height, and Lissa would never have guessed Kent's reliably warm gaze could go as glacial as Cole's.

Of course Rhea looked different than the men, but she also *acted* different. Despite being almost positive of Rhea's guilt, Lissa had expected shock and outrage. Yet the woman shrank away from the husband who'd been holding her, so obviously willing—at least in the moment—to offer a second chance.

And then there was the box Lissa hugged like a child with a beloved puppy.

Cole came forward and put his hands on top of hers. Staring at her strangely, he whispered, for her ears only, "Are you all right?" The unexpected concern made her revelation all the more heartbreaking.

She nodded carefully.

Cole began to pluck her fingers from the cardboard, lifting the box from her grip a scant inch at a time. As she looked into his eyes, she saw alarm and a fierce need to help. "Please," he said gently. "Let me have it. Tell us your story."

Lissa blinked. It was so hard for this man to say *please* that she let go. On a deep breath, she watched Cole retreat with the prize and considered the lifetime that had passed since leaving Trevor and Rhea's kitchen.

Melina had attested to its invasion in more ways than scattered reading materials and dirty dishes. If the house had been pristine, Lissa would still have guessed at Rhea's presence.

The door leading to the basement had been closed.

A person less suspecting—Cole, for instance—might have missed the significance, even though he'd been the one to prop the door open on their departure for India. In their absence, he'd wanted the heat from the main floor to circulate and guard against frozen pipes routed from below. To Lissa, the closed door had meant someone had followed behind them with a visit to the basement, later shutting the door as a reflex.

Rhea being the prime candidate.

She'd sidetracked Cole with a strong suggestion about joining the merrymaking in the rock garden. While Lissa had shared her inklings about a connection between Kate and Rhea—one far fonder than Rhea let on—Lissa had not revealed her fears of foul play. She hadn't wanted to muddle Cole's perception of Kate's death with unfounded suspicions.

Nodding toward the box and then Rhea in turn, Lissa asked, "Recognize the show-and-tell?"

Cole lifted the cardboard higher. Trevor and Kent shifted on anxious feet, both looking confused. All were getting more than they'd bargained for.

Rhea took a step back, but Kate's stone-bound eulogy stopped her retreat.

Don't drag it out. Lissa faced off against the woman who'd once loomed so large. "Your irrational anger flirted with too many minor deceptions. One day you insisted Kate had been a cheating whore who'd violated the sanctity of your marriage. The next you eyed the painting she gave you, constantly monitoring its position but refusing to mount it on the wall. You maintained this gravesite, even after being asked to stay away. Claiming you never wanted Kate 'for a sister' only betrayed the fact that you wanted her for something else. I saw you sit in front of that rock"—Lissa pointed to the headstone—"and trace out the letters now kissing the backs of your knees."

L. O. V. E. D.

Listing Rhea's little reveals made them all the more damning. "You cared enough to see every blade of grass clipped and every flake of snow shoveled, but when she lived, you returned her gestures of friendship and family with veiled threats. Is that because she spurned you?"

Rhea's eyes flared, broken and dangerous. "She *loved* me."

"Yet in the end she didn't *choose* you."

"She *wanted* to."

"Maybe," Lissa countered. "But if yours had been a mutual case of star-crossed love, why—at least after Kate's death—didn't you acknowledge that the Kate-and-Trevor angle had been a mistake? No one would have guessed at what came before. Why did you make a part-time job out of proving your hatred and distrust, in life and in death?"

With each new piece of the puzzle, Lissa drifted closer to Rhea. "You laid a fake trail to make sure no one suspected the infidelity rested on *your* shoulders, which would have pointed right to your violent secret. You're no better than the bookie who bets on the little guy in the fight when you've been supplying the big guy with his steroids. The bet's just a diversion."

"You don't know what you're talking about," Rhea choked.

No? "What's in the box?"

When Rhea looked at the burden in Cole's arms, she shuddered.

Well, well, well. "I'll give you a hint—it's the last you saw of Kate."

Lissa knew the truth to the fiber of her being. The past few minutes had resolved weeks of discordant hunches and lingering doubts.

On the heels of Cole's departure for the garden, and wearing only her winter hat as spider-armor for the sake of an emergency, Lissa had ventured past that closed door and into the basement. She'd found Cole's collection of Kate's belongings in the corner, some boxes unstacked and open as though abandoned mid-search, others lined up and waiting. One box in particular had drawn her attention. In truth, that small, neat package had bothered Lissa on and off since she'd accidentally stumbled upon it in her own search of the basement weeks ago.

The single known quantity had sat high on the discard pile.

Lissa remembered how Cole had caressed the side with a loving hand, seeming loath to leave Kate's things in the dark beneath the house. Then, inexplicably and without a hint of explanation, he'd closed up, flippantly extending his permission to continue on with the box and the hiking gear it contained.

This time Lissa searched for details, any clue or confirmation to help her cause. The top and all four sides of the cardboard were nondescript and unhelpful. Not a name. Not a date. No inventory. But now Lissa knew where to look.

Inside, Kate's Nikon nestled within a familiar yellow shirt. Turning the camera on, Lissa pressed the playback button and saw a blank screen. She looked around at the neat piles in her midst, uncertain whether Rhea had tampered with the contents of this one particular box. With an audible click, the camera went dark. Another press brought the screen back to life.

This time the screen wasn't empty. Confused, Lissa toggled the camera on and off. Sometimes the pictures living in Lissa's memory showed bright against the dim overhead lights. Other times the device hoarded its secrets.

Iteratively working the power and playback buttons, Lissa clicked until she saw a tree-lined sky in early morning and then—yes!—a picture of Rhea pedaling toward the camera, head down above a pair of clunky hiking boots that barely fit over slim pedals. Instinctively, Lissa zeroed in on the date and time stamp—January fourth, 7:27 am, two years prior.

The next photo showed Kate's exuberant selfie in the yellow top—January fourth, 7:57 am, two years prior.

The exact date of Kate's death hadn't been bandied about, but Kate had died in the winter, off the ledge of a hiking trail not far from Melina, approximately two years prior. Right about the time Rhea had been in the same place at the same time despite a damning claim.

The day I'd hike with that woman, Rhea had said.

A day otherwise known as January fourth in the world of non-pathological liars.

As natural as chocolate and red wine, Lissa's mind wandered to Cole. When he'd found her pillaging the wrong end of his man cave, he'd instinctively reached for Kate's box of hiking gear, seeming to channel care through his fingers and, at the same time, forever release the hold the contents had over him.

Like a lover saying farewell.

A whisper in Lissa's mind breathed, *Yes, exactly*. And in that paralyzing instant, the air whooshed from the room. Cold, painful certainty roared between Lissa's ears, leaving her gripping her forehead in a belated attempt to push the knowledge back out.

Lissa had witnessed Cole's last good-bye to his wife's final effects, final effects that included a yellow jersey and a camera placing Rhea where she claimed to never have been.

Dizzy with the horrific implications of the discovery, several competing prescriptions, and tens of hours confined to planes, trains, and automobiles, Lissa melted to the concrete floor, buffeted by the onslaught of too many coincidences—the pictures, the dates, the matching yellow in Kate's good-bye box and the photographs taken on the right winter's day, Rhea's warring obsession and hostility toward the same woman, Kate's withdrawal from her marriage, the breakup Kent swore to have witnessed, and the mysterious decision Kate had contemplated in her note to Cole.

Pulling from her last reserves, Lissa had scooped up the box and ran for the trees.

Horrible days. The worst of Cole's life, Lissa realized now. They'd preceded two years of punishment, and all because Rhea's love had flared out of control.

"Cole," Lissa began, never taking her eyes off Rhea, "open the box. Take out the camera."

At the word "camera," Rhea's brows cinched. She started toward Cole, but Trevor's massive palm thumped to her collarbone, a human fence restraining the woman's ferocity.

So it was true. Unlucky Rhea had been caught on candid camera. Maybe next time she'd look up when pedaling toward her victim on a glow-in-the-dark bike.

Cole pulled the jersey from the box first. The wind caught an edge, and the shirt flared against the whipping snow, its color too cheerful for the weather and the mood. Cole folded the shirt with slow hands and placed it within the protection of the box.

Next came the point-and-shoot. Cole turned the Nikon on and looked up in expectation. "Nothing," he said.

Ignoring Rhea's increasing efforts to escape Trevor's hold, Lissa instructed, "Turn it on and off. I think there's a glitch between the memory card and the internal storage. The thing seems to point to one or the other at whim." Lissa's phone had backfired like that last summer. Half the pictures from an art show had been fine. The other half she'd lost, or so she'd thought, until stumbling over them in another, unbeknownst-to-her memory.

Cole jammed buttons on the camera over and over, suddenly going still. Lissa guessed he'd found Rhea and her bike. With one subtle press of another button, the camera jerked in his hands—Kate's selfie.

Clearing her throat, Lissa prepared to drop the final hint. She didn't want to tell him and restart his loss clock. Yet... licking her lips one last time, she said, "The dates, Cole." A last breath. "Look at the dates."

One heartbeat, and then Cole laughed—a harsh, mirthless noise. The camera fell into the box, and he knelt in the snow and closed the top with precise, economic movements. Even blown away with the cruel reality of his wife loving another and paying the ultimate price, he moved with restrained grace.

Still a joy to watch.

Without looking at Lissa, Cole walked to Kent and handed over the burden. "Give this"—he gave the box a rough shove—"and *her* back to the police. Tell them to do a better fucking job this time."

She shouldn't have told him.

Not any of it.

The lines that streaked from the corners of Cole's cobalt eyes hadn't eased. The unhurried stride he set in approaching Rhea, who still struggled against a stoic Trevor, didn't mask the way Cole's hands spasmed in and out of fists at his sides.

Half-way to his sister-in-law, Cole stopped, hovering like he didn't trust himself to bring the standoff too close.

Lissa had wanted to help, to ride in on a white horse bearing relief. Instead she'd opened a festering wound. "Cole—"

"Don't." The warning sliced through the wind, shutting her up as surely as duct tape to the mouth. To Rhea, he finally asked, "Why?" so low Lissa strained to hear.

Rhea folded in on herself, visibly shaking with suppressed sobs. "I didn't mean to *or* want to. I just..." She tried again to break free, unsuccessfully.

"I wanted her to acknowledge us. I *needed* her to try for us. At the St. Julien, she danced around our future. She called us sisters. *Friends.* On the mountain, she threatened even that. I was to get nothing, to be nothing. Kate was willing to live a lie for *you.*"

This time Cole's fists didn't uncurl. "A lie? What do you call your last two years?"

"Heartbreak." Looking up, Rhea's eyes glittered like liquid glass, and each syllable eked out in a fractured whisper. "I told you I didn't intend this. Like with Kent. One minute he was hounding me with questions. The next he was on the floor, and I stood over him, meds in hand. Kate was walking ahead of me, insisting we stay apart. Then she was screaming, falling."

Lissa tamped down sympathy that had no place. "You *pushed* her."

Momentum, the police had said.

A pained gasp from Rhea said Trevor struggled for control. "I *want* to kill you," he growled at his wife, squeezing her too hard. "Not on accident. Not because I've lost control…"

"Because you *need* killing." Cole dove. In a blink, Rhea lay flattened over Kate's gravestone with Cole's strong hands around her throat while Trevor stood by, contemplating the scene with curious detachment.

Shock. From the only person this side of Boulder with the strength to stop the madness.

"Yes." Rhea choked, no longer struggling like she had in her husband's embrace. The woman relaxed into Cole's merciless grip. "Please."

Shaking her by the throat, a rabid dog with a ragdoll, Cole snarled, "My pleasure."

Trevor merely watched and nodded—a zombie, but an approving one.

The sickness that had chased Lissa from India rose up in a heated rush, pricking over her skin and clenching in her stomach. Bile scalded the back of her throat. "No."

She'd wanted to free Cole from the perceived burden of killing someone. She couldn't—wouldn't—let him substitute imagined guilt over Kate with real guilt over Rhea. "*No.*"

Cole either didn't hear or didn't care. He muttered against Rhea's slack chest. "Too bad you won't be joining Kate up top. You'll have to wait for me in hell."

Refusing to lose the contents of her stomach, Lissa tripped forward in a jagged path through the rocks. "Cole, stop. *Please.*"

Rhea's eyes slipped closed. An aching remnant of a smile curved her lips, and Lissa realized the woman craved release in any form she could get it.

Afraid to touch but more afraid not to, Lissa laid a gentle hand on Cole's straining shoulder. "*Stop.*" She swallowed frozen air in an attempt to calm her revolting stomach and watering mouth. "Cole," she pleaded again, "look at me."

God, the fever and nausea felt like *fear*.

Still hanging on, Cole turned his head and stared at her, eyes blank.

Unseeing and unreachable.

"I'm not okay," Lissa said. The plea was both a desperate bid for distraction and a real cry for help. Her hand slid off his arm. Like it or not, she was going down. Not out, maybe, but definitely tapping the mat.

The last bit of Cole's jacket slipped from her fingers, and she reeled backward, stung by her failure. She deserved to pass out in the snow. Maybe a couple frostbit fingers would teach her to mind her own business.

She tensed for impact.

And never hit the ground.

"Goddamn it!" Cole had wrenched himself from the trance. His face, flushed and fully inhabited by frustrated, thwarted, *concerned* male, swam above. Clarity had broken the blankness. "You won't even let me murder a murderer in peace. I *hate* that I love you."

She did, too. Wait? What?

In Lissa's peripheral vision, Rhea rolled off the rock, gasping for air but coughing most of it up. Old Red would live to sue Cole for assault and battery from a prison cell. Lissa wouldn't die of hypothermia, left for the coyotes. Or wolves or bears or whatever foraged for frozen people in January in the Rockies. Kent had answers to fill most of the remaining blanks in his head. Trevor at least knew why his wife had turned so terribly cold, not that Lissa imagined knowing of his wife's struggles would be much consolation.

And Cole.

"Kate didn't leave you." Lissa grinned up at the woozy sky. Up at him. "She chose you."

He didn't smile back, but the tension leached from his muscles and eased his fierce expression. Testing her cheeks with the back of the free hand not supporting her torso, he said, "You're hot again." His knuckles trailed over her forehead, making her skin ripple with pleasure instead of pain.

"Always am—"

"All this destruction"—he looked over his shoulder at his felled sister-in-law—"when I could have let Kate go."

You never would have. "You didn't know."

He shook his head, as though clearing out cobwebs of negative thought trying to stand their ground. "I'm glad I didn't."

"Know Kate had fallen for Rhea?"

"Give Kate my blessing to be with Rhea."

"Why?"

"Rhea was a time bomb, hurting people without rhyme or reason, even in her own mind. She would have ended Kate eventually, but she would have hurt her first, like she did Trevor. You wouldn't have been here to stop my retaliation. The circumstances of Kate's death—or at least what I thought were the circumstances—brought us together."

Right, she hadn't let him commit a Class Two felony. Go her. Lissa swallowed, willing the dizziness away. "I didn't give you absolution."

"No."

Heart sinking, Lissa nodded.

"You taught me that I didn't need it. Or *want* it."

If that was true, then Lissa *had* healed him.

"And not because you revealed that Kate didn't kill herself. Because this whole time you knew she loved me more than I thought. She would have wanted me to be happy, not constantly fighting having loved more than she could love back."

Yes.

Beyond the breadth of Cole's shoulders, Trevor hauled Rhea to her feet. He didn't lift her or comfort her, but he supported her weight as she limped from the clearing, Kent trailing behind with the box.

If nothing else, Rhea's journey to incarceration would be humane. The woman's face held not happiness, per se, but a truckload of resignation and even a glimmer of peace. Forgiveness may never come from the Rathlen men, but telling the truth might have been the first step toward forgiving herself.

Lissa closed her eyes and let snowflakes clutter her lashes. "They say those who love the most, love again."

"Do they? You remind me, *my* Lissa, wheeler-and-dealer for all that she wants, I've a bargain for you."

Lissa lifted heavy lids to examine Cole, who looked down at her in all his rattled, serious, battered *glory*. "Do you?" she asked with unconvincing nonchalance.

Mmmhmm. And just like your offer did, mine will require practice. And compromise. It'll probably be challenging. It may take us to crazy places with squat toilets and inquisitive locals.

She waited, dizziness be damned.

"If I can be your first," he said finally, "then you can be my last."

The tears froze to her damn face. "You already are, Cole. You always will be."

L. O. V. E. D.

EPILOGUE

Two weeks after Lissa accepted Cole's pact, he locked her out of their bedroom.

But only for an hour so he could set up.

International travel had been postponed in lieu of all the activity surrounding the reopened investigation into Kate's death, Rhea's arrest, and transitioning the supportive might of the Rathlen clan to Trevor, who was proving that Cole hadn't known the meaning of the word reclusive.

Cole lit candles but didn't turn down the sheets. The frenzied beat of Lissa's favorite Indian pop song pulsed through the room, and Darjeeling tea brewed on a hot pad by the bed, its calming floral scent spicing the air.

He'd sent Lissa to Boulder for food. Now that the Supper Solutions' deliveries had ended, he and Lissa were inching into the culinary arts one burnt chicken breast and sliced finger at a time. Mostly they kept Boulder's take-out industry in the black.

"A man who banishes his woman to the hall rarely samples the chicken vindaloo for which she drove seventy minutes round-trip." Lissa's muffled voice tapered off on the other side of the bedroom door. Then he heard her cooing, asking Sasha if he enjoyed Indian food.

Hell, no. Last week she'd fed the pup meatballs stuffed with herbed mozzarella. The consequences of feeding a two-hundred pound dog an entire plate of rich food had been... epic, in a replace-the-carpets kind of way.

Cole jerked the door open to find Lissa standing on the threshold with a brown paper bag. Sasha leaned into her side, head stretched to the bottom of the sack. She stroked his muzzle and lowered the booty to give him a good sniff.

"You wouldn't," Cole predicted.

"Try me," Lissa countered. "This is why he likes me more than you."

"He likes you because you smell like strawberry shortcake." Or Frosted Flakes. Or cinnamon Red Hots. Cake batter. Juicy Fruit. *God*, one day she'd managed to smell like Skittles. In another life, she'd *totally* been a confection perfumer. Should the prize he'd set up on the mattress be rejected by the masses set to view it, edible scents could be her second career in this one.

She beamed and brushed passed him with a breezy, "Like father, like son. Who doesn't want—"

The joke died on her lips. "Cole," she breathed. Knowing what was coming, he stepped forward, ready for the moment the bag of food landed in his waiting hands. In slow motion, Lissa approached the bed. "It's us."

"Our work," he corrected.

Cole had done as she'd asked in a bronchitis-muddled moment—his-and-hers mixed media. Spread before Lissa's wide eyes lay a collage of sorts. Lissa's painting of the children playing in the Delhi traffic circle served as an enlightened backdrop for Cole's more somber photos of the same.

Where she'd layered illusions of fenced-in entrapment beneath the carefree hope of children the world over, he'd shown the harsh reality of homeless kids without access to medical care.

The pictures lived within the painting, part of an integrated whole. Separate, his and Lissa's philosophies presented drastically different takes on the same subject—literal versus whimsical, black and white versus living color, what was versus what could be. Together, the combined work read like a silent and subtle self-help book.

"The sheer creativity"—Lissa's voice cracked—"in how you set the scenes, in how they play off each other. It's like a dream, reminding us we filter existence through a personal lens, equally valid and unique for each individual, yet if we dare, we can see the gifts we have over the ones we crave."

Always so astute, his Lissa. "You taught me that lesson. Now you can show everyone else."

Lissa threw herself at him, her smile dazzling. The bag of rice and curry hit the floor with a wet thud. "You taught me I *could* show everyone else."

Cole left the food. Sasha might have a snack, Styrofoam and all. After all, that's why they made carpet cleaners.

The kiss lingered, long and hot and *patient* with the knowledge of a future of intimacy.

"Cole," she whispered, breaking away, "you took a while to love me, but you're really good at it."

He couldn't resist. "Baby, I *know*."

THE END

THANK YOU!

Thanks for reading *Art-Crossed Love*. I hope you enjoyed the read as much as I enjoyed the write!

Would you like to know when my next book is available? You can sign up for my new-release e-mail list at www.libbyrice.com.

I post regular snippets from novels, pictures of character adventures, and other fun extras on my Facebook page. I also post tidbits about what's going on with me. Come join us at www.facebook.com/libbyrice.author.

Or you can follow me on Twitter at @libby_rice, Instagram at libby_rice, and/or Goodreads at https://www.goodreads.com/LibbyRice.

Reviews help readers find books they'll love. I welcome and appreciate *all* reviews, whether positive or negative.

You've just read the second book in the Second Chances series. *Love Drunk*, Trevor's story, will be available in the summer of 2015. If you would like to read an excerpt, please read on.

LOVE DRUNK: EXCERPT

Available Summer 2015

Wine importer London Whitley dots her I's and crosses her T's. Her meticulous nature insulates her from fears that she might just be crazy, as in certifiably, medically nuts. When her almost ex-boyfriend winds up dead at her hands and she's soon accused of importing counterfeit wines, London's carefully constructed world begins to crumble. There's help to be had, but only in the form of an imposing stranger who threatens her ruin.

Trevor Rathlen is lucky to have escaped his marriage to a murderess alive and merely indebted to men who think the exquisite London Whitley's innocence is a façade. A computer security specialist by day and hacker by night, Trevor agrees to return the favor owed by learning London's secrets. The task should be an easy one, except Trevor is short on trust, London is long on lies, and together they battle an infinite attraction…

July—Denver, Colorado

Two weeks ago, London Rose Whitley had started a date with a living man and ended with a dead one. If she'd ever needed to arrive on time, today was that day. Latching the door behind her with an audible click, she spied a gleaming casket sitting too still down a center aisle. Stainless steel edges peeked from beneath at least a hundred wilting roses, the metal just shiny enough to catch stray rays of dusty summer light and hurl rainbows across a silent, mourning crowd.

A dead Dillon Farro still managed to rule the room.

"Always late," her mother whispered as London squeezed herself into the end of an oak pew. Dr. Victoria Whitley subjected London to a round of slow scrutiny, no doubt taking in the wrinkles in her black skirt and the way the buttons on her shirt pulled ever-so-slightly around the middle.

"Late and not looking your best. You realize," her mom said casually, now fighting a droning organ for supremacy, "we're five minutes from downtown Denver, five minutes from your apartment. Your disrespect is unconsciously deliberate."

Same criticism, different day.

Up top, London shrugged the shoulder her mother would easily see from the corner of an eye. Below, she wound a discrete arm around her waist, pressing hard against the ache that spiked at the woman's complaint. Some psychiatrists—at least the ones who'd raised London—automatically sought reasons for behavior. A late client, they would deduce, exhibited signs of suppressed hostility. Ten extra pounds cried depression. A person who bawled out the checker at the grocery store felt resentful about having his power usurped by an hourly wage earner.

According to Dr. and Dr. Whitley, actions manifested themselves like the jerking reflex after a good tap to the knee. Every last move reflected deeply-seeded roots in the psyche. Lateness never sprang from a traffic jam. Weight gain didn't come from a craving for jelly donuts. Acting like a jerk could never be attributed to a bad day.

"Yes, Mom,"—what to say?—"my being late and frumpy is an expression of power. I want to stick it to a dead man... show him he'll have to stand in line for something not particularly worthwhile."

Her mother stiffened against the unforgiving pew. "You make light of this?"

London balled her good hand. For once her mother's outrage sounded genuine, not the product of a test to see how her daughter might react. Perhaps London ought to appreciate the show of support on this baddest of bad days.

Support nearly withheld.

Her mother had insisted London's presence at Dillon's funeral was, "a rash choice, reminiscent of the one that put Dillon in a casket in the first place." Instead of looking angry over London's audacity, her mom had grabbed her chin and peered into her face with concern, with a strained grief that implied the woman's daughter had finally tipped over the precipice between compulsive and crazy, between rash and dangerous.

They're wrong. Two psychiatrist parents didn't always know best. Their labels wouldn't rise to the level of self-fulfilling prophesies, no matter how many times words like impulsive and compulsive fluttered her way.

Even Freud had acknowledged that sometimes a cigar is just a cigar.

"I don't make light of today," London insisted quietly. They could do only so much sparring from the back pew before attracting unwanted attention. "You do by insinuating I would ever want, consciously or otherwise, to show Dillon disrespect."

244

She'd loved him, after all.

But love had grown silent, their relationship stale, and on the day she'd tried to break things off, Dillon had died.

Before her mother could bombard her with the usual, "Why, then, were you late?" or "What, then, do you mean to say with your shabby clothing and extra pounds," a more sinister problem fell in London's lap. A shadow crawled across her exposed knees, silencing the battle of wills raging between mother and daughter. Then came a pained scrape of a voice that nearly choked on swallowed anguish before words made their debut. "How can you sit there? Only a few feet from my murdered son?"

London looked up into a hollow, pinched face. All her determination to do the right thing vanished. Defiance crumbled to dust as deep as the kneeler crowding the tops of her tapping toes. Her mother had been right.

Nothing but insanity had tinged London's decision to mourn Dillon openly. Maybe her late arrival and ugly outfit did amount to a tacit admission of something deeper, like guilt and lack of belonging.

Instead of offering grudging support, Doc Victoria ought to have met her daughter on the church steps with a white jacket and a promise of padded walls.

London swallowed and stood. Gaze averted, she slunk around the man blocking her path to freedom. When her arm brushed his in passing, he emitted a low howl, as though her limbs were coated in battery acid. Jerking away, London realized pain had a sound, one that would ring in her ears long after she fled the echoing church.

Pain sounded like a father confronting his son's killer.

Pain sounded like Mr. Farro confronting her.

******

Trevor gazed up at his buddy through a shiny bar bisecting the view. "Add twenty-five to each side." A cumulative three-fifty would max him out, yet he hesitated to go for gold. The trainer nearby with the do-rag, patterned track pants, and a set of eighteen-inch tatted biceps would take note. Then Trevor's numbers would end up on a white board behind the gym's front desk.

He shouldn't be anybody's goal.

Metal clanked above his head, foreshadowing the extra weight joining the bar. Not even the sound of an oncoming challenge dented Trevor's vague sense of disinterest. Once, he'd been proud of the number three-fifty, or at least felt a sense of accomplishment. A guy who could bench three-fifty was strong. Strength meant speed, distance, endurance. Strength meant power.

Hoisting hundreds of pounds in the air had built him up, helping him do all the things that mattered, like *winning*. Now it provided an easy distraction—*up, down, up, down*—which helped him forget that none of his former priorities mattered at all.

Plus a beer only weighed around a pound, give or take the bottle.

Still, his routines had become more than habit. They'd become *him*. If Trevor stopped pushing, if he quit training and never completed another Ironman or triathlon or ski race, he might as well hand his murderous ex-wife a weapon and let her pick him off, too.

Not happening.

With movements honed by two decades of repetition, Trevor curled his calloused hands around the bar. He squeezed and felt a welcome tension grow in his torso. With a deep breath, he drove his feet into the floor, locked his hips, and unracked the weight.

His friend Kevin spotted Trevor's movements with a low oath. "I won't be coming by later with an ice pack for your crying, whining pecs."

Ignoring the taunt, Trevor gulped another breath and rowed the weight downward until it touched his old T-shirt. Then he drove the bar back to lockout on a burst of coordinated power.

Resetting his lungs, he managed a quick, "Fuck off," before his second rep. Then another before his third. On the forth, Kev no longer looked on with that smarmy, self-satisfied grin.

"What have you been eating, man?"

Mostly anger strapped to the back of grilled chicken breasts. Lots and lots of chicken breasts.

Before Trevor could share about protein overload, Kevin's chin lifted and came to a slow stop. The attention once focused on keeping Trevor from wrapping the bar around his own neck homed in on something across the gym.

No doubt a woman.

Kevin's reasons for prompting a change of gym scenery in the last month had become painfully obvious. Where their old gym had been about function over form, this one had yoga classes and soaking tubs and expensive shampoo in the showers. While those things meant fuck all to Trevor, they did result in one very important distinguishing characteristic— the presence of chicks.

As Trevor stared up at a textbook case of distraction, Kev's look changed. A patient interest, able to bide its time, morphed into surprise, then panic. Without a word, Kev wrestled the bar back to the rack and disappeared from Trevor's line of sight. So much for number five. Trevor rocked upward and let his focus follow his friend.

A developing emergency about thirty feet out hooked Trevor's cloak of apathy and jerked. *Hard.* After six months of *fuck everything* but the basics— exercise, work, sex—he saw something worth effort.

She was… indescribably gorgeous, with black curls swept away from her face, exposing a delicate profile.

She also had about twenty seconds left on her feet. Her ponytail swished less and less with each step, legs swaying heavily on the moving treadmill. A small hand groped for the machine's front rail.

Instead of flushed from her workout, the woman looked to have lost every drop of blood in her soft, plush body. At the same time, she seemed unaware of her plight, almost confused about what was happening. That hand missed the rail and fluttered to her face, graceful despite her obvious disorientation, and she rubbed at her eyes like she could shake the dizziness.

Trevor lunged off the bench, the urge to protect fueling his flight across the gym. He chased Kev around equipment and people, all as oblivious to the woman's plight as the woman herself.

"Kev, *wait*," he gritted. Trevor would handle the saving. If Kev did the honor, things would end up all wrong. Kev had a simple way with women: He crooked his finger, and they sucked his dick.

Not today.

Instinctively, Trevor muscled his friend into the crevice between two elliptical machines. Kev flailed for purchase, barely staving off the unexpected jostling.

"Not sorry," Trevor said as he slid past, reaching the woman's side the moment her time ran out.

Sweet, sweet skin slid beneath his hands. Her shoulders sagged as he gripped their sloping curves. When the weight of her slumped, he plucked her off the machine and lowered her ever-so-gently to the floor through buckling knees. Once flat on her back with him crouched overhead, he took a good, long look, ignoring Kev, who buzzed in the background about "dickheads" and "disrespect" and how Trevor might have "hurt her worse."

Never. A fall would have meant a concussion and broken teeth. Landing against his chest had meant a slow, careful trip to the ground, a relaxed journey with time for her plump breasts to give him a good, long *hello*.

Now her chest waved through a thin shirt with every breath. Recent months had revealed how much he liked soft, forgiving breasts that could fill huge hands. Before her defection to one of Colorado's finest correctional facilities, his wife had defined feminine fitness—tall, statuesque, *tough*. In everything but brute strength, his stunning ex had held her own. His ten-mile run had become her eleven. His forty push-ups had become her forty-five.

Rhea's stamina had won his respect. The one-upmanship—with his *wife*, of all people—had crippled his desire. Sinew and bone had a place on a woman. They belonged under a layer of softness he could sink into.

Some women had bodies built for clothes, for the drape and the crease.

Others for sports, for speed and power. This one, in her pink leggings and loose tank, had a body built *for him.*

www.ingramcontent.com/pod-product-compliance
Lightning Source LLC
Chambersburg PA
CBHW030915120626
46554CB00001B/153